Sally Ann's S

Leo McNeir

BEFORE GETAWAY WITH MURDER

enigma
publishing

Also by Leo McNeir

Getaway with Murder (ISBN 0 9524052 6 1)

Death in Little Venice (ISBN 0 9524052 7 X)

Kiss and Tell (ISBN 0 9531742 1 2)

Devil in the Detail (ISBN 0 9524052 2 0)

No Secrets (ISBN 0 9531742 4 7)

and published by enigma publishing.

See the author's website: www.leomcneir.com

enigma publishing

PO Box 1901, Milton Keynes, MK19 6DN

First published 2007

Text © Leo McNeir 2007

Cover art © Alex Prowse 2007

The moral rights of the author have been asserted.

The events and characters described in *Sally Ann's Summer* are entirely fictitious, and any apparent resemblance to real people, companies or occurrences is entirely coincidental.

A CIP record for this book is available from the British Library.

ISBN 978-0-9531742-5-6

Typesetting and cover design by *specialist* publishing services ltd, Montgomery

Printed in Great Britain by Bell & Bain Ltd, Glasgow

The author

Leo McNeir is a linguist and lexicographer and has edited ten dictionaries in fifteen languages in the past decade, the standard works in their field.

Sally Ann's Summer is his sixth novel, following the successful publication of *Getaway with Murder* (2000), *Death in Little Venice* (2001), *Kiss and Tell* (2003), *Devil in the Detail* (2004) and *No Secrets* (2006).

He lives with cookery writer Cassandra McNeir and their cat, Mog, in a 300-year-old cottage in a Northamptonshire village.

They have a narrowboat on the Grand Union Canal.

Dedication

For my mother
Jessie Eileen McNeir (1921 – 1995)
in love and gratitude

For Beth Baldwin (1906 – 2003)
in loving memory

And for Marilyn
whose chance remark was the start of it all

Foreword

All the events described in this novel are fiction, and any similarity between names or boats is entirely coincidental. While some of the locations are based on real places, others are invented. In reality, Little Venice is not only one of the most beautiful parts of the waterways system, it is also one of the most peaceful.

Reference is made to British Waterways because it seemed unnecessary to invent a body to fulfil its functions with a different name. The BW staff mentioned in this book bear no relation to my knowledge to any actual member of its personnel.

The first books about boating that I ever read were the writings of the young women who volunteered to work on narrowboats during the Second World War. They came to be known as the Idle Women because of the linitials 'I.W.' on their badges, denoting 'Inland Waterways'. Their books, like their lives, became an inspiration. I hope that Iris Winterburn, who features in this book and, like all the other characters, is entirely fictitious, does not disgrace those extraordinary women.

As far as the central mystery is concerned, I leave it to the reader to decide where the facts end and the fiction begins.

Leo McNeir

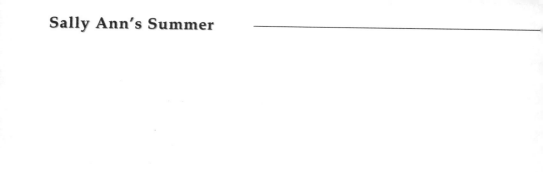

Sally Ann's Summer

Prologue

This was where it all began.

Marnie Walker was rummaging in the back of a locker on the boat when her fingers touched something unexpected, a notebook, weather-beaten as if left out in the rain, oil stains on its cover, a grimy thumbprint clearly visible in the corner

She had been looking for torch batteries, but now abandoned her search and sat down at the table in the saloon. A few years had passed since she had last seen the book. The day she acquired it had been a turning point in her life, though she had not realised that at the time. It had been one significant moment in a summer that had led her not only on a tour of the waterways, but which had taken her away forever from the life she had known until then.

She flicked through the pages. Each entry brought back memories. The life she now knew – a life that had for some years been filled with incident and episode – had not just come about by careful planning and hard work. There had been the element of chance. Marnie sat back, gazing out through the window across the still water of the canal to the fields beyond.

Chance has determined the whole course of my life, she thought. At any other time those influences might have worked out differently or never come together at all. What started as a simple holiday trip brought me to where I'm now sitting in the saloon of the narrowboat *Sally Ann*, at our mooring on the Grand Union Canal, fifty miles from London.

It was all down to that summer. Marnie closed the logbook and cast her mind back, trying to remember. It all started, she thought, with a phone call.

1
Shelf

Marnie was on the point of reaching for a cigarette when the phone rang. It was Beth and that was bad news.

'I'm busy, leave me in peace.'

'You're always busy, *too* busy, I keep telling you.'

Marnie definitely needed that cigarette and put the phone under her chin so that she could pull one out of the packet.

'I hope you're not smoking again.'

Marnie thought *Hell – she must be psychic!* and put the cigarette between her lips.

'Whatever gave you that idea?' she mumbled, stretching to reach for the Zippo.

'Very funny. I always did like your Humphrey Bogart impressions.'

If the truth were told, it was more the appurtenances of smoking that appealed to Marnie than actually breathing smoke into her lungs. She especially liked the Zippo, that was just then evading every effort she made to reach it.

'Do you have to ring me at work when I'm really busy, to nag me about giving up smoking?'

'What are big sisters for?'

'Good question. What do you want, Beth?'

'You know what I want. You *promised*.'

Marnie had a vague idea about a distant conversation, but had not registered anything remotely resembling a promise. She had by now given up all efforts to reach the Zippo and dropped the cigarette from her lips onto the drawing board in front of her.

'Look, Beth, I'm not in the mood for promises. In fact, now is not a good time to be asking favours.'

A change of tone. Sisterly concern. 'Actually, you don't sound too cheerful. What's the matter?'

'I'm just a bit fed up, that's all.'

'*Fed up!*' Beth yelled down the line. 'How the hell can you be *fed up*? You've got just about *everything* anybody could want: a good job, big salary, no ties, no debts, your own place, good prospects …'

'Okay! Okay!' Marnie yelled back. She lowered her voice. 'I don't need the inventory. Anyone can feel fed up once in a while, can't they?'

'Is it the work or the private life?'

Marnie sighed. 'It's the work *and* it's the private life.'

'Do you want to talk about it?'

'Of course I don't want to talk about it. I'm sitting in an open-plan office with nine other people. I might as well sell serial rights to the *News of the World*.'

'You're the boss aren't you?' Beth had a logic that was curiously her own.

'It doesn't make the others deaf.'

'I meant that you had more space around you on account of being a senior executive.'

'I am not a *senior executive* or any other sort. I'm an interior designer.'

'Well, you're *senior*,' Beth insisted.

Marnie had had enough of this. 'Look. I am senior in that I have two plants, a bigger chair and a view over the litter in the canal just outside my window. Big deal.'

'That brings me back to the promise. You said you'd look after *Sally* for us and I have to see you to give you the keys.'

There was a pause. 'Look after *Sally?*'

'You promised you would. Don't you remember?'

Marnie had completely forgotten. 'Sure. When and where?'

'Ring me at home tonight. I've just remembered, I have to get to the cleaners before they close. Must rush. Bye!'

That was it. Gone.

Marnie cradled the phone, looked at the plans in front of her and felt stale. She seldom chatted with her sister, but now, with Beth and Paul going away for a year's sabbatical, she realised she would like a confidante for her various woes.

Without noticing herself, Marnie had the cigarette in her mouth and leaned across the drawing board for the Zippo. She enjoyed the smooth feel of the metal against her fingers and flipped the lid open with one movement, just like Bogart or Cagney. The striking wheel felt rough on the edge of her thumb and she looked at it thoughtfully, willing it to light first time. On the point of flicking down on the wheel, she heard a cough over her shoulder. She knew that cough. It was Larry, the office creep, one of her assistants. Of course, he was making his point. They had all democratically decided that the office should be designated a *no-smoking zone*, and she had gone along with the idea because at the time she had given up and thought it would be an inducement to persevere.

She would not give Larry any satisfaction. Deftly, she slipped the lighter and the cigarette into the pocket of her long cardigan and set off towards the loo.

Washing her hands, she glanced in the mirror. Could this really be the promising young designer of not so long ago? It was not that she had totally gone to seed, at least she persuaded herself of that. But the signs were there. Were those bags forming under the eyes, and was the skin becoming just a little slack around the jaw line? She was glad the mirror only showed the top half and had already given up inspecting herself in the full length mirror at home. The weighing scales had acquired a light coating of talc-scented dust, standing alone and neglected in the corner of the bathroom. These were not good signs. She was not a complete person at ease with herself, as the magazine articles were wont to tell her.

Involuntarily, Marnie found herself opening the door onto the tiny patio that everyone in the office called *the shelf*. She stepped out and stood by the murky waters of the canal, lighting her cigarette in the shadow of the bridge and keeping out of the range of vision of those in her office, such as Larry, who would smirk to think she had had to retreat to this forlorn smoker's haven, where she always felt like a schoolgirl skulking in the lavatories for a clandestine drag.

This was meant to be an idyllic waterside social area, where creative people would come to be refreshed by contact with a soothing element. At least that was how they had planned the office building several years before. It had looked good on the drawings, with sketchy figures standing languidly among pots of geraniums, coffee cup in hand, thinking creative thoughts, swapping creative ideas and looking like the colour supplement people they imagined themselves to be. Few came here now, apart from one or two hardened cases who found it impossible to kick the smoking habit.

Marnie flicked the butt into the canal and turned to go. As she did so, she heard the rumble of an engine and, looking round, saw the prow of a boat painted in bright colours in a bold diamond pattern coming under the bridge, swirling the floating litter aside with its light bow wave. She paused on the threshold before going in, drawn by a vague curiosity to watch the narrowboat pass. It was green and yellow with red lining over a black hull and had flowers in tubs on the roof. The effect was cacophonous and jaunty, all the colours merrily vying for attention.

Marnie became aware of a middle-aged couple standing on the minute rear deck, each clasping a mug of coffee. They seemed free of cares, glancing around as the boat chugged along at walking pace. Suddenly, they caught sight of her and raised their mugs, calling out a cheery greeting that was made indistinct by the throb of the diesel. Marnie waved back and noticed that their mugs did not match.

What was the attraction of these slow-moving vessels that led apparently normal people to set off like nomads, wandering at a slothful pace through the oily waters of urban decay? Why did they always seem to throw away any aesthetic sense they might once have possessed, as soon as they boarded a boat?

What on earth was she doing here, she thought, wasting time when there were drawings to be done, colour schemes to be devised? The canal boat was receding into the distance, and the couple were looking up at a hideous block of high-rise flats as if in wonder. She made a mental note to collect the keys to Beth's boat later that evening. Just what she was expected to do with the thing while they were away, she had no idea. She opened the door and went back to the drawing board.

2
Lumbered

'I don't suppose you'll be wanting another drink, will you?' Beth said, perhaps a little pointedly, picking up the bottle and putting it back in the fridge.

'Won't I?' Marnie glanced at the dregs left in her glass.

'Not when you're driving,' Paul said with a smile. He got up and walked to the door.

'Oh, yeah. I'd forgotten I was driving.'

'That's not a good sign.' Paul smiled cheerfully and went out.

That more or less summed up the evening, at least as far as Marnie was concerned. They sat in the kitchen over the remains of a Chinese take-away. Food stocks had been allowed to run down in view of the imminent departure for the year's sabbatical. In a cupboard they had found a medium dry Yugoslav white wine left over from a party and decided to give it the benefit of the doubt. Not a wise decision. If Marnie was honest, she could not regard its disappearance from the table with genuine regret. It was more a reflex action, a matter of principle. Was she drinking too much these days? *Surely not.*

'Do you think you're drinking too much?' Beth asked in an even tone.

'Not much chance here, is there?' Marnie wondered again if Beth was psychic.

'You know what I mean. Is it all part of your being fed up?'

Marnie automatically reached for her bag to get a cigarette, remembered that Beth and Paul lived in what they described as a *no-smoking house*, and pushed the bag under her chair. She felt reluctant to talk about her malaise. This was partly because she was not sure what was causing it and was too lazy for concentrated introspection, partly because she knew that Beth's mind was occupied with other things.

'I dunno. Perhaps I've been working too hard.'

Beth agreed. 'You ought to get out more. It's not as if you're short of friends ... and there's Steve ... unless you've put him off.'

Marnie realised she hardly gave him a thought. Steve lectured at University College like Paul, and they had met the year before at a dinner party. Marnie was convinced that Beth had stage-managed the meeting. 'He's still keen enough, I suppose. God knows why. I don't give him much encouragement.'

'I thought you liked him.'

'He's all right ... if you like people making sheep's eyes at you. I'd rather just go my own way for a while. I'm not into relationships right now.'

'Perhaps you're in a rut. Though I suspect you can't be ... it isn't fashionable.' Beth spoke without malice.

Paul came back with a document folder under his arm and a bunch of keys attached to a bizarre key-ring. It was a short length of thickish red string with a ball at the end, the size of a golf ball. It looked like a ball and chain, and Marnie was surprised that it was so light when Paul handed it to her. The ball was made of cork. There were only three keys, and Paul explained their uses: towpath gate, doors on *Sally Ann*, ignition switch.

'No problem.' Marnie dropped them in her bag. 'I'll keep them in a safe place till you get back.'

Beth suddenly looked shifty. 'It's not *quite* as simple as that.'

Marnie feared as much.

'All you have to do –' Beth began.

Marnie interrupted her. 'You sound like a special offer on a corn flakes packet or a recipe. In the case of Mrs Beeton, she usually tells you to take a dozen plovers' eggs and a pint of brandy.'

Beth was undeterred. 'Pay attention, or it'll be a recipe for disaster.'

Marnie disliked Beth's tendency to speak in clichés. She also disliked her tendency to have the last word.

Paul put on his best lecturer's voice. 'Like all machines, it's desirable to keep the engine in use as regularly as possible. That also goes for the internal systems.'

Marnie looked suspicious. 'What *internal systems?*'

Paul put on his most encouraging smile. 'Well ... there's the water pump, the stern bilge pump, the forward bilge pump, the hot water system, the fridge, the cooker, the shower unit ...' he paused for breath.

Marnie was stunned. 'All that on one little boat?'

'She's not so little,' Beth countered. 'She's forty-five feet long, made of steel and weighs fourteen tonnes.'

Paul picked up the narrative. 'There's also the time switch for the fan that we like to run to keep her ventilated from time to time in the summer, which has to be changed to run the fan heater to keep her free from frost damage in the winter. And ideally, she ought to be opened up and the bedding aired each week, especially in the winter or during a spell of damp weather.'

'Right.' Marnie thought she should be taking notes of all this. 'Anything else?' She sensed the question was a mistake.

'If you had the odd moment ... or two ...' Beth faltered.

Marnie frowned and said nothing, hoping the body language would say it all.

Beth resumed, undaunted. 'Well, you know how bad it is for brass to be neglected for a long period ...'

Marnie could not remember how much brass there was on the boat.

'The Brasso and cloths are in the cupboard under the sink in the galley.'

'That's the kitchen,' Paul added helpfully.

'I *know.*'

'You see, there's nothing to it really.' Beth smiled as if it was a done deal.

Marnie was digesting all this when she noticed the document folder on the table. It was a faded pink with signs of the odd oily thumb-print and was thick with papers. It seemed to exude a faint odour compounded of diesel fuel, gas and old engine oil. There was a stout elastic band round its middle, straining to keep it together. She pointed. 'What's that? Do I have to learn it by heart?'

Paul pushed it nearer. 'The *Sally Ann* file. It's got all the info about the engine, the pumps, the heating system –'

'Okay, fine.' Marnie glared at it. 'I don't suppose I'll be needing anything, but I'll keep it in the filing cabinet.'

'You never know. It's fine now, but when autumn comes there may be things that need doing.' He patted the folder. 'You'll find everything you need to know in here.'

Marnie had already decided that her contact with the boat would be a visit to the mooring once a month to open the windows and air the bedding. She said so.

Beth and Paul glanced at each other. Marnie saw the glance and waited. She put on the expression of someone listening to a used-car salesman.

'It's not quite as simple as that,' said Paul.

Beth opened her mouth to speak. Marnie got in first.

'Don't give me that *all-you-have-to-do* crap,' she said. 'What is it?'

'We rather hoped you might use her a bit,' Paul said.

'From time to time,' Beth joined in.

'Keep her running,' said Paul.

'Shipshape and Bristol fashion,' Beth added cheerily.

Marnie knew she was in a hole. She could advance all manner of arguments, but for each one they would come up with an answer. Worse, they would come up with more and more reasons why it would be good for *her*. The trouble was, she did not want the burden of this boat with its engine and systems and … god knows what. It would be like looking after a St Bernard dog that needed to be taken for an eight mile walk twice a day, mainly up steep mountains.

She became aware that while she was thinking, Beth and Paul were watching her. She suspected that her facial expressions were changing with each thought, so that she was revealing her mind's innermost workings without saying a thing. Beth always seemed to know what she was thinking, anyway.

The two of them sat there studying her, sharp and eager, like Jack Russell terriers, their heads turning from side to side as if waiting for her to throw them a stick. Her shoulders slumped. She sighed in defeat. She knew she was beaten and would have to give in on all fronts.

'I won't do it,' she heard herself say.

Beth looked disappointed, laced with a dash of exasperation. Paul moved off in the direction of hearty encouragement. 'Oh, come on … *Sally*'s not as bad as all that. You'll like her once you get to know her. She can be real fun.'

Marnie put on an expression that said clearly there was no chance of persuading her and it was pointless even to try.

Beth had a moment of inspiration. 'Gary from along the cut has this theory that narrowboats are all about food, wine and sex.' She laughed gaily.

'In that order?' Marnie was stony-faced.

Ten minutes later, Marnie was on the doorstep wishing them a good sabbatical, fumbling for car keys with one hand while clutching the pink folder in the other. As she walked off down the drive, Beth's valedictory message followed her.

'You ought to take *Sally* off for a trip. You could do with a break. Have your own sabbatical. Do you good ... do you *both* good.'

Marnie started the car and drove off, waving through the window.

'Fat chance,' she thought.

3
Pub crawl

Two days later, Beth and Paul set off for America, but Marnie was not there to wave good-bye. She had a big project running in Leicester and spent much of the week in the Midlands, dealing with the client, in this case a major brewery that was refurbishing its pubs. She stayed each night at a different pub to get to know them better. The trip, known in the office as *Marnie's pub crawl*, involved her in interminable meetings to sort out the details of the interior designs of several pubs strung out along or near the Grand Union Canal.

Marnie appreciated the irony of the situation. Here she was, trying to sort out her life and arrive at some feeling of detachment, when all the while she was being confronted by the very objects that recalled to her the burden of boat-minding. It seemed impossible to escape.

She drove from pub to pub, virtuously drinking sparkling mineral water – *designer water*, she called it – and trying to resolve the basic dilemma confronting her. All the pubs were decorated to look like country cottages. She saw every one of them as a cliché, with their reproductions of old canal signs, their panels painted with castles and roses and the inevitable – and dreaded – horse brasses. She tried not to wince whenever she paid her first visit to each pub on her list.

Still full of unresolved questions, Marnie set off on the drive back to London at the end of the week, looking forward to a break. She had nothing planned for the weekend and thought she would just potter about the flat, read a few magazines, ring a few friends. Not high society, but as she sat in the third tailback on the motorway somewhere near Luton, the prospect held many attractions.

The early evening traffic inched its way along in reasonably good humour. It was spring after all. Marnie reached over to the glove box and took out a tape. Without looking to see what it was, she slipped it into the cassette player. It was Acoustic Alchemy, two guitars, very smooth and stylish. Ideal for relaxing after a busy week.

The traffic spread out across all three lanes and was accelerating towards the next bottleneck. Sure enough, there were the familiar signs for roadworks in three miles. Marnie braked to a halt with a mile to go in the inside lane on a bridge over the railway.

Below her, the sunlight reflected off water. It must have been the Grand Union. It was following her everywhere she went, like a stalker. She remembered *Sally Ann*, waiting to be visited, presumably somewhere further south down that same stretch of water. Marnie sighed at the thought of going to the boat to air the bedding, run the engine, see to this, see to that. She tried to recall what the boat looked like, but only had an impression of dull, dark paint and a noisy engine. At least she was becoming aware that all canal boats were not the same. She had seen enough of them during the past week –

enough to last her a lifetime – to know that there were different styles.

A loud blast on the horn from the car behind made her jump back to the present. The traffic had rolled on, and two cars from the middle lane, which was stationary, had already nipped in front of her. She looked into the rear-view mirror and saw the driver behind shaking his head.

'Black mark, *Sally Ann*,' she muttered and pulled up to close the gap. It was the first time she had spoken the name.

———⚏———

Saturday did not turn out quite as Marnie had planned it. Her idea had been to look in on the boat briefly, leaving the rest of the day free. She wanted to see an art gallery that had recently opened in Covent Garden, buy half a dozen paperbacks from her favourite bookshop in the Strand and return via the garden centre to get plants for her window-boxes.

Just after eight o'clock she threw the pink folder and the boat-keys onto the passenger seat of the Rover and set off for Little Venice. The traffic was light and she pulled up by the railings a short distance from the mooring, confident that with luck she could be away by the time the shops were opening. It was a cool morning. Already the sky was clearing, promising a fine spring day. Marnie had only been to Little Venice for occasional short outings on the boat and scarcely knew the place. Clutching the folder, she wandered along the pavement looking at the boats and crossed the road at the traffic lights on the bridge, gaining a vantage point from where she could look down at the pool into which three waterways merged.

It was a broad expanse of water with an island in the middle. There was a public park on one side, and much of the pool was overlooked by elegant Regency houses in white stucco. Through the branches of a mature weeping willow standing on the island she could see three long narrowboats moored on the far bank, painted in a dull livery of maroon or brown: waterbuses. Ducks and swans were swimming with convoys of their young. On the roof of a barge that announced itself as an art gallery a young woman was sweeping energetically. As she worked, a narrowboat appeared under the furthest bridge, and the woman glanced up, wiping the back of a hand across her forehead. Marnie was turning to leave when she heard a shout. The woman was gesticulating urgently to the steerer of the boat. Her voice rang out over the water above the noise of the traffic crossing the bridge.

'Over here!'

The steerer cupped a hand to his ear, reaching down to the controls to slow the engine. The woman was pointing now ahead of the boat and waving it towards her barge. The steerer altered course, drew close to the barge and slowed the boat to a halt. The woman leaned over the roof rail to talk to him.

Marnie could not hear what they were saying, but both had turned to look across the pool, where the woman was pointing. Marnie scanned the water and eventually saw the object of their interest. In the middle of the pool was what seemed to be a wooden crate.

Marnie could see a corner protruding a few inches above the surface, like an iceberg whose bulk was invisible below the water. She wondered whether such a thing could damage a narrowboat. How thick was the steel of a hull? How vulnerable?

While she was pursuing these thoughts, the steerer pushed his boat away from the barge and manoeuvred in a wide arc to cross the pool, heading towards the crate. Reversing up to the mystery object, he knelt and extended a hand down towards it. After struggling for a minute he stood up, looking over to the woman on the barge, shaking his head. He called out, but the traffic smothered his words. Marnie caught snatches, '… about it … the office …' The woman's reaction was a vigorous nodding of the head. The man pointed under the bridge, adjusted his accelerator and slid out of view.

The excitement over, Marnie headed back along the road towards *Sally Ann*.

———✺———

As Marnie left the bridge, the steerer of the narrowboat cruised under it and tied up against the first moored boat on the towpath side. He walked the short distance back to a small house that looked like a country cottage, nestling in the lea of the bridge. Of average height and build, fit and capable-looking, his walk had something of the rolling gait of a seaman. Stepping through the wrought-iron gate, he crossed the tiny front garden and pushed open the front door, ringing the bell as he entered.

The receptionist knew him well and announced him by intercom to the office manager. 'Gary's in reception asking to see you, Mike. Are you in?'

Gary winked at her. She smiled back and asked him to wait. Mike Brent came out from a passageway behind her and thrust a paper into her hand.

'Get me two copies of that, will you, Liz.' He turned to his visitor. 'Gary, to what do I owe the pleasure?'

Gary invited him to step outside and led him under the bridge. The two men stood facing the pool.

'D'you see it?'

Mike Brent scanned the scene. 'Give me a clue.'

'Titanic.'

'Try harder.'

Gary pointed. 'There. Got it?'

'Oh yeah. Looks like a crate of some sort.'

'That's it.'

'What's it got to do with the Titanic?'

'Iceberg.'

'It's big? Hard to tell from here.'

'It's big, all right.'

'You think it's a hazard to shipping?'

'It could do a lot of damage to a tupperware.'

'Mm … true. Trouble is, we don't have a crane in the area at the moment.'

Gary grinned. 'I can get it out … for a small fee, of course.' Mike Brent looked doubtful. Gary put a hand on his shoulder. 'You can't get your blokes to try to haul it out by hand ... Health and Safety at Work regulations. One slipped disc and you're in deep doggies' doo-doos. Industrial tribunal ... compensation ... damages ... early retirement '

'Yeah, yeah, all right, Gary. I get the picture.'

As Marnie drew closer to Maida Hill tunnel, the pavement began to climb. By the time she arrived alongside the mooring, she was a few feet higher than the towpath. She leaned against the railings staring down at the boat that was temporarily in her charge.

Sally Ann was painted maroon and dark blue, with a black hull and had none of the jaunty lines and stripes of some of the other boats. She lay drab at her mooring in the still water and looked abandoned. On both sides of the canal new leaves were sprouting on the trees, but *Sally Ann* had dead leaves on her roof and decking. Dirt from the overhanging plane trees dusted every surface. She seemed to live in a perpetual autumn, grimy and neglected.

Unlocking the gate to the towpath, Marnie found that close-up, *Sally Ann* was not only drab, but scratched and dented. Rust marks showed where she had scraped against walls and other boats. For someone's pride and joy, she was a very sorry sight.

'Excuse me!' An imperious voice from the pavement above startled Marnie. Looking down at her over the railings was an old lady with white hair, tweed jacket and a shopping basket, everybody's idea of a favourite granny.

'Good morning,' said Marnie.

'Good morning. Would you please tell your fellow boaters not to put their bags of rubbish under the trees on the pavement. Some of us try to have standards and keep the area presentable.'

'My *boaters?*' Marnie felt unable to identify herself with such a breed.

'Of course. It's you people who give the place a bad name, you know.'

This was too much. Marnie, virtually a complete newcomer, objected to being made spokesperson for people she did not even know. Strangely, she found it hard to put this idea into words, especially while being looked down on, literally and metaphorically.

'Are you sure that it's us?' She immediately regretted the *us*.

'Who else could it be?'

'Well, it certainly wasn't *me*.' Marnie was regaining her composure. 'You're not the only one to have standards, you know.'

'I'm glad to hear it. It's bad enough having to look out onto these scruffy boats. Look at them.' She gestured grandly in their direction.

Marnie looked, as instructed. The old lady certainly had a point. These were not all like the boats pictured in the publicity photos, moored outside the pubs that she had been visiting. On the other hand, some of them were not bad and a few were quite smart.

'Nothing that a lick of paint couldn't cure,' Marnie said, despite herself.

'Well, I hope you're going to do something with that boat of yours at long last. After all, it is a bit of an eyesore. A lick of paint certainly wouldn't come amiss.'

Marnie looked blank, taken aback at having her own criticisms thrown at her by a stranger. 'Actually, it's not quite as simple as that.'

'I suppose not,' the woman said generously. 'After all, you are just a lot of water gypsies.'

Marnie gaped. *Was this conversation real?* It was certainly becoming one-sided. True, she had put on a brightly-coloured long skirt as a gesture to freedom, the weekend and the onset of spring, but *water gypsy!* And she did wonder if her gold-hoop ear-rings were a touch flamboyant and open to mis-interpretation. She found herself fingering one self-consciously. Before she could formulate a coherent reply, the woman turned and was gone with a moderately cordial flourish.

Abandoned on the towpath, Marnie turned back to *Sally Ann* and climbed onto the deck, fumbling for the right key. She located it at the third attempt, opened the double doors, pushed the hatch forward and stepped down inside.

Her first impression was the atmosphere. Marnie had expected the interior to smell like a caravan. This was different and yet somehow familiar, a curious mixture combining oil, the sharp tang of diesel fuel and a pungent aroma of machinery. Of course, she realised, it was the same smell as the pink folder, only stronger. She hung the keys, in accordance with Paul's instructions, on the hook in the ceiling – or whatever it was called on a boat – and felt strangely satisfied at doing the right thing.

For several minutes she pottered about, opening all the windows and the forward cratch doors. She knew the front part of the boat was called the *cratch*, but had no idea why. There was a small electric fan, which she put on with no result. Then she remembered the *systems*. The boat had mains power at her mooring, but the electricity had to be switched on outside in the engine compartment. She found the isolator and pressed it down.

Back in the cabin, Marnie started as a loud growl came from under the sink.

'*What the hell* ...?' She had visions of wild beasts, but the noise was obviously mechanical and stopped after a few seconds.

'Morning, *Sally*.' She treated the growl as a form of greeting.

The fan was now working, and already the sourness in the air was fainter, or she had become accustomed to it. The bedding, the curtains, the towels hanging in the loo – was that the *heads*? – all seemed to be impregnated with the smell. Without thinking, Marnie heaped everything into a pile on the bed, tut-tutting at the variety of patterns and colours. She found carrier bags under the sink and bundled everything into them.

With more tut-tutting she inspected the crockery cupboard. Remnants of different sets, some chipped, some cracked. *Sally Ann* was kitted out with left-overs and hand-me-downs. Marnie recalled the conversation of the previous week with Beth and Paul.

'You get to know about values on a boat,' Beth had said. 'What if you do drink out of old odd mugs and don't have saucers? It doesn't matter. The main thing is to get away from it all.'

Well, *Sally Ann* was their boat and they could do what they liked with it (or should it be *her*?). Marnie would try to get down fairly regularly to keep it tidy and aired, but she had her own life to lead. She was the wrong side of thirty, with a failed marriage behind her, and she was trying to find a new direction by focusing on her career.

She emptied the water from a vase (chipped) and put the daffodils (dead) into another carrier bag. There were dishes left to dry in the sink. Marnie put them back in the cupboard, where they added to the overall variety. The units in the galley were fairly new and of reasonable quality. There were two round sink bowls with mixer taps and a wall-mounted water heater. The cooker was small but adequate and a gas fridge was tucked neatly under the work surface.

By now, the cabin space was cluttered with carrier bags, so Marnie lugged them outside ready for taking away. On deck she heard the throb of an engine and looked round to see a narrowboat passing. It was much smarter than *Sally Ann* in dark green and gold with shining brassware, moving very slowly, scarcely causing a ripple. A man and a woman were standing close together in the stern, the woman at the tiller. The steerer raised her hand briefly before reaching for a mug on the roof. Marnie smiled and waved back, noticing how beautiful the morning was, sunlight shining through the trees that lined the bank. Two children were sitting on the roof in bright orange life-jackets, dangling their legs over the side. Marnie thought she was starting to get the hang of boating. It was not as hard as she had imagined.

The sight of all the coffee being drunk was giving Marnie a thirst. She picked up the kettle and held it under the tap. The pump growled. She tried to light the gas. *Damn!* She was just thinking how typical it was of her sister to leave without checking there was gas on board, when she remembered the *systems*. No doubt there was a gas tap somewhere.

Out on deck, Marnie pulled off the lid of the gas locker and tried to work the switches. She turned the top one and the connector came away in her hand. She struggled to put it back on, worried that gas might be escaping, huddled over the gas bottle, trying to imagine the newspaper story of the explosion … and its fatal consequences.

'It goes the other way.' A voice at her elbow, a woman on the towpath. Marnie almost jumped with surprise.

'Sorry to creep up on you.'

Marnie straightened and turned. 'I didn't hear you coming.'

'I'm Jane … Jane Rutherford.' The woman held out her hand.

'Marnie Walker. Come in. I mean, come aboard.' She glanced at the gas bottle. Jane reached over and deftly fixed the connector back on, turning the switch, all in one fluid movement. She stepped onto the deck and replaced the lid on the container. Marnie led her into the cabin, put the kettle on the hob and struck a match. Still no flame.

'I think I've probably run out of gas,' she muttered.

'Have you turned on the cooker supply?'

'I haven't quite got the hang of all this.' Marnie fumbled at the side of the cooker, located a valve and turned it on. Still no gas at the burners.

'Keep the switch pressed down,' Jane suggested. 'It'll take a minute for the gas to come through.'

Marnie did so, and this time the gas flowed. The boat gave its low growl. 'All right, all right, I'm doing my best,' Marnie laughed. 'Why does that happen when I'm not turning on the tap?'

'It's just the water pump maintaining pressure in the system.'

'Oh, yes, the *system*. I've heard all about the famous *systems*. There's a file inches thick I've got to learn to recite.'

For the next few minutes while the water heated, Jane gave Marnie a guided tour of the boat's systems. She made it seem easy. Marnie took a few notes. Over coffee, Jane explained that Beth had told her Marnie would be looking in from time to time.

'So you're a neighbour, then?'

'We live in West London, but our boat, *Joshua*, is moored further along towards the pool. It's a lovely spot here. You're a boat enthusiast?'

'Not really. I've been for the odd trip on *Sally Ann*, but I'm not sure it's my sort of thing.'

'Well, be warned. You may find it addictive.'

'I've already been called a *water gypsy* once today. I don't think it's quite me, all this castles and roses stuff.'

'Castles and roses aren't really about gypsies,' Jane said. 'They probably derive from designs on furniture imported from the continent in Victorian times.'

'Really?' Marnie Walker, interior designer, sat up. 'I had no idea. That sounds interesting.'

'I could lend you some books, if you like that sort of thing.'

'I do, thanks.' Marnie was thinking more about her project for the brewery, than about the boats themselves.

Jane stood up. 'I'll drop them in next time I see you here. Thanks for the coffee. I must be off. We're taking *Joshua* to the supermarket at Kensal Green.'

'You do your shopping by narrowboat?'

'Always. Much easier than parking the car. Quicker too … no traffic to worry about. You can tie up right outside *Sainsbury's*. Try it some time.'

Definitely more to this boating lark than Marnie had imagined. She had a sudden thought.

'Jane, if you're going round the island, remember to watch out for the wooden box.'

'Wooden box?' Jane looked blank.

'There's a crate or something floating in the middle of the pool.' Marnie spread her arms. 'It's quite big, most of it submerged. You haven't seen it?'

'No.'

Marnie narrated the sighting by the woman on the barge roof.

Jane frowned. 'We'd better report it to the BW office. It's not likely to harm a narrowboat, but it could put a hole in a GRP.'

Marnie's turn to look blank. Jane explained. 'Sort of fibreglass, usually white, used on small cruisers. More fragile than steel. Thanks for the warning, Marnie.'

'Thanks for the tour of the *systems*.'

When Jane had left, Marnie cleared up, loaded the carrier bags into the boot of the car, carefully went over the boat, turning off everything and fastening all the windows. She looked at her watch. It was lunch time.

'Oh god, where's the day gone?' she murmured.

Behind her, she heard the rumble of a diesel engine and looked round. This boat was different from the others, the hull low in the water, high sides and round portholes, dark grey and dull green, the colours of a battleship from times past.

Marnie was ready to give the usual wave. Only one person stood at the tiller, an old man, thickset and immobile, wearing a grey pullover and a Panama hat, a pipe clamped in his mouth, staring ahead. There was no wave and no smile.

———※———

Gary had wasted no time in putting the word around that he needed some help to lift the crate from the pool. There was a tenner in it for anyone who could lend muscle to the operation, he said. With two or three other men, he reckoned he could get the crate out of the water and charge BW enough to make a tidy profit. The game plan was simple. He would nudge the crate towards the bank with his boat. There, the group would take firm hold of it and heave it clear.

That Saturday evening, on his way home from the pub, he heard footsteps behind him. He turned to look back and was surprised when a man spoke his name. In the semi-darkness Gary could not make out his features and he did not like the way a second man stayed back in the shadows. Knowing better than to speak out of turn, Gary opted for a casual response.

'Hi. I don't think I recognise you in this light.'

'That's all right, Gary.' A deep voice like gravel. 'I just wanted a little word.'

'Sure.'

'You've been asking for help to get the crate out of the cut. Any luck?'

'One or two of the lads might be up for it.'

'Why are you so interested in it?'

Gary shrugged. 'Want to make a few bob. Not often you get a chance to screw money *out of* BW. It's usually the reverse.'

The stranger waited. Gary had the feeling he was assessing his reply. 'A *few bob*.'

'Yeah. If it's yours, well, fair enough. I'll –'

'Not yet, Gary.'

'No?'

'No. Leave it for a while.'

'All right. I can leave it forever. It's not that important.'

'Let's talk about it. Meet me in the pub Monday tonight. Ten o'clock.'

'Okay. Who's paying?'

'On me, Gary. It'll be my pleasure.'

4
Sabbatical

Halfway through Monday morning, Marnie sat at her desk looking through the mail from the previous week. It had been sorted into priority order by her group's secretary. She was pondering the talk she had had earlier with Philip Everett, the senior partner, first about the brewery job, then about her dissatisfactions. He had been sympathetic and had gone through periods like that himself. After long spells of hard work he had sometimes felt stale. He had suggested an extended vacation to *recharge the batteries*. Marnie found herself making a note on her pad to check the battery-charger on *Sally Ann*.

The only snag was that she would have to hand over her current projects to Larry. It would be his big chance. Marnie was not sure she wanted him to have his Big Chance by doing her work. It was not his ability she doubted; it was personal. Although she knew that nobody was indispensable, she liked to think she could be the exception.

The phone rang. For the next ten minutes she discussed the brewery project. When she put the receiver down, she saw that she had doodled a pattern on her note pad: a castle surrounded by roses.

———⟨⟨⟨⟩———

It was a few minutes before ten that evening when Gary took the short walk from his boat to the pub. He felt apprehensive. It was not fear. After all, if the strangers had meant him any harm, they had had the perfect opportunity to do anything they wanted on Saturday night when they accosted him. But he wondered what they might have in mind and was sure it would not meet with approval by anyone on the side of the law. And there was one other small point: would he recognise the man who had offered to buy him a drink? Somehow he did not think that would be the main problem facing him that evening.

He was right. He had not walked two paces into the bar when a hand gripped his elbow and he was guided to a corner table. The man seated behind a large whisky flicked his chin up. Gary got the message. An eloquent invitation.

'I'll have the same as you.'

The guide disappeared. Another head gesture from the man at the table, this time towards a vacant chair. Gary sat down.

'You know my name's Gary, but I don't know yours.'

'Don't worry about it.' The same gravelly tone as before. 'I won't hold it against you.'

'So, er ... what can I do for you?'

The other man was back and placed a tumbler of whisky on the table in front of him. It was a generous measure. The man had not been kept waiting at the bar. Gary was not surprised. He picked up the glass and raised it towards his host.

'Cheers.'

'Cheers, Gary.'

They both took a slug of scotch, eyeing each other over the rim of the glass. Gary's host was middle-aged with a shaved head. He wore a black leather jacket over a black polo shirt. A gold stud in one ear and a gold watch gave him an air of malevolent affluence. Gary decided to wait for Gravel to say his piece. He did not have to wait long.

'Let's talk about the crate, Gary.'

'I did wonder if it might've gone by now.'

'No. That's where you come in. You saw it first. I wouldn't want to queer your pitch.'

'But you are interested in it.'

'A passing interest, you might say.'

Gary's own interest in the crate was diminishing rapidly.

The stranger went on. 'So what are your plans?'

'I had thought of lifting it out ... for a small charge to British Waterways, of course.'

'*Had thought?*'

'It was just an idea.'

'It's a very good idea. We wouldn't want any boats to come to grief on account of it, would we, Gary?'

'I suppose not.'

'No. So I think it would be very public-spirited of you to lift it out.'

'All right. I'll get it lifted tomorrow.'

The stranger shook his head. 'Not tomorrow, Gary.'

'No? When then?'

'I should hold off till Friday. That should give you time to get your team together. No rush, no hassle.'

'If you say so.'

'Who knows ...? You might get covered in the weekend press.'

Gary looked blank.

'Friday would be best, Gary. Trust me.'

The next evening Marnie drove to Little Venice to check the batteries on *Sally Ann*. It was around eight o'clock when she arrived, and some of the boats were showing lights in their windows. The canal had an inviting atmosphere in the dusk, with street lamps filtered through new leaves, and a background glow from the windows of tall houses on either side.

In the engine compartment there were two lorry-size batteries. Marnie changed the leads of the charger from one to the other and stepped down into the cabin. She switched on the lights and grimaced. They gave a harsh white glare. There was an oil lamp on the workbench in the galley, and she took off the globe and chimney to see if the wicks were in place. She lit them with her Zippo, turned them down low and replaced the glassware.

In a storage jar, one of three on the galley shelf – each in a different style – she found a bag of ground coffee and set the filter machine to work. Soon, its smell filled the cabin, and the oil lamp had warmed enough for Marnie to turn up the wicks.

The furniture on board was a motley collection of collapsible kitchen chairs round a drop-leaf table discarded from someone's flat years ago. The impression was folksy but jumbled, and although it irritated Marnie less in subdued lighting, it was a definite eyesore.

She settled herself with coffee at the table in the saloon and began to draw up a list of all her projects at work, writing down the action needed on each one and the timetable for completion. Against the names of the jobs she wrote the initials of the colleagues who would have to see them through if she went away. Larry would have more than half the workload.

'What do I want out of this?' she muttered.

She put a circle round Larry's initials on the list. She wondered if she really cared, as long as she had a break. It was all very unsettling and, since her split with Simon three years before, and now Beth's departure, she felt increasingly isolated. Of course people would say it was just a phase, she knew that, but it was still a problem.

The water pump growled. The boat no longer felt strange to her. She picked up her list of jobs and read through the items, her pen stuck in the corner of her mouth like a cigar. Strangely, she had never had any desire to smoke on *Sally Ann*.

She scribbled on the pad: 'curtains'. She added 'crockery' and looked around the cabin, musing on what she would do if the boat belonged to her. She thought of the patches of rust on the hull and the scratches on the paintwork, the ropes that were frayed, the fenders made of plastic in different colours.

There was so much to do. She was glad it was not her responsibility.

———— ɯɯ ————

Marnie had to stay on late at the office on Wednesday to finish off the schedule for a 'rush job'. That meant the client had dithered for so long that everything had to be done too quickly. Having finished her work, Marnie set off for the loo from which she emerged a few minutes later with hair brushed and make-up revitalised. Philip was perched on the corner of her desk, exhaling smoke from a cigarette, holding a photograph of *Sally Ann*.

'This your sister's boat?'

'Yep. That's *Sally Ann*.'

Philip studied it closely. 'I've often wanted to have a go on one. Looks like fun.'

'From closer it looks like a lot of work. Don't believe cameras. They lie.'

Philip put the photograph down and drew on the cigarette. Marnie recognised the sign. He had something to say. She waited.

'Marnie … have you thought about our chat the other day? Are you serious about wanting a break?'

She hesitated. There would never be the possibility of a clean break, and the idea of just dropping everything was absurd.

'I don't really see it as a practical proposition.'

Philip was smiling. 'Are you indispensable, Marnie?'

'Aren't we all?'

'Seriously, though.' He took another pull on the cigarette. 'Willards Brewery liked your designs, even though you had reservations about them. Perhaps it's not a bad time to have a break. We could organise the work around the office. I know the signs, Marnie.'

'You think I'm getting stale?'

'I think you've had a lot to cope with and you haven't had a holiday in ages. You could regard it as a sabbatical.'

'They seem to be all the rage just now.'

'You could take a month or two ... the whole summer if you wanted ... go on a trip, go abroad somewhere. See new things. That's what I did a few years ago. It did me a power of good.'

'What about the work you left behind?'

'There's always someone to deal with it. You ought to write a list of your projects and who'd handle them. Five years ago we would've been too busy to cope. At the moment, we can manage.'

'The bulk of the work would land on Larry.'

'Ah ...' Philip grinned. 'Well, he's an able chap. *He* certainly thinks so.'

Marnie shrugged.

'Look, Marnie, you said you needed a break. I want to help you ... as a friend. We're offering you the chance while we can. You're a first class designer and it would help you sort yourself out.'

'You really think I could?'

'Just do it.'

Marnie nodded thoughtfully. She picked up her bag and slung the strap over her shoulder, ready to leave. Philip, still sitting on the corner of the desk, looked around for an ashtray. Not finding one, he leaned over and stubbed the cigarette out in the waste bin.

Marnie smiled. 'Enjoy it while you can, Philip. You won't be able to do that when Larry's in charge.'

—✦—

Out in the parking area, Marnie got in the car and took out the jobs list she had written on *Sally Ann*. At the bottom she saw the notes about curtains and crockery. An idea blossomed: today was late night shopping in the West End. She reread the list, got out of the car and headed for the nearest tube. In twenty minutes she could be in Oxford Street.

—✦—

Later that evening, Marnie dumped her briefcase and the Liberty bag on the mat and opened her front door. She had not bothered to carry the box of crockery up the stairs, but had left it in the boot of the car. The flowers on the hall table were fading; yesterday's newspapers were still lying on the sofa in the living room. The flat had an unaccustomed air of neglect.

It was too late for a meal. Over toast and coffee she sat in the kitchen to go through the post. In with the credit card bill and the junk mail, was a card from Beth telling her they had arrived safely in Boston. Cryptically, Beth had added a note: 'Try not to go bankrupt buying things for *Sally*!' Definitely a witch.

Marnie tried to imagine how the curtains would look. They had been a special offer, but even then much dearer than she had planned. It was the same story in Habitat where she had found a new range of crockery, dark blue with a pale cream band.

Now that she had made up her mind, everything seemed easier. She knew what she was doing and was going to get on with it. *Just do it*, as Philip had said. Were there reasons why he was keen for her to be away? She put the idea out of her head, sat at the desk in the living room and switched on the computer. In ten minutes the list of jobs was sliding from the printer. She had written herself out of the office for months to come.

Marnie spent what remained of the evening tidying the flat. Just before ten the phone rang. It was Jane Rutherford. She had the books she had promised to lend Marnie. They agreed to meet the next day.

5
Joshua

Marnie liked Jane's boat. *Joshua* was a sixty-footer, dark blue with gold banding and highly-polished brass mushrooms on the roof. The interior had fitted bookshelves, comfortable seating and a lived-in atmosphere. Almost every inch of the walls seemed to be covered in paintings or framed photographs. There were scenes of the waterways in all seasons and a few ancient black and white photos: strong faces staring out from under flat caps or Victorian bonnets, lads and lasses holding the bridles of sturdy horses, children smiling shyly from cabin roofs.

Marnie arrived at five o'clock. Jane declared that the sun was over the yard arm, so they sat in the saloon, each clutching a gin and tonic. Jane gave Marnie the small collection of books.

Marnie read the titles. 'It'll take me a while to get through this lot.'

'Don't worry, keep them for as long as you need. I'll want them back some time, apart from the one at the bottom. That's for you to keep.'

Marnie read its cover. '*Boat Decoration – styles and techniques* … by Jane Rutherford.'

'It's a spare one I had lying around. I'd like it to go to a good home.'

'So you're a writer?'

'Not exactly. That's my only book so far. I do sign-writing on boats and I teach it too. What about you?'

'I'm an interior designer.' Marnie took out a business card.

Jane read it and tucked it into her shirt pocket. 'Hence your interest in castles and roses. That kind of thing didn't always pay the bills. I've often had to take other jobs to made ends meet.'

'So you taught art?'

'I've taught … done temping … even worked in a job centre, advising on benefits. But now, I've got a steady clientele. Sometimes I have to turn work away.'

The sound of an engine made Jane incline her head to the window. Marnie saw the passing form of the grey and green boat with no name and the old man with the Panama hat, standing rigid at the stern.

'I've seen him before. Do you know him, Jane?'

'Oh yes. That's Old Peter.'

Marnie took another sip from the gin and tonic. 'Old Peter?'

'That's what everyone calls him … rather a mysterious figure. There are all sorts of stories about him.'

'Stories?'

'You'll find that on the cut. People who'd seem very ordinary in the outside world can be real characters on the waterways, and everyone's got a story to tell.'

'So Old Peter isn't just a harmless recluse?'

'Who knows? What I do know is he used to be a working boatman. He's an engineer … a registered boat inspector years ago. I've heard his family history on the canals goes back generations.'

'He told you all this?'

'No. I came across an article on old boating characters in one of the waterways magazines … recognised him from a photo. His real name is Peter William Gibson.'

'I'll have to take out a subscription.'

'There are some back copies over there. Help yourself. I warned you this could become addictive.'

'Thanks. So what have you learnt about him?'

'Two things of real interest … only one of them from the magazine. He was named after his grandfather, the original skipper of *Captain* and *Mate*.' Marnie looked blank. Jane explained. 'Two of the oldest working boats on the cut … steam-powered … built as a working pair almost a century ago. Now they're restored and back together again.'

'So he's like living history.'

'He was already retired when we first came here years ago … lived on a boat in those days, the other side of the basin. Now he lives in a caravan down the arm by the first bridge. You see him tootling up and down, but I don't know where he gets to.'

'*Tootling?*'

'To tootle is to go on a short trip.'

'So a tootle would be such a trip?'

'You seem to've got the hang of it, Marnie.'

'Is that a recognised boating term?'

'Probably not, but it's a term I use.'

Marnie looked out of the porthole. 'You said there were two things of interest about Old Peter. What was the other one?'

Jane shook her head. 'It's just gossip, really … probably Chinese whispers.'

'You've lost me.'

'Well … when we first came here more than ten years ago, Derek, my husband, said he'd heard something about Old Peter – he was called that even then – from another old guy in the pub. It was odd …'

'What was it?'

Jane frowned. 'It seems silly to repeat it … but apparently Old Peter owns something very valuable.'

'Like what?'

'The old boy couldn't – or wouldn't – say.'

'Old Peter doesn't give an impression of wealth … unless he's an eccentric millionaire.'

'I've known one of them,' Jane said. 'We had an old lady living near us when I was at school. She always wore the same ancient coat in all weathers, topped off with a battered black hat in winter. My mother used to take her homemade cakes sometimes … invited her to tea. She accepted the cakes but always turned down the invitations.' Jane's face clouded over. 'She was dead for three days before anyone noticed the milk collecting on the doorstep. You can guess the rest.'

'They found her mattress stuffed with money and a will leaving everything to Battersea Dog's Home?'

'Something like that.'

'And you think Old Peter might be the same?'

'Who knows?' Jane reached for the gin bottle. 'Ready for another?'

'No thanks … better not … got to drive home. Things to do.'

'You've made plans?'

Marnie reflected for a moment. 'I'm not planning to be here that much.'

'Just the occasional visit to check over the boat?'

Marnie hesitated. 'I'm thinking of taking *Sally* for a trip.'

'You mean a tootle?'

'No, a proper journey.'

Jane looked at her quizzically. 'Single-handed?'

'That's the idea.'

'How much do you know about boating, Marnie?'

'Beth and Paul are always telling me how easy it is. That's true isn't it?'

Jane rolled her eyes. 'I think I'd better take you in hand. You've got a lot to learn.'

———— ✠ ————

After leaving Jane, Marnie went along to *Sally Ann*. She opened all the windows to air the boat and went back up on deck to look at the controls. They were surprisingly simple. In the middle of the deck was a tall handle that came up to her chest from a hole in the floor. At the top, it had a grip like the throttle of a motor-bike. The only other control seemed to be a smaller handle attached to the side of the stern rail by a flimsy-looking bracket. It was obviously designed to slide up and down, but when she tried to move it, the whole thing was stiff.

Just inside the door, was a simple control panel with switches marked *Lights* and *Bilge pump* and a prominent red button. After a few moments' hesitation, Marnie pressed it. Immediately, there was a wheezing sound from under her feet, a loud clanking, a puff of grey smoke from the stern, and the engine clattered into life. The elation at this single-handed achievement gave way very quickly to a series of questions. Should it be doing this? Would it overheat? Should she have checked the oil, or added some to the engine? Exactly where was the engine? Should she press any of the other switches? Most important of all: how do you switch it off?

For the moment it seemed happy enough, but Marnie had the feeling, entirely justified, that she was not in control. She realised that putting up new curtains and changing the crockery were just a small part of the great mystery of running a narrowboat. The engine thudded on, no longer smoking, and she could feel a tremor in the decking under her feet. She noticed for the first time that the deck was made up of several sections and decided to lift up the centre panel. Sure enough, there was the engine. It was much bigger than she had imagined, painted a grimy dark red.

Marnie's instincts told her that now was the time to turn it off, before she caused any damage. She would run along and ask Jane. Turning to leap off the deck, she bounced straight into the arms of a man standing on the towpath. She hastily apologised and he grinned back at her. He was about Marnie's age, wearing blue jeans and a black T-shirt. He had short, dark curly hair, a twinkle in the eye and an air of self-confidence.

'Nice motor,' he said, still grinning.

'Do you think so? I want to turn it off, but … I don't know how.'

'It'll cost you.'

Marnie guessed it was meant as a joke, but would feel more like smiling when the engine was silent again. The man stepped nimbly onto the deck and looked at the controls.

'No cut-off switch,' he said. 'You're supposed to have a cut-off.'

'There must be some way …' Marnie began. Before she could finish, the man knelt down, put his hand under the top step, held it there for a few seconds till the engine clanked to a stop. He stood up, looked at the controls and shook his head.

'You didn't have the fuel pump on. Sure way of getting air in the system.'

'I … I had no idea.' Marnie was starting to resent the confident tone of the man in the face of her own inadequacies. She wanted to get back onto her own terrain, but realised that for the moment she was out of her league. Also, she felt she ought to show some gratitude at being released from her predicament. 'I'm Marnie.' She held out her hand.

He took it, perhaps a little more firmly than was necessary, looking her steadily in the eyes, smiling all the while. 'My name's Gary. If you need any help with the boat, just let me know. I'll be happy to oblige. Any time.'

'Thank you.'

'No problem.'

'How did you switch it off?'

Gary lifted out the top step and pointed to a lever at the side of the engine. 'See that? You just push it back and hold it till the engine cuts out.'

Marnie studied this carefully. She had a lot to learn. Gary lifted out the central inspection panel in the deck and looked at the engine. He made a tut-tutting sound and drew in breath between his teeth.

'What's the matter?' Marnie was starting to get worried.

'It's an old'un … probably needs a full service … maybe an overhaul. These can be a load of trouble if you're not careful.'

Marnie thought of the fortune she had just spent on new curtains and crockery, of her plans for a sabbatical and a complete break for the summer. Perhaps it was not so wise after all. She decided on a tone of casual nonchalance.

'Oh well, it's not my boat, actually. I'm just minding it for my sister while she's away.'

Gary looked thoughtful, then smiled again. 'Well, any time.' He turned to go. 'Let me know if you want the engine overhauled. Must be off.'

'Thanks again.'

'My pleasure.' Gary winked and walked off.

6
Crate

Gary had it all worked out. It was a neat plan, an improvement on the original, and it could not fail. They assembled by the pool of Little Venice on Friday morning just after ten watched by random passers-by and two men with notebooks and cameras. Two of his mates were waiting on the bank beside the bridge with ropes contrived into a harness. Gary used his boat to push the crate gently towards them. They knelt down and guided the crate into position. Now came the clever part. A third mate was waiting on the slope up to the bridge in his JCB. He had borrowed it from the building site where he was working, just two minutes drive from the pool. From the bucket of the digger hung another rope formed into a noose. He lowered it carefully towards the water where Gary attached it to the harness with a bowline.

'Okay, Vince!'

At Gary's signal, the JCB driver raised the bucket to take up the slack, and the rope held firm. On the other side of the cut, a small group had gathered, mainly the staff from the BW office. Mike Brent stood in the middle of his team with arms folded, grudgingly admiring Gary's plan.

Gary grinned across at the spectators, looked up at Vince and raised his hand. The engine roared as the machine tugged the box clear of the water. Another signal from Gary and the digger's arm swung over the bank, the two men putting their hands up to prevent it from slipping in the harness. The arm of the JCB stopped, but the crate swayed in the air. It lurched precariously and suddenly slid without warning out of the ropes that had held it. The men jumped clear as the crate crashed down onto the paving, one corner taking the full force of the impact.

The crate burst apart on the bank, water gushing and slime oozing out as it fell to pieces. From his boat, Gary let out an expletive that carried across the water. His two mates on the bank gave a cheer and burst out laughing. Then, abruptly, the laughter stopped. The men stared at the slippery detritus on the canalside, made groaning sounds and simultaneously threw up. Gary stared, horrified. Cameras flashed. On the far bank a woman screamed. Another fainted.

7
Police

On Saturday afternoon, Marnie returned to the boat. She had made the first pair of curtains during the morning and was keen to try them out. They looked good and she wanted to rush home to finish the rest. Before doing so, she rummaged around in the cupboards to see if there were any books on the technical side of narrowboating in general and on *Sally Ann* in particular. The pink folder made no reference to the basic practical matters of making the boat go and eventually stop.

She found a variety of manuals, a servicing guide for the engine, a small volume on knot-tying, maps (or were they *charts?*) of several canals, a copy of the Waterways Code and a well-thumbed paperback of murder on the Oxford Canal featuring Inspector Morse. There was nothing that told her how to make *Sally Ann* actually work.

While she was thumbing through the magazines, Marnie became aware of movement on the boat. A voice hailed her from the stern deck.

'Hallo! Anyone in there?' A man's voice with a ring of authority about it. 'Police. I'm coming aboard.'

'Hallo? Yes, I'm here.' Marnie began walking through the boat and discovered a constable at the foot of the steps in the sleeping cabin. 'Er … you'd better come through.'

She led the way back to the saloon. The policeman was tall and gangling, and even when holding his hat he had to stoop to avoid contact with the roof.

Marnie offered him a seat. 'What can I do for you?'

'We're conducting some enquiries in the area.' He pulled out a notebook. 'Your name, please?'

'Marnie Walker.'

'And this is your boat?'

'Not exactly.'

'Meaning?'

'It belongs to my sister and her husband.'

'You have their permission to use the boat.'

'I'm looking after it in their absence. They're working in America at the moment.'

'America?' He made it sound sinister. 'What are they doing there?'

Marnie felt a ridiculous urge to tell him they were collecting a consignment of heroine and cocaine while setting up a new vice ring and robbing a few banks. 'My brother-in-law, Paul – that's Dr Paul Sutton – is on sabbatical leave. He's a lecturer at University College.' She refrained from adding that he was a biochemist. 'They're in Boston for a year.'

'Oh.' He sounded disappointed and wrote rapid notes. 'Have you seen any odd characters in the area lately?'

Marnie thought of Old Peter, Gary and the weird folk who went by on very tatty craft from time to time. 'Not really. I've only been here once or twice in the past week.'

'So you haven't noticed a wooden crate floating in the pool?'

'Wooden crate? Well yes, I did see a box of some sort the other day … on my first visit.'

'What day was that?'

'Saturday … last Saturday morning.'

'Where were you at the time you saw it?'

'On the bridge … the further one. I found a parking space as soon as I arrived and I was on my way here when I paused to look at the pool.'

'That must be a first.'

Marnie's eyes widened. 'The first sighting of your crate?'

'No, the first time I've heard anyone say they got a parking space as soon as they arrived.'

Marnie smiled. 'Why are you interested in the crate?'

'Have you seen it since then?'

'No. I haven't been along that way. Has it caused an accident? Someone said it could be a real hazard to a GRP.'

The officer closed his notebook and tucked it into a breast pocket. 'Not just to a GRP,' he muttered and stood up. He failed to remember the lack of internal height of the cabin.

'Mind your – '

Marnie was too late. She winced at the sound of the impact as his head hit the ceiling. The policeman made his way carefully out through the boat while Marnie followed him onto the stern deck.

'Thank you, miss.'

'You didn't tell me why you were interested in the crate.'

'You really don't know?' Marnie shook her head. 'Don't you read the papers or watch the news on TV?'

Marnie thought how obsessed she had become with getting the boat ready for her sabbatical. The outside world seemed to have receded into the background.

'Sorry. I've been very busy with work this week.'

The policeman looked at her steadily. 'The crate was pulled out of the water yesterday morning and found to contain parts of a dismembered body. Good afternoon, miss.'

Back in the cabin, Marnie searched in the cupboards and was relieved to find a bottle of brandy. She poured herself a good measure, gulped down half of it and sat at the table. It had been the first time she had ever been questioned by the police. She hoped it would be the last. She had been a boater for just one week.

8
Lesson

'I think you've got to watch that one.' Jane took the cup of coffee that Marnie handed to her.

It was Monday, and Marnie had gone to Little Venice straight from the office. They sat out on deck having a quick cup before Marnie's first boating lesson.

'In what way?'

Jane looked thoughtful. 'Well, for a start, Gary knows a lot about boats, that's for sure. The trouble is, he knows that you don't know about them, and he's the type who'd try to exploit that.'

'I know what you mean. Still, he did help me out.'

'Oh yes, he'd always do that. Boat people are usually a very decent bunch.'

'And he's quite personable,' Marnie observed.

Jane looked thoughtful again. 'Yes, and that's another thing. He *is* personable and he knows it. I never quite trust a man who smiles all the time he's talking to you.'

They both nodded sagely.

'What does he do ... for a living, I mean?'

'Good question. You'll find that's a feature of life on the waterways ... *not* knowing what people do in the ... *real world*, so to say.'

'I don't follow.'

'On the cut – that's what a lot of folks call the canal – you tend to know people mainly just by their first name – or sometimes a nickname – plus the name of their boat as a kind of identifier.'

'So I'm not Marnie Walker round here ... just Marnie, brackets *Sally Ann?*'

'Exactly. I'm Jane, brackets *Joshua.*'

'And Gary? What's he got in his brackets?'

Jane pulled a funny face. 'Doesn't bear thinking about!' They laughed. 'His boat's called *Garrow*, and he lives on it, though strictly speaking he's not supposed to. He doesn't have a residential mooring.'

'And you don't know what he does for a living?'

'I've seen him drive one of the waterbuses. Sometimes he ferries cargo on other people's boats ... does odd jobs. But I'll tell you this, he knows everyone and everything that's going on. If you want anything, talk to Gary, he'll arrange it. The rest of the time ...' She shrugged.

'How curious.'

'That's the cut ... a private world in more ways than one.' Jane stood up. 'Ready for your lesson?'

Marnie remained seated. She had put off talking about the crate, but felt it could not be ignored any longer. 'Before we do that ... have you been visited by the police?'

'The *police*? No, why, should I have been?'

'I would've thought so by now.'

'What d'you mean?'

'You know that box floating around in the pool like an iceberg?'

'Sure. It's about time BW pulled it out. It's going to be bad news for somebody.'

'It already has been.'

'Pulled out?'

'Both.'

'I don't get it.'

'You haven't heard what happened?'

'We were at my sister's for the weekend, remember? I'm out of touch. Tell me.'

'This policeman came here asking questions on Saturday. It seems the box was pulled out of the water on Friday and they found a body inside ... or rather, parts of a body.'

Jane's hand leapt to her mouth. 'Oh my god ...'

'I'm surprised they haven't been along to question you. I got the impression they wanted to talk to everyone.'

'We only got back last night. What did he ask you?'

'If I'd seen the box. I told him I had ... once ... but that was all I could tell him.'

Jane looked shocked. 'Phew! A *body* ... how *horrible*.'

'Jane ...' Marnie hesitated over asking the question that was troubling her. 'Not sure how to put this ...'

Jane saved her the effort. 'The answer is no. We don't regularly get bodies dumped in the canal, if that's what's on your mind. Supermarket trolleys, yes, from time to time ... the occasional beer can ...' She pulled a face. 'The odd condom ... but *not* bodies. This is not gangland.'

'Glad to hear it. I've just spent a fortune on curtains.'

Before the lesson began, Jane did a quick tour of inspection of the controls. She checked the level of diesel in the tank using a bamboo stick. It seemed to Marnie a suitably archaic way of doing the job. On her car a computer measured the fuel in litres to two decimal points.

Jane explained about the bilge pump, the stern gland, the fuel pump, the isolator switches for the batteries, the drop filter and the engine cut-out. Marnie took copious notes.

'Any questions so far?'

'Where do you go for fuel? And how many miles does she do to the gallon?'

'Marinas and boatyards mainly. If you fill up, you can forget it for the rest of the year. Don't drip diesel onto the deck. It's very slippery.'

'Right. What next?' Marnie's pencil was poised over the notebook.

'Something quite important,' said Jane. 'Try to relax. Don't look so serious. Enjoy it. It's meant to be fun. It *is* fun. Write that down.'

Marnie kept a straight face while she wrote. 'Boating ... is ... fun. Got it.'

'Okay. Let's get the deck back in place and take her for a tootle!'

While they were fitting the bulky sections of decking, Marnie saw Old Peter's boat glide by. The old man stood holding the tiller, immobile as ever, without glancing in their direction. Jane did not notice him pass, and Marnie said nothing.

When the deck was replaced, Jane stretched her back. 'Ready for off?' Marnie raised a thumb. 'Good. Routine for starting.'

Marnie concentrated hard. She took a deep breath. Jane laughed and shook her head.

'I know, I know,' Marnie said. 'This is fun and I have to enjoy it. I just don't want to get it wrong, that's all.'

'Of course. Just get the routine clear and it's a doddle.'

Marnie spoke as she wrote the note, 'Tootle equals doddle.'

Jane laughed, disconnected the mains electricity supply and hopped back onto the deck.

'Now, you switch on the fuel pump. It's the same as the bilge pump, only you press it down instead of up.'

Jane moved aside to let Marnie perform the action.

'Then you check the gear lever's in neutral and press the starter button.' Marnie did this and the engine began thumping. Jane looked over the stern at the exhaust, which gave off light grey puffs of smoke. Jane seemed content with this.

They cast off and the bow swung out slowly towards mid-channel. Marnie felt ridiculously thrilled at this and instinctively put a hand on the tiller.

'Over to you, skipper,' said Jane. 'Take her away.'

Marnie pulled the heavy lever to engage forward gear and pressed down on the accelerator. Nothing happened. The handle was rigid. The engine was idling and the boat was barely moving. Marnie had no idea what to do.

'We can go a bit faster,' Jane encouraged. 'We're clear of the moored boats.' She bent down to the accelerator and pressed. Feeling the resistance, she unscrewed it to loosen the grip, pressed it down a couple of inches and left it there. *Sally Ann* gained speed with the wake bubbling behind her, heading for the tunnel. The prow slid forward into the darkness. Jane switched on the headlamp.

Marnie was not sure whether to tell Jane she had never actually handled the boat before. She was becoming aware that steering *Sally Ann* was not as simple as she had thought. Now, under power and in a dark, narrow tunnel, Marnie felt disoriented and found it hard to keep the boat pointing straight ahead. Every now and then, Jane gave the tiller a prod to adjust the course.

Jane said something. The engine was too loud for Marnie to hear properly but for one ridiculous moment, she thought Jane had said that a boat was coming in from the opposite direction. She stared in horror. The far end of the tunnel had become much brighter. She was looking at a headlamp. A boat *was* coming in from the opposite direction.

Marnie felt panic-stricken. *What do I do now? Are we going to crash? How deep is a canal, anyway?* She was wondering which side you were supposed to pass on – *try* to pass on – when Jane pointed to the right. By now, the other boat was almost upon them. Marnie held her breath as she squeezed *Sally Ann* as close as she could up against the wall.

Just as Marnie was congratulating herself on a brilliant manoeuvre, *Sally Ann* struck the retaining barrier and bounced off. The noise as they hit the other boat amidships was like the striking of a great bell and it echoed down the tunnel. Marnie found that she had closed her eyes and, when she dared to open them, the boat had passed. She gripped the tiller hard, looking straight ahead, breathing heavily. When they emerged at the other end, Marnie experienced a feeling of gloom far darker than the tunnel.

Jane was laughing jubilantly. Marnie thought she was laughing at her mistake, but she was looking back into the tunnel.

'Well, that'll teach him. You're not supposed to enter the tunnel when another boat's in already.' Jane adjusted the tiller, still laughing. 'He won't do that again in a hurry!'

'Who won't?'

'Gary, of course. Didn't you recognise him?'

'No.' Marnie bit her lip. 'I was … too busy … concentrating.'

'Well you're a cool one and no mistake.' There was admiration in Jane's voice.

'Concentrating … on keeping my eyes shut.'

They both laughed out loud.

———※※———

After Jane had left, Marnie sat at the table in the cabin – no, the *saloon* – and wrote notes of what she had learnt. She was starting to feel she was making progress. The boat was becoming less of a mystery.

It was also becoming less of a jumble. She had brought with her the remaining curtains, and spent half an hour taking down the old ones, putting up the new. During the course of her work, she needed more light and turned on the oil lamps.

Still fired with energy, she cleared the cupboards, putting everything that seemed out of keeping or just plain ugly into a black plastic sack. Standards were going to rise under Marnie's stewardship.

In the lamplight the new curtains transformed the whole interior. She pondered. If she replaced the flooring with new carpet tiles and spread a new cover on the bed, *Sally Ann* would be a completely different boat.

Dusk had changed to night now. Little Venice was lit up, looking its most theatrical. Marnie wondered if the waterways could be her world for the whole summer. Then she remembered the crate floating partly submerged in the attractive waters of the pool. Was this world as charming as it appeared on the surface, or did it have a sinister side that she had barely glimpsed?

———※※———

Gary hopped ashore from *Garrow* that evening just before ten and set off for the pub. He was uncertain about the reception he might receive from Gravel, but sure he would be around, even though they had made no arrangement to meet. It came as no surprise when he found himself flanked by two dim shapes in a dark corner.

Gary played it cool. 'Hi.'

'Hallo, Gary.' The unmistakable gravelly voice. 'You've been a busy boy.'

'It was tricky, getting it out. The crate was covered with slime and –'

'I know, my friend. I was there. It had to be opened anyway sooner or later. You just made it that bit more ... dramatic. I see they've cleaned up the puke from the bank.'

'Doesn't go down well with the tourists ... piles of vomit and bits of dead body lying about can give a place a bad name.'

'You could have a point there, Gary. Why don't we go to the pub for another little chat?'

'Fine ... but it might be crowded.'

'Don't worry, I expect we'll squeeze in somewhere.'

The pub was busy, with standing room only, but by a quirk that Gary did not think was a miracle of coincidence, Gravel's usual table in the corner was unoccupied. They had scarcely had time to sit when Gravel's sidekick placed tumblers of whisky in front of them.

'You've been round here quite a while, Gary.' Gravel was scanning the bar as he spoke.

'A few years.'

'You must know a lot about what goes on.'

Gary shrugged. 'I try to keep out of most of it.'

'But you hear things ... gossip ... rumours. Know what I mean?'

'Yeah ... s'pose so.'

'Talk to me about the old geezer with the boat down the Paddington Arm.'

'Old Peter?'

'That's the one.'

'What about him?'

'Gary ...'

'I dunno much about him, really. He used to do work on boats, but he's getting on a bit now. Must be well in his seventies.'

'I hear he's eighty-three.'

'There you are, then.'

'Tell me about the rumours, Gary.' There was an edge of impatience to the gravelly tone.

Gary racked his brain. 'Rumours,' he murmured. He sipped the scotch, scratched his ear. 'Oh ... that was *ages* ago. I didn't believe it then.'

'What didn't you believe?'

'Stands to reason. No one would own something valuable and live in a beat-up old caravan on the bank.'

'Something *valuable*,' Gravel repeated. 'Like what?'

'Dunno. No one ever said. There was something about him having this ... valuable stuff, that's all.'

'You used to know him, Gary. You were mates, or so I heard.'

'Not mates, really. I helped him with a couple of jobs … changed a fly-wheel on an old engine once … two-man job that was … stuff like that. He never said much … didn't drink … didn't bet. Not an easy bloke to be mates with.'

'You must've formed an opinion about what it might be. Think back. Did he ever mention anything that might give you some idea?'

'I told you … he never said much at all. I don't know where you got the idea he had valuables. Always seemed skint to me.'

Gravel took a long pull at his whisky. Gary waited.

'Do you remember Arthur Fredericks, Gary?'

'The name does seem familiar.'

'Working boatman … one of the old breed … worked Joshers way back.'

'Yeah … I remember. Doesn't he live down Limehouse way?'

'Not any more.'

Gary had a vision of body parts falling out of a smashed crate. He took a hasty sip of scotch.

'He died a few weeks back. At his funeral someone told me he'd been big buddies with Old Peter yonks ago.'

'Doesn't surprise me. All these old boys knew each other. They're dying out now.'

'Which is why it's important to find out about them while they're still with us, Gary.'

Gary was getting the picture. 'You want me to find out about this valuable stuff Old Peter's supposed to have stashed away under his pillow?'

'That's right. Then we can have another little drink together.'

Gary downed his scotch. 'That'll be nice.'

———

Marnie got home around ten o'clock and headed straight for the shower. The phone rang while she was undressing.

'Hi Marnie, it's Beth.' Her sister's voice was as clear as if she was in the next room.

'Where are you?'

'In Boston, in the apartment with my feet up. Just been shopping. How's things?'

'Okay. How's the sabbatical going?'

'Fine. Paul's enjoying being in a department that actually has some money for research. What about you? Any improvement with Steve?'

'Er no … haven't seen him. I'm much too busy.'

'Work isn't the only thing, Marnie.'

'I know. In fact, I've asked for a sabbatical. Phil's agreed I can take the whole summer.'

'No *kidding*? That's *great*! So you're coming over? We've got loads of room here.'

Beth's suggestion took Marnie off guard. She had been to the States once before and had had a great time. It surprised her to realise that she had not even considered that as an option. 'Well, actually … I had thought about going somewhere on *Sally Ann*.'

This time it was Beth who paused. '*Sally Ann*? You want to go for a trip on the *boat*?'

'Yes. That's all right, isn't it? You said I could.'

'Sure. It's just a surprise, that's all. I didn't think you were that keen. Who are you going with … Steve?' There was a suspicious smile in her voice.

'No, nobody … just by myself.'

'*Really?* Well, you'd better get some practice in. There's a fair bit to learn if you want to go solo. You could ask Jane Rutherford for advice. Her boat's called *Joshua* … she's very helpful. There are one or two others along the cut. But watch out for a character called Gary. You might bump into him.'

Marnie winced. 'I already have.'

'Don't say I didn't warn you.'

'Do you know an old man with a grey and green boat … Panama hat … pipe?'

'That's Old Peter. Everybody knows him. He's what's known as a *character*. Can't say I've ever spoken to him. Why do you ask?'

'Nothing in particular. I've seen him go by a few times.'

Beth gave Marnie her phone number and reminded her there was a five hours' time difference between them. Marnie said nothing about the body parts in the crate.

She showered in the white and blue tiled bathroom she had designed when she bought the flat three years before. Lathered with her favourite gel, she stood under the powerful hot jets. After *Sally Ann*, her home seemed so spacious. She wondered how she would cope with a shower on the boat that was so narrow you could hardly move.

Marnie dried herself on a blue and white striped towel. In the bedroom she switched on the CD player and let Corelli waft around her like a summer breeze. Would a trip on *Sally Ann* be a big mistake? She had once read that if you have a four-star lifestyle, you would not be happy with a one-star holiday.

She sat up in bed with a notepad and pencil and started to redesign the boat. When she nodded off, her head was filled with colours, the patterns of oriental rugs, designs for towels and tiles. And with the echo of the clang that had rung out when she bumped into Gary in the tunnel.

9
Plans

The handover of Marnie's jobs to her team was going well. The day after the boating lesson, she went direct to *Sally Ann* after work. She parked near the pool of Little Venice and calculated the meter had almost enough time left to take her up to the end of the charged parking period. A good sign, she thought.

Marnie walked slowly along the towpath looking at the boats. There must have been about forty, most of them reasonably presentable, but even the smartest had scratched paintwork. The canals were evidently not designed to keep up appearances. They were built of stone and steel, with hard surfaces and sharp corners.

Marnie wondered how she could smarten up *Sally Ann*'s drab, dreary colour scheme without a total repaint. She took a chair and notebook out onto the towpath and sketched the boat. The bow area looked a mess, so Marnie unhooked the cover that sagged sadly over the cratch and dumped it on the ground. Now *Sally Ann* had an almost raffish look, and for the first time Marnie could see a certain charm in her lines.

Lost in thought and concentration, Marnie spent more time than she realised imagining the boat in different colours. She had no desire to spend the summer stuck at the mooring with a paintbrush, but what if she just lightened the roof, touched up where necessary and eliminated the rust?

Suddenly she noticed that dusk was coming down. She heaved the defunct cover into the cratch-well, locked up and set off along the towpath in high spirits. It was a mild evening; the air was warm; swallows were swooping over the water. That had to be a good omen.

It was only when she was in the car that Marnie noticed the parking ticket stuck to the windscreen.

———✦———

Marnie arrived back at the flat, still fuming from the parking ticket. The red light on the answering machine winked at her, and she prodded its button irritably. After the beep, a cheerful voice.

'Hi, Marnie, it's Jane, Jane Rutherford. I seem to have been inspired by your enthusiasm and the fine weather. We've decided to take *Joshua* for a short trip, not just a *tootle*, a few days out in the country. Back at the weekend. Talk to you soon. Bye!'

Marnie wandered through to the kitchen. It was too late for her to be bothered with making a meal. This was becoming a habit. Rummaging in the fridge, she found a packet of smoked salmon. She pulled off two slices from a granary loaf in the freezer and popped them in the toaster. With the smell of hot toast permeating the kitchen, her appetite and morale revived slightly. She buttered the toast, laid salmon on each piece, sprinkled them with lemon juice and black pepper and ate at the workbench, perched on the stool, reading her notes on *Sally Ann*.

Sipping designer water, Marnie felt she was entering a kind of half-life, no longer fully engaged in the office, not yet part of the boating fraternity, on the brink of jeopardising a career with its stability and certainties to go off wandering like a gypsy on a canal boat. It would be exciting if it wasn't so scary.

On Wednesday night Gary's relationship with Gravel took a new turn. Watching a football match on TV he heard a knock on the boat's window. He opened one flap of the centre doors. In the faint illumination from a street lamp along the towpath, Gravel was standing, hands in the pockets of his leather jacket. Behind him, his sidekick waited in shadow.

Gary opened both doors wide. Watching the men coming down the steps backwards, he was reminded of the old threat, *We know where you live*. The visitors seemed to fill the cabin, even with Sidekick lurking behind his boss. Gary switched off the TV and gestured to the dinette.

Gravel shook his head. 'Thought I'd just drop in, Gary, as I was passing by to see how you're getting on with our mutual friend. What have you found out about his … *valuables?*'

'I'm working on it.'

'That's good, Gary, but don't take too long. You've just got to get your head round it.'

'I am trying to find out about it.'

'Fine. Find out about it … and then find it.'

'The trouble is … it may not even exist. I've talked to people who know Old Peter – in a roundabout sort of way – and they all think it's just a rumour.'

'Do they now? Is that what they think?'

'That's what everybody thinks.' Gary wanted to add, *That's what I think*, but he thought better of it.

'Find it, Gary.'

'Like I said … I'm working on it. I'll let you know if I find anything.'

'*When* you find something, Gary. Then, when we've got our hands on it, we'll cut you in.'

'Cut me in?'

'That's right. You'd rather be cut *in* than cut *out*, Gary. Think about it. Think about it tomorrow.'

'Why tomorrow?'

'Who knows what tomorrow might bring?'

Marnie was stuck at the traffic lights in Swiss Cottage on her way to the office on Thursday morning. She was paying scant attention to the radio until she heard the name Little Venice.

… the dismembered body found in the crate when it was lifted from the pool last Friday

morning. The police now believe the killing was probably linked to a drugs ring that has been under surveillance for some months. Detective Inspector Bruere of the Metropolitan Police appealed for anyone who might have information to come forward …

—∽∿∿—

Gary sat at the dinette enjoying his usual hearty breakfast: a cup of black instant coffee and his first fag of the day. His first job of the day was to find out about Old Peter and his supposed *valuables*. Gravel wanted him to think about it today, so that was what he'd do.

A sudden coughing spasm, also his first of the day, seized Gary and he reached for the cup to drown it with coffee. At that moment the eight o'clock news headlines were interrupting the flow of noise from the local pop music channel on the radio. One item almost made him choke. He grabbed for the switch to turn up the sound.

… has now been confirmed that the body was a member of a local drugs gang, caught up in a battle for control of organised crime in the area.

Gary sat stunned. *What sort of people am I getting involved with?* He sipped his coffee and grimaced. It tasted bitter. Suddenly everything about his life was bitter. *Why did they contact me?* He could hear Gravel speaking … *think about it tomorrow, Gary …* He returned to his question … *why me?* It was obvious. There would be no trails leading back to Gravel and his friends. They only came out of the shadows when they wanted publicity, and they knew some imaginative ways of getting it.

10
Engine trouble

By mid-morning on Saturday, Marnie had sandpapered the boat's roof and painted half of it with undercoat. She was aching in every joint and feeling uncomfortably warm in her overalls. The worst problem was the discomfort of kneeling on solid steel for hours on end with only folded towels as a cushion.

Soon after Marnie started sandpapering, Gary went by on a working boat and gave her a friendly wave. It turned into a mime reminiscent of scrubbing. He obviously thought it was humorous. Marnie drew two conclusions: (a) he did not understand what she was doing; (b) Gary and hard work were not the most regular companions.

Marnie straightened her back and stretched. There was no turning back now. The sun was climbing and the roof was warmer to touch. It also seemed to be getting longer. As she dipped her brush in the tin, a grey and green boat cruised slowly past. The old man at the tiller gave no impression of having seen Marnie.

Passers-by on the pavement overlooking the towpath called out encouragement. At one point she noticed three children staring down at her through the railings. She carried on painting.

'Hey, lady!' one of them cried out.

Marnie pretended not to hear.

'La-a-a-dy!' all three chorused as loudly as they could.

Marnie looked up. They were three boys, aged about eight or nine.

'Is that the boat we seen on the telly?' the first one called. 'Rosie and Jim's boat?'

'Sorry, 'fraid not.'

'Is it your boat?'

'Yes.'

Then came a staccato flow of questions in quick succession:

'Do you live on the boat?'

'Has it got a loo?'

'Have you got a telly?'

'Have you got kids?'

Marnie looked up and they fell silent. 'My answers are no, yes, no and no, in that order.'

For three seconds they said nothing. Then the first interrogator started again. 'Can we come for a ride on your boat?'

Marnie shook her head.

'*Please!*' they shouted in unison.

'You can see I'm busy. I've got all this painting to do.' She pressed on, hoping they would take the hint and leave her in peace.

'Is she called *Sally Ann?*' It was one of the others who spoke.

Marnie nodded in reply. She was sure they would tire of this and go away.

'Lady … can we have a drink of water?' another of them called out.

Marnie pictured chilled tumblers of sparkling iced mineral water. The children thought she had not heard.

'La-a-a-' the chorus broke out in a raucous three-part harmony. Before they could reach the end of the word, Marnie looked up sharply and they stopped in mid-flow.

'If you give us a drink of water, we'll go away.'

One of the children interpreted her hesitation as a sign that she was thinking what to give them. 'Or orange,' he said tentatively.

'I haven't got any.' Marnie could feel her resolve weakening.

They looked at her incredulously. 'They have on the telly,' said one.

'*And* orange,' said another.

'But *I* haven't.' Marnie hoped she sounded adamant.

'In the tap in the kitchen,' insisted one that had not spoken so far.

Marnie sighed and relented. It was a relief to climb down from the roof and give her knees a rest. In the galley, she found some paper cups with the name *Sally Ferries* on the side. She filled three of them with water, it was all she had. Even so, she felt she was carrying the canal tradition of hospitality quite far enough.

She passed the drinks up through the railings. To her surprise, one of the children thanked her. The other two took them quickly, as if they thought she might change her mind, and began drinking in hasty gulps. The first one to finish looked down at Marnie.

'Why can't we come for a ride on your boat?'

'I told you. I'm not going anywhere. I've got painting to do.' She turned and went back to the boat. By the time she had climbed onto the roof, the children were running off down the road. With renewed energy, she had the last section undercoated in twenty minutes. In the dappled sunlight through the trees, she could imagine how the fresh cream paint would look when it was finished.

'I say, hallo there!'

Marnie recognised the imperious voice of the neighbour who had called her a *water gypsy*. She braced herself for the onslaught and looked round.

'I thought you might like something to drink.' The old lady was holding a tall glass filled with a pale cloudy liquid and chunks of ice, complete with beads of condensation trickling down the side.

Marnie was almost speechless. Could it be a mirage? 'That's *very* kind of you.' She climbed down from the roof and reached up to take the glass through the railings.

'It's my home-made lemonade. I always make it when the weather gets warm. I see you've been out here all morning.'

'It's delicious …' It had a cold sharp tang and Marnie felt the ice cubes touching her lips. '… *wonderful*.'

'My mother and grandmother used to make it every summer when I was a girl in

Hampshire before the war.'

'I'm sorry, I don't know your name. I'm Marnie, Marnie Walker.'

'Everyone calls me Mrs Jolly. At my age one becomes accustomed to it.'

Marnie took another sip. 'There were some children here asking for a drink a while ago and all I had was tap-water from the galley.'

'I know, I saw them. That's what gave me the idea. My mother always said that any act of kindness is its own reward, but I thought you could do with something a little better.' She smiled down at Marnie. 'You've been working hard.'

'Yes and there's a lot more still to be done. I'm sure the boat's grown since I started.'

'Your curtains have made a big difference already. It's nice to see her looking better. She wasn't always so shabby. The people before you never lifted a finger. Just used it to entertain their friends and show off.'

These *people* were presumably Beth and Paul. Marnie opted for diplomacy and sipped the lemonade without comment.

'Are you doing all the work yourself?'

'Yes ... just trying to smarten her up a bit.'

'I can remember when it was owned by a naval officer. He used to stay on the boat during the week and go home at weekends. He painted her navy blue and maroon. She was smart in those days.'

'How long ago was that?'

Mrs Jolly calculated. 'Must be about ten years. I think he retired seven or eight years ago. That's when he sold it to the other people, the ones who let it get scruffy.'

Marnie nearly choked, but drank to the bottom of the glass and returned it through the railings. 'That was *marvellous*. You must come and have something with me on *Sally Ann* when I've made a bit more progress.'

'That would be nice. Well, I mustn't hold up the good work. Good-bye, my dear. Such a pity about the weather forecast.'

The weather forecast? Marnie was wondering about this when her eye fell on something bright among the shrubs. There were three paper cups, bearing the name: *Sally Ferries*. She picked them up with a sigh and turned back to the boat. Surveying her handiwork, she was pleased with what she saw.

It looked pretty good, apart from the large splash of pigeon droppings in the middle of the roof.

———⟨∭⟩———

The decision to go for a first solo run that evening was a pure impulse. By seven o'clock Marnie wanted to eat but had no desire to cook. She wandered up to the café perched over the canal and sat on the balcony, giving her a view along the cut. Over an omelette and salad, she watched the boats go by and tried to remember how life had been before *Sally Ann*.

Waterbuses in dark maroon and cream contrasted with brightly-coloured pleasure boats with scalloped awnings. Old Peter's boat approached, running as straight as if on rails hidden under the water, as he lined up to enter the tunnel that led to London Zoo and Camden Lock. Lights began to appear along the banks. Little Venice glowed, inviting and festive, and Marnie felt refreshed. She decided there and then to take *Sally Ann* for a run.

Back on board, Marnie went through the checklist she had learnt from Jane.

Disconnect lead to mains electricity.

Start engine.

No.

Switch on fuel pump.

Right.

Then start engine.

Bang, bang, clatter, clatter.

Check puffs of grey smoke (no idea why).

Good (presumably).

Cast off and push away from the bank.

Pull gear lever into forward position.

Press down accelerator.

And go!

Marnie knew better than to expect a surge of power, a thrust of acceleration, or the wind in her hair. *Sally Ann* hardly dug holes in the water. But when they slipped out into the channel, the engine thumping and the water bubbling behind her, it felt good. It felt like freedom.

———⟲———

Gary did not look his normal carefree self as he hopped from his boat onto the towpath that evening to nip round to the other side of the pool. With hands thrust in his pockets he turned under the first bridge and quickened his pace along the arm for Paddington Basin. Here the atmosphere changed. This part of the canal existed in almost permanent gloom, crossed by bridges in dreary succession.

It was around fifty yards from the pool to the mooring where Old Peter kept his boat and caravan. Gary stopped abruptly. Before him was a gap where the grey-green boat should have been lying. Cursing under his breath, he looked up and down the cut and turned to face the caravan. It was no bigger than a garden shed and reminded Gary of a tea cosy. The bodywork had dulled to a matt shade of cream; the Perspex windows had faded to an opaque tinge of yellow. So this was the private residence of a man with valuable possessions? No way.

Gary turned and walked quickly back towards his own mooring. But now he strode out. There was a gleam in his eye; this was his Saturday night out.

———⟲———

The maiden solo cruise almost went well. *Sally Ann* burbled happily along and Marnie felt almost in control. At the moorings beyond the tunnel, boaters looked up and waved. Some raised wine glasses to her.

Sally Ann's Summer

Under the grey railway bridges where gloomy grey pigeons huddled on the girders just above her head, Marnie guided *Sally Ann*, the engine booming and echoing in the confined space. A moment later they emerged into Regent's Park, where trees now coming into full leaf hung over the water. Set back all around were smart mansion blocks and impressive residences in landscaped grounds.

The engine hesitated momentarily, gave a cough and settled back to a steady rhythm. Strollers on the towpath smiled. A young man on roller-blades, solemn-faced with spiky crew cut, dark glasses and walkman headset raised a laid-back hand and swept past. Everyone was out enjoying the warm evening.

The plan was to take *Sally Ann* down to the pool, turn round the island, go back to the tunnel, then through the park before turning and heading for home. Just a short practice tootle. All too soon she cruised through the zoo and saw the right-angled turn by the bridge at Cumberland Basin up ahead. She hove-to while a pleasure boat pulled round the bend and came towards her. On board, a quartet was playing Dixieland jazz, a few couples were dancing, others eating from baskets.

The pleasure boat's steerer waved all clear and on impulse Marnie changed plans. Instead of going back, she headed off towards Camden Lock. This stretch of the canal ran behind the gardens of tall houses as old as the cut. People were sitting out talking, eating, laughing.

At Camden Lock the canal widened into a basin. Music blasted from loudspeakers; the smell of food wafted from stalls and booths; people milled about in the market on the left bank. Many were dressed in bright costumes with fringes, coloured headbands, beads and armlets. It was merry but with a hint of menace, like a mediaeval fair.

This was a very public place to attempt a manoeuvre by herself for the first time. Marnie took a deep breath, threw the tiller hard over and accelerated to push the stern round. While she was reversing in the middle of the three-point turn, a restaurant boat went by, its broad beam blocking access to the channel, its wake pushing *Sally Ann* to the side.

Marnie was dismayed to find that the bank was formed by a low platform on a frame of scaffolding. She left the tiller and walked along the gunwale towards the bows. The nearest part of this pontoon was just above water level. As she struggled to reach down to it from the gunwale, a man detached himself from the crowd and began moving towards her in a heavy lumbering shuffle. He was built like a wrestler, with black hair shaved at back and sides leaving a tuft on the top and a pony-tail at the back. Marnie saw him coming and her heart nearly stopped beating. She strained desperately to touch the pontoon, but could barely scrape it with her fingertips.

The man wore a studded leather jerkin over a torn khaki T-shirt. His arms were bare with exotic tattoos over thick muscles. Marnie could hear his boots thudding on the platform and in a few seconds he was upon her. She froze.

'Let me help you.' His voice was quiet.

Marnie was conscious of his bulk looming beside her. 'I got pushed over by the restaurant.'

'I saw.' He moved past and took up a position near the bows. 'It often happens. If you'd like to get back to the tiller, I'll push you clear.'

She backed along the gunwale while he began pushing the boat away. Marnie pulled the lever into gear. The engine coughed once before picking up speed.

'Thanks!' Marnie pressed on the accelerator. 'I'm really grateful.'

The man raised a hand and his tattoos rippled.

Sally Ann was now clear, but the way ahead was blocked by the dead slow restaurant boat creeping along. There was no room to pass for at least half a mile. Rather than inhale its exhaust fumes, Marnie tied up at the bank to watch the world go by for the next twenty minutes.

When she pressed the starter button, the engine fired at once and only wheezed slightly. Approaching Cumberland Basin it coughed. Marnie blipped the accelerator to clear its throat and made the turn under the bridge. Running slowly the engine gasped, but when Marnie increased revs it picked up speed. Her relief was short-lived. The engine spluttered, gave a few more coughs and wheezes, faltered and coughed again. Marnie thought of Gary: *probably needs a full service ... maybe an overhaul. These can be a load of trouble, if you're not careful ...*

It settled back to a steady thumping. Marnie crossed her fingers that the obstruction was cleared, but passing through the zoo, the gasping returned. Little Venice was twenty minutes away, and the light was fading fast. The engine began coughing in earnest, worked itself up to a real forty-a-day spasm ... and cut out.

What now? Marnie reviewed the situation. She was a long way from home, alone, with a dead engine, and night was falling. Not promising. *Sally Ann* drifted under a bridge and pushed her nose into a clump of tall grasses by the bank while her tail swung slowly out.

Marnie pulled the pole from the roof and thrust it down into the water to try and punt the tail in. She struck the bottom, pushed as hard as she could and the stern began to swing. She tried again with the same result. At the next push, the pole slipped from her grip and floated clear. She cursed out loud as it drifted out of reach in the dark water.

Marnie looked up at the tall pillars supporting the bridge behind her. The canal was deserted. She flicked the fuel pump switch and pressed the starter. The engine retched a few times and gave up. Options. She could wait for someone to come past and give her a tow. But didn't the trip boats stop at sunset? She could call out to a passer-by to get help. What help? What passer-by? She remembered the gates to the park were locked at sunset.

In the undergrowth something rustled. She looked round. It stopped. Probably a duck or a coot or maybe a rat. The red fuel pump light was glowing; she switched it off. There was more rustling. Wild animals never escaped from the zoo, did they? Marnie hoped they were all safely tucked up in their cages for the night. There it was again.

Somewhere in the zoo an animal called out, a long hooting cry from darkest Africa ... darkest Regent's Park. There were few lights along this part of the canal. Marnie heard the shuffling again. It seemed to come from the darkness under the bridge.

Marnie sat on the lid of the gas bottle locker. There was that sound, a distinct shuffle

... then another. *Sally Ann's* water pump growled faintly. This time she saw movement in the gloom under the bridge, heard murmurings. There was no doubt about it. Marnie was not alone. Not normally given to panic or fear of the dark, she had a healthy sense of self-preservation. Something was approaching in the darkness and it was no small creature. Time for action.

Marnie got up and raced along the gunwale, trying to find a firm bank to push *Sally* off with her foot. It was hopeless. The long grasses kept her clear of solid ground. She hurried back to the stern deck, flicked the fuel pump switch and pressed the starter button. The engine clattered and came to life. Marnie sighed with relief and pulled the heavy lever into forward gear. In the same movement she turned to press down the accelerator. The engine spluttered and died. In the shadows Marnie made out the shape of a man coming towards her very slowly under the bridge.

Turning in desperation, she saw the pole floating beside the boat and threw herself down on her knees to grab it. Suddenly, she was flooded with light and jumped with shock. From nowhere, a boat was pulling in alongside her. The light from its headlamp passed by and she heard the engine revving as the boat came to a halt. From the stern deck, the steerer bent down and pulled the pole from the water, lifting it clear and setting it on the roof of *Sally Ann*.

'I think you will be needing this.' The steerer had an old voice, dry and brittle. He pronounced each word distinctly, as if he was speaking a foreign language.

Marnie took a deep breath. She felt foolish. 'I didn't hear you coming.' She spoke in a breathless half-whisper.

'It's the men ... they sleep under the bridge.' Old Peter spoke with slow deliberation. 'I always slow down here and switch off the light.'

What men? Marnie wondered. 'You don't want to disturb them?'

'That ... and other reasons.'

'My engine cut out. I thought I was going to have to stay here all night.'

'You have diesel in the tank?'

'Yes,' Marnie said confidently and hoped she was right.

'Fuel filter,' he said, though whether it was a question or statement she was not sure.

Marnie tried to remember what she had read about the engine. 'I don't know,' she said simply.

'I will check it.'

Old Peter tied his boat to *Sally Ann* round a T-bracket at the stern. Marnie went forward to secure the bows and returned to find him standing on her deck with a toolbox. He lifted out part of the decking, knelt on the steps and switched on a lamp to light up the engine. He had white hair thin on the top, with broad shoulders and powerful forearms. Close up, his features were sharper than she had expected. He loosened a nut under the bowl of the fuel filter. Fluid dripped out as the old man removed the filter drum.

'Water.'

'Water?' Marnie repeated.

'Condensation in the tank. It gets into the fuel line when the level falls.'

Marnie watched as he wiped out the bowl with a rag and held the filter in the beam of light, twisting it slowly between his fingers.

'Have you a can of diesel?'

Marnie had no idea. 'No.'

Old Peter went back to his boat and returned carrying a fuel can and an empty jam jar. He knelt on the steps, poured some fuel into the jar and dropped the filter drum into the pink liquid. The air was filled with the whiff of diesel. From his toolbox he took out an elderly toothbrush and worked it round the drum, wiped it with the rag and re-assembled the filter. The process took two minutes.

'Try now.'

Marnie pressed the starter button. The engine turned over several times before firing. The old man wiped his hands on the rag, listening to the note of the engine. He stood up. Marnie was so relieved, she wanted to hug him. She had to raise her voice over the noise of the engine.

'Thank you. Thank you *so* much.'

'Uh-huh.' He nodded and untied the rope attaching the boats. 'You go ahead. I will follow in case of trouble.'

'Okay, but I'm sure it'll be fine.'

'Perhaps.' He paused while turning. 'Best not to come along here in the dark. It can be … unpleasant.'

'Dangerous?'

The old man hesitated before replying quietly in his cracked voice. 'In the last four years I have pulled … three bodies out of the canal in this place.'

The *other reasons* why he slowed down … '*Bodies?*' Marnie breathed the word.

'The men drink too much … fall asleep … roll down the slope into the water.'

'So these men aren't dangerous?' Marnie indicated under the bridge.

'Only to themselves.'

'How *sad.*'

'Yes … but perhaps a gentle way to go.'

They set off in convoy. *Sally's* engine ran sweet and true all the way home. Marnie took great care to pull in smoothly, so as not to make a fool of herself in front of Old Peter. He brought his boat in close alongside and leaned towards her.

'It's running fine,' Marnie told him. 'Better than ever.'

'Good.'

'Thank you so much.'

Old Peter made that sound again, just two syllables … *uh-huh* … but it summed up everything that needed saying. He nodded, reached for the accelerator and was gone.

After he left, Marnie felt bone-weary. She quickly checked all the systems, windows and catches. Back on deck locking the doors, she discovered Old Peter's fuel can standing in the corner.

Sally Ann's Summer

Gary did not *walk* to Warwick Avenue tube station to meet his date earlier that evening, he *wafted* along. He had splashed on far too much aftershave and hoped the evening air would dilute some of its power.

His date, Sheena, came up the steps from the station just seven minutes later than the time they had agreed. This confirmed Gary's view that she was an *up-market bit of totty*. By his reckoning, if a girl arrived on time she must be desperate; more than ten minutes late, she was trying to make a point about who was in control. It was their second date, and Gary had high hopes for the evening. That, and his *up-market* assessment, was why he had chosen to take her to dinner in the small restaurant above the entrance to Maida Hill tunnel.

Wearing high heels, Sheena was as tall as Gary, and he was pleased to see that she had made an effort for their evening out. Shoulder-length honey-blonde hair and a dress that covered the essentials under a short pink jacket were just the job. When she came up the stairs from the tube station, she took his hand and let him kiss her on both cheeks. In the shoot-out between his aftershave and her perfume, Gary reckoned the result was a score-draw: *Aramis* – 1, *Issey Myake* – 1.

He guessed correctly that she had bought the perfume in the local chemist's where she worked and where he had met her the previous week.

They arrived at the bistro with no unwanted attention from Gravel, though Gary had the feeling these days that all his movements were being observed. He had asked for a table on the enclosed balcony over the water so that Sheena could enjoy the lights coming on along the canal while dusk descended. It would also provide a subject for conversation if they needed one. Gary's anxiety proved unfounded; Sheena kept up a bubbly chatter while they read through the menu and began their meal.

Each time a boat passed under them, Sheena asked Gary what sort it was and whether it was like his. He promised to let her see his boat some time and knew exactly when he planned that time to be. She seemed genuinely interested in boating, and the evening passed pleasantly. Gary asked about her work in the chemist's and, as she told him of the tribulations of working with a very fussy pharmacist, he noticed idly that *Sally Ann's* mooring was empty. The idea flickered across his mind that *Sally Ann's* new owner and Old Peter were out together somewhere on a date. The thought brought the suggestion of a smile to his face, which pleased Sheena who was describing an embarrassing incident involving a customer and a prescription for suppositories.

Gary was pouring wine for Sheena when he saw *Sally Ann* emerge from the tunnel and pull over onto her mooring, closely followed by Old Peter's boat which stopped alongside. Marnie and Old Peter exchanged a few words before he went on his way. Odd. What were they doing, travelling together in the dark like that?

He was still mulling this over when Sheena leaned towards him.

'Tell me, Gary, are you going out with anyone at the moment?'

The directness of the question startled him. '*What?* … No darlin' … course not.'

'Yes, you are.'

'I'm not ... I *swear*.'

'You are ... you're going out with *me* ... or you're supposed to be. Can't you take your mind off boats for two minutes?' Sheena looked down to the water. A streetlight showed a woman in tight jeans bending over a mooring ring. 'Or are you taking an interest in more than just the boats?'

Gary followed her gaze down to *Sally Ann's* and Marnie's rear ends, shook his head and smiled back. And for the rest of the evening – and much of the night that followed it – gave her his undivided attention.

11
Old Peter

Marnie remembered hearing the alarm clock, but not turning it off. She half-opened one eye and waited while it focused. Nine-fifteen. The sky was sitting on her head. Everything was aching and she lay there trying to work out what day it was.

Images from a dream were circling inside her brain. She was wading chest high through grass across a flat plain, a vast African sunset ahead of her, something indistinct shuffling along behind, just out of sight. Suddenly she was falling, with fronds of long water grasses wrapping themselves round her legs. She went under, the air bubbling from her lips, feeling cool, without pain or fear.

Marnie turned onto her side, wishing she was back in the watery dream. Her whole body throbbed. It must be Sunday.

The hot shower and the thought of breakfast began the revival. She stood under the sharp jets and let them massage her limbs, joints and other moving parts back to life. Stepping out of the cubicle, she risked a glance in the full-length mirror, ready to wince … But what was this? Could she be mistaken? It was hard to believe, but she seemed to be in better shape, firmer in most departments, the slackness round the chin tightened, the stomach flatter.

By the time she reached Little Venice, the first raindrops were falling, and she just made it on board as the downpour started. Undismayed, she put on the kettle and settled down to finish the curtains, telling herself it was only a shower. The first clap of thunder made her jump.

She worked on steadily while the storm banged around her and did not notice it had stopped until she went out to inspect the boat with its new curtains in place. In bright sunlight, steam was rising from the roof. By mid-afternoon she was able to give it another undercoat. By early evening she was aching again in all the old familiar places, plus a few new ones. Clearing up to go home, Marnie remembered Old Peter's fuel can. She switched on the fuel pump and pressed the starter button before untying the mooring ropes. The engine fired first time.

She cruised round and found Old Peter's mooring in the side arm off the pool. If Little Venice was a 'good address' in the boating world, this was the part you did not talk about, a Sargasso Sea of flotsam and jetsam, lined on one side with boats that had known better days.

Marnie located the grey-green boat, huddled beside a low bridge of black iron, with an elderly caravan tucked in the corner against a tall fence, opposite an office block car park. It was too narrow to tie up alongside, so she pulled in further down behind a shabby cabin cruiser, long retired from the hire trade. The old man's boat in contrast had simple lines, clean and purposeful. Marnie knocked on the door by the stern deck. The hatch slid open without a squeak. Old Peter looked out.

Marnie smiled. 'Good evening. I've come to return your fuel can. You left it last night.'

'I did.' The old man climbed out, surprisingly nimble for his age and stocky build. 'You are thinking I forgot it.'

'Yes.' Marnie had considered no other possibility.

'You said you had no can. I left it in case you should be needing it again.' His voice had a strange intonation and he pronounced every word clearly and slowly.

'I didn't realise.' Marnie was touched by this act of kindness from a stranger. 'That was very good of you.'

The old man stood quietly on the deck, as if waiting for her to make the next move. Marnie put the can on the ground. 'Oh, and er ... my name's Marnie ... Marnie Walker.'

Normally she would have offered a hand, but on this occasion she held back as the old man remained immobile. He said nothing, as if registering her name in his mind.

'Actually, I do have a spare can,' she continued. 'I found it in a cupboard, I mean a locker. Thank you for lending me this one.'

Old Peter stepped onto the path, picked up the can and tucked it behind the door. He walked along to the bow and sat down on the side of the foredeck. Marnie followed, unsure if the conversation was at an end. The old man shifted to make room for her to sit beside him.

'You have done a lot to your boat,' he said impassively.

'Yes. I'm glad to take the weight off my feet.'

'The people who had it before did nothing.'

'I know. That's my sister. It's still her boat, actually. I'm just looking after it while they're away.'

The old man turned to look at her. His eyes were faded brown under grey brows and his skin was tanned like a countryman. 'You do all this and it is not your boat.'

'Well, yes. I started to make one or two improvements and I never realised how much there was to do.'

'There is always much to do on an old boat.'

'I'm trying to get it right, but it's one thing after another. And I want to take it away for a journey.'

'Make sure the windows don't leak,' the old man said. 'The rain will spoil your new curtains.' Marnie jerked her head round. He seemed not to notice. 'The topsides will be protected by your paint, but it is hard work. You will need at least two top coats.'

'Yes. The trouble is ... I've got to sort out all the problems with the engine. I'm starting to wonder if I'll ever get away.'

The old man looked thoughtful. 'Problems with the engine?'

'Gary thinks it might need a complete overhaul.'

'There is nothing wrong with the engine.'

'But what about the water in the fuel filter?' Marnie felt pleased at using the right word.

'Fill your tank … you will reduce the condensation.'

'But other things could go wrong,' Marnie protested.

Old Peter sat with his inscrutable expression for some time. 'Listers are good engines. They turn cement mixers on every building site in Britain.'

It seemed a strange recommendation to Marnie. 'That's good?'

'They endure the three worst things ever invented for engines.'

'What are they?'

He held up a thumb. 'Dust.' His index finger. 'No maintenance.' The next finger. 'Irishmen.'

Marnie felt a conflict of emotions at this announcement, ranging from relief at his faith in the engine, to amusement at the turn of phrase, via slight indignation at his prejudice. 'So you don't think it needs a complete overhaul?'

'If it is running, leave it alone. An oil change would do no harm. Have you a manual for the engine?'

'Yes.'

'Read it and do what it says. Maintenance. How far are you going on your journey?'

'I'm not sure. I just thought I'd set off and see how far I got.'

'You have no plan?'

'I just want to get away.'

'Get away,' he repeated quietly. 'What are you looking for?'

'I need a change. I'm an interior designer and … I'm feeling stale. That's all.'

'You design things.' The old man seemed interested.

'Yes. I design the interiors of buildings, not the actual structures.'

'You like doing that?'

'Usually, when I'm not feeling … jaded. It's what I'm trained for.'

'And you like … structures, as well?'

'Very much. I work within the structures, if you like. Buildings and structures are an important part of my work … part of my life.' It surprised Marnie to be speaking like this with a virtual stranger.

Old Peter sat staring ahead. Marnie could not tell if he was thinking or had lost interest in the conversation. She thought it may be time to go, but just sitting there on the side of the boat with the old man felt comfortable.

'You like canals?' he said, suddenly.

'Yes … yes, I do. I like the structures, of course, and the designs on some of the boats interest me. I'm attracted by the textures … brick, stone, iron … and water, naturally.' The old man nodded and Marnie thought she detected a half-smile. 'Everything's so solid.' This time, she was sure there was a smile.

'Not everything.' Was there a twinkle in Old Peter's eye? 'The walls up to the tunnel at your end are not very solid. They have no proper foundations.'

Marnie pictured the walls at the mouth of the tunnel. They had stood there, as high as a house, for nearly two centuries. How could they have no proper foundations? And how could the old man know this?

'Are they dangerous?'

He shrugged. 'They need attention … more than your engine does.'

'That's reassuring … I think.'

'Your boat is built for long journeys.'

'That's good. I want to get away and find some space.'

'You think you can get away on the canals?'

'I just need a change. The boat gives me that opportunity.'

'Yes. What you see will be different, but it may not be what you are looking for, unless you are lucky.'

'I'm not really looking for anything in particular. I just need to be away.'

Old Peter nodded. 'We all have to be away sometime.'

Sheena left Gary and *Garrow* on Sunday after a hasty breakfast with promises of more times together. Gary would ring her soon. He put on his overalls ready for a day in the engine room of a trip boat. It needed extensive repairs: replacement of fuel injector nozzles, the exhaust manifold and a full service, the kind of casual cash-in-hand arrangement that Gary liked. Strangely, although his Saturday night with Sheena had been all he could have wished, his thoughts kept returning to Marnie and Old Peter. Could she be the key to finding out more about the old man and his valuables?

The work on the engine demanded full attention, and it was not until he emerged from the bowels of the trip boat that he returned to the everyday world. Pocketing the rewards of his labours, Gary walked quickly back to *Garrow* where a hot shower awaited him. Lathering himself all over, he made up his mind to pay a call on Old Peter and tried to work out how to broach the subject of his … treasure.

So … I hear you've got something very valuable hidden away under the mattress …

Perhaps a little too direct?

My partners are looking for someone to invest heavily in the commodities market …

The image of a geriatric caravan with peeling paintwork flashed across his mind. Try again.

I don't suppose you could see your way clear to loaning me a large amount of …

Forget it.

For Chrissake, Pete, where's your bloody money … how much have you got?

This was getting ridiculous. He rubbed his palm over the bathroom mirror to make a hole in the condensation and stared at his face.

'All right, you're so bloody clever … *you* think of something!' He wagged a finger at himself. 'Come on … what do I say?'

But it was no use. He simply could not find the right words to question the old boy. Not the sort of person you could casually interrogate. Gravel would have to understand that. But that was another conversation for which the right words did not exist. Gary padded along to the sleeping cabin, thumped the pillows into shape and flicked the duvet straight for the first time that day. As he dressed, he tried to imagine explaining to Gravel why he could not find out about the treasure.

You see, it's like this … I don't think he's got anything valuable … nobody does …

That wouldn't work. Gravel would just send him back like before. Maybe slightly rearranged.

I've spoken to him. He's not got anything of value. Any fool can work that out …

Better rephrase that.

If he had anything valuable he'd enjoy a higher standard of living …

He'd already tried that.

I beat the old guy to a pulp, roasted him over a slow fire and pulled out his fingernails. Before he snuffed it, he confessed he had nothing …

Get real, Gary. You're not cut out for this tough-guy lark. Perhaps an appeal to reason. *You've just got to accept that there's no way …*

No. That was no use. He could not argue like that. He wouldn't have a leg to stand on.

Ha! Gary laughed out loud at his joke then stopped suddenly. It was definitely not funny. He remembered the crate splitting open, the slimy mess of body parts slithering onto the canalside. Gravel would not be inclined to see his point of view. Both Gary and Old Peter could well end up bouncing around on stumps. Nothing else for it, Gary would just have to go round to chat to the old man and see what came up.

He ran the razor over his jaw, went light on the aftershave, pulled on a T-shirt and jeans and headed off to the Paddington Arm. He had two plans. If OP was outside the boat, he would stop for a chat as if in passing.

Hi. Haven't seen you for a while. How yer keeping?

If OP was on the boat or in the caravan, he would vary the approach, tap on the door.

Hi. Just passing by and realised I hadn't seen you for a while. How yer keeping?

What else could he do? The old guy never went to a pub, never went anywhere except up and down on his boat. Perhaps if Gary came up with a special offer on red diesel from an unspecified source? Worth a try. It would do for starters. He was feeling better already.

His mood improved still further when he rounded the corner from the pool and caught his first sight of the old man. OP was walking along towards the front of his boat and sitting on the bow. Just right for a casual encounter. But what he saw next stopped Gary in his tracks. Who was following him along the bank and sitting down beside him? Marnie. What was going on between those two? Gary shrank into the wall to think through the situation.

In one way it would be easier to chat if he saw Marnie with Old Peter. Just being sociable. Against that, he could hardly raise the question of the secret horde with her present. It would give away his interest. It might even set Marnie thinking, and a woman would stand a better chance of getting information out of him than Gary would. With a shiver, he suddenly realised she might already have done so. Why else would an attractive woman like that be spending time with a man older than her own grandfather? He looked out from under the bridge. Their heads were close together in intimate conversation.

Gary needed time to think, needed to know more about Marnie and her links with OP without arousing her suspicions. This was a development he had not foreseen.

—⟨⟨⟨—

Marnie was getting used to arriving home worn out. She went straight to the bathroom and loaded the towels and bed linen from *Sally Ann* into the washing machine. They smelled of boat.

She pressed the button by the red light on the answerphone. The machine buzzed.

'Hi, it's Steve … wondered how you are. I thought we might talk. Be in touch … if you want to.' Click.

Marnie sighed and frowned. It buzzed again.

'Have you gone into hiding or what?' It was Beth. 'You're never in any more. I've been ringing all day. Anyway, I expect you're out having a good time, so that's good. I just wanted to find out how things are. We're okay. The weather's fine. I've met a *dishy* architect. You'd really like him and he'd like to meet you. If you're still having that sabbatical, why not come over for a few weeks? I'll ring again soon. Oh, yes, one other thing. You won't forget to see the boat's all right, will you? We wouldn't want her to sink! Talk to you soon. Bye!'

Within minutes, Marnie was ready for bed. Her last conscious thought was about stern glands. She was convinced she would dream that *Sally Ann* had sunk.

12
Transatlantic call

Monday mornings had never been a problem for Marnie. At least, not in the days when her body functioned without the aid of pain killers and embrocation. She launched herself cautiously into the week without the usual spring in her step, thankful that she could sit at her desk briefing the team. As the days went by, the aches in her joints faded.

The high point of the week came when Willards Brewery announced they were reassessing their business plan, which meant delaying the refurbishment programme until the end of the summer. That made everything easier. Marnie's only slight anxiety was whether she would remain indispensable. Philip told her she need have no worries and asked about preparations for the Great Journey.

'How do you manage all those locks and things by yourself?'

Good question, Marnie thought. She had never been through a lock by herself. In fact, she could not recall going through a lock at any time.

'It's just a matter of technique,' she said, as casually as she could manage.

—◦∭◦—

By mid-week Marnie had everything under control. On Wednesday evening she paid a flying visit to the mooring and gave *Sally Ann* a once-over, now a familiar routine. She got home at eight. While she was making a sandwich in the kitchen the phone rang.

'I don't believe it. You're actually there. What happened – did they run out of champagne at the wine bar?'

Hi Beth.'

'Seriously … is everything all right?'

'Yes. Why shouldn't it be?'

'Well, you're never in when I ring. Are they still working you like a slave at the office?'

'What's new about that?'

'Are you still getting this sabbatical? Are you thinking about coming over here to visit with us?'

Marnie winced. It was always like this. Beth usually took about two weeks to reprogramme her speech patterns to American. Marnie had been waiting for the first signs to creep in. 'No, thanks. I've got no plans to come and *visit with you* at the moment.'

'That's too bad,' said Beth, undeterred or unaware of the subtleties.

'Yes, it's a *pity*, I'd like to see New York again.'

'Marnie, we're in Boston. You know that.'

'Oh, sorry … by your accent I thought you'd moved to Brooklyn or maybe the Bronx.'

'Okay, okay. But you're really not coming Stateside?'

'No, really, thanks. I'm planning to take a trip on the boat, as I told you.'

'You were serious about that? I thought you were putting me on.'

Marnie took a deep breath. 'I'm almost ready to set off. Beth … I've been meaning to tell you … I've been doing things to … well, smarten her up a little. I didn't think you'd mind.'

'A designer narrowboat!' Beth remembered just in time not to add 'yet' or 'already'.

'Not exactly. Just one or two touches here and there.'

'Sure, sure, I mean yes, that's fine. You're not painting roses and castles all over it, are you?'

'Not quite. Listen, are there any special things I need to know about operating locks when I'm out travelling?'

'Well, there is one golden rule. Take along a hunky guy with big muscles. You never know when he might come in handy.' Beth hooted.

'I'll try to remember. Seriously, though, are they hard to operate?'

'It helps if you're a Sumo wrestler. I'm sure you'll be fine. I'm sorry you aren't coming over, though. Perhaps when you get back from your trip, you'll change your mind?'

'I'm … er … planning a longish trip.'

'I give you one week at most. *Sally's* pretty cramped and you like the finer things in life.'

After disconnecting, Marnie sorted through the post. Among the bills and junk mail was a postcard from Jane Rutherford.

Hi, Marnie. We're travelling up the Grand Union in the company of kingfishers and herons. You'll love it. Charming scenery. Very secluded and dreamy. Far from the madding and all that. Decided to extend the trip. Hope your preparations are going well. See you soon, Jane and Derek.

The picture on the card showed two traditional working boats side-by-side in a lock, the crews, men and women, dressed in Victorian costume. The men all seemed to be busy, operating the lock paddles. How would she cope with this?

Before turning in, Marnie settled down with canal charts and cruising guides. *Very secluded and dreamy. Far from the madding …* But it was only just outside London. She would be cruising the inner reaches of commuter country, not quite the same league as Francis Drake or Vasco da Gama. The guides contained no warnings of the danger of falling off the edge of the world, showed no areas marked *Terra Incognita*, or badlands infested with dragons.

13
Bitch

It was Friday lunch-time when the reality struck Marnie: there was no turning back. A client rang about a riverside warehouse conversion, an imaginative design that Marnie had produced and handed over to the group. The client asked for the project designer. Marnie was about to confirm that was herself, when he added … *Miss Faye Summers*. Marnie looked at Faye across the office, a talented young woman whose skills she had nurtured, and transferred the call. After an initial twinge, she felt strangely liberated, like a ghost haunting the office.

She reached for the diary and consulted the things-to-do list. By now most items were crossed through. On the other hand, the *Sally Ann* list was as long as ever. There and then, Marnie decided to take the afternoon off.

The phone rang again. Marnie hesitated for a moment, then got up and left. Someone else could answer it.

———

Earlier that morning Gary had a call from the BW office in Little Venice. The manager wanted to talk about a job. Once Gary had clarified that it was nothing to do with shifting any obstructions in the water, he agreed to look in as soon as he could find a 'window' in his busy schedule. He disconnected, picked up his cigarette and returned to the horse racing pages of the *Daily Mirror*.

Try as he might, he could not concentrate on the chances of Apprentice Lad winning the 2.30 at Haydock. His thoughts kept wandering to Gravel and Old Peter, who were constantly on his mind these days. He had run out of ideas about anything to do with the old man and his supposed valuables. The only remote prospect seemed to be Marnie.

The problem was the same as for Old Peter. How could he find a way of just happening to pass by and fall into conversation with her?

Hi. I was wondering if you'd like to come for coffee or a drink some time …

No good. If she didn't fancy him and refused, she'd be on her guard every time they met.

Didn't I see you travelling along with Old Peter the other day?

That would only work if she was chatty. In his experience that was unlikely.

That's funny … I haven't seen Old Peter for a while. Do you know him?

Improbable, and how would he get to that point?

Somehow he had to find a way of getting into conversation with Marnie and gradually steering her towards the subject of Old Peter. But how? He tilted back in the chair, closed his eyes and pondered, thinking back to the first time he had seen Marnie when she had literally jumped into his arms.

He had the beginnings of an idea and was just letting it develop in his mind when the mobile rang.

'It's me, Sheena.'

'Hi, darlin'! I was just thinking about you.'

'Oh yeah?'

'Of course. Who else?'

She laughed coyly. He felt himself suddenly want very much to see her again and soon. All thoughts of Marnie were immediately, if only temporarily, put out of his mind.

———✠———

Marnie slotted the Rover into a parking space and fed as much change as she had into the meter. She was determined not to get a ticket and noted the time available. It was a short walk to the mooring and, as the gate clanged shut behind her, Marnie felt she was entering another world.

Putting the key in the lock, she found a piece of paper tucked into the steel doors. Inside the cabin she drew back the curtains, put the kettle on and read the message. She read it a second time and frowned.

BITCH
TIME YOU THOUGHT ABOUT IT
LET ME KNOW

There was a smudge in the bottom right-hand corner that might have been a letter Q. Was someone threatening her? What could it mean? Marnie pinned the note on the cork board in the galley and considered the options.

Steve? No. He was unhappy with her, but would not resort to extreme measures. His main act of violence would be a long sulk. Anyway, he would not know about her spending time on the boat, and the writing looked too primitive.

Perhaps the message had been intended for Beth? Unlikely. She had her annoying little ways, but if anyone was tempted to feed Beth to the piranhas, it would be Marnie herself.

There was something odd about the note that she could not quite fathom. Shaking her head, she put it out of her mind and concentrated on the boat.

After a good rub down with sandpaper, she gave the roof its first top coat. At the halfway point she sat back on her heels and rubbed her forehead at the moment when a boat emerged from the tunnel and passed slowly by. Old Peter raised his hat and smiled. Marnie raised her paintbrush.

An hour or so later, on her way back to the car, aching in the usual places, Marnie bumped into Gary.

'Hallo,' he said. 'Did you get my note?'

'Your note?'

'I left you a note in the door. Do we need to have a little chat?'

Marnie was astonished. Here was Gary in broad daylight, apparently talking about a threatening letter in the most casual tone. She had a vision of a 1920's gangster holding a Tommy gun: *Sorry lady, this isn't personal, it's business.* Then, she suddenly realised what it was about the note that had struck her as odd: that Q, or whatever it was in the corner. The anonymous threatening letter had been signed.

'Was your note personal or business?'

Gary thought for a moment. 'Business, I suppose. I put one on all the boats.'

This was not what Marnie expected. 'Tell me about your note. I don't get it.'

'You ought to have it done. God knows when the other people last did it.'

'Did *what* exactly?'

'Had the hull bitched.'

'*Bitched?*'

'Yeah. Old boat like that, you ought to take her out of the water at least every two years and get the hull painted with bitch. You know … bitumastic.' He stumbled over the word, as if unaccustomed to using so many syllables at one go.

Enlightenment. 'Ah … But what was that squiggle in the corner? It looked a bit like a letter Q?'

'Q?' Gary looked blank. 'No, not Q. It's a G. That's me. G for Gary.' He laughed. 'I may be a lot of things, but I'm certainly not a Q!'

Marnie felt foolish but laughed with Gary, who was trying to think of a way of getting round to Old Peter.

'You ought to think about the hull, Marnie. Ask anyone. They'll tell you it's got to be done. Ask your mate, Old Peter. He'll tell you it's important.'

'My mate?'

'Yeah. The old boy down the side arm. You know him, don't you?'

'Why is it important … about the hull?'

Gary shrugged. 'The other day when I went past I noticed you were looking a bit weedy. Your bottom could definitely do with a good rub down and blacking.'

Marnie kept a straight face. It was a struggle. 'We'll talk about it some time.' She looked at her watch and started walking.

'Talking of Old Peter, Marnie, I was wondering –'

'Sorry, gotta go.' She quickened her pace. 'Time, tide and parking meters wait for no man … or woman.'

She left Gary standing.

———⚬———

Back at the flat, Marnie went into the kitchen and began assembling ingredients on the workbench. Reaching for her favourite, dog-eared cookery book, she turned on the oven and rolled up her sleeves. In a short while she was sliding baking trays into place. While the smell of biscuits emanated from the cooker, she was busy in the spare bedroom, now the supply dump for the Great Journey.

Marnie had bought twelve plastic crates from the local garage to stow in the cratch lockers. Into these she piled stores for the summer: tins of food, soap, towels, toilet rolls, matches, tissues, washing powder, even sketchbooks and a box of pencils. The list seemed endless. All her casual clothes were neatly stacked on the bed.

On the floor stood a few other essentials, comprising four cases of wine: two red, one white, one rosé. A smaller box included Pimm's, gin and Bacardi. It looked like being a wet summer.

14
Gift

By nine o'clock on Saturday morning, Marnie was already aching. She forced herself to keep going, rubbing down ready for the next round of top-coating, spurred on by the knowledge that the end of her labours was in sight.

It was another two hours before she applied the last brushload. She climbed down to the towpath, stretched her back and admired her handiwork. *Sally Ann* was becoming a new boat. Back on board, she cleaned herself up and changed into fresh clothes. A tupperware box stood on the workbench. Marnie picked it up before leaving the boat to dry in the warm air.

She took a short walk round the pool of Little Venice and turned into the side arm.

———✕✕✕———

Gary enjoyed his day out and was confident he would enjoy his evening still more. While Marnie was working steadily to transform the appearance of *Sally Ann*, he was spending Saturday taking a top-of-the-range boat down to Docklands for a couple who had given up their prized Little Venice mooring for a slot in an exclusive marina outside their new home.

During the journey he had plenty of time to think about Gravel, whom he had not seen for a few days, Old Peter and … Marnie. He was sure she was the key to the OP mystery, or at least a way of getting closer to the old man. By the time he had reached the Thames he had a workable plan all figured out. He would go round to see Marnie and offer to check the boat over thoroughly before she began her journey. That would give him the chance to get her to relax and chat with him.

He decided to go and see her as soon as he returned to Little Venice, before he had Gravel and his chum breathing down his neck again.

———✕✕✕———

The walk round to the Paddington Arm helped to ease Marnie's tired muscles. She found the grey-green boat at its mooring and tapped on the centre doors. When one of them opened outwards, she met the impassive gaze of the old man and wondered fleetingly if she had committed a *faux pas*. She had read somewhere that in the Romany world no man was ever permitted inside a caravan with a woman other than his wife or immediate family. Perhaps in the world of boat people it was considered inappropriate for a woman to call on a man, even one of venerable age who had shown her kindness.

'Hallo. Remember me … Marnie … Marnie Walker?'

Old Peter murmured his customary, *uh-huh*, and a warmth came into his expression. He pushed open the second door and came out to join her on the bank.

'Sorry just to turn up like this. I … wanted to see you before I set off … on my journey.'

'Oh …'

'I'm planning to leave next weekend.'

'So you are ready.'

'Yes … well, almost. I've got to put another top-coat on the roof, but apart from that …'

'A good solid boat.'

'I'm glad you think so.'

'Fill the tanks – water and diesel – and she will take you …' He made a gesture with his hand. '… wherever you desire.'

'I will.'

Marnie reached into her shoulder bag. 'Oh, I … I brought you something.'

'Oh?'

'I wanted to thank you for coming to the rescue the other night in the park when I broke down.'

'There is no need. No traveller ever leaves another boatman in difficulty. It is the way.'

'Yes, I know. Even so …' She pulled out a tupperware box. 'It's just a small thank-you gift. I, er … well, I made these for you.'

Marnie held out the box. When Old Peter made no move to take it, she added, 'Half of it is shortbread, the other half, flapjacks. Of course, I realise you may not like that sort of thing … I couldn't think how else to thank you.'

Old Peter took the box carefully from her slim fingers with his strong hands. 'You know what they say …' He enunciated every word clearly. 'Sweet tooth … and an eye for the ladies.'

He was smiling, and his old eyes seemed a little more moist than before.

Marnie smiled back. 'You like that kind of thing?'

'I like that kind of thing … both kinds of thing.' His voice faded away.

He must have been over eighty and he was flirting with her. On impulse, Marnie stepped forward and kissed him on the cheek, surprised at the smoothness of his face. 'There. Now you have both.'

———— ⌇⌇⌇ ————

Gary sat on the Docklands Light Railway train and watched the world go past the window. It went past slowly. He wondered if the DLR was the railway equivalent of a canal.

He was running – if that was the word – late. After delivering the boat to its new mooring, he had been hailed from another craft by someone he had worked with in the past. Invited on board for a quick chat, it was not long before a bottle was opened and the chat turned into a discussion about business opportunities.

Sitting on the train, he forced himself not to look at his watch every two minutes. He estimated that by the time he got home – assuming he ever reached civilisation again – he should just have time to fit in everything he had to do. His reckoning proved to be optimistic. A long wait on the Bakerloo Line for a tube back to Little Venice all but scuppered his plans, and he barely had time to shower and change on *Garrow* before his date.

Waiting by the tube station, he fretted that his talk with Marnie would have to keep for another day. Then Sheena walked up the steps. One look at her shining blonde hair, the pink glossed lips parting in a smile and the clinging short dress, and all thoughts of Marnie floated out of his mind.

———❦———

Marnie was surprised at the interior of Old Peter's boat, as surprised as she had been when he invited her in. He gestured her to a chair in the saloon with a single word, 'Tea?'

'Thanks.'

She wanted to ask what she should call him and what was the name of his boat, but sensed that questioning would feel like an intrusion. While Old Peter attended to matters in the galley, Marnie looked at her surroundings. The saloon was lined in tongue-and-groove pine that seemed to have been lime-washed rather than varnished. Muted cream and light green were the other colours, with natural rush matting on the floor. The overall impression was old-fashioned but soothing. It was cool and restful, completely uncluttered, neat and orderly.

Tea arrived on a tray in a Brown Betty teapot. The crockery – all matching from the same set – was white with a floral design in green and pink. Its style was dated, but in perfect condition. The best china. He had set out the shortbread and flapjacks on a larger plate from the same series. No cast-offs here.

The tea was strong, and Marnie accepted one finger of her shortbread. Old Peter took a flapjack and nodded as he tasted it, like a gourmet sampling a delicacy.

'Good … good,' he murmured.

'Glad you like it.'

'You have done much work on the boat.'

'I've done almost everything I can, I think.'

'You have prepared yourself?'

'Myself? I'm ready to go, yes … ready for a change.'

'It is always a good idea to be ready for change.'

Marnie smiled. 'Well … I hope I'll cope with whatever comes along.'

'Yes. You will cope.'

'You think so?'

'What else can you do?'

It was a good point. She would be out in the country, on her own, responsible for running and maintaining the boat. This was no time to be having doubts.

'You said that what I find on my travels may not be what I expect. I think that's right. All I know is, it will be a change from my normal life.'

The old man paused, looking into his teacup. 'Everything has changed in my life.'

'On the cut?'

'On the cut … everywhere else.'

'Do you regret that?'

'No. There is no point regretting. You just … move on … to the next lock.'

'I find that a comforting thought.'

'There is nowhere else to go.'

15
Paint

Sunday morning, and Marnie could not believe she had set the alarm for seven. Arriving home the previous evening, she had found five messages on the answerphone, friends asking why she had become a recluse. Being Saturday evening, they had all been out, so she left messages, explaining she had been tied up with a project and was going away for an extended cruise. After nibbling crackers and cheese she had showered and heaved her weary limbs into bed.

Now, amazingly, she felt pretty good when she turned off the alarm. She pushed back the duvet and went straight to open the curtains. Dry and bright, ideal weather for painting. One last effort, one last coat, and *Sally Ann* would be ready.

Marnie bolted down breakfast, grabbed her bag and headed for the door.

———————

Sunday morning, and it was warm under the duvet on *Garrow*. Gary was having a lie-in with Sheena, untroubled by thoughts of Gravel, Marnie or Old Peter's hidden valuables. He had promised her a day out on the boat, and twitching the curtain over the porthole with one finger, he could see clear sky. A perfect day.

He stretched and looked at Sheena's face on the pillow. Her eyes were closed, lips slightly parted. Seconds later she woke up, saw him, smiled.

'Steady … you'll spoil my make-up,' she murmured softly.

'You're not wearing any make-up.'

'Oh, well … that's all right, then.'

Sheena closed her eyes and began breathing slowly and rhythmically. In the pale light that was seeping into the cabin Gary could see her clothes carefully folded on the shelf at the foot of the bed. Definitely up-market, this girl. Not one of those who throws everything on the floor and wakes up next day with smeared lipstick and mascara on the pillow. She stirred, turning onto her back, clasping both hands above her head.

'When will I see you again, Gary?'

'When you open your eyes?'

She giggled. 'After today, idiot.' Her voice was sleepy.

'I told you, I've got this job on. It'll keep me out of town till the end of the week. We'll be working all hours, not worth coming back into London.'

'What is it, this job?'

'I told you.'

'I know. Tell me again. I don't remember … it had a funny name.'

'It's a fit-out.'

'Who are you fitting up?'

'We're not fitting anyone up. It's a fit-out ... on a boat ... I'm helping a mate to finish it off, then he'll be selling it.'

'Where is this?'

'I told you that, too.' Was she testing his story, he wondered. Or was she thick?

'At a marina.'

'Where exactly?' Was she suspicious? On balance, he would prefer her suspicious to thick.

'Up near Tring ... Hertfordshire. It's called Cowroast.'

'What kind of a name is that?'

'It's just the name of the marina.'

'Why?'

'I dunno.'

'Sounds like a barbecue.'

Gary laughed. He wondered if she found the name so improbable, he had to be telling the truth. Sheena hit him playfully. He took hold of her hands to ward off the blows.

'Now don't start a fight.' He grinned at her. 'It'll spoil your make-up.'

'I'm not wearing any, I told you ... or anything else, come to think of it ... you should know that.'

Laughing again, he pulled her towards him under the duvet. It was a perfect day.

—✺—

Marnie had had a good day. She arrived home that evening, exhausted but happy. *Sally Ann's* new livery of navy blue and cream was completed; the jobs-to-do list had been cut down to size.

After a supper of scrambled eggs on toast she ran the bath while sorting through the mail and checking her clothes for the journey. As she dozed in the bath, a question began to trouble her.

Am I becoming some kind of anorak? Is this boat enthusiasm a sign of that? A bad sign?

She ran her hands over her stomach. Whatever else, she was definitely getting thinner.

Could I be getting obsessed with the boat? Is this Obsessive Boat Disorder? Could I be anoraksic?

She laughed at her joke, then quickly stopped. A thought. All-weather clothing. Perhaps an anorak would not be a bad idea.

On that note she climbed into bed and fell into a dreamless sleep.

16
Blur

Monday morning, bright and early, the last Monday in the office for a long time. Marnie's desk had a strangely tidy look, and fleetingly she wondered if she would ever come back.

'You're an early bird.' A voice from the other side of the room, Philip in the doorway.

'I wanted to make sure everything was ready.'

'And is it? Are you ready for off?'

'Just about.'

'I was telling Janet about your plans. You've got us thinking about a boating holiday, now.'

'Watch out,' Marnie said. 'They can be habit-forming. The next minute you'll find boats have taken over your life and you haven't got a job any more.'

Philip crossed the office. 'That isn't the case for you, Marnie. This is your desk and your team. You can come back when you're ready … any time.'

'Thanks.'

'Don't forget we're having drinks and nibbles in your honour, lunch-time on Friday. Just a little gathering in the office.'

'It's in the diary.'

Philip grinned. 'Nothing formal, no speeches … just to wish you *bon voyage*.'

'That'll be nice.'

Philip nodded. 'I think Larry's organising it.'

Marnie held his gaze. 'Super.'

Gary was waiting on the bridge when the white van arrived. He climbed in beside Brendan, hoisting his bag behind the seats and they drove north out of London in sluggish traffic. Neither spoke much; incessant pop music blared from the van's radio. Gary let his thoughts wander. There were four people on his mind, each one with a question mark.

Where was he going with Sheena? He had had many girlfriends over the years, but rarely had he got on so well with one like her. She was nearly ten years younger than him. Who cared?

Where was Gravel these days? Had he really left Gary space and time to find out about Old Peter? Not so long ago, Gravel seemed to pop up every five minutes. Now, nothing … silence. Gary had a horrible suspicion that Gravel told you to do something and waited while you did it, probably waited only a very short time. After that … He had an excuse this week. He could hardly keep on his enquiries about the old man when he was away working out of town. Somehow he didn't think Gravel was very interested in excuses.

And what about Old Peter? Gary could not believe the old boy had anything worth worrying about. Was he the kind of eccentric who stashed a fortune away under the bed and left it to a sanctuary for retired donkeys? Nah! It was just a daft rumour thought up by some idiot in the pub. The trouble was, how could he persuade Gravel of this?

Then Marnie. How had she become so pally with Old Peter so quickly? One minute she was a total stranger, the next, she and the old bloke were big buddies. What was going on?

The van arrived at Cowroast Marina and Gary got his first sight of the job. He was amazed how much work there was to complete the re-fit in only five days. At least it would help take his mind off Sheena.

———⚍———

For Marnie the week went by in a blur. Everything was falling into place, at the office, at home, on the boat. On Wednesday evening she was in the flat checking her lists when the phone rang.

'You're in! I don't believe it.'

'I live here, Beth, remember?'

'You don't feel like changing your mind, coming over here?'

'Nope. I set off on Saturday for the Great Journey. Crack of dawn on the morning tide.'

'How far are you going on the, er … morning tide?'

A pause. 'Sainsbury's supermarket, Kensal Green.'

'I'm impressed.'

'That's just my first port of call. After that … wherever the mood takes me.'

'So, you're really serious. What about work?'

'They've organised a wake for Friday.'

'Well, I hope you have a good time. Remember all the things we told you.'

'Sure. You don't have to worry about the stern gland.'

'Marnie, tell me something. What actually *is* the stern gland?'

'What do you mean?'

'To be honest, I haven't the faintest idea what it is. It was just something Paul was always muttering about.'

'See you, Beth.'

'Bon voyage!'

Marnie was relieved her sister did not add, 'Have a nice da-a-ay!'

17
Casting off

On the whole, Marnie thought the Friday lunchtime drinks and nibbles went well. There were no speeches, just a chance to do the rounds, chat to everyone and say her good-byes. When no-one was paying her any particular attention, she slipped out to the car park. They did not even notice her go.

Outside, she could not believe her eyes. Under the windscreen wiper was a parking ticket. *In a private car park?* Then she saw that one of the wheels was clamped. *What the hell was going on?* She pulled the ticket from the windscreen. *The Council had no right!* Then she noticed that the fine imposed was one million pounds – her jaw dropped – and the signature of the City Treasurer of Westminster Council looked suspiciously like … Mickey Mouse.

Closer inspection of the wheel-clamp revealed that it was made of cardboard. She pulled it off and stuffed it in the boot of the car. Musing on the potential for fraud offered by modern word-processing packages and the inventiveness of interior designers, she climbed in and switched on. The heater fan came on full, the windscreen wipers leapt into action at double speed, the cassette player blasted her with heavy metal.

Setting the controls back to normal, she found the rear-view mirror was pointing at something strange lying in the back. Wrapped in an old sack, it looked like a tramp. She got out of the car, extracted the bundle and unwound the sack. Inside was a black plastic rubbish bag, which she opened to reveal a Buckby can, the traditional water container from the old days of boating. In typical boat fashion, they were painted with flowers, and the one Marnie now held by its wooden handle was in dark blue with cream bands dividing the floral sections around the name, *Sally Ann*. Specially commissioned, it was a beautiful and generous gift.

Then she saw them. The whole company was lined up at the windows of the first floor, waving. Marnie held the can up like a trophy, grinning and blowing kisses. Back in the car, she fastened the seat belt round the can beside her and accelerated out into the street while the firm cheered her off. Ten seconds later she pulled up at the kerb for two reasons. The first was to wipe her eyes. The second was to untie the string holding the row of tin cans to the exhaust pipe.

Arriving on *Sally Ann*, Marnie carried out an inspection and was pleased with what she saw. The boat had been transformed inside and out. The table in the saloon was laid for tea with the new crockery and within minutes of her arrival, Mrs Jolly came on board; the first guest of the new regime, bringing a parting gift of homemade shortbread.

'And when does your adventure begin, my dear?'

'At crack of dawn on the morning tide.'

'Of course.'

After Mrs Jolly had gone, Marnie felt restless, an eve of departure feeling. While she washed up, a question came to mind. Why wait until tomorrow? She rushed back to the flat, phoned for a taxi and carried her last bag downstairs to the hall. She was setting time-switches for security lighting when the doorbell rang.

In just over an hour she was back on the boat.

———✠———

The traffic bulletins on the van's radio told Gary and Brendan what they already knew: the Friday afternoon traffic round north London was congested. But they were feeling good. The work had gone well and each of them had a bulge in his pocket that bore more than a passing resemblance to a thick wad of banknotes.

Gary had also had time to think about Old Peter and make a plan. When they got back to Little Venice he would go round and see Marnie before his date with Sheena. He would say he had been thinking about *Sally Ann's* hull and wanted to check it over before her journey. Then, he would get round to the old man.

Don't just take my word for it, Marnie, ask Old Peter. You know him, don't you?

And:

I think we should get a second opinion about the mechanical side, too, while we're about it. Why don't we ask Old Peter to take a look? Do you want to ask him or shall I?

What could be simpler?

———✠———

The journey would begin now, no waiting for the *morning tide. Sally Ann* was kitted out and ready to go. Marnie took a deep breath, turned the ignition key and pressed the red button. The engine began thumping, even and steady like a healthy heartbeat. As she pushed off from the bank, Marnie imagined the boat was trembling with the anticipation of the journey ahead.

This evening, the supermarket at Kensal Green. Tomorrow, the world. But first, there was something she had to do. On the hatch cover that was shining in new paint, stood two tupperware containers. One contained shortbread, the other ginger biscuits, lovingly baked at home, carefully packed in greaseproof paper.

———✠———

Gary threw his bag into the saloon on *Garrow* and went quickly round to *Sally Ann*, desperate to have something to report when Gravel showed up and asked for progress. But where *Sally Ann* should have been moored there was only empty water. He did not want to believe it.

He was standing on the path wondering what to do next when a voice hailed him from behind.

'Hallo. Excuse me.'

Gary turned. Looking down through the railings stood an old lady.

'I'm sorry to interfere, but were you looking for *Sally Ann* by any chance?'

'That's right … Marnie. I'm a … friend of hers. I have to talk to her about the boat.'

'Oh …'

'I'm worried that *Sally Ann* might need attention … *urgent* attention, before she sets off.'

'Oh dear, I see.'

'I don't suppose you know if she's left already? I've been away all week and I've come straight round.'

'No, she's not left yet. She did say something about going to the supermarket. She'll be back soon, I'm sure.'

Gary was relieved. 'That's great. I'll catch her later.'

'It's very nice of you to be so concerned about her.'

A choirboy's smile. 'No problem at all.'

Marnie brought *Sally Ann* to a halt and tied up outside the supermarket. Her elation at setting off from Little Venice had given way to a feeling of disappointment. The boxes of biscuits were still standing on the hatch cover.

She had steered down the side arm where Old Peter lived, looking for the grey-green boat, only to find an empty mooring by the bank. It had not occurred to her that she would leave without saying good-bye. She had wanted a few words of valediction from the old man to send her on her way.

Returning to the pool of Little Venice, Marnie had circled the island to see down to the tunnel. There had been no familiar shape coming towards her, though she fancied she recognised Gary walking briskly along the towpath.

She had taken her decision to set off and there would be no wavering. She had pointed *Sally Ann* towards the other end of the pool and her journey began, with one glance back. Certain that no-one was watching, she had turned and blown a kiss towards Old Peter's mooring and whispered good-bye.

Gary legged it back from Marnie's mooring, glancing at his watch. He had barely time for a shower and a change of clothes before Sheena arrived, but he had to see Old Peter. He turned smartly left and crossed the canal by the bridge, quickening his pace, checking his watch again as he hurried past the waterbuses. Time was against him. He had to force himself not to run. A breathless casual encounter would seem less than convincing. A minute later, for the second time that evening, he found himself staring at a gap where a boat should be standing.

'I don't believe it!'

He ran a hand through his hair.

'Hallo, Gary.'

Gary snapped round. A head was protruding from the boat beside him, a man in his fifties with short grey hair.

'You looking for Old Peter?'

'Er … yeah. Seen him?'

'He's been out all afternoon.'

'By himself?'

The man looked puzzled for a moment, then a smile spread across his face. 'Yeah, by himself.'

'What are you grinning at?'

'You were thinking he might be out with … *her*, weren't you?'

Gary's turn to look puzzled. 'You mean …'

'That's right … that smart-looking woman. She was here with Old Peter at the weekend. You won't believe this … she even went on board with him.'

'You're kidding!'

'I kid you not. D'you think the old boy's found himself a girlfriend.'

They laughed together at the idea, but Gary's mind was racing.

———❦———

The supermarket occupied a site near the gasworks, opposite Kensal Green cemetery on the other side of the canal. Marnie made *Sally Ann* secure at the bollards on the towpath close to the entrance to the shop.

She hoped to do her rounds and be away in half an hour, but through the glass doors she could see the Friday evening crowds. Progress with the trolley was slow and she bumped and wriggled up and down the aisles, estimating how much she could store on board. *Sally*'s fridge was the size of two shoe boxes and the freezer compartment was big enough to hold a walkman.

———❦———

Gary showered, shampooed and changed into fresh clothes like an automaton. He ought to be thinking about Sheena, but he could only think about Marnie and Old Peter … and whatever it was that had brought them together.

By the time he jumped off his boat and dashed for the station he had persuaded himself they were up to something, or rather, she was. It was with a shock that he realised he was nearly twenty minutes early. *Calm down, Gary!* He had time to kill. There was only one option.

He pushed open the doors of the pub and went in, anxious to tell Gravel he had been away, getting in first before he had to go on the defensive. There was no sign of Gravel, no sidekick. He walked up to the bar.

'Hi, Gary, what'll it be?'

'Er … I'm looking for a mate.'

'Oh yeah? Who's that, then?'

'Middle-aged bloke … very short hair, leather jacket, gold ear-ring.'

'No name, your mate?'

'He's trying to give it up.'

'You described half my customers, Gary. It could almost be you.'

'He usually has that table over there.' Gary pointed.

'We have a lot of customers, Gary. I don't know 'em all.'

'But you know this one, Benny – deep gravelly voice, drinks double scotches, has a sidekick who seems to manage to get served first even when the place is crowded.'

'Like I said, we have a lot of customers. Some of them have more forceful personalities than others. Anyway, what can I get you … double scotch is it?'

'Er … I've got a date … better be going. Thanks, Benny.'

'For what? Bring her back here. You can sit over there if you want. I don't think anyone'll be using that table tonight.'

But Gary had other plans for the evening.

Marnie struggled from the checkout, looking like a refugee fleeing a battle zone with all her possessions piled high. After an hour in Sainsbury's, the shopping was too heavy for her to cross the cattle grid that was designed to keep trolleys away from the canal. She humped the bags across to the boat and shuffled through to store them away in the galley.

She was standing at the workbench panting from her exertions when an unmistakable boat passed by at close quarters. Marnie leapt out on deck just as *Joshua* pulled in to tie up behind *Sally Ann*. Jane waved from the tiller as Derek jumped onto the bank holding mooring ropes.

Five minutes later the three of them were sitting in *Joshua*'s comfortable saloon drinking red wine. Derek spread the map of the southern waterways on the table and traced their journey. Eventually he pushed it towards Marnie.

'So where are you making for tonight?'

Marnie glanced out of the window. 'Kensal Green, by the look of it.' The evening was drawing on and already the sun was dropping below the gasholders.

Jane suddenly looked serious. 'Did you hear the news on the radio?'

'News?'

'You remember the crate they dragged out of the pool in Little Venice?'

'The murder.'

Jane nodded. 'Unless he'd chopped himself into bits, jumped into the box and floated off for a jolly wheeze.'

Marnie grimaced. Jane continued.

'Well … it seems the police have identified the victim.'

'Leroy Monroe,' Derek chipped in. 'In his thirties, heavily involved in drugs. A *gangland* killing.'

Marnie recalled Jane's words: *This is not gangland.* She frowned. 'Strange way to conceal a body … leaving it floating around in the canal.'

'Ah, but that wasn't the idea, apparently. This was intended as a very public warning to his gang.'

'God, how awful! To think he was in there all that time …'

Derek topped up Marnie's glass. 'Sorry, perhaps we shouldn't be going on about this when you're just starting a long journey … alone.'

Jane agreed. 'No, perhaps not. But I don't think Marnie's the nervous type. Are you, Marnie?'

'Probably not, but I'd prefer to give murderers a miss, if possible.'

Jane held up her empty glass. 'Derek, what about opening another bottle? This red's not bad.'

Marnie made to stand up. 'Not on my account. I'm supposed to be on the journey of a lifetime. So far I've made it to the supermarket.'

Leaving her friends to do their own shopping, Marnie returned to *Sally Ann*, her head filled with thoughts of the body in the box. She made a decision. Much as she liked Colin Dexter's Inspector Morse books, she would not be reading his canal murder story for a while.

Time for another decision. She had had a few glasses of wine, nothing to eat and dusk was coming on. She would tie up for the night, have a bite and make an early start in the morning. On the other hand, it did seem pathetic to spend her first night virtually in a supermarket car park. She thought she should at least chug over to the opposite bank.

Slightly further on, she spotted a grassy patch between the trees where she could hop off and knock mooring pins into the ground. It offered a good view of the gasworks. After tying up, she stood on the bank enjoying the quiet and the mild evening air. An armada of ducks cruised by to explore the prospects for dinner. Behind her, there was a rustling in the bushes. Marnie ignored it, went inside and lit the oven. By the time she had wrapped a salmon steak in foil with a little butter, a bay leaf and a sprinkling of chopped onion, she had forgotten the sound completely.

Once the salad was made and a chunk of French bread was warming, Marnie debated with herself whether to have a glass of dry white wine with the meal. It was a close vote and she looked out at the gathering dusk as she reached into the drawer for the corkscrew.

She took her wine out on deck while the fish baked, its smell mingling in the air with the scent of the vegetation and the cool breath coming from the water. Marnie perched on the stern rail and took a sip, feeling more free than she had been for years.

There was no towpath by the cemetery where *Sally Ann* was moored, just an unkempt bank with trees overhanging the water's edge and a high brick wall. Further back, the wall gave way to tall railings. Marnie knew the tombs of several eminent Victorians were nearby. Thackeray was there, she thought, and Trollope, Wilkie Collins and Leigh Hunt, their graves set in amongst the bushes and trees. Hardly a sound reached her, only a distant murmur of traffic.

She lit the oil lamps and sat down to eat, reading a cruising guide, planning her next day. One lamp went out almost immediately. After she had finished eating, it was cool enough to refill. Screwing the top on the oil bottle, Marnie thought she saw movement outside. She stood quite still, making a determined effort not to think of dismembered bodies floating in crates.

Curiosity led her out onto the stern deck, grabbing the torch from its hook by the door. All was silent in the darkness.

Was this going to be the pattern for the whole summer, she wondered, creeping about, fearful of her own reflection in the window? Or was this just sensible caution, obeying a deep-rooted instinct to be wary and alert in strange surroundings? She told herself to do something practical and stepped ashore to check the mooring ropes.

At the bow end Marnie stood up quickly from inspecting the rope, and the sudden movement made her dizzy. She stopped to let the feeling pass, holding on to the roof rail. Through the windows she saw the light fade in the saloon as the second oil lamp went out. She walked to the stern, flashing the torch briefly to check that the mooring pin was firm.

Back on board, not wanting the glare of the electric lights, she groped her way in darkness past the sleeping berth and into the galley. She knew the exact location of the oil lamp that she had refilled. The Zippo lay on the work-surface and she flicked it on to light the dual wicks, carefully replacing the globe and chimney, leaving the flames at their lowest setting to allow the glass to warm up slowly.

It was while she adjusted the lamplight that Marnie became aware of a change in the cabin. She looked up, at first sensing the movement before her eyes had focused. The intruder must have gained entry while she was inspecting the bow-ropes. Now they faced each other across the galley and the saloon.

In the glow of the lamplight, Marnie found herself looking into the eyes, the unblinking amber eyes, of a sturdy black cat.

18
Visitor

Saturday, and the bows of *Sally Ann* were cutting through the water at a steady four miles per hour heading westwards on that first cool morning of the Great Journey. Marnie had made an early start as planned. It was just after six, a mug of coffee stood on the hatch, steam faintly rising, and she was yawning at the tiller. London was just waking, and she had escaped.

She had hurriedly washed and dressed, checked over the boat, given the cat some milk and sent it home. This would be her daily routine from now on until the end of summer. Correction. This would be the routine, apart from dealing with the cat.

Marnie had been surprised the previous evening to find the unexpected black shape on board. Under interrogation it had revealed nothing, but had simply paused in washing itself, blinked at her and continued licking its foreleg. It had been a one-sided conversation.

Where could it have come from? On this side of the canal there was only the cemetery. Marnie knew little about cats and wondered whether they had wide-ranging territories. This was no feral creature. It was calm, placid, relaxed. It even allowed itself to be stroked gently on the head and began purring, bringing a homely feeling to the saloon that went well with the lamplight.

Marnie was encouraged enough by this reaction to look for a collar. She reached forward to touch its neck while it was distracted with washing its chest. In one continuous movement it inclined its head slightly and licked her hand. The unaccustomed roughness of the tongue on her skin made Marnie withdraw, and the cat resumed its ablutions. There was no collar. There was also no chance she would let it stay on the boat.

The cat allowed Marnie to pick it up and carry it to the door.

'It's been nice knowing you. Now off you go home like a good cat.'

She set it down gently on the deck and reached out to shut the doors. Immediately, the cat turned and skipped back into the cabin before Marnie could react.

'Hey! Come on! You've got to go home. They'll be wondering where you are.'

The cat was back on the chair, turning round and round as a prelude to curling up. Marnie had no intention of abducting someone's pet. She resolved to take firm action.

After the third attempt to get the cat to stay out, it occurred to her that it might be wanting something and she suspected that might be milk. It surprised her that the cat showed no inclination to rush at the saucer, but took its time to approach and sniff at it. When the saucer was licked clean, Marnie picked the cat up carefully and placed it determinedly outside on the stern deck. She had made it quite clear who was in charge and was pleased to have had her first visitor of the journey and to have sorted out the first problem.

When Marnie woke early in the strange bed, she remembered the events of the night before. She leaned out and looked towards the saloon. The cat was curled up on its chair, fast asleep. Marnie washed and dressed. When she slid back the hatch to let the morning in, the air was cool and clean on her face. She lit the gas under the kettle and popped a croissant in the oven, her mind on the journey ahead. All this time the cat did not stir.

Marnie poured some milk into a saucer.

'Breakfast! Come on, cat. Time to get up … and go home.'

The cat yawned and stretched, looked briefly at Marnie and jumped down. When the milk was gone it walked slowly through the cabin and stood by the stern doors. It had got the message. Marnie stroked its head and let it out.

'So long! See you when I get back, perhaps.'

The cat placed its front paws on the gunwale, looked from side to side and jumped ashore, walking off into the undergrowth, tail held high. Marnie smiled. A visit from a black cat. Must be a good omen.

———⚏———

Gary woke early that Saturday morning to find Sheena looking at him, her head nestled on the pillow. He smiled. There was a delay of some seconds before she smiled back.

'You all right?' His voice sounded croaky and he cleared his throat.

'Uh-huh.'

'Sleep okay?'

'So-so.'

'You sure you're all right?'

'What's bothering you, Gary?'

'Me? Bothering *me*? You're the one who's acting strange.'

'You've been rolling around all night.'

'I've been –'

'And you've been muttering things.'

His face clouded. 'What things?'

'Dunno. Couldn't make 'em out. What's up, Gary?'

'It's nothing.'

'It's not nothing if it means I go around yawning all day at work with dark circles under my eyes.'

'Must've been something I ate, disagreed with me.'

'We both had the same. The only thing likely to disagree with you is me.'

'Look, I don't know what it was, okay? It was just a bad night … no big deal … let's leave it at that.'

'I thought we had a … relationship.'

'We have, sweetheart.'

'I thought we were getting close. If we aren't, I don't know what I'm doing in this bed.'

'We are … course we are. You know that.'

'Then tell me.'

Gary propped himself up on one elbow and squinted at the clock. Still early. He had no excuse that he had to rush and put it off till later.

'Talk to me, Gary. You're worrying me.'

He dropped back onto the pillow and put an arm round Sheena's waist. 'Where do I begin?'

'Try the beginning.'

He told her about the encounters with the stranger with the gravelly voice, fearing that once Sheena made the connection with the body in the crate and the gangland war she would be up and away forever. She made no comment about Gravel and waited for him to continue. He told her about Old Peter and his presumed valuables, how he was trying to find out what they might be. He did not mention Marnie.

When he stopped, Sheena turned her head on the pillow to look up at the ceiling. 'So this bloke with the gravelly voice thinks the old man's got something worth a lot of money stashed away. If he has, it must be on his boat or in his caravan.'

'Yeah.'

'So why not just break in and search the place?'

Gary jumped. 'What? You can't be serious. I'm not some kind of burglar.'

'Not *you*, Gary … *him* … or his thuggy mate. Why don't they just check out the caravan while the old man's away from his place?'

'In broad daylight?'

Sheena turned to face him again. 'Who's gonna see anything down there? You said it was under a bridge, tucked out of sight.'

'Ye-e-es.'

'Well, then?'

'I'm not sure I follow this. You think I should tell Gravel to get his mate to break in?'

'No. Of *course* not. I'm wondering why Gravel doesn't just get on with it.'

'Don't suppose we'll ever know the answer to that.'

'We already do, dibbo.' Sheena punched him lightly under the duvet. 'It's obvious.'

Gary was bewildered. 'Is it?' Sheena was a sales assistant in a small chemist's shop and she was talking like a fully paid-up member of the Mob. 'So what is the answer?'

'He can't be seen in public.'

'Mm …'

Sheena looked thoughtful. 'The real question is … why not?'

'And I suppose you've got that worked out, too?'

'He's worried about being recognised, obviously, especially now.'

'Now?'

'Yes. The police have been all over Little Venice and Maida Vale while you were away, since they found out who that body was in the crate you pulled out of the canal.'

'*That's* why he's lying low, why I haven't seen him …' Then, a sudden thought. 'They found out who it was in the crate? Who was it?'

'Leroy Monroe.'

'Never heard of him. Have you?'

'No ... course not. Gary, how would I know a gangster?'

'You remembered his name well enough.'

'Gary, I'm a shop assistant. I work in a chemist's. I'm not some gangster's Moll.'

'So how come you remember his name?'

Sheena smiled coyly. 'Easy. Monroe's like Marilyn Monroe. One of my boyfriends used to say I looked like Marilyn Monroe when she was young.'

Gary felt the first stirrings of carnal interest. 'Good point.'

'Only I'm not as *voluptuous* as her. It's one of my favourite words, *voluptuous*.'

'And Leroy?'

'Well, that's different.' The coy smile again.

'Don't tell me he thought you looked like someone called Leroy.'

She giggled. 'It's one of my favourite names. I've sometimes thought that ... well, if ever I had a little boy ... I might like to call him Leroy.'

Gary frowned. *Leroy!* The situation was worse than he had imagined.

Sheena laughed. 'I know what you were thinking.'

'What was I thinking?'

'Over my dead body ...'

Gary laughed too. 'Yeah ... great choice of words. *Blimey*, is that the time?' Gary grabbed the alarm clock and stared at it. He flicked the duvet aside and leapt out of bed. 'I'd better be getting up. Gotta see a man about a job.'

Sheena sat up and stretched. 'Did I say something that scared you, Gary?'

He looked at her as he grabbed his jeans from the floor. She was naked, and for a moment his resolve faltered. 'No. It's just –'

'This Gravel bloke has got to you, hasn't he? Did he threaten you?'

'No ... well, not in actual words.'

'Did he ask you to do anything you couldn't do?'

'Not really. He just told me about Old Peter's valuables.'

'And?'

'Just said he wanted me to get my head round it.'

Sheena shrugged. 'That's all right, then.'

Gary pulled a sweatshirt over his head. 'Not quite. The trouble is, I get the feeling that when he tells me to get my head round something, he could be thinking of an axe.'

————〰————

Marnie steered *Sally Ann* through a district where factories went on for miles. Crossing the aqueduct over the North Circular Road, the contrast stunned her. There she was, suspended high above the dual carriageway in her boat, using a waterway from the eighteenth century, while below her the morning traffic trundled along, most drivers unaware that the aqueduct existed at all. It seemed to Marnie indecent that she had so much space all to herself. And it felt like she was playing truant.

At mid-morning Marnie slowed to a crawl for the right-hand turn at Bull's Bridge.

She inched round the corner, ears pricked, ready to throw *Sally* into reverse and bring her to a sudden halt. But there was no other boat, and she turned quietly under the bridge, straightened the tiller and increased power.

Marnie had made the first change of course of the journey, normal life was receding and she was on her way on the main line of the Grand Union Canal. She weighed each word as she said the name to herself.

The Grand Union Canal.

It had a grand sound, promising to unite her with waterways the length of England and beyond into Wales.

———⟨∽∽⟩———

Gary had almost stopped in his tracks as he reached for the door handle, when Sheena squeezed past him on her way to the shower. He wanted to grab her and drag her back to the sleeping cabin. With enormous self control he had forced himself to open the door. Sheena reminded him she had to be at work by nine o'clock and promised to have breakfast ready for when he returned,

It was seven-thirty and overcast when he walked rapidly towards *Sally Ann*'s mooring. He covered the distance in two minutes. His shoulders sagged; the boat was gone. Marnie had already left. Damn!

He cursed himself for believing the silly old biddy who had told him Marnie had only gone shopping. Now, there was no-one around to ask. He scratched his chin. Or was there? He retraced his steps at double-quick time. Sheena was not the only one who could work things out.

Of one thing he was certain. Marnie and Old Peter were in cahoots, up to something together. It was weird. Everything was changing. Women were different these days, he thought. They were calling the shots.

He thought of Sheena with her beautiful body, meticulous grooming, perfect white teeth. He knew what she wanted. Not much doubt there. And Marnie, also attractive, well-groomed, smart – when she wasn't up to her elbows in paint or grease. What did she want? In particular, what did she want from Old Peter? To that question he was convinced there could be only one answer.

———⟨∽∽⟩———

Marnie had been waiting for this moment; her first lock. The black and white balance beams loomed up ahead, one gate standing open, beckoning her in. She motored in and climbed up the wall ladder to close the lock. The boat rose smoothly, held steady by Marnie with a rope round a bollard, and she was sad there was no-one around to witness her competence. The procedure had taken just under fifteen minutes. Before setting off, Marnie wrote in the log book her time of arrival and departure. Very soon she would have another entry, something altogether unexpected.

The engine gave only a faint puff of smoke as they left the lock behind them. Marnie felt a new confidence, conscious that she was young and strong and glad to be alive.

She smiled at the sky, at the passing gardens and canal banks. She smiled at the sight of *Sally Ann's* long freshly-painted roof extending before her, with its poles and gang-plank. She looked down into the interior and admired her new curtains, carpet tiles and bedspread. She smiled at the cat stretching on the bed, yawning.

The cat!

'Mind your wash!'

The shout came from a moored boat and it startled Marnie. She leapt to the accelerator and reduced speed at once, turning to raise a hand in apology. Seeing her embarrassment, the man changed his protest to a smile and waved back, shaking his head.

The cat was now sitting up on the bed, washing. Marnie was assailed by questions, all of them seeming to lead to only one answer. She would have to turn back.

She could not steal someone's pet, even if it was not her fault. The initial shock changed to surprise and gave way to calmer reflection. Above all, she could not bear the idea of going back, at least not on day one after such a good start. There had to be another way.

Marnie chewed her lower lip, trying to think calmly, while the cat was oblivious to the problems it was causing. They were still only in west London. It ought to be possible to find a tube station somewhere nearby. Marnie could take the cat back to Kensal Green, assuming there was a station there. She looked at the stowaway. No chance. It would hardly sit quietly on her lap and allow itself to be taken on the tube. She had no carrying box and no lead.

Suddenly, she had inspiration. Didn't Jane say that she and Derek lived in west London? Marnie dived into the cabin and grabbed her filofax and mobile.

'Hallo, Rutherford.'

Marnie told Jane about the stowaway. 'Look ... I was wondering ... do you live in this part of London?'

A pause. 'You want me to collect the cat and take it back?'

'Jane, I really hate to bother you but –'

'No problem. But ... are you sure it's the best thing to do?'

'Well, I don't want to abduct it and I can't just let it go.'

Another pause. Jane was thinking. 'I wonder where it came from. Of course, cats do often wander.'

'Do they? I don't know much about them.'

'Some do ... especially in the summer ... if they want a change of scene.'

'Why would they do that?'

'All sorts of reasons: unsettled after moving house, noisy new baby, wanderlust, who knows? The thing is, you don't choose *them*, they choose *you*.'

'You think it might be looking for a new home?'

'Possibly. I'll gladly take it back, if you want me to, but I suspect it'll carry on wandering. Does it show any sign of anxiety?'

'It looks like it owns the place.'

'That's normal for cats.'

'Right.'

'I'm not being much help to you, am I, Marnie?'

'Well, I just thought it would want to go home, but if it's going free range ...'

'Look, here's a plan. I'll be at home for the next hour or so. If you decide you want me to take it back, give me a ring and I'll come and collect it. If I don't hear from you, I'll assume the cat's taken command of the boat.'

———∽∽∼———

Gary passed under the first bridge to enter the dingy arm that led to Paddington Basin. Prepared to find a gap where the old man's boat should be, he was relieved to see it at its mooring. Relief turned to elation when Old Peter crossed his path, walking from the caravan to the boat. It was the perfect chance encounter. The old man would never know that Gary was deliberately coming to find him. Gary composed his features to register surprise.

'Oh, hi.' No one ever addressed Old Peter by name.

'Uh-huh.'

'How're you doing?'

'About the same.' The old man continued on his way.

Gary held his ground. 'I, er ... see you've got a girlfriend these days.'

Old Peter stopped and turned to face Gary, his expression serious. He said nothing. Gary spoke again.

'I came by the other day and you were chatting with that new woman ... Marnie, I think she's called ... *Sally Ann*.'

'Oh?'

'Quite a looker, that one.'

The old man pulled out a bunch of keys. Gary was determined not to be deflected.

'That boat of hers could do with a proper overhaul before she goes off on her trip. She's going away for the summer, you know.'

'Good.'

'Except it's got a lot that needs sorting out before she goes ... could have big trouble with that boat. I said I'd see to it before she went.' Old Peter looked thoughtful. Gary continued. 'I'm not sure when she's actually going, but I think she wants to go soon. Perhaps she mentioned it.'

'What trouble?'

'Oh ... this and that. Boat's been neglected for years. The engine's dodgy for a start.' There was no reaction. Gary persisted. 'Like I said, I don't know when she's wanting to go.'

'You could ask her.' Old Peter pushed a key into the lock and turned it. Pulling open the doors, he went down into the boat without another word.

Gary remained on the path for a few seconds, deflated, before setting off at a brisk pace back to *Garrow* and Sheena, unaware that he was being observed from behind a lace porthole curtain on the grey-green boat.

Old Peter filled the kettle and lit the gas stove, watching Gary's departure, noting that he was going back the way he had come. While he attended to his ablutions, he wondered what Gary was doing and why he had come. It had been no chance meeting. So why was he asking questions about Marnie?

Gary was devious like a fox, but lacked that animal's intelligence. He did not have the sense to cover his own tracks. Something was motivating him, and the old man had a fair idea what it was.

———

Marnie turned Jane's comments over and over in her mind until she reached the next lock.

… cats often wander …

The journey was barely one day old and already she had picked up a passenger,

… you don't choose them …

a stowaway,

… they choose you …

another mouth to feed.

She pulled over to make the boat secure at the bank and reached down for the windlass. At that moment Marnie took a decision. She would take on her first crew member and give it half a tin of tuna for breakfast. But in that same moment the crew member took its own decision. It slipped past her and neatly jumped onto the towpath. Typical! Marnie thought. I offer you hospitality and you jump ship without so much as a 'thanks for the ride'.

The cat walked off up the towpath without a backward glance and disappeared into the bushes. Was that it? Marnie wondered if she would ever see it again. Would it leave her to continue its walkabout? Curiously, she found herself disappointed at the idea.

'Come on, cat!' she called out. 'I've got some lovely tuna for you.'

Marnie worked the lock with no further sighting of the cat. Feeling warmer after her exertions in the sunshine, she slipped down to the cabin to grab a T-shirt. A sound reached her from the saloon. She looked in to find the cat had taken up station by the fridge and was purring. The amber eyes of the stowaway transfixed her.

Marnie wondered what cat meal times were. She reached for the tin opener and the cat meowed. *Sally Ann*'s water pump growled.

'Okay, okay! Don't rush me. I've got a lot to learn, all right?'

Oh god, she thought, this is how eccentrics begin. I talk to the boat and the cat and they both answer me back. She selected two saucers from the cupboard, put food in one and milk in the other. For herself, she put out bread and cheese with a glass of cider, but first picked up the mobile and redialled Jane's number.

'Hi, it's Marnie.'

Before she could say more, Jane interrupted.

'Right, listen up. Cats usually get two meals a day, one in the morning, the other at tea-time. Don't overdo the milk, but make sure there's always some fresh water in a bowl.

Are you getting this?'

Marnie grabbed the logbook and began rapid scribbling. 'Yes. Are you taking psychic lessons from my sister by any chance, Jane?'

'Pay attention. I'd advise you to get some crunchy food as a basic … good for the teeth and gums … easy to store, too. What have you fed it so far?'

'Skipjack tuna steak … half a tin.'

'You've got a friend for life. It'll think it's in cat heaven. You could give it something like that every other day.'

Marnie heard the cat purring in the background.

'What about …?'

'Yes. You'll need a litter tray.'

'Where on earth am I –'

'I've thought about that. Get an engine oil drip tray at the next chandlery you pass.'

'That's a good idea. What about –'

'You can use sand or even dig up some soil. It'll be okay.'

Marnie finished scribbling. 'It doesn't seem too difficult. I was getting worried … not knowing what to do.'

'You'll be fine. It's all about training.'

'But this is all new to me. I've never trained a cat before.'

'Not what I meant, Marnie. You're very intelligent. I expect the cat will have you trained in no time at all.'

19
Dolly

Marnie surprised even herself. By the next day she was feeling like a veteran of the boating life. The world went by at a gentle pace, locks came and went, the engine thumped on steadily. Her only doubts concerned the cat, though it too had adapted to a new rhythm and seemed contented with its lot.

She could not go on calling it 'the cat' all the time, and this led to another thought. What sex was it? If it was male, did they have undesirable habits or make dreadful smells? If it was female, would it suddenly produce a litter in a cupboard? Would the boat be overrun by tiny fur-covered shapes, doing unutterable things in every corner? Perhaps that was why it was wandering, looking for somewhere to have kittens. Oh gawd …

First priority was to give it a name, assuming she could work out what sex it was. If not, she would have to come up with something neutral like *Puss* or *Mog*. She remembered that Brigitte Bardot used to call her duck *Canard* and her dog *Chien*. So would this one be *Chat* … or *Chatte*? Open to misunderstandings. She sighed. It was becoming a habit.

So … a name. Inspiration. She would adopt one from a boat they passed. It would give her something to do while chugging out of London, like the games she used to play with her sister on long car journeys in their childhood. A line of moored boats appeared.

September Dawn … Windrush … Desiree … Bulrush …. Castle Rose … Hector.

Tricky. *Dawn … Hector?* Back to the sex thing again. She put the exercise to one side to negotiate a lock. Waiting in the boat for the chamber to fill, she decided to check the visitor. As she approached, it gave her a speculative look, as if it knew she was up to something. Marnie picked it up and it made no protest. She cradled it in her arms and began stroking its tummy. It purred while Marnie ran her fingers up and down, trying to part the fur in the lower area. She rummaged around while the cat lay happily back with its eyelids drooping. Marnie could not find anything protruding.

'Oh well,' she muttered. 'I suppose that eliminates *Hector*.'

Underway again, the canal now offered more open views, with lakes and fields visible between the trees and bushes lining the banks. At the edge of the water stood a heron, immobile as a garden ornament, the colour of damp concrete.

Ahead, another line of boats presented her with a new opportunity to find a name.

The Minstrel … Wanderbug … Camelot … Dun-Ernin … Old Harry … Escape-aid

By late afternoon it was time for another decision. Marnie had been on her feet since early morning with only a sandwich and the odd cup of coffee to keep her going. If she stopped for a meal now, she could go on as long as she wanted, rather than find herself too tired to prepare food at the end of the day. There was a line of boats moored up ahead. She would take a break after passing them.

Mephisto … Liberty Belle … Kingfisher … Genevieve … Ramblin' Rose … Joylen

Nothing very promising in that lot, Marnie thought, looking at the cat and trying to imagine it (or probably her) as a *Genevieve*. No, not really. *Rose, Rosie, Rosa?* Perhaps not, even though it had a certain boatish ring to it. The cat rubbed its flank against her legs as she stood at the workbench in the galley.

Marnie had devised a simple food policy for the journey based on easy recipes, ingredients as fresh as possible, with tins for backup. While an egg boiled on the hob and a small baguette warmed in the oven, she blended half a ripe avocado, chopped onion, mayonnaise and seasoning. She laid the table and fed the cat. The chopped hard-boiled egg joined the other ingredients to form a pale green purée. On the table she placed a small side salad of lettuce, tomato and sliced red pepper with a vinaigrette dressing and a sprinkling of herbs and opened a bottle of dry white Orvieto that had been cooling all day in the fridge.

A feast in minutes. It looked wonderful, and the interior of the boat smelled good enough to eat. Sitting down was bliss. Marnie found some Monteverdi on the radio, and the cat purred along while washing herself in the middle of the floor.

After the meal Marnie cut a small bunch of green grapes to eat on deck and set off on the next leg, scrutinising every boat she passed for a suitable cat name.

Still Waters … Willow … Argonaut … Badger … Laurel … Straight and Narrow

After another couple of locks and no more inspiration, Marnie resolved to take the very next name and adopt it, come what may. Ahead, she saw a boat approaching and called down into the cabin.

'Okay, cat, this is it!'

The boat drew nearer, the family on board waved and it passed by in a bright livery of green, yellow and red.

Pigling Bland

Ah … Never mind. Another boat was waiting up ahead to enter a lock. Marnie crossed her fingers as she drew nearer.

Dolores

Marnie groaned inwardly as she pulled alongside. How could she call the cat *Dolores* … *Doll* …? The steerer, a curvaceous woman in bulging pink sweatshirt and blue jeans, smiled over at Marnie.

'Shall we go in breasted up?'

'Er …' Marnie became aware of a more than ample bosom and tried to avert her gaze. '… sorry?'

'Go into the chamber together … side by side?' She pointed ahead. 'My husband and the kids will work the lock.'

'Right … yes, of course.' Marnie tried to sound confident as if travelling *breasted up* was something she did every day.

They eased forward close together and entered the chamber while a man and two teenagers tackled the gates and paddles with expert skill.

'Travelling alone?'

'Yes ... apart from a cat.'

'So I see. What's he called?'

'Er, well, actually ... Oh, can you see her?'

The woman gestured towards the windows. 'Yes. There's a black face looking out.'

'Excuse me.' Marnie stepped down inside, went through to the galley and found the cat standing on the workbench.

'Hey, puss! What are you doing up there? That's not allowed.'

The cat blinked at her but did not move. Through the window Marnie could see the name emblazoned on the side of the other boat ... *Dolores* ... She picked up the cat, put her on the director's chair and returned to the deck.

'Nice cat. What did you say its name was?'

There was the name staring at her. 'Dol ... er, well, it's ... *Dolly*, actually.' Marnie sounded doubtful.

The Amazon on *Dolores* smiled again. 'Very nice. *Dolly*. Yes, that's nice. I'm sometimes called *Dolly* by my husband.'

'Really?' Marnie had visions of inflatable dolls. Time for a change of subject. 'Nice boat you've got there.'

'We're pleased with it. Daft name, though. Who ever heard of a canal boat called *Dolores*?'

Marnie agreed. 'It is a bit exotic and voluptuous, I suppose. Perhaps it's named after somebody.'

'It is ...' The woman smiled. '... me.'

———— ⚬⚬⚬ ————

It had been a busy day for Gary, taking over for a waterbus driver who had phoned in sick. He waited for Sheena as usual that evening at the tube station, even though she now knew the way to his boat. She was the kind of girl you went to meet; she did not come to you. Life was treating him well, with good money coming in and a great girlfriend.

The only smudge on the horizon was Gravel. And where was he these days? One minute he's lurking behind every shadow, the next he's disappeared.

Sheena arrived for the evening carrying an overnight bag. He loved meeting her there, seeing her come up the steps from the underground. She was a 24-carat blonde bombshell.

On *Garrow*, Sheena dropped her bag on the bed in the sleeping cabin and went to the bathroom to check her make-up. Leaving the door open, she called out.

'Where are we going tonight, Gary? What's the plan?'

'I thought we might go to the place over the tunnel again. That all right?'

At times like this he felt the lack of a car. It was the downside of living on a boat in the middle of London. A night out usually meant somewhere within walking distance, unless he wanted to bump up the cost of the evening by taxi fares.

'Great. Tell you what … it'll be my treat.'

Gary could not believe his ears. It was the first step on the downward slope. No up-market girl ever expected to pay for anything.

'Did you hear me, Gary? I'm treating you tonight … if you see what I mean.'

It was a warning bell. When a girlfriend offered to pay for the evening out, it meant one of two things: she was starting to get serious; or she thought he didn't have enough money to keep her in the style to which she was – or wanted to be – accustomed. Either way it meant the beginning of the end. At least it had so far in his life.

'How do I look?' She presented herself in the gangway.

'Good enough to eat.'

She flashed him a sparkling smile. 'I told you it was my treat.'

'What do you do for a first course?'

She adopted a coquettish pose, began humming the tune, *The Stripper*, peeling off imaginary long gloves. Gary swallowed. It was time to go, before it was too late.

Walking along the towpath, Sheena returned to her theme. 'So there's no argument … I'm paying tonight, okay?'

'You know I can't let you do that, sweetheart.'

'Why not?'

'Because. No question. You're my girlfriend, I take you out. I don't mind women's lib, it's all right in its place, as long as it doesn't interfere with our lives, but if I take you out, I pay. End of story.'

Sheena knew an immovable object when she saw one, and even though she had no doubts about her ability to be an irresistible force, she knew when to hold back.

'All right, here's what we'll do.' She looked at her watch. 'It's early, so I'll take you for a drink before we go to the restaurant.'

'Why this sudden urge to start paying for things?'

'It's only fair. Deal?'

Gary sighed. 'All right … deal.' He was surprised when she pulled on his arm to take a side street as they crossed the road by the bridge. 'What's this?'

'There's a pub round the corner.'

Gary hesitated. It was usually around there that Gravel loomed into his life. 'Pub?'

'Yes. It's a like a big house where they sell drinks. You know the sort of place? Come on.'

In the pub Sheena led Gary straight to the table where he had previously sat with Gravel. As usual it was free. He felt uneasy, but no-one materialised threatening to cut his legs off. He was automatically reaching into his pocket when she put a hand on his shoulder and made him sit down. She turned and crossed to the bar. He had only just realised she had not asked what he wanted when she returned holding two glasses.

'How'd you get served so fast with all those guys already at the bar?'

She winked, leaned across the table and shimmied with her shoulders. One glance at the scooped front of her dress and he got the message.

'I've never had to wait long to get served at any bar, and at least two blokes asked what I was having. I nearly told them it was *you* ...' That smile again.

The second shock came when Gary looked at his glass. It contained two lumps of ice and a generous measure of golden liquid. 'Scotch?'

'Yeah. I got you a double ... thought you might like a treat. Cheers!'

—————〰—————

Marnie cruised on till the sun went down. The air cooled, the sky changed colour, a hundred shades from blue to grey to pink and darker blue. The houses and factories of that morning had given way to fields and farms. In open country the silhouettes of trees stood out against the fading background.

Perhaps tomorrow she would learn the names of trees from one of her books or identify the various types of waterfowl. Waterfowl! She was starting to sound like an expert already.

A procession of boats passed her from the opposite direction, all crewed by families who waved happily at Marnie as if they had been waving and smiling all day. They probably had. She wondered what impression she gave them, a woman travelling by herself with only a black cat for company. The witch of the waterways! She put aside such fanciful thoughts and waved at the passing boats, reading the names as they went by.

Diane ... Lily ... Samantha ... Luisa ... Daisy ... Little Mo ... Rebecca ... Lizzie Bell

Marnie shook her head and wondered where they had been when she needed them.

The world settled down for the night, Dolly curled into a ball on the duvet and Marnie held the tiller, watching the night come down, filled with a sense of peace and freedom. That stretch of the canal twisted its way along a contour line. The banks were too shallow and overgrown for mooring, but she was in no hurry, happy enough to cruise a while, knowing that a stopping place probably lay just around the corner.

—————〰—————

Gary lay in the darkness of the sleeping cabin. Beside him he could hear Sheena breathing softly, feel her warmth under the duvet, smell her fragrance. He had laughed when she told him she had brought her night things and clothes for the next day. When he asked about the 'night things' she had giggled.

'I'm wearing them already, got them on under my dress.'

Of course, he should have realised, she only wore perfume at night.

He liked her things around him, but he was under no illusions. Everything was fine for now, and it was pleasant to find her make-up and sponge bag in the bathroom, her smells in the boat generally, a faint tang of scent hovering in the air. But he knew that sooner or later the novelty of the boat would wear off and she would be asking him pointed questions: did he want to live on a boat all his life; was he content to earn a living by doing odd jobs? Still, that could wait till later. For now, things were good, except ... Something wasn't right. He had felt that ever since she had offered to pay for their meal. He was drowsy now after the exertions of bedtime, but he had to work out what was troubling him. Begin at the beginning, he told himself.

First, there had been the offer to treat him. He put that aside. Second, there had been the choice of pub. Perhaps it was just the nearest, and anyway, he had accepted the drink as a compromise. Third, the choice of drink. It was exactly what Gravel had given him. Had Sheena asked the barman what Gary had been drinking of late? An outside possibility. Fourth, the choice of table. There were others unoccupied. Fifth, the speed with which Sheena had been served. Was it really down to a glimpse of cleavage? Were these really all just coincidences?

And then there was the name of the victim in the crate. How many people remembered names after hearing them on the news? Was that *Monroe* story plausible? He looked at her face on the pillow in the dim light seeping round the porthole curtain from the street beyond. Perhaps she did look like Marilyn Monroe. She was certainly a blonde bombshell. But *Leroy?* Was she *serious?*

More than that, more than all those coincidences – if that was what they were – there was something else. Sheena had come into his life at about the time he had first met Gravel. He did not want to believe it, but he had to face facts. She had flashed him a come-on look in the shop that day, one of her brilliant white smiles. He was sure it was genuine. He could not believe she had anything to do with the world of gangs and drugs. He pictured her there in the chemist's, all fresh and neat in her white coat, standing at the pharmacy counter. He was convinced that she was ... wait a minute ... chemists! ... He almost sat up in bed. Sheena worked in a place that dispensed drugs.

She was breathing gently and rhythmically beside him ... in his bed, on his boat, in his life. Was she a coincidence too far? Maybe Sheena was a bombshell in more ways than one.

20
Lazy Sunday

Marnie did not realise how tired she had been until she turned over to look at the alarm clock on the floor of the sleeping cabin. A habitual early riser, she was amazed to see that it was already eight-fifteen. Even on a Sunday, that was late for her.

Slatted sunlight was patterning the wall from the Venetian blind in the galley. Marnie sighed and rolled onto her back. How far would she travel that day? Did it matter? On *Sally Ann*, the journey and the destination were the same, while the world rolled past at walking pace.

A narrowboat journey was like a journey back in time, she thought, living with the technology of the past. It was a journey that was an end in itself, a state of being. *Hold on, Marnie ... isn't this all a bit mystical for first thing in the morning?* But then another idea came to mind. Perhaps she was on a journey *away* from somewhere, rather than a journey *to* somewhere.

I'm rambling, she thought, and took a decision. She would take it easier than she had done the previous day. She would spend some of her time sketching plants, trees, animals and birds. While she was wondering how many different types of sheep she might learn to identify, and for what ultimate purpose, she heard the cat scratching about on her litter tray. Marnie decided it was time for her to get up and do the same.

—— ⚞ ——

Gary was in a quandary. These days he seemed to spend all his waking hours asking himself questions to which he had no answers. After a cup of black coffee he escorted Sheena to the tube station. She was visiting her parents that day. Walking slowly back from the underground, smoking his first cigarette of the day, Gary wondered what he was going to do about Old Peter. It was hopeless. He knew direct questioning would get him nowhere.

At the crossroads by the bridge he turned left and walked along the pavement towards the tunnel where *Sally Ann* was moored. Or rather, where an empty space marked the spot where *Sally Ann* used to be. The empty stretch of water seemed to mock him. Everything he did came to nothing. Where was Marnie? What was her connection with Old Peter? Did it matter? Questions, questions. No answers.

He pictured Marnie working on the boat. She had arrived in Little Venice at the same time as the crate was seen floating in the pool. He pictured Sheena. She had appeared in his life at the same time as Marnie and the crate ... and Gravel. Was it all just coincidence? Why now?

—— ⚞ ——

Marnie travelled further than she planned that day, enjoying the life of the truant, the wanderer, enjoying the locks, though the gates were sometimes heavy to push and the paddles stiff to turn.

Exiting each lock, she told herself she would tackle just one more before taking a break. And then another. Becoming well practised in managing by herself, she could lock through in about fifteen minutes. The cat, now firmly established as *Dolly*, took up position on the hatch, sitting, dozing or washing herself as the miles slipped by.

It was well into the afternoon by the time Marnie found a pleasant spot to pull over and tie up. After a ham salad sandwich and a glass of cider, she set up a safari chair and settled down with sketch pad and pencils. Before her the ground rose up to a tree-crowned summit. Sheep were grazing in the meadow. Somewhere back down the canal, in what felt like another life, architects and designers were sitting in the offices where she worked, dealing with issues that by now seemed strangely irrelevant.

Marnie turned and looked back down the stretch of water that was gleaming in the sunlight. Then she gazed at the sketch pad on her lap.

What am I doing here? she asked herself.

* * *

Gravel was sitting opposite Gary in the dinette on *Garrow*. He had arrived one minute after Gary returned to the boat from checking *Sally Ann's* mooring. This startled Gary, partly because the visit was so unexpected, on a Sunday morning, partly because Gary realised he was being watched. Gravel's sidekick lurked behind Gary, a menacing presence out of his line of vision.

'So Gary, what news?' It was the usual growly voice in the usual quiet tone.

'Old Peter's not talking. I've been round to see him, but he won't answer directly … just avoids questions. He's not easy to talk to.'

'I never said it would be easy.'

'I think he's more likely to talk to …' Gary faded. An idea was forming in his mind.

'You're not going to say he's more likely to talk to me, are you Gary? That would be like keeping a dog and doing your own barking. Barking, I'm not.'

'No. I was wondering … I don't suppose you've got someone else on the job, as well as me?'

Gravel's eyes narrowed. 'Someone else?'

'Marnie?'

'Marnie.' Gravel repeated the name. 'Tell me about this … Marnie.'

'You don't know her?'

Gary sensed a stirring behind him as if Sidekick had moved closer. It was an uncomfortable feeling, a reminder of who asked the questions.

'Just tell me about her, Gary.'

Gary was desperate to buy time to sort out his thoughts. 'D'you want a drink?'

'Marnie.' The voice was quieter this time, and Gary was sure Gravel's eyes flickered momentarily over his shoulder.

'She first came here when the … crate … was in the pool. She's doing up a boat … down the tunnel end.'

'What boat?'

'Sally Ann.'

'Go on.'

Gary shrugged. 'That's it.'

'Why do you think she might be involved in … something?'

'I've seen her with the old man … a few times. They travel around together.'

'Could she be an old boating mate?'

'Nah. Marnie's new to all this. I'd know her otherwise.'

'Then what's the connection?'

'I dunno, but I'll tell you something. She's even been on his boat. They talk.'

'People do talk, Gary.'

'Old Pete never talks to anyone … hasn't for years. Then this Marnie woman arrives on the scene … all of a sudden they're big buddies.'

'Your point being?'

'I don't reckon it's because she fancies him. There must be more to it. That's why I wondered … well, if she was …'

'An approach from a different angle?'

'Yeah.'

'You think she's the kind of woman who might work for me?'

'No, she's too …' Gary stopped himself just in time. He hoped. 'She seems too la-di-dah. But you never know. She might be a good actress.'

Gravel seemed to consider this idea. After a few moments he nodded. 'Women can surprise you sometimes … but not this time. What do you know about her, Gary?'

'Not a lot.'

'Think.'

'Well, if you don't know her, I don't suppose she can have anything to do with Old Peter's valuables.'

'I'll be the judge of that. What do you know?'

'Only what I've told you already. When I was in the café I saw them going along together on their boats.'

'Coincidence?'

'Don't think so. They were in tandem, I'm sure of it. He pulled alongside when she stopped … they spoke before he went off.'

Gravel absorbed this. 'What else?'

'I went round to see him and she was there, all matey, sitting with him on the side of his boat. They were talking, like *real* talk, not just passing the time of day. Then, when I went round again, he wasn't there but someone told me she'd been there before me and had actually gone on board.'

'People do go on each other's boats, Gary.'

'Not *women* … not with a *bloke*. If a woman comes on my boat, she's not there for polite conversation … well, not just that.'

Gravel looked pained. 'Old Peter's in his eighties.'

'That's my point. Why does a woman go on a boat with a bloke old enough to be her grand-dad?'

'So what's your answer?'

'They want to talk in private. Got to be. End of.'

Gravel was silent for so long, Gary began to feel even more nervous. He almost jumped when Gravel stood up.

'Seems like it's time you and this Marnie had a little chat, Gary.'

Gary scrambled to his feet. 'I can't.' He was sure Sidekick was closer behind him now.

'Can't?' There was an edge to the gravelly voice.

Gary knew his next answer had to be good. 'I mean, she's not at her mooring at the moment. She's gone on a trip.'

'You mean … you let her get away?'

'I figured if she'd gone, she wasn't likely to be following a trail with Old Pete. I mean, why would she just leave if she was trying to get something from the old boy?'

'There's an obvious answer to that, Gary. I'm a bit disappointed you didn't think of it. Try this. She might leave if she'd found what she was looking for.'

'Right. So, er … where does that leave me?'

'Good question, Gary.' A pause. 'This Marnie … what's she look like?'

'Not bad. Medium build … dark hair, wavy, down to her shoulders … taller than average.'

'How old?'

'Thirtyish?'

'Has she got a bloke?'

'I haven't seen one about.'

'But she'd need someone with her to run the boat, presumably, Gary.'

'She said she was going solo.'

'Really? You sure about that?'

'That's what she told me.'

'*Sally Ann* you said? What sort of boat is it?'

'Forty-five footer … oldish … cruiser stern …nothing special.'

'Colour?'

'Dark … er … maroon and navy.'

Gravel made a slight gesture with his head. Sidekick pushed the side doors open. Turning at the bottom step, Gravel looked Gary in the eye.

'I suggest you get back to Old Pete and find out where this Marnie woman has gone. End of.'

———〰———

Gravel dialled a familiar number and spoke without preamble.

'I've got a job for you.'

'Talk to me.'

'I want you to find me a boat. Listen carefully … write this down. Narrowboat …

Sally Ann's Summer

Sally Ann … maroon and dark blue … forty-five foot … oldish. Only one person on board … a woman, age about thirty, dark hair, medium build, tallish, name is Marnie. Got that?'

'Marnie … got it.'

'She's heading west out of Little Venice. Don't know how far she's got. At Bull's Bridge she's either gone south towards the Thames or north up the Grand Union.'

'How will I know?'

'My guess is she's gone north. She's a novice. The Thames is tricky. Anyway, that's where you try first.'

'When I find her?'

'Just let me know. Don't approach her. Don't let her see you.'

'You're sure she's alone?'

'She's the independent type.'

'How far could she 'ave got?'

'Could be up around Watford? After that maybe Hemel Hempstead … Leighton Buzzard. People pull in there for supplies. But check it all out. She could be anywhere along the line.'

'I'll find her.'

'Do that.'

21
Routine

Over the next few days Marnie settled into a steady routine. She rose with the lark each morning to cruise quietly through the countryside until early afternoon. Around mid-day she would stop in a quiet spot to make a sandwich for lunch and eat it while underway again. Afternoons were spent sketching or walking footpaths. She retired early each night, contentedly weary. She had never slept so well.

Despite the open-air life, Marnie felt little inclination to make substantial meals. Supper – prepared and eaten to the accompaniment of the radio, usually Classic fm – would be pasta with a quick sauce made of tomatoes, onions, garlic and peppers, or tuna steak with a salad, or rice with herbs and chicken seasoned with paprika. Simple meals with a glass or two of wine.

In the mirror, she noticed a subtle but perceptible change. Her face and arms were becoming lightly tanned. She applied moisturiser morning and evening, used sun cream during the day and thought no more about it.

On Wednesday evening she sat out on deck with the remains of her second glass of wine, flicking through one of Jane's boating magazines. The world it described no longer seemed foreign. Her life had become pared down to a simple regime that was surprisingly satisfying. The demands of managing the boat, with its engine and systems, had taken over and transformed her existence.

She could imagine nothing more relaxing than a summer spent cruising sedately and only hoped it would not just become a dull routine.

That same evening a man sat in the living room of a flat high in a tower block in Hackney, north-east London. The room was sparsely furnished: sofa, armchair, low table, wall unit containing a television with video and hi-fi equipment. He had poured himself a scotch on the rocks and was sitting with a canal cruising guide on his lap. A road atlas lay on the sofa beside him.

Sections of the cruising guide were marked in yellow highlighter, recording the lengths of canal he had covered so far in pursuit of Marnie. He took a slug of whisky and felt its warmth in the back of his throat as he consulted the road atlas. In three days of searching he had only moved a few centimetres from London on the map.

He checked a new page in the guide, scanning the text, watching for symbols that could be useful to him. How could there be whole areas of country described in the book as remote, rural and isolated so close to London? And why would anyone want to travel through these god-forsaken places on a boat at walking pace? It defied belief. And people actually paid to hire boats for holidays. Incredible.

He was annoyed, impatient. At the start he had expected to find the boat by the afternoon of the first day. Trouble was, the canal wandered through countryside and only crossed the road network at rare intervals.

Another slug of whisky, another page in the cruising guide. Then he saw it: a supermarket beside a junction, his first target for the next day. Two pages later, another chance: Leighton Buzzard, a town with a boatyard, stores, pubs, take-away. It was a watering hole, a supply depot. She'd be stopping there for sure.

He made quick pencil calculations on the page. He would check the whole stretch from his finishing point that day and if he had not tracked her down by noon, he would arrive in good time to catch up with her at Leighton Buzzard. Whenever she reached the town the next afternoon, he would be waiting for her.

22
Anne (with an 'e')

Marnie had been surprised by Bedfordshire. Previously just a place she had rushed through on the motorway without a thought, by canal it had been a revelation. On impulse, even though she had hardly begun that day's journey, she pulled *Sally Ann* over to the bank beside a bridge. It seemed to serve only a cart track, perhaps leading to a farm or hamlet. She dug out the sketch pads. Silence. A feeling of remoteness, woodland all around, countryside probably unchanged since the canal was built in 1794.

She sat on the prow, feet dangling over the side, to sketch the bridge. It had rained in the night, leaving the air cool and damp. The brickwork curving up over the canal was still moist, and vegetation sprouted from gaps in the pointing.

Marnie's concentration was broken by a sound, little more than a rustling of leaves. But there was no breeze and the air was still. She remembered the shuffling under the bridge in Regent's Park the evening she had first met Old Peter. A minute passed before she carried on sketching. After another minute she set the pencil aside.

'Why don't you come out?' She spoke a fraction louder than normal.

There was no response but a muted scuffling behind the parapet, as if something had jumped in surprise. Marnie waited. Round the end of the bridge, a face peeped out. Marnie smiled in an effort to look friendly.

'There's no need to hide.' She hoped she sounded encouraging.

The thought fleetingly crossed her mind that she might be about to encounter a psychopath armed with a meat-axe in this remote place. The stranger stood up. It appeared to be a girl in her teens, thin with short blonde hair, wearing jeans and a T-shirt.

Marnie was unsure what to say, confronted with this juvenile. She decided to combine the wisdom of her thirty-something years with a dash of applied psychology and play it straight down the middle.

'Hallo,' she said. That went well, she thought.

The girl stood by the bridge, looking at her. Marnie removed her sunglasses as a friendly gesture, but it brought no reaction. Intrigued as she was by the sudden arrival of the girl, Marnie was finding the conversation too one-sided.

'Good-bye,' she said casually and began sketching again.

Perversely, the girl began to move slowly towards *Sally Ann*. She stopped on the path a short way from the bows, both hands stuffed into her pockets. It made her look even thinner. Marnie was uncertain how best to proceed. There was something odd about this encounter.

Why had the girl hidden on the bridge? Where was she going at that time of the morning? Marnie checked her watch; it was barely eight o'clock.

'Is this your cat?' The voice was thin like the girl.

Dolly was standing in front of the new arrival, who bent down to stroke her.
'Yes.'

'What's her name?'

'Dolly.'

The girl squatted down. Dolly rubbed her sides against her knee, tail standing upright.
'Hallo, Dolly.' She gave all her attention to the cat.

Marnie looked on. Squatting like a child, the girl seemed vulnerable. She had sharp features and pale skin. Her hair had been expertly styled in an urchin cut, sculpted to the shape of her head.

'Is that your boat?'

'Yes. Well, not actually … it belongs to my sister. I'm borrowing it for a holiday.'

The girl looked at the prow. 'Is that your sister's name?'

'No. It's just the name the boat had when she bought it.'

The girl looked up at Marnie. 'I'm an Anne, too … but it's Anne with an 'e'.'

Gary had spent the days following Gravel's visit trying to plan a strategy, but it was hopeless. He knew how to get things done, not always within the strict letter of the law, but all this poking and prying was way outside his range. It irked him that Marnie had disappeared when the old lady had told him she was not yet ready to leave. But perhaps she wasn't mistaken, perhaps Marnie hadn't left after all. Perhaps she had had a problem with the boat and left it somewhere. It could be anything. For want of a better idea he went back to Sally Ann's mooring, just in case.

Once again, the abandoned space taunted him. He stared at the empty water at a complete loss and swore under his breath. He couldn't get anything out of Old Peter, couldn't talk to Marnie, had no idea where she'd gone.

As a last resort he went to see Jane Rutherford. He knew before he knocked on the door of her boat that she would not be there. More muttered cursing. He was just turning to leave when a voice called out behind him.

'Gary!' Jane was coming along the towpath. 'Were you looking for me?'

He quickly struggled to look casual. 'Oh, hi. Yeah. I was just checking … wondered if you needed any diesel … or coal or logs … or anything.'

Jane, who was wearing a summer dress, looked pointedly at her bare arms. 'Coal … logs? You've obviously been listening to the wrong weather forecast, Gary.'

'What? Oh … right. No, I mean I can get you a good price at this time of year.'

'Thanks for the offer, but I don't fancy going round all summer with sacks of coal on the roof. They're hard to lie on when I'm sunbathing.' She rummaged in her bag for the boat keys. 'Was that all?'

'Yeah. Fair enough. If you see any of the other boaters, you could let them know I've got some special offers on at the moment.'

'Okay.' Jane put the key in the lock.

Gary hesitated. 'Although, don't worry about it. I've seen most people already … only missed one or two ... like the new girl down by the tunnel ... what's her name ... you know ... *Sally Ann*. If you see her, you might just mention it. Oh and er ... tell her I'd like a word about the boat.'

'You mean Marnie?'

'Yeah ...' Dead casual. '... that's the name. I don't suppose you know what's happened to her?'

'*Happened* to her? She's gone off on a trip. I thought you'd know that.'

'Are you sure? Only, the old lady opposite her mooring said she wasn't ready to go.'

Jane shrugged. 'I saw her on Friday evening at the supermarket in Kensal Green.'

Gary's face registered concern. 'You did?'

'Come to think of it ...' Jane looked furtively up and down the towpath and lowered her voice. 'I think I spotted an Arab dhow moored there. Perhaps she's been taken by white slave traders. She could be in Neasden by now.'

'Ha ... ha ...' Gary was not amused.

'Gary, Marnie's a big girl. She'll be fine. What are you worried about?'

'It's just ... well, I'm sure that boat needs attention before she can go on a long journey, especially by herself. Do you have any idea how to contact her?'

'Look, she's going on a trip to get away from it all. That usually means you can't be contacted ... or don't want to be. It amounts to the same thing.'

Gary smiled. 'Sure. I'm fussing over nothing.' He turned to go.

'Nothing to worry about,' Jane agreed, pulling open her door.

Gary hesitated. 'D'you know if she has any relatives who might know where she's gone?'

Jane took a deep breath before replying, slowly. 'She has a sister who owns the boat.'

'Great. D'you know where she lives?'

'Boston, I think.'

'Blimey! That's up in Lincolnshire, isn't it?'

'Massachusetts.'

'Shit!'

'Pardon?'

'Oh, sorry. Doesn't anybody stay in one place any more?'

Jane's expression manifested infinite patience. 'That would rather defeat the purpose of building two or three thousand miles of waterways, Gary.'

On the way back to his boat Gary wished he had never got involved with Gravel, wished he was returning to the arms of Sheena and could forget the whole Marnie and Old Peter business. He was tired of frowning all the time. He had tried everything to get in touch with Marnie and failed. It was only the last part of that equation that would interest Gravel. He was also haunted by the image of that empty space where *Sally Ann* normally lay. He hated to see a prime mooring going to waste like that.

Back on *Garrow* he slumped down at the table. Marnie had definitely gone and had deliberately laid a false trail. What else could it be? If she was after something, why

Sally Ann's Summer

disappear like that? The answer was simple. She had found out the location of what she was looking for and had gone to get it.

———— ∽ ————

Jane phoned home on her mobile. She had been pondering what to do while the kettle boiled and now she was sitting in the saloon on *Joshua* watching the steam rise from her mug. The phone was picked up after the third ring.

'Hi, it's me.'

'Everything all right?'

'Yes. Listen, Derek, I want you to do something for me.'

She outlined to her husband the conversation she had had with Gary.

Derek was quick on the uptake. 'You think he fancies her?'

'Possibly, but … I'm not sure.'

'You think there's more to it?'

'He gave the impression of being worried about Marnie. If it was anybody else I'd believe he was sincerely concerned about her. With Gary you can never tell.'

Derek agreed. 'Whatever it is, there's not much we can do about it, is there?'

'I suppose not, except … there may be. Have a look on my desk. I'm sure there was a mobile phone number on Marnie's business card. See if you can find it and ring me back.'

———— ∽ ————

Marnie smiled at the girl on the bank. 'Hallo, Anne … Anne with an 'e'. My name's Marnie.'

'Marnie.' Anne repeated the name quietly to herself. 'That's nice.'

She remained squatting beside Dolly, who had rolled onto her side and was licking a foreleg. Anne looked up at *Sally Ann*.

'We went on holiday on a canal boat once.' She stood up and put her hands back in her pockets. 'It was bigger than this one.'

'On this canal?'

'No. We went to Wales. It was great.'

'When was that?'

'When I was about … nine.'

'Do you think you'll do it again … have a canal holiday?'

Anne shook her head. 'Can't have holidays. Dad's out of work.'

Marnie felt awkward at this turn in the conversation. 'I was thinking of making some coffee … unless you have to be somewhere?'

The girl arranged two safari chairs and a folding table on the stern deck, while Marnie was occupied in the galley. Dolly jumped onto the roof and curled up on the hatch. By now, the sun was climbing and the air was warm. There was a haze in the woods and over the water. Marnie poured coffee and offered biscuits. She pointed at the bridge.

'Where does that track lead to?'

'Nowhere, really … just to a barn. It's derelict.'

'Perhaps I could sketch it,' Marnie suggested.

'There's not much left of it now. Some kids burnt it down … for a laugh.' Anne said this in an even tone without trace of praise or blame. 'Where are you going on your holiday?' The girl asked her question without making eye contact.

'I'm not sure. I'm just travelling … thought I'd see what I found on the way.'

'How long are you going for?'

'I've got the summer off. It's like sabbatical leave.'

'They let you go … just like that?'

'They thought I could do with a break. So did I.'

Anne stared into her cup in silence. Marnie sat quite still, looking at the fingers of sunlight through the trees, noticing the flies and insects picked out in the rays of light. She poured herself another cup of coffee. Anne remained immobile. When she spoke again, her voice was quiet and seemed deeper than before.

'That's what I want to do.'

Marnie waited. Anne stood up as if to leave and stepped forward to stroke Dolly. She leaned against the roof caressing the cat's head, while Dolly purred.

'Does this canal go all the way up to Wales?'

'Eventually.'

'How long would it take to get there?'

'I'm not sure. A few weeks maybe. It depends how many hours a day you travel.'

'Might you go that far? You've got all the time you want, haven't you?'

'I might. I have thought about it. What about you, Anne? Do you have plans?'

The girl made no reply. Marnie got up and stood beside her. Anne was looking towards the bridge but her eyes were unfocused. If she had plans, she seemed to be staring into a bleak future.

———∞———

Jane was putting her mug away in the galley on *Joshua* when the phone rang. It was Derek, triumphant.

'I've found it! Marnie's business card. Here's the mobile number. Got a pencil?'

Jane hesitated before phoning. She wanted to respect Marnie's desire for privacy, but if there was a problem with the boat, as Gary said there could be, it would not be doing her a favour to keep that from her. Gary may have had a reputation as a Lothario, but he would not want to see Marnie run into trouble on a long journey.

Jane picked up the phone.

———∞———

After they had finished doing the dishes and Marnie was putting them in the cupboard, Anne stepped out into the cratch. She looked at Marnie's sketchpad.

'Were you taught to do trees like that?' Anne pointed at the drawing.

Marnie came over to look. 'I suppose so. They're just meant to give an impression of trees, really. I'm more interested in the shape of the bridge. Do you draw?'

'Sometimes.'

'Would you like to do some drawing here? I've got another pad and more pencils.'

Anne stared at the drawing. 'If you like bridges, there's a nice one a bit further on.'

Marnie checked the cruising guide. 'Mm ...there's a lock and a footbridge about half a mile north of here. Would you have time for a trip? Or ... perhaps you have things to do?' It was the closest she came to asking why Anne was not at school that morning.

'Just a mo'.' Anne jumped off the boat. She ran to the bridge, returned with a rucksack and dropped it on the deck without explanation. 'Shall I undo the ropes at the front?'

Marnie let Anne take the tiller for the ten-minute journey. The girl steered straight and true and they moored clear of the lock.

They took chairs, pads and pencils and stepped onto the bank in warm sunlight. Suddenly, Marnie stopped. 'Hold on!' She dived back into the boat and emerged a moment later carrying two wide-brimmed sun hats. 'That one should fit you all right.'

Anne hesitated and put it on, smiling for the first time, turning her head to strike a pose like a fashion model. A warbling sound emanated from somewhere in the boat. Marnie hopped back on board and reappeared pressing the mobile phone to her ear. After a brief conversation she disconnected.

'That was a friend in Little Venice. She's an artist. You'd like her.'

'Everything all right? Oh sorry ... I shouldn't ask questions.'

'That's okay. It appears someone's trying to get in touch with me ... seems he's concerned *Sally Ann* might have an engine problem.'

'That's worrying.'

'Not really. Another neighbour – a nice old guy – sorted it out for me. It was nothing serious.'

'So will you let this man know that it's sorted?'

Marnie shook her head. 'No need. If anything goes wrong with old *Sally*, I'll get it fixed on the way.'

'But if he's concerned about you and asking after you ...'

'He probably just mentioned it to Jane in passing. It's fine.'

For the next hour they sat sketching, Marnie concentrating on the bridge and lock, Anne working on the lock-keeper's house at the edge of the woods, Dolly lying under Anne's chair, flicking her tail.

After a while, Marnie spoke over her shoulder. 'Do you have brothers and sisters?'

'An older brother. You?'

'An older sister.'

'And it's her boat?'

'Yes. She's in America. Her husband's on sabbatical at a university there.'

'Are you married?'

A pause. 'I was, but ... it didn't work out.'

'Oh, sorry. I didn't mean –'

'That's all right.'

They went on sketching. Marnie turned to ask how the work was going, but Anne spoke first.

'Do you have children?'

'No. I would have quite liked to, but there's not much likelihood at the moment.'

Anne bit her lip. 'I keep saying the wrong thing.'

'Don't worry. I grew up in a secure family and had a happy childhood. There are always compensations.'

Marnie waited, but there was no reply. She heard Anne's pencil drop. There was a sound like a sigh. Marnie glanced round and saw Anne bent double in her chair, her back shuddering. She heard a sob, the breath vibrating in Anne's throat. Tears were falling onto the dusty ground. Marnie leapt up and in one movement was kneeling beside her on the towpath, an arm round her thin shoulders.

They left the chairs where they were, and Marnie led Anne back to the boat. In the saloon she sat her down, put a box of tissues on the table and lit the gas under the kettle. The girl sat for a few moments, head in hands, then pulled out a tissue and blew her nose. It was a loud blow in the multi-megaton range, causing the cat to sit up and take notice.

Marnie stared at Anne. 'Blimey! That was seven point nine on the Richter scale.'

Anne spluttered into the tissue and laughed through her tears. 'I'm sorry, I'm sorry, I'm really sorry …'

'Any more blasts like that and I'll be advertising for a new ship's cat.'

Anne forced a smile as she wiped her eyes.

'I don't know why I'm making tea.' Marnie thought of Mrs Jolly. 'Do you want any?'

'Not really … thank you.'

'Nor do I.' She leaned back against the workbench. 'Look, Anne, I don't want to pry, I really don't, but I don't like to see you so upset.'

Without any preamble, Anne began. 'Dad had a good job at the lorry factory but they had to get rid of a lot of people. His redundancy money ran out so Mum went back to hairdressing to help out. Then they started having rows … Dad said he didn't want to live off Mum's money.' She sniffed and blew her nose again.

'That explains why your hair's so well cut.'

'Yes. Anyway, Dad did a bit of van driving for a friend, but the police stopped the van for a check-up or something and they reported him for not having the proper papers. So now he's in trouble and might have to go to court.'

'And the rucksack?'

'I thought if I could get a job somewhere it would help. It would be one less to feed.'

'How old are you, Anne?'

'Fifteen.'

She put the box of tissues on the table. As she did so, she dislodged the sketchpads and they slipped over the edge. Marnie reached forward and caught them. She opened the pad that Anne had been using and glanced at the drawing. Unintentionally, she gave a small exclamation of surprise. Anne looked up at her.

'You've done a lot. Do you always work this fast?' Anne shrugged. Marnie went on. 'I see what you mean about the trees. Yours are really good.'

'My dad showed me how to do them. He's good at drawing, good at making things.'

'I'd say you have a real talent, Anne.'

'That's what my teacher said. She wanted me to go to art school.'

Marnie noticed the past tense. 'To do what?'

'Not sure ...'

Marnie laughed. 'Beware! You could end up like me!'

'Is that what you are ... an artist?'

'I'm an interior designer. I did a foundation course at the local college and then went to art school.'

'You must have been really old after all that.'

Marnie grinned. 'Ancient. I was twenty-one when I started work.'

Anne frowned. 'My parents couldn't keep me for all that time.'

'They wouldn't have to. You could get a grant or a loan.'

Anne became thoughtful and for a few seconds a determined look came into her eyes. Then her anguish returned. 'I wish I knew what to ...'

'Play to your strengths, Anne. That's how you'll find your way. Build on what you're good at. Focus on that and don't let anyone persuade you otherwise.'

The girl stared at Marnie. 'Yes.'

'Work out what you want to do, in broad-brush terms –'

'Like going to art school?'

Marnie nodded. 'For example. Then take one day at a time and give it your best shot.'

'Yes ... yes ... When you put it like that, what else could I do?'

'That's what I think.'

'It makes sense. But I suppose even then I might not get a job at the end of it all.'

Marnie reached for her bag, took out her wallet and produced a business card.

'Here, take this ... just in case. You never know. I might be able to advise you. You can ring me any time you want.'

Anne read the card. 'It's a nice design.'

'Thanks. Actually, I designed it for the company. It's what we call the house style.'

'I'll keep it safe.' Anne zipped it into a side pocket on her rucksack.

'Do you feel like finishing off your sketch?'

Outside on the towpath, they donned sun hats and resumed sketching, side by side.

'Is it a good art department at your school?'

'We do interesting things ... go to exhibitions. Also, they talk to us like grown-ups ... like you do.'

In that moment, Marnie sensed that Anne was starting the journey back to her world. The thought crossed her mind that at some point she too would take the same step, even though it seemed a long way off just then.

'What do you think will happen to my dad?' Anne spoke calmly.

'Nothing much. He'll probably just be told he mustn't do it again, I expect.'

Anne stopped drawing and turned in her seat. 'Would you say you were a drop-out?'

Marnie laughed. 'I'm just taking a break. I was starting to feel drained. Creative work can be like that sometimes. My ... marital problems didn't make things any easier. *Sally Ann* came along just when I was offered the chance to have a change of scene.'

'And you do want to go back?'

'Of course. What else would I do? That's where I belong.'

'And what do you think will happen to me?'

'Oh ... I think that's fairly clear. You've got time to change your mind, but I can imagine you doing A levels and going to art school, as I did.'

'What about now ... this morning?'

Marnie looked at her watch. 'It's nearly noon. Is there any particular teacher you get on with very well?'

'There's Mrs Robertson ... head of the art department.'

'I think you should talk to her ... tell her how you felt this morning.'

Anne's eyes widened. 'About running away?'

'You could tell her you needed time to think things over. You'll find your own words.'

'What about Mum and Dad? What should I tell them?'

'Well ... I think it's probably best that they hear about your worries from you rather than from anyone else. Best to talk about them ... no secrets.'

Marnie got up and went back to the boat, leaving Anne to think things over. She returned with a camera.

'Why don't you go and take some photos of the bridge and the lock for my collection while I make us an early lunch?'

While Anne was lining up her first shot, Marnie shredded a lettuce and put a baguette in the oven. A knob of butter and two cloves of pressed garlic were melting in the frying pan while she completed the salad with slices of cucumber, diced red pepper and a French dressing. She drained a tin of prawns and tipped them into the pan, stirring the mixture gently together.

Outside, Anne was kneeling to take a shot under the bridge. Marnie turned off the flame under the pan and quickly laid the table. She called Anne through the window, cracked four eggs into a mixing bowl, added milk, ground black pepper and sea salt and beat them lightly with a fork. She looked out as she worked, but Anne was no longer in view.

'I hope you're going to like this,' she said as Anne came through into the saloon.

'It smells wonderful! And it looks like a feast.'

Marnie passed her a glass of apple juice. 'No, just a simple meal. It's what I'd call *peasant food*.' Marnie turned on the gas under the pan and added another knob of butter. While it heated, she took the bread from the oven and put it in the basket on the table.

Anne watched with interest. 'Can I do anything to help?'

'No, just have a seat. This'll be ready in a minute or so.'

'What peasants eat this kind of food?' Anne was staring at the table.

'It's a Spanish recipe.' Marnie poured the eggs into the pan with the prawns and garlic and stirred them with a wooden spatula. In a trice she had produced a scrambled mixture that she divided onto their plates. 'It's called *revuelto de gambas*. Eat it while it's hot.'

Anne needed no further encouragement. While they ate, they talked about photography, angles and apertures, structures and shapes. Afterwards they ate grapes on the stern deck in the sunshine, comparing their sketches and raising a hand at passing boats.

Anne looked thoughtful. 'This is strange. I never imagined today would turn out like this. It's as if I've ... stepped out of my world.'

'You have, but just for a little while. It's the same for me. I've left mine behind in London.'

'It's weird, Marnie. It feels as if I've known you a long time.'

It was the first time Anne had addressed her by name.

'Where is your school exactly?'

'In town, near the centre.'

'Near the canal?'

'Not far.'

'Would you like to drive us there ... or at least as near as we can get on *Sally*?'

A pause. 'Yes. I'm ready to go back now.'

—⚏—

The search had produced no results. Gravel's associate had discovered that following a canal through and out of London by car was no easy matter. Maps failed to tell the whole story. The fact was, canals followed devious routes as if they had a mind of their own. He had had to leave the car and traipse for miles along the towpath. By the third day he had seen enough of the cut to last him forever.

At lunchtime that day he bought a sandwich and a Coke in Leighton Buzzard and, after strolling along the line of moored boats, sat on a low wall beside the towpath, keeping watch.

Suddenly, he spotted her, a woman with dark hair, alone at the tiller, and the boat was blue. He leapt to his feet, leaving the half-eaten sandwich on the wall, and moved slowly to avoid attracting attention, waiting for the bows to come into view. The boat's name slid into his line of vision. *Dolores*. Damn! In the same moment a child emerged beside the woman. False alarm.

This was a stupid job, he thought. You'd think it would be child's play ... a boat travelling at walking pace on a single strip of water. But he was beginning to wonder if this could be the wrong strip. Maybe she had gone south to the Thames after all. Maybe she knew more about boating than anyone realised.

The stalker returned to his place on the wall to find two sparrows finishing his lunch. Cursing, he decided to change vantage point and moved to take up position on the bridge. It could make him conspicuous but it was near a bend and would give him a better view in both directions. One boat had passed while he was turning onto the bridge. There was no name at the stern, but he knew it was not the boat he wanted. There was a woman on deck, but a girl was steering, and they were wearing similar sun hats. Mother and daughter, no doubt. Also the colour was wrong. This one had some dark blue paintwork, but the roof and centre bands were cream. And there was a cat. Definitely not a solitary woman, definitely not *Sally Ann*.

After passing through the lock, it took them less than half an hour to reach the town centre with Anne at the tiller. Dolly sat up on the hatch, having the inevitable wash. They glided into town, cautiously taking a series of bends, passed under a bridge and found a place to pull in at the end of the line of moorings.

'I can walk it easily from here.' Anne picked up her rucksack and gave Dolly a final stroke.

'You'll be all right?'

'I'm fine. I'll be in time for afternoon lessons. It's double art after lunch.'

'Good. Here, take these.' She gave Anne one of the pads and some pencils. 'Well, good-bye, Anne with an 'e', and good luck. Perhaps we'll meet again some day.' She kissed Anne on the cheek and watched her walk off. The girl turned and waved before she stepped from the path.

Marnie went inside to check that everything was secure, ready for the next part of the journey. Turning to go back out, something caught her eye on the pin-board in the galley: a tiny pencil drawing of *Sally Ann*, moored by the towpath against a background of trees. It must have been executed at great speed but it was perfect in detail, with the dark shape of a cat sitting on the roof.

Marnie cast off and pointed *Sally Ann* out into the channel.

23
Captain **and** *Mate*

Gary had drawn a blank with Jane. Despite his subtle – he hoped – way of bringing Marnie into the conversation, Jane had not so much as nibbled at the bait. Sheena was sitting opposite him in a small Italian restaurant tucked away in a side street off Little Venice. He had to make an effort to concentrate. She was chatting about another assistant in the chemist's shop who was always making things up, dreaming of doing impossible things.

'Are you paying attention, Gary?'

'Sure.'

'Only you've got that glazed expression.'

'No, it's fine. I'm interested. Go on.'

So she went on, and Gary slipped back to wondering where all this Old Peter business was going. And where was Marnie going? Where the hell was she?

'Anyway, so she said she was planning her next holiday on the moon ...'

'Right.'

'Or was it Mars?'

'Could be.'

'Only the moon gets booked up so early these days ... doesn't it ... Gary?'

'Yeah ... probably.'

When Sheena brought her hand down hard on the table, Gary jumped so much he staggered back and fell off his chair. Red in the face and squirming with embarrassment, he scrambled to his feet, righted the chair and attempted to sit with as much dignity as he could muster, all the while feigning a coughing spasm. A waiter rushed to his side and quickly poured him a glass of water. With Gary reassuring him that everything was fine, the waiter withdrew, rolling his eyes at the other guests who were mostly trying to pretend that nothing had happened.

Gary wheezed at Sheena under his breath. *'Jesus!* What did you do that for?'

She was unrepentant, indignant. 'You weren't paying attention. You were miles away.'

He took a deep breath. 'Look, Sheena, I'm sorry. It's just ... I've got a lot of worries on my mind ... big worries.'

'It's not still this Old Whatsit thing, is it?'

Gary's eyes shifted from side to side as if he expected Gravel and Sidekick to jump up at any moment. 'Yeah.' His voice was barely audible.

Sheena sighed. 'Gary, if you're going to have your wicked way with me, the least you can do is humour me while I prattle on about my apparently insignificant and uninteresting life. After abandoning me all week –'

'Darlin', I had a lotta work on!'

'I said … after abandoning me all week, the least you could do is give me some of your valuable attention when we're together. Going out is supposed to get you *away* from your worries … refresh your spirits or whatever.'

'That's what everybody's doing these days.'

'What are you talking about?'

'That Marnie's doing the same … getting away from it all. That's why I can't trace her.'

'Why do you want to trace this *other woman?*' Sheena invested the last words with heavy meaning. 'Why are you going on about this … Marnie … when you're supposed to be out with me?'

'You know why … darlin'. It's *business* … nothing *personal.*'

'So she's fat and ugly, got bandy legs and a squint, has she?'

'No, she's … all right …ordinary looking.' A flash of inspiration. 'Must be about ten years older than you. How old are you, actually?'

'Don't change the subject.'

'I just wondered.'

'Twenty.'

'Oh, well … she's *more* than ten years older, I'd say.'

'So … nearer your age than mine.'

'Now you're changing the subject.'

'Gary, I thought you were going to tell this Gravel bloke you couldn't find anything out.'

'It doesn't work like that.'

'Why not? He can't expect miracles.'

'Sheena, the situation is … Gravel thinks Old Pete has got something valuable. He thinks Marnie might know something about it. Why? Because I mentioned her to him. Do you understand?'

'Go on.'

'So this is how it is … I can't get anything out of the old fella, Marnie's hopped it and Jane up the cut knows where she's gone but isn't telling.'

'Why not?'

'She says Marnie's gone off to get away from it all and she can't contact her.'

'Or won't.'

'Right.'

'So, Gary, where does that leave you?'

'Nowhere … up a well-known creek without a paddle.'

Sheena giggled. It made Gary remember why he liked being with her. She leaned towards him. He liked that too. 'Well. if there's no-one who can give you any clues about this … pot of gold at the end of the rainbow … there's nothing you can do about it, is there? I mean, you'll just have to tell … wotsisname … Gravel … won't you?'

'I told you, it doesn't work like that.'

Sally Ann's Summer

Sheena spread her hands. 'What more does he want?'

Gary gave the question serious thought. 'Miracles.'

———— ɱ ————

After dropping Anne off in Leighton Buzzard, Marnie had taken the boat several miles out into open country, all the while thinking about the girl, with her problems and her future. Strangely, it had helped Marnie gain a perspective on her own situation. Both of them were facing difficult circumstances, both looking for a new direction, both needing time and space to find it.

Play to your strengths ... you'll find your way.

She had spoken so confidently, as if she knew all the answers. It had certainly had an impact on Anne.

The following evening, standing under the spray in a cubicle so narrow that she could barely turn round, Marnie longed for the powerful jets in the shower at home. By the end of the day she was weary and wanted nothing more than a reviving blast of hot water to restore her spirits. It had been a long day travelling alone, and each lock had seemed heavier than the one before. But she had no regrets. *Sally Ann* was giving her the chance to look at her life and think of the next steps.

Build on what you're good at ...

Makes sense. Marnie agreed with herself.

Take one day at a time and give it your best shot ...

Good thinking. Maybe Marnie should listen to her own advice.

She was sure she would never see Anne again, but knew she would often think back to their meeting. Marnie wondered if the moment when their lives had touched briefly had been a turning point for both of them.

———— ɱ ————

Thirty miles away in Little Venice Old Peter poured himself a cup of tea. It was dark and strong, the way he liked it, sweetened with two sugars. He stared into the brown liquid, thinking of the woman who had not long before sat with him in the saloon drinking from his best china. He had made the tea less strong that day, more like gold than mud, and she had drunk it there with a small dash of milk and no sugar. He would remember that, if she ever called in again.

It was strange to have someone on board. He could not remember the last time he had had company like that, especially not a woman. Marnie. He muttered the name to himself. He had not spoken a woman's name since he knew not when.

Even stranger, he seemed to be getting more than the usual amount of attention these days. It was not chance that had led Gary to call round. Gary had been asking about him, too. He was after something. That was certain. And the old man knew what it was. The question was ...

It had happened before, years ago. He had dealt with it by keeping his mouth shut. Saying nothing was an option back then. But now things were different. Everything was more organised, people more determined. Even the petty crooks were part of something bigger. They were all under someone's control, someone's protection.

Gary was no crook, never had been. A drifter, maybe, but not a villain. Even so, Old Peter was convinced he was not ferreting about on his own account. So who was pushing Gary, and what could one old man do about it? More to the point, what could he do about what they were searching for?

He had been the custodian for decades, for most of his life, as had his father before him, and his before him. At first he had thought of it as a kind of nest egg, an insurance for the future. He had always known it was valuable, though he could not understand why. It made no kind of sense, but then so much of the world was incomprehensible to him that he had long ago given up trying to fathom it. He had not had the education.

Of one thing he was in no doubt. Many people had tried to get their hands on it, and no-one could be trusted. His father had impressed that on him. He was not to pass it on to anyone unless he was absolutely certain they would know what to do. His father had chosen to do nothing for half a century rather than risk taking the wrong course. Now he had done almost the same. But doing nothing did not seem such a safe bet any more.

He drank the hot sweet liquid. All his life he had followed the simple path handed down to him by generations of his family. He looked back on their concerns, backwards through the mists of time, repairing a damaged engine, setting a broken leg after a locking accident, treating an ailing horse, breaking through the ice and even further back, digging the next section of canal ditch, further still, deciding to come to England to work on the navigations. Now he had a clear choice to make. He needed to find someone who could be trusted with absolute certainty.

He drank again. Now that the decision was forced on him, he was surprised at how easy it was to choose that person.

———〰———

After a rub down with the towel Marnie felt refreshed. She slipped on a white shirt and a skirt in a pattern that Mrs Jolly would describe as pure water gypsy, poured a glass of white Bergerac and took the cruising guide onto the deck. It was a fine evening and Dolly was already installed on one of the safari chairs.

The wine evoked past holidays: Greek islands, Venice, the Valley of Kings, weekends in Paris. Now here she was, eagerly planning a canal run from Stoke Hammond to Milton Keynes.

She had to admit she was loving her new life. Boats, she had discovered, were gregarious. Each evening she tied up in some remote place. The next day, she usually found one or two other craft moored in line with *Sally Ann*, like elephants gathered at the same waterhole. On that particular evening half a dozen or so boats had already formed up behind her at the bank.

Marnie went below and had just begun preparing supper, when a sudden clamour filled the air. It began with a single blast on a boat's horn. At once others took up the call, until the canal reverberated to the sound. Had the elephants been thrown into panic by the intrusion of a predator? In the midst of all the uproar came a more sonorous tone, haunting and high-pitched. Marnie heard voices now, calling out across the water. She abandoned the lettuce that she was cutting and ran up onto the deck, ready for any emergency.

It was a scene from another age, a working boat from the beginning of the century, seventy feet long, with a fine jutting prow, the cargo area covered in black tarpaulin, smoke curling from its funnel. The unmistakable smell of a steam engine filled the air.

Marnie gave a blast on *Sally Ann's* horn. The crew waved at her. One man blew a kiss. As the lead boat came by, Marnie saw a famous name emblazoned on the side of the cabin. This was *Captain*, one of the last of its generation, towing its equally famous butty, *Mate*.

Marnie had read about them in one of Jane's magazines. Now, seeing them out here in their working environment, she had a glimpse into the past. Such craft had mobilised the industrial revolution that changed the world. Now, their commercial usefulness past, most of them had been scrapped or left to rot where they lay. A few, like *Captain* and *Mate*, had been rescued from watery oblivion by enthusiasts who brought them back to life.

Marnie knew their story. One of them had been found barely afloat in Wakefield, the other half-submerged in Dudley. Members of the Waterways Restoration Club – known as WREC – had taken four years to rebuild them. Crewed by volunteers led by the redoubtable Jack Hadley, the pair had become a famous sight, touring the country, prominent in every campaign to preserve some part of the canal heritage.

In bed that night Marnie's head was filled with images of blazing coals in the fire box, shining paintwork and polished brass. As she drifted off to sleep, she dreamt she was showering under hot jets of turbo-spray, enveloped in steam, with the wail of *Captain's* whistle calling out over the countryside.

24
Stalker

Marnie breakfasted early the next morning. Dunking a croissant in a bowl of coffee, she listened to the weather forecast: the fine spell would continue; a heatwave was on the way. Great!

Then she thought of the locks ahead of her and groaned. She hoped she would not be facing them alone. It would be warm work.

In T-shirt and lightweight pale blue jeans, she applied sunblock and set off while the neighbours were still asleep in their cabins. It already felt like high summer, and Marnie turned her face to the rising sun. It felt good to be alive.

———✺———

The traffic crawling out of London that Friday morning was unbelievable. Stalker sat drumming his fingers on the steering wheel, staring at the rear end of a milk tanker he had been following for at least twenty minutes.

This would be the day when he finally caught up with Marnie. He had it all worked out. There were three supermarkets along the section of canal that he was searching, and he knew she could not be further north than there. He would watch the first at Leighton Buzzard for an hour. If that produced no result he would move on to the next one. Then the next. She had to stop somewhere along that stretch for supplies and on that day he would catch up with her. About that he was absolutely determined.

The traffic in his lane began to roll and Stalker felt elated at managing to reach second gear before it stopped again. Taking another cigarette out of the pack, he reflected that narrowboats travelled at three or four miles an hour. At this rate, *Sally Ann* would be leaving him behind.

———✺———

Gary was in high spirits. He had just collected a week's rent in advance from a boat on *Sally Ann*'s mooring and felt very pleased with himself. No cost, no risk, easy money and everyone was happy. Well, everyone who knew about it. What the eye doesn't see ... he told himself. He felt a great need to see Sheena again, even though she had only left his boat to go to work less than two hours earlier.

As he strode out along the towpath, he had no idea he was being observed from behind net curtains by an old lady on the other side of the road.

As soon as he entered the chemist's, Sheena came out from the back of the shop and advanced towards him. He liked her white coat and wondered how she would look in a nurse's outfit.

'Good morning, sir.' She smiled coyly, lowering her voice, 'What can I do for you?'

'How about –' Her expression stopped him going in that direction. 'I was just wanting to see you. Do I have to buy a tube of toothpaste every time I want to say hallo?'

Sheena turned and walked back to the pharmacy, reappearing seconds later minus the white coat. She took his arm and led him out of the shop.

'Come on. You can take me for a coffee. Old Grumbleguts let me have my break a bit early. But I've got to be back in fifteen minutes Gary. Okay? Not sixteen.'

'You bet.'

'And there's one other condition. You don't talk about Marnie or any other woman. And you give me your full attention.'

'That's two conditions.' Sheena stopped abruptly. 'Only joking,' he added quickly.

There was a café a short way along the pavement, and they ordered cappuccinos at a table in the window.

'So what's new, Gary?'

'Since you left the boat after breakfast, you mean?'

'I did wonder what could be so important you came to find me at work.'

'Nothing much, really. Do I need a reason to want to see you?'

'No ... and that's very nice. It's flattering. I like that.'

Gary beamed, pleased that he was doing the right thing. But he could sense a but coming.

'But you do have something that's cheered you up. I can tell.'

'Yeah. I've done a nice little deal.' Pleased with himself.

'Oh.' Disappointment.

'That's good. Doing deals is what it's all about.'

'If you say so, Gary.'

She took her first sip of cappuccino, which left a thin line of froth along her top lip. She ran her tongue from one side to the other, and Gary realised that doing deals was not what it was all about.

'I thought you'd be pleased.'

'Sure. I am. It's just I thought you might have done something a bit more important.'

'Like what?'

She leaned forward and lowered her voice. 'You were going to tell this bloke with the gravelly voice that there was no way Old Peter had anything valuable and that was the end of it.'

'I've told you before, darlin'. It's not as simple as that.'

Sheena sniffed and drank more cappuccino. Gary was mesmerised again by the tongue-froth routine, but he felt the atmosphere was cooling. Perhaps coming to see her was not such a great idea after all. To his surprise Sheena broke the silence.

'Oh Gary ...' She shook her head wearily. 'You may be good at little deals that earn a few quid here and there, but you're not so good at tackling the things that matter ... the bigger things.'

'Darlin', I can't just tell Gravel he's wasting his time, that he's got it all wrong –'

'No? Well, perhaps I'd better tell him. I'll go and find him and –'

'Don't even joke about it … you are joking, aren't you?'

'Someone's got to tell him, Gary, because it's messing up our relationship.'

'Is it?'

'Gary, I'm not some harmless little bimbo who's too dim to think for herself. I can see what needs to be done … and perhaps I ought to just get on and do it.'

Now Gary really was sorry he'd come. 'No, that would not be a good idea, darlin'. No way. End of.'

He frowned. *Harmless* was not the word.

—⟋⟋⟋—

Marnie's next stop was a canalside supermarket handily located beside a watering point. Stores were running low and, above all, the time had come for the taking on of water and the dreaded emptying of the *Porta Potti*.

She tied up and connected the hose. While the tank filled, she detached the base of the *Porta Potti* and lugged it along to the sluice. The emptying process was not as ghastly as she had expected.

Those tasks completed, she collected a trolley. On her way in to the store she ducked into a telephone kiosk and interrogated her answerphone.

The first message was from Steve.

'I hear you've gone away. I hope it wasn't because of me. I hope you'll find what you're looking for.' Click.

The nerve of the man! The ego! The mournful voice made Marnie cringe. She almost missed the start of the second message from Beth.

'… it's me. If you haven't sunk or anything, give us a ring some time. There are problems in Paul's department. We may not be able to stay a whole year. Tell you about it when you call. Remember the stern gland. Bye!'

Marnie tried to figure out what the time was in Boston. The third message took her by surprise.

'Hallo, Marnie? It's Anne … Anne with an 'e'. I tried your mobile but got no service. You said I could leave a message for you. Well, I told Mrs Robertson about meeting you … told her about my dad and what I'd done. She was very nice about it. Anyway, I'm ringing to say I've chosen my GCSE Art project. I'm doing studies of the canal. You gave me the idea. I've already started. Hope you'll see it one day. Thanks … for everything, Marnie. Bye! Safe journey! Love to Dolly!'

Marnie was smiling in the phonebox. Two more messages followed, both from Philip, both about projects with problems that were now resolved. It had been a kind thought, but Marnie was surprised to realise that she had virtually forgotten about the projects. It was nice to know the firm had not forgotten about her.

In Boston they would still be sleeping, but she had other calls to make. First she dialled Jane's number. No reply. She rang Philip.

'He's in a meeting. Can anyone else help you?' A new voice on the switchboard.

'I'd like to leave a message. It's Marnie Walker.'

'Sorry. Would you say the name again?'

'Marnie Walker.'

'One moment, please.' The line went dead as she was put on hold. 'I'm afraid we have no-one here of that name.'

A pause. 'You're new.'

'Yes. I'm temping. The other girl's on holiday.'

'Okay. I'll try again later.'

Marnie felt as if she had died and her ashes had been scattered to the four winds. She needed to make contact with someone to prove that she still existed. She phoned Mrs Jolly and after several rings was about to hang up when it was answered.

'Oh, hallo, my dear! How are you getting on? Are you in foreign parts?' She giggled.

'I'm in Bedfordshire, or it may be Buckinghamshire by now.'

'Very exotic. Are you having a nice time?'

'Very interesting. Quite a change from my usual routine.'

'Do you have one of those mobile phones?'

'Yes, but the battery's low and I can't recharge it at the moment. I'm calling from a kiosk at a supermarket.'

'There's nothing like a complete break, that's what I always say.' She giggled again.

'I don't think you're taking me very seriously, Mrs Jolly.'

'Sorry, dear. I've been playing with my grandchildren in the garden and it's making me rather skittish.'

'Good. Well, I just thought I'd ring to say hallo.'

'I'm glad you did, because there's something I want to ask you. *Sally Ann*'s mooring. It is yours all the time isn't it?'

'Yes. It's a prime mooring. We pay the rent for it.'

'Even when you're not there?'

'That's right.'

'Well, another boat has been moored there. I thought you might have given it up while you were away.'

'Perhaps they just pulled over to check something on their boat.'

'But then why would they plug in to your electricity point?'

Marnie was making indignant sounds when her phonecard ran out.

———— ∞ ————

Stalker was wishing he had gone in for drystone-walling, or anything more exciting than his chosen career. He had hung around the first supermarket until boredom drove him further on. Another hour of watching boats and their crews and he was ready to throw himself into the nearest lock.

He knew how to blend into any background and avoid security cameras, but loitering by a canal, he was as exposed as if wearing a neon sign saying *Suspicious Character*.

When a party of schoolkids arrived he had to think quickly. They installed themselves along the towpath, about twenty teenagers, spread over a hundred yards with stools and sketch pads, settled in for the duration. His chances of not been noticed dwindled to nothing. One or two of them pulled out cameras and began clicking away in all directions.

As he folded up his paper and turned to leave, a boat pulled in at the bank in front of him. The steerer apologised to the two kids at that spot for taking their view. There was some good-natured banter. Stalker saw his chance. He nodded at the man from the boat who hopped off to tie up at a mooring ring.

'Morning! Come far?'

'Up from Hemel.'

'Some mates of mine are doing that run … don't suppose you've seen them? Boat's called *Sally Ann*.'

The man pondered. 'Don't think so.'

'Thanks.'

Stalker took off. He did not notice that one of the artists on the bank was watching him. She was a thin girl, pale with very short blonde hair and a thoughtful expression.

———— ‰ ————

Gary was on his way back to *Garrow* from the café when he passed two women chatting on the pavement. One of them was Jane Rutherford, the other an old lady. He nodded at Jane and walked on, worrying about his conversation with Sheena, hoping she would not do anything rash. Both women watched his retreating back.

'That's him, isn't it?' said Mrs Jolly. 'The man I was telling you about.'

'That's Gary, yes. He seems to have something on his mind. Not the usual swagger.'

'He ought to have something on his conscience.'

'I doubt if he has one.' Jane smiled. 'So you think he's sub-let Marnie's mooring to these other people while she's away?'

'And her electricity supply.'

'Sounds like a typical Gary kind of scam.'

'He'd have been called a wide boy in my day … or perhaps a spiv, though his clothes aren't flashy enough.'

Jane chuckled. 'Spiv, yes … lovely word.'

'But it amounts to the same thing. Dishonesty. And Marnie's the victim. She'll end up paying the bill.'

Jane looked serious. 'Mm … Are the people there now, do you know?'

'They were there when I came out. Do you think there's anything we can do about it? They didn't take any notice of me when I spoke to them.'

Jane thought for a few seconds. 'We'll see.'

———— ‰ ————

The first lock was heavy to operate and Marnie was sweating in the heat. If no other boats were around by the time she reached the next one, she would pull over, find some shade and wait until someone came along to share the locking.

In half an hour *Sally Ann* reached the last bend before the flight. Turning the corner, Marnie could see a boat pulling away from the bank towards the lock. Her rejoicing was short-lived. It was unmistakably *Captain*, with *Mate* firmly tied alongside. They were breasted up ready to go through together, leaving Marnie to fend for herself. She sighed and pulled over to the bank.

The working pair made an impressive sight, and Marnie strolled along the bank to watch them. She was in no hurry now.

The boats were skippered by Jack Hadley himself, founding father of WREC. He guided the craft expertly into the chamber. The crew, all volunteers from the organisation, seemed to swarm over the lock, operating the paddles, holding ropes and generally looking purposeful, even if they were not actually doing anything. Marnie looked on with envy.

'Excuse me. Sorry to disturb you.' A quiet voice.

One of the crew needed Marnie to move to allow the gate to shut. She stepped round the beam and moved back from the edge. As the boats came to a stop, the man heaved on the beam. He was about the same height as Marnie and lightly built. She pulled with him to shut the gate, ruefully noticing how heavy it was.

'Thanks for your help,' the crewman muttered as the gates from both sides of the lock bumped together and Marnie caught a whiff of warm oil in the air.

'Excuse me.' The quiet voice again. 'Is that your cat by any chance?'

Dolly was walking up to investigate the action.

'Yes. We're from *Sally Ann* ... back there.'

The man bent down to stroke the cat and she leaned against his jeans.

'These are the oldest working boats still going, aren't they?' said Marnie.

'Among the oldest steam-powered, yes ... built about 1906 ... worked together for over fifty years.'

'Did you work on the restoration?'

'No.' He pointed over to *Captain*, now slowly descending in the lock chamber. 'Jack was in charge of all that.' There was admiration in his voice.

Jack Hadley was leaning on the tiller, talking quietly with one of the crew, emphasising a point by jabbing his pipe in the air. He was in his sixties, lean and wiry with an aquiline profile. In loose-fitting dark trousers and collarless striped shirt, he looked the epitome of the enthusiast. A black peaked cap of unquestionable vintage, perched on a thatch of silvery hair, completed the ensemble.

'He's a remarkable man,' said the voice behind her.

'So I hear.'

Captain and Mate were making steady progress to the bottom of the lock chamber, filling it with their bulk, and already members of the crew were poised by the balance beams. Marnie looked back along the canal, but there was no sign of any other boat that could lock through with *Sally Ann*.

'Excuse me again, miss.' The quiet voice sounded amused. 'Your cat seems to be getting curious.'

Marnie turned just as Dolly leapt from the side of the lock onto *Captain*. She landed on the cabin roof directly in front of Jack Hadley, who was still addressing the steerer on *Mate*.

With a grin the latter called out, 'Stowaway!'

Hadley turned to find himself confronted by an inquisitive black face. He looked up to the lockside, raising his hand against the sunlight. Marnie knelt down on the stone edge.

'I'm sorry, Mr Hadley. She's escaped.'

'That's all right.' The voice was lighter than she had expected. Hadley set his pipe down on the hatch to pick Dolly up and stroke her head. He was tanned like a seaman, with light blue eyes, and handed Dolly up to Marnie, smiling with long teeth.

Holding the cat in her arms, Marnie felt the eyes of the crew turn towards her.

'I'd better take her back to the boat. I don't want her being a nuisance.'

Hadley was still smiling. 'You could keep her on board ... let your husband lock through.'

Marnie hesitated. It was a reasonable assumption.

By now, the crew was pushing the gates open, and Hadley returned his attention to the boats. The pair moved forward, *Captain*'s steam engine rumbling gently.

The crewman spoke again. 'If you want to signal your boat to come up, I'll do the gates for you.'

'That's kind of you, but ... I'm not in any hurry. I'm probably going to wait a while for another boat to come along.'

'Waiting for friends?'

'No ... actually, I'm travelling solo. I'd rather wait to share. The gates are heavy on this section.'

The man looked thoughtful. 'I could work these locks for you.'

'Oh, I couldn't ask you to do that.'

The man shrugged. 'There's more than enough hands for our two boats.'

It was a tempting offer.

'Well ...'

Before she could finish the sentence, the man was already turning the first paddles to fill the lock.

'Go on. I'll have it ready by the time you get your boat here.'

———※———

Sheena busied herself tidying the shelves on the display cabinets and putting out new stock. It was a monotonous job but she liked doing it whenever she had something to think about. It also brought approval from her boss, the pharmacist. He looked up from the high counter of the pharmacy and his expression, though not actually a smile, was recognisable as the face of approval.

Sheena was thinking about Gary. He was a nice guy and they had a lot of fun together, but he seemed to have limited horizons. She was beginning to worry that he was a drifter. Other boyfriends had been less entertaining but they had had careers, prospects, their own place to live and a car. Gary lived on a boat, walked everywhere he needed to go and seemed to earn a living from one day to the next.

But what really bothered her was this business about Old Peter and the bloke with the gravelly voice. Gary didn't seem to realise that he had to stand up to him. People respected you if you told them straight. She wasn't daunted at the prospect. Past experience had taught her that if you just came out with what you wanted to say, everyone knew where they stood. Of course she did have certain advantages. She smoothed the white coat down over her hips, a manoeuvre not lost on the boss, who liked to keep an eye on what was happening in the shop.

So what should she do? And how could she find Gravel? She lined up a special offer on dental floss and rearranged the toothbrushes. The more she thought about it, the easier it seemed. She would ask for him in the pub. The landlord would know when he came in, if he was a regular. She would tell Gravel about Old Peter and that would be that. Easy. No more worries.

The pharmacist watched Sheena reaching up to the top shelves. It made the white coat ride up, so she had to smooth it down after each action. He liked that. In fact, he liked Sheena. She was a good worker and pleasant to the customers, as well as having other qualities. She could go far, if she wanted to. He could see a future for her. He could help her.

When Sheena returned behind the counter, Diane, the other assistant, had just taken herself off to the loo. The boss saw his chance.

'Sheena, can you come here for a moment. I want to have a quiet word with you … in private … just the two of us.'

—⚜—

Sally Ann entered the lock, as *Captain* and *Mate* were almost at the lowest level in the next, with one more to go. They eased into the last lock while Marnie was still descending in the second and were through to open water as her helper set to work on the paddles. Marnie had nothing to do but hold *Sally Ann* on a rope while the water level rose.

It was at the point when she left the third lock that Marnie realised there was a problem. She emerged to find that *Captain* and *Mate* were out of sight, leaving no more than a thin plume of smoke in the distance. Her helper was now stranded. He closed the gates, seeming unperturbed. Marnie pulled *Sally Ann* into the bank and waited for him to catch her up.

'Don't worry. If you want to stay here a while, I can walk to the next lock. It's not far.'

Marnie protested. 'It's nearly three miles.'

'Forty minutes. No trouble at all.'

Marnie shook her head. 'No, no. I can pull in at that lock just as well as here.'

'It'll be lunchtime soon. They'll be stopping there. I'll easily catch them.'

Mention of lunch made Marnie realise how long it had been since breakfast. She looked around her. It was an attractive spot, the canal running through rolling countryside in noonday sunshine, pastures dotted with small areas of woodland.

'Are you sure they'll stop there?'

'Absolutely. It's Jack's favourite pub. The landlord's an old friend.' The man half turned to set off.

Marnie acted on impulse. 'No, stop. I know it's early but let's eat here. We'll catch them up afterwards.' The man hesitated; she held out her hand. 'I'm Marnie, by the way … and my cat's called Dolly.'

'I'm Mick.'

They moored *Sally Ann* by the towpath.

While Marnie produced lunch, Mick wrestled with the parasol on the stern deck and set up the folding table and safari chairs. Lunch consisted of pâté, herb omelette, a mixed salad, cheese and fruit. A bottle of claret completed the scene. Mick stared at the table before they started.

'Is everything all right?' Marnie said.

'It … er … well, it looks like a picture from a magazine.'

'Least I could do.'

—⚭—

Stalker studied the cruising guide. The next crossing point was a village beside a lock. Its attractions included a canalside pub, a fourteenth century church, a Georgian rectory and Jacobean almshouses. Maybe Marnie would have a pub lunch and do the tourist thing.

He checked the road map. By the time he reached the village it would be well into lunchtime. Perhaps she would be tempted to take a break. It was the only eating opportunity for miles. He had a feeling about this place.

—⚭—

Mick pointed ahead. The first sign of the lock was the outline of a bridge, and as they drew nearer, the roof-line and chimneys of the pub came into view. As he had predicted, *Captain* and *Mate* were moored nearby. Several people were sitting out, finishing lunch. Marnie brought the boat into the bank while Mick hopped ashore to tie up.

'Thanks for lunch, Marnie. It was great. Are you staying here or do we go on?'

'I'd like to look around … make a phonecall or two. I might travel on later.'

They shook hands.

'Leave the keys. I'll take *Sally Ann* through so she'll be ready for you.'

Marnie went into the pub and bought a phonecard. The phone was in a narrow corridor by the front door and was being used by a young woman speaking in a hushed voice. She frowned at Marnie and turned away to resume her whispered conversation.

Marnie went back to the bar. 'Is there another phone round here?'

'Just up the road by the post office.' The barman winked. 'It's cheaper than this one.'

—⚭—

There was something familiar about one of the boats tied up before the lock by the pub. Stalker was sure he had seen it before, but he was convinced he had seen practically every boat registered on the waterways of England in the past few days.

He switched off the engine. From where he had parked, he could not quite read the name. If the boat had been the right colour he would have got out and walked round to the front to read it, even at the risk of revealing himself to the owner. He had begun to wonder whether Gravel had been right about the colours. He had seen several boats painted in dark blue, but none with maroon. This one was the right shade of blue, and it was in the right place, but the cream was all wrong.

He lit his last cigarette, crumpled the packet and tossed it on the floor. Just then, he spotted activity on the boat. Someone was taking it forward to the lock. Stalker sat up in his seat, exhaling smoke through his nostrils. No luck. The boater was the right height and build, but definitely a man.

Despondent and wondering if he was ever going to find the wretched boat, Stalker got out and crossed the road to buy cigarettes in the pub. In the corridor he had to squeeze past a woman on the phone, who seemed to be having a crisis in her private life. She glared at him as if he was an intruder, and he glared back.

When he came out, there was movement on the canal. Two bigger boats were approaching the lock, and the smaller one was all but invisible inside it. Stalker headed towards the towpath, hoping that if he just wandered along it for half an hour, his prey would come to him. His luck was due for a change.

———∽∞∽———

It was hot in the kiosk and Marnie wished she had remembered to put on a sun hat. She dialled Jane's number.

'It's Marnie, hi.'

'I know what you're ringing about and it's all sorted.'

'What do you mean?'

'Your squatters. They've left ... half an hour ago. Gary is not pleased.'

'Tell me more. And how's Gary involved?'

'He told them it was his mooring and his boat was in dry dock. He sub-let it to them for a month, generously throwing in the electricity at no extra charge.'

'*Cheek!*'

'Quite ... but not untypical where Gary's concerned.'

'So how did you get rid of them?'

'I went to see them this morning ... told them you were the chairman of the British Waterways Board of Governors, head of the local magistrate's bench and were due back at any minute. They remembered an urgent appointment halfway up the Grand Union. They should be overtaking you about now.'

Marnie laughed. In the background she heard the wailing of *Captain*'s steam whistle. After disconnecting from Jane, she dialled her home number and listened to the answerphone. There was one message.

'Hi, it's me again ... Anne. Sorry to keep pestering you, Marnie, but there's something I think you ought to know. My class went to the canal in town this morning. Mrs Robertson liked my project so much she thought we could all do some sketching. A man was asking about a boat called *Sally Ann*. I didn't say anything because he said he had some mates travelling on the boat. Obviously not you. But afterwards I wondered if it might be that man who's worried about your boat. Perhaps you've got a problem that needs attention. That's all really. I promise not to bother you again. Have a good trip. Bye!'

25
Sun

On Saturday morning Marnie was feeling jaded. For the past few days she had been unsettled. The weather had been fine and warm with endless sunshine from cloudless blue skies. *Sally Ann* was running well, and they had passed through beautiful countryside. But something was wrong.

Even Dolly seemed affected by the atmosphere. All day long she stayed out of sight … except at meal-times.

Milton Keynes had surprised Marnie. The new town, so often the butt of jokes, revealed a care for the canal, its bridges and towpaths that so far was unsurpassed anywhere she had seen outside Little Venice.

Leaving the ultra-modern town behind, she found herself cruising through a timeless landscape. It seemed to drift in and out of focus. A feeling of lethargy came over her and she brought *Sally Ann* into the bank in the shade of a line of willows. A glass of mineral water would revive her.

In the saloon, Dolly was curled into a ball, asleep on a chair. Marnie poured a glass of Perrier water. She tipped some milk in a saucer for Dolly and sat opposite her, taking deep breaths, glancing at the cruising guide on the table.

Suddenly, she found herself laughing quietly. It was partly at the thought that she might curl up like Dolly, partly the idea that she might plan a different route with *Sally Ann* than the one shown in the guide. She had a vision of *Sally* taking off across a field as an alternative to following the canal. In her mind she saw the boat sliding between the sheep, over the cattle grid and off up the high street of the next village. It could save her a lot of bother with locks, she thought.

Feeling revived, Marnie started the engine and pulled away, not noticing that she had forgotten to tie up and the boat had drifted into mid-channel. She was in high spirits and took in every detail of the canal, its bridges and planting as she cruised along.

What kind of men built the canals? She tried to picture the engineers: velvet waistcoats and white frills, powdered wigs and buckled shoes. Long-lost voices came into her mind, men arguing technical details, pointing at plans. There were disagreements, rivalries, reputations.

Today, everything seemed sharper than on other days. Marnie felt the texture of the surfaces beyond the water, stone, wood, iron, brick and steel, every one hard and shining. She could feel the shapes of the bridges as she ran through their reflections in the water. In her head there was the sound of an old man's voice.

You like … structures?

She wanted to answer, but no words came. She cruised on. *Sally Ann* glided between willows and elders. Marnie felt she was linked with every waterway in the world. If she stayed on course she would run into the ocean and eventually the Amazon, the Zambezi and the Yangtze-Kiang, all one great highway. She heard herself laugh out loud.

The deck moved under Marnie's feet as if she was at sea. She steadied herself against the stern rail, throttled back and put a hand up to her throat. She blinked and stared. The water was utterly calm and only *Sally*'s bow wave was breaking its mirror surface. Marnie took deep breaths and gripped the tiller firmly. The air was stifling. There was no breeze, no shade. Her hat was in the cabin, but she could not trust herself to leave the deck even for a few seconds to fetch it.

Stalker had seen a church tower on high ground from miles away and had set out to find it, hoping for an observation post where he could survey that whole sector of the canal. Arriving in the village he drove through looking for a suitable spot, casting covetous eyes at the tower itself.

The best he could find was a field affording views over the waterway to north and south, glimpsed between trees and bushes. He pulled out his binoculars and swept the scene. It was the usual problem; for much of its length, the canal and road never met. The strip of water disappeared to become no more than a tantalising vision in the distance.

He fiddled with the focus ring as he scanned. One boat ... two boats ... three ... Moored along the bank, partly concealed by overhanging trees. A fourth ... a fifth. Not as easy as he had expected. The distance and the reflected light from the water made them all seem the same colour, a uniform indistinct dark shade that could have been green, blue or maroon.

Then there was movement, a boat in the distance in mid-channel. Stalker strained, adjusting the focus. The name on the bow sharpened just as it slid under a tree. *Yes!* That could have been *Sally Ann*, but something seemed wrong. He had to wait minutes before seeing it again. *Damn!* Even allowing for the distortion of distance and back lighting, the boat he was watching was the wrong colour. The roof may have been white or cream, but it was not maroon.

Quickly, he swept back to the tiller. There she was, a woman. Solo. He had only a few seconds before she was swallowed again by the trees on the bank. Stalker chewed his lip. He had been in the business long enough to know that whatever anyone told you, it could be wrong. He walked back to the car, where he could use the mobile without being noticed.

Gravel answered almost at once. Stalker explained the dilemma.

'My informant told me it was navy and maroon.'

'How reliable is he?'

'Good question. Navy and cream, you say?'

'White or cream.'

'Make up your mind. Which is it?'

'A mile away through binoculars it could be either ... light, anyway.'

Gravel paused. 'Keep it under observation. I'll check and let you know. Don't let her out of your sight.'

'I've got her.'

———∞∞———

Marnie had no recollection of bringing *Sally Ann* to shore. Mooring with one line at the stern, she switched off the engine and leaned against the tiller to catch her breath. Her eyelids were heavy. She went below, desperate to find shelter from the heat, but it was no good. The cabin was airless and stuffy. She grabbed her hat and went out.

The world was deserted. A short way from the bank there were trees, and she thought she glimpsed chimneys among the branches not far away. There would be shade where she could rest awhile. She half stumbled over the lip of the deck onto the bank.

Once there had been a fence, but it had long since rotted away. Marnie stepped over it and walked in among the trees. In the shade she steadied herself against one and rested her back against its rough bark. She remembered that she had been learning the names of trees from a book and turned to look up to identify it. In turning, she lost her balance and gently slid down onto the ground, her hat rolling off to settle beside her. She had no energy or desire to sit up, but lay there, her head spinning, breathing fitfully, until the world went away.

———∞∞———

Gary hated having to do it, but he cancelled his date with Sheena for Saturday night.

They had not made a firm arrangement, but things between them had reached the point where it was understood they would see each other at every opportunity. That weekend he had been offered a good job, moving new boats down from Cowroast to Docklands for customers of his Limehouse friend. It was well paid, and there was no point coming back to London on Saturday evening. They would have to finish late and start early to get there in a weekend.

He went round to the chemist's to explain. To his surprise and relief, Sheena was understanding. She gave him a discreet kiss behind the shampoo and conditioner stand and wished him a pleasant journey. As he went out, she stayed in the shop, tidying shelves that needed no tidying. She had things to think about.

Leaving the shop, Gary's mobile rang. He frowned as he heard the gravelly voice.

'Tell me about Marnie's boat, Gary.'

'What's there to tell? It's a forty-five footer ... *Sally –*'

'Colour.'

'Colour? Dark blue with maroon.'

'You're sure of that.'

Gary stopped walking. Why was Gravel asking this? There must be a reason. He pictured the boat, dark paintwork, faded in places, some of it peeling, in need of ... He saw Marnie, that rear view as she bent to her task. What was she doing? Scrubbing ... or could it be sanding?

'I'm waiting, Gary.'

'She may have ... touched it up ... here and there.'

'Changed the colour?'

Gary was cautious now. 'Not when I saw it last, but ...'

'Could she have changed it?' The voice was flat.

'I don't think she had the time. I'm sure she couldn't have given it a complete repaint in the short time she was in Little Venice.'

'Really sure? Or is it a possibility?'

'You think she altered the colour ... to what?'

'White ... maybe cream.'

Gary thought about it. 'She could've changed part of the colour, but nobody paints narrowboats white or cream. They're not practical colours.'

'Is that definite, Gary?'

A pause. 'Not definite.'

The line went dead. Gary realised he had made a mistake.

———

Gravel disconnected and immediately dialled another mobile.

'It could be cream.'

'That's definite?'

'It's the best we've got. Go for it.'

'She's mine.'

Stalker was back on the hillside. The cruising guide showed that the canal skirted round the village where he was waiting. No need to chase her any more. She was coming to him. The map indicated a wooded area down by the water. There was a farm nearby, but he needed a secluded spot.

Voices. He stiffened. Someone was coming down the track. He pressed himself against a tree, only risking a glance when he was sure they had passed. He could not believe his eyes.

———

It was the music that brought Marnie back. For how long she had been unconscious she could not tell. The sun was obscured from view by the canopy of trees around her, but was still high in the sky. The music came from nearby, a light baroque air played on strings. Even in her befuddled state, Marnie knew this was no recording.

She struggled to sit up and leaned against the tree, taking deep breaths, her eyes closed, listening to the sound that drifted her way between the bushes. She blinked and focused, not without difficulty, and pulled herself up from the ground, locating the source of the music ahead of her. Curiosity gave her the strength to go on. Pushing herself away from the tree, she stepped cautiously forward, concentrating hard to keep her balance.

The ground was bumpy and more than once she stumbled until, inevitably, she tripped over a root in the grass and fell flat onto a bed of dead leaves. She spat soil from her lips and rubbed her mouth with the back of her hand. Beyond where she lay was a courtyard bounded on two sides by ruins. Marnie eased herself up onto her elbows.

She made out a dilapidated house, in honey-coloured stone with tall chimneys and gaps among the slates on the roof. Close by stood a cluster of barns. The music was emanating from between the buildings. They were probably eighteenth century, perhaps earlier, and the music from the same period. Marnie closed her eyes and listened. The scene was unreal. Everything was unreal. She was unreal.

When she looked again, she blinked and froze. Along the track, not thirty yards away walked a man and a woman, arm in arm, followed by two children, skipping and laughing. The man was in bottle green frock coat and pale grey breeches over white stockings. The woman wore a full length dress of cream and dark red, gathered in at the waist, with hooped skirt. Both wore powdered wigs, and the children were dressed in miniature versions of the same style. All were absorbed in animated conversation and took no notice of Marnie lying among the bushes. Fragments of speech drifted towards her.

'... and I don't know what she was thinking of, especially at *her* age ...'

'... not much else they could do in the circumstances ...'

'... it was *bound* to come out in the end ...'

The group passed the barns and turned behind the buildings. Marnie lowered her head, deeply confused. The music still hung in the air. What on earth was happening?

She resolved to go round to the other side of the barns and dragged herself to her feet. But vertigo struck. The ground swayed, the trees swirled around her on all sides, the buildings tottered and blurred. She felt she was struck from behind and staggered, but there was no pain when she hit the ground.

The barman shook his head, polishing a glass. 'Don't know who you mean, love.'

Sheena repeated herself more slowly. 'Middle-aged, bald, black leather jacket, earring, gravelly voice. He's a regular here ... sometimes drinks with a friend of mine ... Gary from the boats? ... double whiskies? Always got a mate with him. Now ... which bit of that don't you understand?'

'Are you ordering?'

'I'm asking for information.'

'Yeah, well this is a pub, not an information centre.'

Her eyes bore into his. 'I think you know who I mean.'

The barman put down the glass and stared back. 'Even if I knew who you meant, I wouldn't know who you mean. Get it? And if you tell me you're asking for information about him, I'd say it'd be better if you didn't ask. Now ... which bit of that don't *you* understand?'

To Marnie it seemed as if only a few seconds passed before the world came back to her. It was a sound, not music this time but voices. She wanted to ask the people what they were doing. So many questions ...

She desperately needed to know their attitudes to the canals, to life, to everything, but she had no strength and knew they would go away before she had a chance to talk to them. But the voices did not go away. They grew louder, coming nearer. She wished someone would help her up. Then she felt hands on her shoulders.

'Take it easy.' A low voice.

She tried to turn and focus, but blinding sunlight flashed through the trees. Her mouth was dry and dusty.

The voice again. 'We're just getting you some water. Are you hurting anywhere?'

Marnie's leg was twisted under her. She tried to straighten it and groaned with pain. The man raised her slightly and eased her position.

'Try this.' She felt the mouth of a bottle at her lips and sipped. 'Just take it slowly.'

Marnie took a couple of sips. Something soft brushed against her arm. She blinked and looked into yellow eyes. A sturdy black cat.

'Dolly.'

'Yes.' A familiar voice.

'Mick?' Marnie was still not focusing.

'Jack … Jack Hadley from *Captain*. Do you think you can walk by yourself?'

Marnie thought about it and shook her head. 'Not for the moment.'

'Come on, then.'

Marnie felt the arms tighten round her back and under her legs. With a grunt, the man lifted her and carried her through the trees back to *Sally Ann*. With eyes still closed, she felt him step up onto the deck.

'I'm going to have to set you down here. It's too narrow to get you in through the entrance.'

'Okay.'

Marnie took the weight on her feet and let herself be led unsteadily down into the cabin. She sat on the bed, aware of men's voices in the background. Breathing steadily, she heard the clink of glass in the galley.

Jack returned to the cabin. 'Try this. It'll help. Just a sip or two, now.'

He held a glass to her lips and the smell of brandy made her eyes water. She managed a sip and opened her eyes. Faces were peering in from the hatchway.

Jack was speaking again. 'Can you tell me your name?'

'Marnie.'

'Okay. Now listen, Marnie. You need to rest awhile. We've opened the windows to let in some fresh air. I'll come back soon to see how you are. I don't think you need a doctor, but if you do, we'll find one. Try and sleep.'

Marnie swung her legs up onto the bed and lay back on the pillow. She heard the growl of the water pump in the galley. With eyes closed, she tried to smile. Her last memory was a cool damp flannel on her forehead.

On Saturday evening Gravel paid Gary a visit, but found his boat empty. While Sidekick made enquiries, Gravel took up station in the pub. His backside had hardly warmed the seat when the barman appeared with a double scotch.

'Thanks, Benny.'

The barman bent down and spoke quietly. 'A bird's been in asking after you.'

'After me? You sure it was me? Did she use my name?'

A shake of the head. 'She asked for someone who fitted your description.'

'What description would that be?'

A pause. 'Good-looking bloke … ear-ring … black leather jacket … uses this table.'

'What did you tell her?'

The barman raised an eyebrow.

'Good lad. Now tell me about the girl.'

'Blonde.'

'And?'

'Blonde.'

'Try harder.'

Another pause. 'Good boobs … legs up to her armpits.'

'Name?'

'Dunno. Doesn't come in here much. Seen her once with a bloke.'

'What bloke?'

The barman hesitated. Gravel's turn to raise an eyebrow. 'Gary … off the boats.'

Gravel nodded. The audience was over.

Gravel sat staring into his whisky. He knew the girl, easily recognised from Benny's detailed description. Why was she looking for him? Why now? What was Gary up to? These days it was all questions. It was about time someone started giving him answers.

Sidekick came in and took the opposite chair.

Gravel looked up. 'I hope you've got an answer for me.'

'Yeah. The boat was repainted by the new woman. She kept the blue … changed the maroon to cream.'

At last Gravel had an answer that told him something. It told him he had had Stalker wasting his time for the best part of a week.

'Find out where Gary is. I want to talk to him. And see what you can find out about his girlfriend.'

'You want to talk to her?'

'No. She wants to talk to me. Maybe my luck's changed.'

As sidekick left the bar, Gravel reached for his mobile.

———— ∽∽∽ ————

It was hard to tell how long she had slept, but she woke to find Dolly curled up at the foot of the bed, purring. Something was different. Marnie propped herself up on one elbow. Through the window she could see more trees than she remembered. Behind her in the saloon there was a rustling sound as if the page of a newspaper had been turned.

'Hallo?'

'You're awake. Good.' Jack Hadley came in and perched on the corner of the bed. 'How do you feel?'

'At the risk of sounding like an old film script …' Her voice was croaky. '… where am I?'

'We bow-hauled you here … more shade.' He got up and went into the galley, returning with a glass of water. 'You'll have to drink quite a lot of this.'

Marnie sipped. 'I'm not sure what happened. I feel rather foolish. Did I pass out?'

Jack laid cool fingers on her forehead. 'A touch of the sun, I think. We came upon *Sally Ann* tied up at the stern … the bow drifting across the canal. We made her fast and wondered why there was no-one on board except the cat. Then we saw your hat lying under a tree.'

'So you organised a search party.'

'Found you lying in the undergrowth.'

'I'm sorry to give you all this trouble.'

'No trouble. And it looks as if you're on the mend. Do you feel like eating anything?'

'Not really. I'll just drink this.'

'Okay. If you need anything, we're just along here. You'll not be disturbed. Contrary to popular belief, we don't sit up all night singing boat shanties and chewing tobacco.'

'I'm glad to hear it. Thanks for all you've done.'

'Don't mention it.' He turned to go.

A sudden memory. 'When you found me back there, was anyone else around?'

'I didn't see anyone.'

'You didn't hear anything … people … music?'

'No.'

'There were buildings, though … I didn't imagine that?'

'An old farm … abandoned, I think.'

'You're sure there were no people?'

'Quite sure.'

———❧———

Stalker returned to his flat that evening, bursting with frustration. He had finally found the boat he was searching for, but it seemed to have become part of a fleet and was now travelling in convoy with two others. Worse, the other boats seemed to be crewed by a gang of heavies.

On the map the canal passed by the village in a lonely spot sheltered by trees. It was ideal for his purpose. But there was just a field track leading to a farm at the bottom of a hill. Worse, when he tried to follow it, he found it was as busy as Piccadilly Circus in the rush hour. All the people going up and down the track were in period costume. It was like a film set.

In the village high street banners announced a village fête, celebrating the two-hundredth anniversary of the canal, built in 1793. Stalker skirted round the main track and made it down to the water some way along the cut. There he had caught sight of his prey, nestling against the bank in line with the two other boats a hundred yards further up the cut. What now? He would have to bide his time … again.

26
Glebe Farm

When Marnie woke on Sunday morning she still felt slightly spaced out. The air in the cabin was fresh and cool. Someone had partly closed the windows, leaving a gap for ventilation. She rose cautiously, slid open the window opposite the bed and leaned out.

It was a golden morning. Water and sky merged into one, and the boats seemed to hover in the air. Marnie showered and put on a new sweatshirt and jeans. While the kettle boiled she walked a short way along the bank, feeling fragile, as if convalescing after an illness.

At breakfast on the stern deck under the parasol, Marnie studied the cruising guide and discovered a village a short distance to the left on higher ground, linking up with the derelict farm buildings she had seen the previous day. She was studying the guide when Jack Hadley appeared. He accepted her invitation aboard, but declined breakfast.

His thick crop of white hair gave Jack a leonine appearance and contrasted with his deep tan. Marnie had Indian friends who were paler than Jack Hadley. He reminded her of old paintings of seadogs, an impression compounded by the dark trousers and striped collarless shirt. She had designer friends who were less stylish than Jack Hadley.

He indicated the cruising guide. 'So … already planning your getaway?'

'My *getaway*, yes. I'll just take it gently today, maybe do some sketching.'

Jack looked up at the sky. 'We're in for another fine day … a real scorcher.'

'And I'll be wearing a sun hat. What about you? What plans for *Captain* and *Mate?*'

'Slowly making our way round to Banbury. There's a big rally there in a couple of weeks.'

'Are you the star turn?'

There was a gleam in his eye. 'One of them, perhaps. There'll be quite a gathering.'

'You seem to have captured the public's attention for the waterways.'

Jack laughed. 'That's not quite true. I may have helped a little, but there were many others before I came along … Tom Rolt, Charles Hadfield and of course, the *Idle Women.*'

'*Idle* Women?' Marnie repeated. The concept of being a *woman* and being *idle* was an odd combination in her experience.

'They were volunteers … like the Land Army Girls … only they worked on the boats while the men were away serving.'

'I've never heard of them.'

'Oh, I could tell you some stories about them, but I don't want to tire you out, and I must get along. If you're interested, try and get their books. A good read.'

He stood up. Marnie rose carefully.

'Thanks again for yesterday.'

'You take it gently now.'

Jack held out a hand. Marnie took it but reached forward and kissed him on the cheek. He stepped onto the towpath, grinning.

'See you again some time. Go safely.'

He went back to his boats, walking briskly like a young man.

<hr />

That Sunday morning Stalker returned to the village, determined to catch up with Marnie. He parked a short distance from the open five-barred gate and walked quickly down the field track. Finding a secluded spot with good views, he pulled out his binoculars and began scanning the countryside.

His search only revealed tantalising glimpses of the canal, reflections of light off the water. Then he saw it. A smudge of grey smoke in the distance. The flotilla was on the move. The thin sound of a steam whistle reached his ears like a taunt. He hastily focused and picked up the tail of a boat a second before it was swallowed by rows of trees. Was that *Sally Ann*? He guessed it was.

From memory he knew the next contact with the canal by road was at a lonely pub. The boats might almost be there by now, but it was his last chance for miles.

<hr />

Marnie decided on a lazy day. It was late morning before she even stirred from under the parasol where she had spent an enjoyable couple of hours reading. *Captain* and *Mate* were long gone. The sound of the farewell whistle had hung in the air as the old boats slipped away, leaving a tall plume of smoke and the whiff of steam in their wake. Rested and revived, Marnie picked up her sun hat and set off through the trees.

The spinney extended perhaps fifty yards back from the canal, and she followed a clear path that might have been in use since the coming of the waterway. Today the farm buildings were deserted. There was no music, no people in ancient costumes. She wandered among barns and cottages, saddened to see them so dilapidated. The house was handsome, well-proportioned, double-fronted, with stone mullions and steep-pitched roof of blue slate. Gardens had become jungles of impenetrable weeds. The place had stories to tell, but now there was no-one to listen.

Marnie went in search of the village. Between the house and a small stone barn she found a track and followed it up the hill to a gate on the road. Turning right towards the church, she passed houses and a school set back in its playground. Opposite the church stood a pub and outside it was a shiny red phonebox.

Marnie dialled her answerphone.

'Hi! It's me.' Beth did not sound as bouncy as usual. 'Well, it looks as if we'll be coming back in September. Paul's department is having to make savings, and if he wants to keep his job he has to return for the new academic year. So that's that. What about you? Have you gone home yet or are you still gallivanting about on *Sally*? I expect you've got bored with it by now. You never were one for the outdoor life. Give us a ring when you can. Bye!'

The next message was Steve.

'Hallo, Marnie. Haven't spoken for a while. I wondered if you knew about Paul's department. They have to save four staff and their research budget's been cut by ten per cent. I don't know what Paul's going to do, but it's not looking good here at present. I hope things are okay with you. Be nice to hear from you some time.'

The next voice was unmistakable.

'Hallo, my dear! I hope you get this message. I'm not very good with these gadgets. Anyway, your visitors haven't been back, and I hope that means no-one will be using your electricity from now on. I've made a sign and I'm going to put it up as soon as I see someone who'll let me onto the towpath. It says: Mooring of N/B *Sally Ann*, Strictly Private. That should make it clear to all. Hope you don't mind. Have a nice time, dear. Good-bye.'

Marnie rang Mrs Jolly back, but got no reply. She left the stuffy confines of the phonebox, crossed the road and bought milk and a newspaper at the village shop. It was time for lunch.

The pub was at least as old as the derelict farm, spacious, cool and airy with dark beams and a broad inglenook. It was only just gone noon and Marnie was alone in the bar. She took in the traditional decor of horse brasses, harness and old prints. It was a cliché, but comfortable and welcoming.

'Good morning, or rather good afternoon.' The landlord's voice startled Marnie.

'Hallo.' Marnie glanced at her watch. 'Yes, afternoon, just. I was admiring the bar.'

'I sometimes think we ought to change it, but to be honest, I'm not sure what else we'd do. Anyway, the customers like it. It's what they expect. What can I get you?'

While she waited for a Stilton ploughman's and glass of red wine, Marnie read a notice pinned to a beam. It depicted men and women in old-fashioned clothes, with a horse-drawn narrowboat in the background. The Knightly St John summer fête, held on the last Saturday in June, commemorated the bi-centenary of the canal. Prizes would be given for the best costumes. Mystery solved. Marnie learnt that the fête was held in the grounds of Glebe Farm.

The landlord arrived in the bar with cutlery, paper napkin and wine. Marnie indicated the notice.

'Glebe Farm … that's the ruined place down by the canal, isn't it?'

'That's the one. Almost everyone in the village dressed up, including the vicar. Mind you, he didn't take much persuading.'

'You had lovely weather for it.'

'Too hot for some. Course, I'm not complaining. I ran the bar and we've never sold so much drink.' He chuckled and went out.

Too hot for some, Marnie thought.

27
Idle Woman

The weather stayed bright and warm over the weekend and on Monday Marnie opted again to take life gently. She cruised only a few miles before stopping to sketch an old boat-horse stable by a canalside pub. This trip is becoming another version of the *Marnie Pub Crawl*, she thought.

At noon she was sitting in the pub garden with a glass of cider, waiting for food to be brought out, poring over the map and cruising guide. Ahead she would face two long tunnels at Blisworth and Braunston. After that came the choice of several routes, all of them potentially interesting.

'Toasted tuna sandwich and salad!'

A motherly woman of jovial appearance was weaving between the tables. She put the plate down in front of Marnie.

'Are you going to do the BCN?'

'I'm not sure.'

'They say there are more miles of canal in Birmingham than Venice.' The woman snorted. 'I know where I'd rather be.'

Marnie ran a finger over the map. 'I was wondering about the Shropshire Union.'

'You could do a lot worse.'

Marnie ate the sandwich and traced the canal route via the Shropshire Union and on to Wales, thinking of Anne's boating holiday with her family.

When she was getting up to leave, the woman came back to clear the table.

'Made up your mind, then?'

'Maybe the Shropshire Union.'

'Very nice, the *Shroppie*.' The woman looked up at the sky. 'Enjoy it while you can.'

———— ⚓ ————

Gary arranged to meet Sheena for lunch on his boat that Monday. He decided not to go with his first choice of pork pies and pickled onions and had opted instead for ham sandwiches and tomatoes. They were more Sheena's style.

They sat in the saloon with all the windows open. Sheena removed a crumb from the corner of her mouth with her little finger and took a sip of orange juice.

'Did you ever do history at school, Gary?'

'Course I did. Everyone does history ... 1066 ... 1666 ... 1966.'

She pondered. 'What happened in 1666?'

'Great Fire o' London.'

'Oh yeah. You must've been great for anything that happened in something sixty-six.'

Gary grinned. 'Won the school prize for that – the Clickety-Click Prize for History.'

'So what was in 1966, then? Was that the year they invented bingo?'

Gary looked pained. 'England won the World Cup.'

'So you did do modern history?'

'That was sort of extra-curricular.'

Sheena pursued her theme. 'Did you ever study Marx?'

'Nope ... nor Spencer.'

'*Gary!*'

'Sorry, love. What's Marx got to do with anything?'

'He said you're either with us or against us. At least, I think it was him.'

Gary was beginning to wonder where this was all leading. 'So?'

'Are you with me, Gary?'

'Ah ... one of your trick questions. Try this one. If I said you had a lovely body, would you hold it against me?' He laughed.

Sheena rolled her eyes. 'That's an *old* one.'

'The old ones are the best ones.'

'In your case, Gary, they're the *only* ones.'

'Oh, come on, darlin', what's up?'

Sheena put down her sandwich and looked him in the eye. 'I keep getting the impression you're only half here. Your mind keeps wandering ... probably takes after your hands ... but even so, it would be nice to have all your attention when we're together.'

'Sorry, darlin'.'

'What is it, then?'

Gary hesitated before replying. This could be tricky. 'I'm a bit worried about something.'

'About what?'

He frowned. 'You won't like this.'

'Try me.'

'I'm worried ... about Marnie.'

'You're right.'

Gary looked relieved. 'I knew you'd understand.'

'You're right ... I don't like it.'

'It's not like that.'

'How is it, then? And this'd better be good.'

Gary lowered his eyes. 'The bloke with the gravelly voice has got someone following her.'

'So?'

'I think he might want to ... take her out.'

'You're not telling me you're jealous?'

Gary looked up. 'I didn't mean that sort of 'take her out'.'

Sheena's turn to frown. She picked up her glass and took a sip. No wonder Gary seemed preoccupied, she thought. She tried not to reveal how scared she felt. She did not want him to know she had tried to make contact with Gravel. She also did not tell him she had had a message to meet Gravel after work the next day.

—⟋∞⟍—

Stalker was watching and waiting. The convoy of boats was passing though countryside where the road seldom met the canal. The only aspect of his pursuit that made life easier was the smoke from the funnel. It was a useful marker.

It was Monday afternoon before he realised something was wrong. He had worked out a master plan, lying in wait in the village of Stoke Bruerne. He figured that he could blend in with the tourists and not be noticed. It was a good plan, in theory. The drawback was that a Monday outside the main holiday season did not produce enough visitors.

Stalker was sitting on a bench about twenty yards from the locks, eating an ice cream, when the wail of the steam whistle announced the coming of the convoy. Within seconds, a small army swarmed over the lock; the air was filled with the sound of paddle gear turning. They had scarcely arrived when the far gates swung open to admit the working pair.

From nowhere a small crowd had formed to enjoy the spectacle. Stalker got to his feet and walked as casually as he could to stand at the back of the onlookers. He wandered onto the bridge where a handful of spectators were looking down. Unlike them, he crossed to the opposite side. His heart sank. There were two other boats waiting to use the lock. Neither of them was *Sally Ann*. Neither was crewed by a woman. Stalker strained his eyes to look into the distance. Nothing.

Where was she? Could she have come on *ahead*? Stalker left the bridge to check out the long line of boats moored beyond the museum. He strode out, walking the entire length of the towpath through the village. It took several minutes to reach the end of the line.

Suddenly the air grew chilly. He stopped abruptly. Ahead was the mouth of a tunnel. The guide book told him it was about two miles long. He swore loudly and slammed the book to the ground.

—⟋∞⟍—

Marnie pondered the pub lady's valediction, *enjoy it while you can*, as she pushed off from the side. No more than a few fluffy cumulus floated across the sky, and Marnie kept the sunhat firmly in place.

The cruising guide showed a lock about half a mile ahead. Rounding a bend she had a first glimpse of the balance beams and was disappointed to find no other boat in view. At least the lock was in her favour, the water at the lower level on her side, one gate hanging half open.

She was lining up for the bank when a group of ramblers came along, about six of them, young men and women, with back-packs, in shorts and walking boots. They paused to look at *Sally Ann* as she drew nearer, and one of the group pointed at the lock, shouting something indistinct. Marnie made out the words '... help you ...'

She cupped her hands and called back. 'Just the one gate will be fine.'

Sally Ann's Summer

The rambler raised a thumb, the group seized the gate and they pulled it wide with ease. Marnie piloted *Sally Ann* smoothly into the chamber and the gate was already closing behind her as she engaged reverse and brought the boat to a halt.

She shaded her eyes to look up at them. 'That was great, thanks.'

'No problem.'

It was a deep lock, eight or nine feet down. The ramblers loomed above her, tanned and fit, with muscular legs. One caught the rope from Marnie and looped it round a bollard, dropping the rest of it down to Marnie's waiting hands.

'Is that all right, then?' A Yorkshire intonation. 'Anything else we can do?'

'No. That's fine. I can manage from here.'

They set off with a wave. Marnie made *Sally Ann* secure on the rope, picked up the windlass and stepped along the gunwale to climb the rungs of the ladder built into the wall. Dolly sat up on the hatch and Marnie gave her a stroke as she went past and turned to mount the ladder.

'Silly me!'

She spoke to the cat, realising there was no ladder on this side of the chamber. She made her way back to the stern deck and stepped onto the gunwale on the opposite side of the boat. Halfway along, Marnie stopped and looked up at the wall, puzzled.

Knowing that all locks have built-in ladders, she deduced she was looking in the wrong place. She inched her way towards the bow, climbed onto *Sally Ann*'s roof and rotated through a complete circle. But there *must* be a ladder, she told herself. *Every* lock has a ladder.

She cupped both hands to her mouth and called out. Her voice echoed back from the grey, wet walls of the chamber. Nobody came. The ramblers were well out of earshot.

Back on deck, she switched off the engine. There was no way of scaling the walls, no foot-holes in the gates. The front gates were backed by thousands of tonnes of water. There was no way of pulling the rear gates open from inside the chamber. She was trapped.

'Hallo-o-o-o!'

No reply. It was two-fifteen. She resolved to call out every five minutes. It was a fine, sunny afternoon and she was on the Grand Union Canal, the spine of the whole waterway system. This was no desert island. Soon, another boat would come along and she would be on her way, a little wiser than when she first pulled into the lock.

A cloud momentarily crossed the sun and the air in the chamber felt suddenly cooler. Marnie slipped into the cabin for a sweater. Dolly had stopped washing and was sitting up. Two-twenty.

'Hallo-o-o-o!'

A few more clouds drifted overhead. Marnie remembered a French novel about a man who imagined himself caught in the trunk of a tree, only able to see the clouds crossing the sky above him. He had concluded that that was enough to make life worth living, or something like that. She had not been wholly persuaded by the argument when she read it then and felt even less convinced now.

The sky was darkening. A voice came into her mind … *enjoy it while you can*. At that moment, a raindrop hit the roof beside Dolly, followed seconds later by a rumble of thunder in the background.

Stalker hurried back to the locks, grateful that the weather had at least turned cooler with a few sparse clouds taking the edge off the sun's heat. He told himself Marnie would be in the lock when he reached it, that she had just been travelling more slowly than her friends on the older boats. By the time he reached the first buildings the working pair were moving very slowly past the boats lining the bank. He avoided eye contact with the crew and pressed on as quickly as he dared without drawing attention to himself.

The lock was unoccupied and the crowd of onlookers had dispersed. On the bridge Stalker stared down at the empty stretch of water beyond. Where was she? He could not believe it was so difficult to find a boat that crawled along at walking pace on a single strip of water. The trouble was, these things were unpredictable.

He tried applying logic. There were only three possibilities. One, she was not travelling with the working boats at all. Two, she was running behind them. Three, she had gone on ahead of them.

First, he knew she had been travelling with the other boats because he had seen her with his own eyes. Perhaps when they met on Saturday she had given the men something and they were now going their separate ways. It horrified him to think that Marnie might have turned back and now be heading south again.

Second, she had held back behind the working pair for some reason. What reason? He had no answer to that.

Third, it was possible she had gone on ahead. Why? Again, he had no answer. He heard the wailing of the steam whistle. The working boats were approaching the tunnel.

It was decision time. Stalker dredged up everything he knew about their situation. *Sally Ann* was travelling with the other two boats. Fact. She had been in front. Was that significant? He heard the echo of the whistle, remembered the smell of the smoke. He felt the chill air at the mouth of the tunnel … the tunnel. Of course! She had gone on ahead to go first into the tunnel. Anyone following would be engulfed in the smoke from the engine. If they were in convoy, she would have to be in front.

He checked the map. Beyond the tunnel was another village, Blisworth. The cruising guide estimated that a boat would need over half an hour to get through. He hurried back to the car and paused before switching on the engine. Was this the right thing to do? The map showed him there were several points up ahead where the road connected with the cut. He could leapfrog from one to the other until he found her.

It was time to report in. He grabbed his mobile, pressed buttons and opened the car window. A cool breeze fanned his face.

'It's me.'

'And?'

'I'm closer.'

'Than what? You've been close for days.'

'She's travelling with two other boats.'

'Can you get her alone?'

'I will do soon. And when I catch her up?'

'Find out what she knows about Old Peter and his stuff. Use any means you have to. Find a lonely spot.'

———⚬⚬⚬———

Dolly was safely tucked away on her favourite chair in the saloon before the rain came down. It was a heavy shower and put a temporary end to Marnie's efforts to attract help. She pulled her wet-weather gear from the locker and laid it out on the bed. While she was making tea, the rain began to ease off.

She put her head out through the rear doors. It was worth a try.

'Hallo-o-o-o!' And again, just in case. 'Hallo-o-o-o!'

Some way off she heard thunder, a short rumble like a car going over a cattle grid. She waited, smelling the damp air of the lock chamber, every surface shining with rain. There was no reply and she returned to her tea. After a few minutes she thought she heard voices. Pushing open the rear doors, she went up the two steps to the deck.

'Hallo-o-o-o!'

The rain had almost stopped. Looking up, Marnie saw a dark shape at the lockside. She smiled at the recognition of a human form and as her eyes focused, the newcomer spoke, but not to her.

''Ere, come an' 'ave a decko at this! Look what I've found!'

The man was joined by a few others, looming against the sky. Skinheads. A host of images rushed through her mind: a magazine photo of a crane pushed into a lock by vandals, football hooligans on the rampage, gangs of thugs in a street fight. Some inner instinct told her that a politely worded request for assistance might not be met by selfless, willing co-operation.

''Ullo, darlin'! What you doin' down there?'

The speaker seemed to have a large curtain ring in one ear and a swastika tattooed on his forehead. Marnie hesitated before replying. The situation was obvious. She was stuck at the bottom of a deep hole, unable to move several tonnes of boat, being loomed over by a bunch of people whose reputation for philanthropy was limited.

'Got trouble 'ave yer?' said one of the others.

Marnie knew she could not stay silent for ever and tried to think herself into a matter-of-fact, monosyllabic style of speech to suit the occasion.

'I need the gates open.'

The skinheads stared. The idea that they might open the paddles and bring *Sally Ann* up to their level was very unappealing. Marie was comforted by the certainty that they would have no idea how a lock functioned and would not know how to operate one.

'Throw us yer key and we'll open the paddles.'

Marnie's heart sank. She glanced down at the windlass lying on the deck. It was her best one, moulded in solid aluminium. The idea of handing it over brought little comfort.

'Just a minute!'

She dived into the cabin to fetch the spare windlass, an older cruder version. She emerged onto the deck, hoping they might have gone away, but they were still there, still looming. They were good at looming.

'Come on darlin'! Can't wait all day.'

Against all her instincts, Marnie swung the windlass, her anxiety that the key might fall back into the lock only matched by her anxiety that it would be caught. On the third swing she let it fly and watched it arc upwards.

'Ow!'

The cry of pain was followed by laughter from the ones who had not been hit, growls of annoyance from the victim. Marnie sensed that everything could become highly unpleasant. What now? she wondered.

Stalker soon realised that Marnie was not running ahead of the working pair. The roads in and around Blisworth made it easy to check the whole area. Angry and impatient, he turned back to Stoke Bruerne and parked by the bridge. Rain clouds were threatening as he ran up to the lockside. There was no movement on the canal, and the spectators had vanished. The breeze was now turning to a wind, scudding across the water.

He took the road south to the next bridge and checked the locks. Here too there was no traffic on the cut, no *Sally Ann*. He headed south again, convinced that Marnie had to be in that sector. From a lay-by he had a good view into the distance through the binoculars. Nothing. He wondered if she would be travelling with a storm coming on.

The canal passed close to the next village south. He stopped by the road and watched as rain began to fall. Marnie had definitely parted company with the other boats. He knew she had to be somewhere in the open country ahead of him. Apart from the rain, the situation was perfect. Near a country pub he pulled off the road, zipped up his jacket, pulled on a baseball cap and set off up the towpath.

The sky had become unseasonably dark for a summer afternoon. Another shower hit him. Stalker tried to ignore the elements. He knew he would overtake the boat if he could walk fast enough, but his progress was hampered as the towpath churned into mud.

He caught sight of a group of ramblers up ahead, coming along the path towards him. Their hoods were up, the peaks of their caps sticking out like beaks. He pushed himself into a cluster of trees and bushes, watching the group go past, rain glistening on their legs. None looked in his direction. A blast of wind lashed him with rain. He cursed in silence, knowing he had to go on.

Stalker strode out, elated when the rain moderated and all but ceased. His jubilation lasted less than five minutes. Ahead he saw black and white balance beams and knew the lock would slow down the boat's progress. Then he saw the skinheads, their attention focused on the lock as he crept closer.

Not far from the lock stood an old brick shed, open on one side. Stalker approached it cautiously and dived in, relieved to be out of sight and out of the weather. But what if the skinheads had the same idea? Reluctantly he slipped out and hid behind the building. There was nothing for it but to wait.

A blast of wind brought rain, this time heavier than before. It also brought the skinheads. They charged down from the lock and piled into the shed. But to Stalker's surprise they quickly piled out again and began slithering down the path, swearing at the mud. He watched them go. But something was wrong. Were they fewer in number, or was it his imagination? Had one of them stayed behind? One skinhead would cause him no trouble. He could eat one for breakfast. But his priority was not to be seen.

His other priority was not to die of exposure. A short way off he saw a clump of trees that would give more protection than where he was now standing. Moving rapidly, he concealed himself among them, their canopy of branches keeping off the worst of the rain, but showering him in drips with every puff of wind.

—∙∙∙—

The sky was now much darker. Marnie could hear the skinheads still arguing and she did not like the feeling that decisions were being taken about her. Just then, something like spit struck her in the face and she stepped backwards. Various strategies raced through her mind. Locking herself into the cabin was the most realistic and only risked damage to the boat if they attacked it. Grabbing the boat hook to fight them off might work, but probably not for long and could have dire consequences.

Another spit in the face, followed by another and another. The skinheads began to move. The rain was back. Great drops were splashing onto the deck, the roof, the hatch, as black clouds rolled overhead and emptied their load like bombers. Marnie saw one of the skinheads turning the paddle with a convulsive jerking movement, but the others had now vanished. She dropped into the cabin and pulled on her wet weather gear. In moments she was back on deck, ready to drive *Sally Ann* out of the lock. The skinhead was no longer at the paddle. The windlass hung on the spindle and the rain lashed down.

Marnie stood for some seconds taking in the new situation. The threat from the skinheads had passed, at least for a while, but she was still stuck. The rain was beating down like a tropical storm and *Sally Ann* began to move around in the lock, slipping back towards the gate. Marnie automatically took hold of the rope that was attached to the bollard and held the boat steady. It dawned on her that something was not quite as it should be.

The noise of the rain hammering on the roof was incredible. In the distance, thunder rolled again. Surrounded by sound and spray, Marnie held the rope firmly to stop *Sally Ann* drifting further back. But why was the boat drifting backwards? There could be no wind in a lock chamber this deep. Enlightenment came. The skinhead had partly opened one of the paddles.

Slowly, the level of water was rising. An age went by as the boat inched upwards. Gradually they rose to where Marnie could see over the side of the lock. The rainswept country was deserted. Soon she would be able to open one of the gates and bring *Sally Ann* out at last. She was leaning into the cabin to turn on the fuel pump when a sound made her freeze. Were the skinheads back?

There it was again. But it came from bushes on the opposite bank, away to her right. Marnie started the engine, secured *Sally Ann* on the bollard and ran to push open the gate. Behind her, the diesel was a faint throbbing, barely audible in the storm. As Marnie heaved on the balance beam, she heard the cry. She scanned the whole area. The only structure in sight was a brick shed, about thirty yards or so back along the cut on her side. With the rain easing off, Marnie accelerated out into the channel, crossing to the far side.

'Hallo-o-o-o!' *Sally Ann* drifted in neutral, the engine idling. 'Hallo-o-o-o!'

In seconds came a reply, a high, frail cry. Marnie nosed *Sally* into the bank, swung the tiller to bring the stern in and quickly tied up to two saplings, fore and aft. She set off towards the cluster of bushes standing some way back from the canal. At her first step the storm erupted again. Lightning slashed across the sky and the rain fell harder than ever.

Marnie struggled forward in the mud against the downpour while thunder crashed. Despite the weatherproof clothes, her face was soaked, rain was running down her neck inside the oilskins. Her trainers turned instantly from white to brown and her feet were drenched.

'Hallo-o-o-o!'

She reached the bushes, tripped and half sprawled into a tangle of branches. Thunder and lightning crashed again almost together. *What the hell am I doing out here?* Marnie got to her feet, at once hearing a sudden sound on her left, like an animal moving in the bushes. Wary of plunging into an unknown situation, she hesitated. Thunder roared and a blast of wind blew her sideways.

'Damn!'

The exclamation startled Marnie, a light voice barely audible between thunder and wind. She knelt down and peered under the nearest bush.

'Hallo!' she called and waited. Twigs lashed at her face. 'Hallo!'

'Is someone there?' The voice was incredulous, petulant.

Marnie found a gap like the entrance to an igloo and crawled through the opening. Facing her, lying on the wet ground, was an old lady in anorak and tweed skirt, mud-stained and soaked. She stared at Marnie.

'Where have you come from?'

The question sounded like an accusation. Marnie wondered bizarrely if the woman was a retired school teacher.

'I was on the canal ... I thought I heard a call.'

'You certainly did.'

The scene was ridiculous, the two of them squatting under a bush in a thunder storm, making conversation. The old woman winced.

'Are you hurt?'

'Of course I'm hurt. I'm not lying here for fun. I've twisted my ankle. I fell over some damn' roots while I was trying to shelter.'

Marnie crawled forward to look. The ankle was swollen and she loosened the laces on the walking boot. 'It looks like a bad sprain. Do you think it could be broken?'

'It wouldn't surprise me.'

Marnie eased the sides of the boot away from the injury. 'It doesn't look too good.'

'It'll look even worse if you remove the only form of support for my ankle.' She spoke breathlessly, pausing between blasts of wind and thunder. 'I suggest you do up those laces so that the ankle is strapped. I'll be able to move more easily if my foot isn't flapping around uselessly.'

'You won't be able to walk like this.'

'What else am I going to do ... take up residence here?'

Marnie shook her head slowly. The storm was still raging. She tugged off her sou'wester and made to put it on the old woman's head.

'No! You keep it on. There's no point in both of us being soaked through. Someone has to be fit to get about.'

As the younger of the two, the rescuer, Marnie had the idea she should be the one taking the decisions, as she did at work. Now, she could do nothing right. She had the feeling she was in the presence of someone who knew about action.

'How far away is your boat?'

'It's just over there.'

Marnie indicated the rough direction as a huge clap of thunder shook the air. Her companion made no reaction, lying back on her elbows, working things out, with beads of water on her face.

'It looks as if I'm stuck for the time being.' She sounded impatient.

Marnie admired her spirit. There was no self-pity, no complaint, except about Marnie, and no apparent fear. Even lying in this rough shelter, spattered with mud, she had an air of dignity. She was undefeated. Marnie leaned towards her.

The old woman frowned. 'What are you doing?'

Marnie reached round her head, fumbling. 'Just a moment.' She opened a flap at the back of the anorak and pulled out a hood. 'There. That's better than nothing.'

The woman blinked at Marnie from under the hood. For a moment it seemed she might complain again. 'I'd forgotten about that ... other things on my mind. Yes. You're right ... better than nothing.'

'Are you in much pain?'

'Better not to think about it.' She spoke quietly. 'Let's just concentrate on getting out of this.'

'Yes.'

'Iris Winterburn.'

'Marnie Walker.' She smiled faintly, not wishing to impose on such independence.

Another flash of lightning. Marnie counted the seconds in her head, as she had done since childhood. She had reached five when the thunder crashed at the same time as Iris Winterburn spoke.

'I'm sorry. I couldn't hear you … the thunder.'

'Oh, it was nothing. I just said *Blitz*.'

'*Blitz?*'

'It's the German word for lightning.'

'Oh, yes, of course. Did you teach German, perhaps?'

'No, I didn't teach German. All my generation knew that word … and a few others.'

The rain was falling as hard as ever, and Marnie was trying to work out a plan, but there seemed no way of escaping through the storm.

The old lady read her thoughts. 'We seem to be stuck here for a while.'

'Can I make you more comfortable?'

'*More* comfortable! That's a joke.' She sighed and laughed simultaneously. 'I don't suppose you have a cigarette?' Marnie shook her head. The old lady looked around, still propped up on her elbows. 'It was like this the last time I was here.'

'When was that?'

'1944, I think, or forty-five. Of course, that was long after the Blitz. We were bringing coal down from Derbyshire to Rickmansworth. It was that day when the Luftwaffe bombed the railway yards at Wolverton and Rugby.' She smiled a pale smile. 'Sorry. You're not interested in an old woman's stories of the war.'

'Yes, I am. What happened?'

'Nothing much. Nothing out of the ordinary. Several of the bombers could not get near their targets … Ack-ack, Spitfires, Hurricanes, you know. So they dropped their bombs where they could. They were falling all over the place. One of the girls thought they'd seen the water and the boats and tried to get us. We were worried they'd breach the banks and wreck the canal.'

'Weren't you worried about yourselves?'

She shrugged and winced. 'We were used to it. We just wanted to get our load through.'

More lightning. Marnie counted to ten before the thunder came.

'I don't seem to have much luck when I come here,' Iris Winterburn said.

'Do you believe in luck?' Marnie was beginning to have doubts.

'You get to believe in all sorts of things when people are constantly trying to drop bombs on your head.'

A weariness was creeping into the old lady's voice, and Marnie wished she could get her to shelter. She had a flashback to old war films, with bombers over Britain. She saw the markings on the aircraft, the black and white cross on the fuselage, the swastika on the tailplane. The thunder was rolling again like a wave of bombers. She could see the pilot at one end and the swastika at the other, that strange hooked shape. The image registered in her mind. *Yes!*

'Yes what?' said the old lady.

Marnie was not aware she had spoken out loud. 'Will you be all right if I leave you for a few minutes?'

'Well, I'm hardly planning to run away!'

'There's something I must do. I'll not be long.'

Marnie backed out of the bushes. Nearby was the comforting sight of *Sally Ann* waiting quietly at her mooring, a safe haven herself, if only she could get the old lady on board.

———〰———

Stalker pushed himself as deep as he could in among the trees. The rain was bucketing down, thrown about by gusting wind. The noise was unbelievable.

Peering out to assess the situation, he was amazed to see a boat beyond the lock on the far side of the canal pointing north. He could scarcely believe his eyes. Just as he was looking out, a skinhead emerged briefly from the shed. Stalker ducked quickly back, his mind racing.

Was that the boat he was pursuing? The colours could be right. *Find a lonely spot*, Gravel had said. It didn't come much lonelier than this.

———〰———

Marnie cast off, catching a glimpse of Dolly's face at the window as she ran past. Fleetingly she realised the foolishness of what she was about to do, but put it aside. There was no choice. Like the *Idle Women* in the war, she just had to get on with it and finish the job.

The rain was soaking her face in the pelting wind as she reversed *Sally* towards the bollards by the lock. She left the engine running and ran back down the towpath, slithering on mud and pebbles as she reached the little brick stable. She peered into the gloom inside. It smelt of damp and mice. In the corner something stirred.

'Is anyone there?' Marnie shouted.

'Yeah.' It was a young man's voice, rough and ugly. He came forward, a skinhead, a nasty bit of work, his ears thick with rings and on his forehead a tattooed swastika.

'Where are the others?'

'Wha' uvvers?'

'Your ... mates.'

'Dunno ... scarpered.'

This must have been the one who tried to open the lock paddles. Marnie was not sure if this was a good or a bad sign, but she had not time to care.

'Come on! I need help!'

She turned to go. The skinhead did not move.

'There's an old lady injured in the bushes. She may have broken her ankle. I can't lift her on my own. You've got to help me!'

He seemed to be sizing her up. The thunder rumbled again. Marnie lunged forward and grabbed him by the shoulder.

'I haven't got all bloody day! Move yourself!'

To Marnie's surprise, he did. They stumbled back up the towpath in the rain. Passing the lock, the skinhead grabbed the windlass and brandished it at Marnie. She thought he was going to hit her.

''Ere. You left this.'

Marnie took it, dropped it on the deck, and cast off. She had no weatherproof clothing that would fit Skinhead, but she grabbed a sou'wester and thrust it onto his shaved head. He grunted a protest but left it in place.

On the opposite bank Marnie tied up again and was urging Skinhead forward when an enormous peal of thunder stopped them both dead.

———

Stalker wished he was anywhere but among those trees, miles from civilisation. Sodden from head to foot, he wondered if the storm was the end of the world.

He could imagine his quarry sitting snug and comfortable in her boat with a cup of tea, beyond his reach on the opposite bank. He looked out. The boat was still there. At that moment, an enormous clap of thunder made him jump so hard he nearly lost his balance. He suddenly realised that he was sheltering under a tree … in a thunderstorm.

One unlucky thunderbolt and he would be a crisp … smoky bacon and mud flavour. He legged it for the shed and was relieved to find it empty.

———

Marnie dragged Skinhead through mud and water, fearing for the old lady. She crawled first into the gap in the bushes.

'Are you all right?'

Iris Winterburn opened her eyes. 'Well, I'm still here.'

'I've brought help.' Marnie reached behind her for Skinhead. 'This, er … young man will help me carry you to the boat.'

The sou'wester had slipped down over his face and, as the 'young man' pulled it back, Iris Winterburn beheld her saviour. She saw the swastika tattoo and glanced at Marnie.

'What sort of boat do you have … a U-boat?'

Marnie thought it might be tactless to say this was the best she could do. Skinhead looked blank.

Marnie crawled forward. 'Let's try and get you out of here.'

The rescuers each put an arm round the old lady's shoulders and Marnie supported her legs. They shuffled on their knees, inch by inch until they got her out into the rain, and stood up slowly. The incongruous trio made steady progress across the muddy ground. The most awkward manoeuvre was manhandling the injured woman through the cabin doors and down the steps.

'Don't put me on the bed!' Iris Winterburn barked. 'I'll ruin it and you'll have nowhere to sleep. Put me on the floor.'

Marnie's protests were dismissed with a toss of the head, so she pulled a blanket from the locker, while the old lady balanced on one foot, held upright by Skinhead.

Marnie spread the blanket on top of the bed. 'Come on. No nonsense. I can't possibly put you on the floor.'

They lowered her gently until she lay back with a sigh. Marnie knew what the next step should be.

'I'll put the kettle on.' She began tugging off her waterproofs.

'Good idea.' Iris Winterburn spoke with eyes closed.

The storm seemed to be passing over, but still the rain was heavy. Marnie was worried about the old lady. They were out of the storm but uncomfortably wet, dripping pools of water, a long way from medical help. While the water heated, Marnie fetched towels and began drying the old lady's face and hair. She eased off the sodden anorak and folded a large bath towel to make a pillow under her head.

Iris Winterburn let Marnie ease the boot off the good foot and sat up to watch when she turned her attention to the injured ankle. She had an impish face. Marnie could see she must have been a very pretty child and a striking young woman, with a slightly Roman nose, light blue eyes and small, determined chin.

Marnie undid the laces and eased the boot open. Her patient looked on impassively.

'It's quite swollen. Am I hurting you?'

'I've known worse. I don't think it's broken, though at my age these things happen easily.'

Marnie was steadily slipping the boot off when the old lady spoke again. 'Aren't you forgetting your other guest?'

Marnie had forgotten Skinhead. He had taken off the sou'wester and was waiting by the foot of the bed. His black leather jacket and slashed jeans, made an odd contrast with the Liberty curtains.

The old lady laughed. 'You look like Attila the Hun at a vicarage tea party.'

Skinhead looked confused. The kettle started whistling and Marnie went to make tea. She heard her visitors talking. Iris Winterburn called out.

'I suppose you frown on smoking in the cabin?'

'Yes … normally. I don't mind if you really can't do without … just this once.'

'What about alcohol? Do you object to that, too?'

'No, not at all.'

'A drop of Scotch might liven up the tea.'

Marnie poured a dram into one cup and returned with the tea to find Skinhead sitting on the blanket, lighting cigarettes. She sat with them and they drank in silence. The thunder had moved away, but the rain was steady.

'That's better.' The old lady gave Marnie the cigarette. 'I've had enough of that.'

Marnie ran it under the tap and threw it in the bin. 'I'm wondering how we get you to hospital. Where's the nearest?'

'Northampton General, I suppose, but it's a fair distance.'

'The best bet is to get you to the next village.'

'I live there.' Skinhead's voice surprised them.

The idea that Skinhead lived somewhere, perhaps with a family of real people, struck Marnie as novel.

Iris Winterburn looked at him. 'Is there a doctor in your village?'

He shook his shaved head.

Marnie had an idea. 'I could get a taxi to take us in to Northampton.' A sudden thought. 'Are you staying round here?'

'Not anywhere in particular. I'm walking the canal path, staying at B-and-Bs. My car's miles away.'

Marnie eyed the tiny rucksack on the floor. 'You're travelling very light.'

'No, no. My friend Rosemary Gwent has my proper rucksack in her car. She found the going a bit too tough, so she's driven on to the next place south. I was going to meet her there tonight.'

Marnie took a decision. 'I'll get us underway. Are you warm enough?'

'I got a car.' Skinhead again.

'Where is it?' Marnie said.

'In the village.'

'Could you get us to the hospital?'

'Only got two seats.'

'If it's a van, I could go in the back,' Marnie said, thinking, *as long as there's nothing evil lurking there* …

'Sports car.'

Marnie had a vision of Attila driving a Lamborghini along the Promenade des Anglais in Nice. She was deciding to opt for the taxi when Iris Winterburn spoke.

'Would I be able to get in your car?'

Attila grunted. 'Yeah. It's got big doors.'

'And you could get me to the hospital in it?'

'Yeah.'

'What sort of car is it?' Marnie asked.

'Spitfire.'

'*Spitfire?*' The old lady looked amused. 'Sounds promising.'

'I used to have one,' Marnie said. 'They haven't made them for years. Is it very old?'

'Yeah.'

'Taxed and insured?' A hint of suspicion.

'Yeah.' No hint of offence.

The old lady sighed. 'I think it's time we made a move.'

'You want to go in the Spitfire?' Marnie was incredulous.

'If you can load me into it.'

'The doors *are* quite big,' Marnie conceded.

'I learnt to put up with a lot during the war. It doesn't bother me.'

'If you're sure …' Marnie tried not to sound unconvinced.

'It's probably not the first time I've been rescued by a Spitfire.'

———◦———

Stalker shivered. He had a plan worked out apart from one small detail. This was a lonely spot; Marnie was alone on her boat; the storm would keep people away. The only snag was how to make the final move.

A single woman was unlikely to let a complete stranger onto her boat in a remote place like this. And what if she was not alone? What if one or more of the heavy mob from the working boats was travelling with her to handle the locks? He needed to suss out the situation, which meant watching her once she started off again.

He peered out from the shed. The rain immediately struck him full in the face. He wiped his eyes and was horrified to see that the boat had gone. For the next minute he cursed and swore.

The rain was still falling in buckets, but he had to go on. He jerked his jacket zip as high as it would go, yanked the baseball cap firmly onto his head and strode out. He had a foreboding that this was going to end badly.

—◦◦◦—

Marnie needed all her concentration to keep *Sally Ann* on course. The winds were buffeting her in all directions. Raindrops were crashing in waves on the roof. At any other time she would have pulled over.

The countryside was deserted, though once or twice, looking back, Marnie caught sight of a solitary figure plodding along in the far distance. Normally she would have stopped to take him or her on board out of the tempest, but this was an emergency. Mentally she apologised to the walker and gripped the tiller firmly.

Twenty minutes later a church tower came into view. Roofs appeared over the trees, rising up a slight hill against the backdrop of grey and black clouds. Ahead was a bridge and before it on the right bank was a place to moor.

Marnie brought *Sally* in and Skinhead came out on deck.

'How long will it take to get your car?'

'Not long.' He stepped ashore and disappeared into the rain.

Marnie went below and found Iris Winterburn sitting up. Attila had propped her up with pillows.

'Is this the village with the bridge? I stayed here for a while in the war. We had engine trouble … had to wait for spare parts. You're travelling solo?'

'Yes.'

'There were three of us girls in a crew: one to drive the motor, one to steer the butty, one lock-wheeling. Day in, day out.'

'And to think you were known as the *Idle Women*!'

Iris Winterburn stared at her. 'You know about that? Perhaps you know it came from the initials of the Inland Waterways on our badges. Mine's in that bag. Have a look if you want. It's in the zip pocket on the side.'

Marnie took out a small plastic badge, shiny with age. Around the top were the words *National Service* and below that the initials, *IW*.

'I got that when I began my training at Marsworth … *Maffers*, the boat people called it.'

'And you've carried it with you ever since?'

'Good heavens no! I came across it in a drawer a few weeks ago … haven't seen it for years. I've got no time for sentiment.'

Marnie zipped the badge back in its pocket. 'It must have been strange to come and work on the canals.'

Iris Winterburn shrugged. 'Learning to handle two seventy-footers carrying fifty tonnes … that's no joke. But other women were driving lorries and buses. We all had the same perfume – not Dior … diesel.'

There was a rumble like distant thunder. It continued rolling and seemed to be getting closer.

Marnie looked towards the window. 'Do you think that could be …?'

Her guest nodded. 'That's what I was thinking.'

A car drew up by the towpath. It was worse than Marnie had feared. The Triumph Spitfire's orange paintwork had dulled with age and was decorated with an iron cross design on the door and an American Confederate flag painted on the bonnet. A furry tail hung limp and sodden from the radio aerial. The horn blasted out the first notes of *Colonel Bogey*.

Marnie and Skinhead supported Iris Winterburn out onto the stern deck where she regarded the car dispassionately.

'Did you say you used to have one of these?' she said to Marnie.

'Well, er, yes … sort of … not quite so …'

They stood in the rain for a few moments.

Marnie chewed her lip. 'Perhaps … we ought to phone for an ambulance, after all. It would probably be –'

A dismissive gesture. 'We've got transport. Our friend's car will be fine.'

Our friend!

'Well, if you're –'

'Come on. Let's make a move.'

Attila had been right about the doors. They were long and opened wide, and it was no problem to slide the patient into the passenger seat. Her rucksack fitted neatly in the space behind. Skinhead climbed in and the Idle Woman wound the window down.

'I think this is going to be an interesting experience.' Drops of rain were splashing her face, but she ignored them.

'Are you reasonably comfortable?'

'Sublime.'

She turned away to speak with Attila. When she turned back, she had a cigarette between her lips.

Marnie raised an eyebrow. 'I think he likes you.'

'I knew my luck would change.'

Before she could say another word, the car accelerated away. *Colonel Bogey* rang out in the rainy afternoon as they bounced over the bridge, and Marnie heard the raucous engine growling its way up the hill through the village. Soon it had disappeared like fading thunder.

Stalker was grateful for the tree, even though it offered little protection. He had been filled with dismay when *Sally Ann* reached a village and pulled into the bank. She could decide to stay there overnight. He huddled under the sparse canopy, about fifty yards from the bridge, and sneezed loudly. The sound was covered by the downpour. Perhaps his luck was changing.

He shrank back when someone came out of the boat and loped off as if on a mission. One of the skinheads; this was incredible. First, the working boats, now the skinheads … they were in cahoots! This was no chance stop-over. They had come here deliberately for a purpose. What was going on? Back at the lock when he had first seen them, they must have been waiting for Marnie. Why had Gravel not warned him about this? The answer was simple. Gravel did not know.

He sneezed again. Again the sound was camouflaged, this time by the strains of *Colonel Bogey*. Stalker wondered if he was hallucinating. There was the skinhead again, bounding onto the boat as if he was part of the crew. Stalker pulled back, soaked through to his bone marrow.

He risked another look. Now, there was a group of them on the deck. In the rain, it was like looking through a net curtain, and a vast striped umbrella hid them from view. Could this be another handover?

Stalker was beginning to realise how perfect the canals were for criminal activities. They went everywhere, but were invisible most of the time. The boats were slow, but they could travel day and night. Stick a few tubs of pansies on the roof and they looked as innocent as Little Red Riding Hood.

Another look. He heard an engine revving, powerful and throaty like a getaway car, tyres biting into a gravelly road surface. There was *Colonel Bogey* again. These people were so confident, they didn't care who heard them.

He tried to make sense of it all. Working boats … all those crewmen … skinheads … meeting places … the canal network … remote country. He had never thought of the possibilities before, could not work out if he had hit upon an amazing truth or was rambling because he was getting feverish from exposure.

He wondered how many were on board *Sally Ann*. He would have to watch and wait. His next sneeze was not covered by the rainfall, but he was past caring.

———⟨⟨⟨———

Marnie stood the golf umbrella to drip in the shower tray. It had been a day of strange encounters. She had never expected to mix with war veterans and skinheads.

Suddenly an imaginary conversation came into her mind, a police officer asking questions and taking notes.

'This injured lady, Mrs Walker. How did you arrange for her to receive medical treatment?'

Marnie explained. The policeman licked his pencil.

'Just let me get this straight, Mrs Walker. You handed over this *elderly* lady to a *skinhead* with a *sports car* to take her to some hospital that you *think* was the Northampton General. What was the name of this skinhead?'

She did not know, but he was known affectionately as … *Attila*.

'Can you describe the skinhead, Mrs Walker?'

She did. The policeman checked his notes.

'I see. He had several rings attached to his person, and a *swastika tattoo* on his forehead. Is that right?'

She confirmed it was.

'Can you describe the car? Did you notice its number plate?'

She gave a description.

'So … an *orange* sports car decorated with an *iron cross* to match his *swastika tattoo*. I think we're getting somewhere. Tell me, Mrs Walker, do you think that was very wise? I mean, would you have taken that course of action with your own grandmother?'

Marnie shuddered. Outside, the rain was still falling. Inside, she surveyed the scene. There was the mud-stained blanket lying in a heap on the bed and wet patches on the floor. There was the stale smell of smoke in the air. Cups and saucers littered every surface. The whole place looked as if a bomb had hit it.

Stalker checked his watch. Nearly twenty minutes had passed since the last movement on *Sally Ann*. Decision time. With heavy cloud cover, an early dusk was coming down. If the boat was going to stay there all night, it was a no-go, too conspicuous. If there were no developments in ten minutes, he would have to begin the trek back to the car. The rain was falling steadily. He sneezed again.

After ten minutes Stalker moved off and had gone barely twenty paces when the boat's rear doors swung open. A hooded figure came on deck as the engine clanked into life. Marnie was alone. She untied the mooring ropes, glanced over her shoulder and in seconds the boat was gliding under the bridge. He waited a few minutes and began to follow.

The map had shown a lock not far up the cut. He was closing in.

Despite the rain Marnie was glad to be on the move again. With the boat tidied, she was running with cratch and stern doors half open to clear the smell of cigarette smoke. She wanted nothing more than to find a quiet mooring, prepare supper, enjoy a glass of wine, listen to some music and have an early night.

Glancing back, she wondered briefly what had become of the solitary towpath-walker. A quarter of an hour later she found her quiet spot, tied up and went below, pulling the doors together to shut out the wet evening. She switched on the heating, lit the oil lamps and drew the curtains.

Corelli chamber music was playing as she turned up the lamp wicks, boiled water for rice and opened a jar of mild korma sauce. A glass of chilled *sauvignon blanc* fortified her while she chopped a red pepper, shallots, courgettes and aubergine. Civilisation had returned to the Grand Union. With two pans on the cooker, she took a sip of wine and had a pang of conscience. The stern gland!

She pulled out a jacket from the locker. Reaching into the shower-room, she grabbed the golf umbrella, pushed open the doors, thrust out the umbrella and snapped it open with a flourish. She heard movement on the towpath: a gasp, an expletive, a swishing sound, a muffled plop. A man lay sprawled in the mud. He sneezed loudly.

Marnie held out a helping hand.

'I've been wondering about you. You'd better come aboard.'

Stunned, wary and shivering, Stalker clambered onto the deck and went below, relieved to find no welcoming heavy mob or gang of skinheads. He turned to speak, sneezed again and passed out.

Marnie contemplated the man lying in a heap on the saloon floor.

This seems to be my day for rescuing orphans of the storm.

28
Envelope

The storm had blown itself out in the night. Marnie awoke the next morning to stillness peppered with birdsong. The landscape looked as if it had been rinsed and hung on the line to dry in the pale sunshine. A haze hung over the countryside. It reminded Marnie of a line from *The Shepherd's Calendar* by John Clare.

The village sleeps in mist from dawn till noon ...

She took the boat through the first lock of the day and returned to find her guest sitting on the gas bottle container. He looked crumpled and miserable.

'Good morning.' Bright but not too breezy, she hoped.

He croaked in reply.

Marnie went below and came back a couple of minutes later with a mug of Lemsip, a remedy against colds. On her next appearance she draped a blanket round his shoulders. He was halfway through the Lemsip when she came up on deck with toast and coffee. The man looked at the tray and winced.

Marnie breakfasted in silence while the visitor gradually revived. He blinked in her direction, which she took as a good sign. She spoke quietly.

'You're on the narrowboat *Sally Ann* somewhere in Northamptonshire. It's about seven-thirty. You came aboard last evening and passed out. You spent the night on the floor under the blanket that you're now wearing. That's the story so far.'

The man nodded.

'Oh yes, and my name's Marnie Walker.'

The man cleared his throat. 'You said something ... last night ... when you saw me ...'

'I do things like that ... say something when I meet someone ... it's a sort of habit.'

'You were expecting we'd meet ... something like that.'

'Well, I'd seen you – or someone – walking the towpath. I couldn't stop. I had an injured old lady on board ... I needed to get her to hospital.'

'What about the skinheads?'

'You saw them?'

'Yeah.'

'There was one skinhead on board ... helping me with the old lady.'

'You usually mix with skinheads?'

'Skinheads and old ladies, yes. I collect them. It's a hobby.'

He frowned.

She laughed. 'Sorry, I'm being flippant.'

'So where are they now?'

'Good question ... hospital, I think ... I hope.'

He drained the Lemsip. 'You've got plans?'

'Not really ... just cruising ... a sort of extended holiday.'

'Where d'you start off from?'

'Little Venice. That's in London, but you must know that.'

'Why must I know it?'

'You sound like a Londoner. Could you manage a cup of coffee now?'

'Yeah.'

'Now it's my turn to ask questions.' The man looked suspicious. 'What are we going to do with you?'

'*We?*' More suspicious.

'A manner of speaking. Presumably you'll need a hot bath and a change of clothing. I can't provide those.' Marnie stood up. 'But I can provide coffee.'

Alone on deck, Stalker tried to work Marnie out. Was she as straight as she seemed or was she boxing clever? Was she confident and relaxed because she had back-up? She certainly looked relaxed enough when she returned.

'I've got an idea.'

'What d'you have in mind?' A croak.

'A road crosses the canal by a pub about a mile further on. We could get you a taxi from there.'

He hesitated. Marnie sensed a problem.

'Do you have money?' she asked.

'Money?'

'I could lend you some, if that would ... you know ...'

'*Lend* me some?

'Sure. You could pay me back later.'

'How ... how could I get it to you?'

She reached into her back pocket. 'Here's my business card. That's my office in London.'

'You're actually offering me money?'

'Just enough to get you where you need to be. Please don't be embarrassed.'

He looked at the address on the card. 'No. it's all right ... thanks. I'm fine.'

'You're sure?'

'Yeah ... I'm sorted.'

Gary was on his way to see a man about a job but gave himself an extra ten minutes for a diversion. He was the shop's first customer that morning. A figure emerged from behind the pharmacy partition at the rear to meet him, but not the figure he expected.

'Can I help you?' Auburn hair, glossy lips, brown eyes. Nice. But not Sheena.

'Where's Sheena?'

The assistant glanced back over her shoulder. Gary studied the display of toothpaste.

'I er, need a tube of er ...' He picked one up at random and looked sideways at the girl. Lowering his voice he murmured, 'Is Sheena in?'

'No, not this morning.'

'What d'you mean she's not in this morning?'

'This morning's now, right?'

'Yeah.'

'Well, she's not here. That's what I mean. She rang in sick.'

'Sick?'

A cough from the pharmacy. The girl raised her voice. 'Will that be all, sir?'

Gary scowled and walked out of the shop leaving her holding the toothpaste. He pulled the mobile out of his jeans pocket and pressed buttons. A distant voice spoke to him.

The number you are phoning is not available, please try later.

He was crossing the road when he realised he did not have a home phone number for Sheena or even her address. She was out of reach. His pace faltered momentarily. Behind him a car honked a warning.

———※———

After the taxi had left, Marnie sat in the saloon, deep in thought about the towpath rambler. Had he really been just out walking and got caught in the storm? Where was he going? Why? That was the problem: she had a bucketful of questions, but no answers.

It had been an ordeal to act naturally and make polite conversation. Two things bothered her: the stranger had had plenty of questions of his own; he knew much more about her than would have been apparent to a casual observer. He had seen her with the working boats; he had seen her with the skinheads; he had seen her alone yesterday evening.

Could he really have been watching her for days? Marnie could think of no reason why he should. She was about to dismiss the idea as absurd when she remembered Anne's second message on the answerphone.

A man was asking about a boat called Sally Ann …

———※———

Old Peter had rounded Browning Island and was pointing the grey-green boat towards Maida Hill tunnel when he saw Gary hurrying along the towpath looking preoccupied. He seemed less relaxed these days. Someone was causing him grief. He had seen Gary with his latest girlfriend. Girls could always cause grief, especially that sort, blonde, flighty, skirts too short to keep out the draught.

But was she the problem? Why was Gary so worried? Why was he looking for Marnie? Lots of questions, the old man thought. One simple answer.

He steered past the boat called *Rumpole*, which he knew belonged to a solicitor. He had often seen him pottering about, glass of wine in hand. Some of the windows were open, which meant he was there that afternoon. At the end of the line of boats *Sally Ann's* mooring was empty. The old man lined up for the bank. He had reached a decision.

———※———

Marnie needed a quiet morning after the storm to finish tidying the boat. She pulled onto one of the pub's moorings and, as soon as it opened, she went in to use the payphone.

'General Hospital.'

'Can you put me through to casualty, please.'

'One moment.'

'Accident and emergency. Staff nurse Andrews speaking.' A trim, Scottish voice.

'Hallo. I'm phoning to enquire about an elderly lady who came to you yesterday with an injured ankle.'

'Her name?'

'Iris Winterburn.'

A pause. 'Are you a relative?'

'Well, no, not actually. I'm the person who found her … in a field by the canal. I got her onto my boat.'

Another pause. 'Are you related to the, er, person who brought the patient in?'

'No.' Marnie tried to sound emphatic. 'I'd never met him before.'

'We don't give information about patients except to relatives, normally.'

'I'm just concerned about her. I wanted to be sure she was okay, that's all.'

Silence.

'Are you there? Look, I'm sorry if the skinhead gave you any trouble, but I would really like to know –'

'The *skinhead*? He was no trouble at all. He wouldn't leave her side all the time she was here.'

'Then what's the problem?'

Hesitation. '*She* was the problem. She told us we were doing it all wrong and we wouldn't survive five minutes in a real emergency.'

Marnie groaned. 'Have you admitted her?'

'Oh, no! She allowed us to put a tubigrip on her ankle – it was a bad sprain – and then she insisted on discharging herself into the custody of her friend … *Attila*.'

'*Attila?*'

'That's what she called him.'

'Where is she now?'

'No idea. The last we saw of her, she was being pushed down the corridor in a wheelchair by Attila. She was asking him if he knew what *wheelies* were.'

Marnie thought that on balance that was a good sign, at least in the circumstances. She thanked staff nurse Andrews and hung up, wondering whether it was the patient or the nurse who deserved her sympathy.

———— ⚞⚟ ————

Stalker was up to his neck in hot water. He took a slug of hot toddy, lay back and closed his eyes. A double measure of bath salts had produced foam like deep snow, but he could not smell a thing. He sneezed and blew a gap in the froth like an Inuit's fishing hole. It was positively the last time he would ever attempt to follow anyone on a canal boat.

When he had reported back to his client he had described his results in the best light.

'I hope this is good news.' The voice like gravel.

'I got her.'

'Did you get her to talk?'

'Piece o' cake.'

'And?'

'She knows nothing.'

'I need to be sure of that.'

'Guaranteed. She's not carrying anything, not hiding anything, doesn't know anything.'

'She could be lying.'

'I searched the boat when I got her out of the way.'

Alarm. 'You took her out? Was that necessary?'

'A diversionary tactic. I didn't think you wanted her … taken out.'

'No. But you got her talking.'

'Oh yes. In the end she was offering me money.'

Gravel chuckled. 'I bet you really hung her out to dry, eh?'

Stalker winced at the choice of words. 'In a manner of speaking.'

He took another slug of the toddy. If he had had a conscience it would have troubled him.

------~~~------

Roger Broadbent took the afternoon off to do some odd jobs on the boat. He was in the galley on *Rumpole*, turning the corkscrew in a promising bottle of Australian Chardonnay when he heard the knock. He was convinced that some of his boating neighbours were equipped with radar when it came to wine. Still holding the bottle, he pushed open one of the doors with his free hand. For a few moments he could not believe what he saw.

Old Peter was standing on the footpath in flat cap and shirtsleeves, the bowl of a pipe protruding from the top pocket of his dungarees. He did not speak.

Roger quickly regained his composure. 'Ah, it's er … er, won't you come in?'

'Uh-huh.' With surprising agility for his age and bulk, Old Peter stepped onto the gunwale, swivelled and reversed down the steps into the galley.

'Er … can I offer you a glass of wine, perhaps?'

'No thanks.' Old Peter reached into his top pocket, pulled out an envelope and held it in front of him. Roger took it. There was no writing on it, front or back, no name or address, just a plain buff business envelope, sealed down.

'Am I to open it?'

The old man shook his head. 'It is for … Marnie.' He spoke slowly as if weighing each word.

'Marnie? Who is Marnie?'

'*Sally Ann*.'

Roger pondered this information. 'Along by the tunnel? Young woman, dark hair, nice looking, doing up the boat?'

'Yes.'

'What do you want me to do?'

'You are a solicitor?'

'That's right.'

'Keep that safe and give it to her.'

The obvious question was: why not give it to her himself? Roger realised that *Sally Ann* had not been at her mooring for a while.

'Is this a legal matter?'

Old Peter looked serious. 'It is not illegal.'

Roger suppressed a smile. 'I mean, is it a legal document ... like a will, for example, or something of that sort?'

'Not exactly.'

Roger could feel there was more than one sheet of paper inside. 'Does it contain any money?'

'No.'

'Are you aware that some types of document need to be witnessed?'

'Not that one.'

'I see.' He did not see. 'So you just want me to keep a lookout for ... er, Marnie – do you know her surname?'

'Walker.' He answered without hesitation. 'She is Marnie Walker ... of *Sally Ann*.' He made it sound like an official endorsement of her status as a boatman.

Roger repeated the name as he picked up a pencil and wrote it – the whole title – on the envelope. 'Okay. I'll make sure she gets it as soon as she returns. What should she do with it? Is there any other message ... anything else I should tell her?'

'She will decide.'

'Is it urgent? Do you want me to try to get her phone number and ring her, perhaps?'

'No.'

'You can't give it to her yourself?'

'She will understand.'

Roger looked at the envelope. 'I see.' For the second time he did not see. 'This is important, isn't it?'

'It is important to me.'

———— ∞ ————

Marnie ordered coffee and sat in the saloon bar. She wanted to use the pub's moorings for a while and felt guilty at taking up space without buying anything. The barman arrived with her cup.

'Did you want sugar?'

'No thanks. Do you have a payphone?'

'In the hall over there. Do you need change?'

'No. I, er ... I want to ask you a favour ... two, actually.'

'Try me.'

'I need to call my sister in America.'

'The phone takes credit cards as well as cash.'

'Good, but the favour is … I can't phone her until some time this afternoon.'

'Time zones … yeah. So you want to stay on our mooring.'

'Would that be possible?'

'What are you doing for lunch?'

'Eating here.'

'Then you're a customer. No problem. Did you say two favours?'

'I don't suppose there's any chance I could put my mobile on charge?'

The barman held out a hand. 'Give it here. How long?'

'An hour or two, max.'

The barman left with the phone and charger but returned a minute later carrying a newspaper.

Marnie smiled. 'That's kind of you.'

'Try page seven … bottom of the page.'

She found the article under the heading, *Canal Tunnel Closure.*

British Waterways have temporarily closed the Ashted tunnel in Birmingham following reports of cracks in the roof lining. A spokesman regretted the inconvenience and hoped the tunnel would soon re-open. 'It's a bad time for this to happen in the middle of the holiday season. Boaters should expect some congestion.' A similar problem caused the closure of the two-mile long Blisworth tunnel for four years in the early 1980's.

Marnie knew the Ashted tunnel was on her planned route. There were other ways through Birmingham, but the thought of queuing at locks in the shadow of Dickensian factories was not appealing. The cruising guide had given an ominous warning: *a risk of vandalism.* Perhaps the congestion was because the boats would be travelling in convoys with destroyer escort.

She returned to the boat for a council of war with Dolly. After a lengthy and one-sided discussion, a change of plan was agreed. The BCN and the Llangollen Arm were dropped in favour of Oxford and the Thames.

Marnie reported the news later that afternoon when she dialled Boston and spoke with Beth, who seemed surprised that Marnie was still travelling on *Sally Ann.*

'Beth, it's *your* plans I'm more concerned about. Paul's sabbatical … what's happening?'

A sigh. 'It's the old story. Government funding cuts. They have to make economies. The guy covering for Paul is one of them, so we have to come back early.'

'Is Paul's job secure?'

'For now, but he can forget about promotion. We'd stay here permanently given half a chance.'

'Is that possible?'

'Not at present, at least not for a tenured post.' Beth mentioned the names of Paul's colleagues whose positions were 'under review'.

'*Under review* doesn't sound too bad.'

'It's a euphemism, Marnie. At universities they only ever use words that sound harmless. Say *the department is going to close* and they dismiss it as a rumour. Say it's *under review* and they know they're dead flesh.'

Marnie spent the evening reading the cruising guides and every article she could find in the old magazines about the South Oxford Canal and the river Thames. On balance, she thought it was a good decision. Like so many decisions that summer, it would change her life.

29
Blisworth tunnel

Wednesday morning, and Marnie awoke to the stirrings of the country. Somewhere in the distance a sheep was bleating. Others followed in an erratic chorus. A few birds singing. A random cow.

She reached up for the alarm clock. Just after five, much earlier than she thought, but she was wide awake, the day was bright and it was time to move on. Oxford beckoned. She thought of 'dreaming spires', bookshops, art galleries, museums, bistros. After that, the home run via the Thames.

With a muted warbling, Dolly leapt up onto the duvet. Marnie stroked velvety ears and heard the purring start up. It was a summons. The day had officially begun.

Once underway, Marnie worked steadily up the Stoke Bruerne flight with a clear head and energy revived. It was still early when they glided gently past the sleeping craft lined up through the village.

Trees crowded in on both sides as Marnie accelerated to cruising speed, approaching the entrance to Blisworth tunnel. It seemed strange pulling on a waterproof jacket over a jumper on a fine summer morning. There was warmth in the sun, but Marnie dutifully followed the advice in the guide book.

Dolly appeared on deck, licking her whiskers and sniffing the air. She jumped nimbly onto the roof and took up her customary position on the hatch. With collar turned up, Marnie flicked on the headlamp as the entrance to the tunnel loomed ahead in the hillside. Suddenly, Dolly stopped in mid-lick, sat up straight and stared towards the bows. Seconds later she hopped down and disappeared below. The air at the mouth of the tunnel had turned icy cold.

Marnie zipped the jacket up to her chin as the bows entered the portal, thinking of her first run through the tunnel in Little Venice an age ago. Nosing through darkness, the note from the engine echoed around her. She found it hard to steer a straight course, despite the headlamp, and even harder to believe men had actually *legged* it in times past, walking against the sides of the tunnel, while the horses were led over the top along the bridleway.

At intervals, air vents let down a pool of pale daylight. Marnie tried to look up one of them to gain an impression of the depth of the tunnel, but had to leap aside to avoid a shower from the opening. In that sudden loss of concentration, *Sally Ann* veered over and clouted the wall with a resounding clang. Marnie was glad there were no spectators.

Half an hour later they emerged from the gloom, the engine noise diminished and the brightness overwhelmed her. Marnie tugged off the jacket.

'We did it, Dolly!' She took a deep breath. 'You can come out now.'

But Dolly stayed hidden for the rest of the morning.

Gary had spent a restless night. He was not sure if he should be worrying about Sheena or whether this sudden absence was just the first move in the brush-off. Somehow it did not feel like that. Nothing in her behaviour had suggested she wanted to end their relationship. It did not fit in with his past experience, but you could never be quite sure where women were concerned. They were unpredictable. Take that Marnie. She had told him one thing and done the opposite. Totally unreliable. Just like a woman. But he thought he knew Sheena better than that.

He got up and prepared breakfast. It did not take long. With the first drag of the day, breathing the smoke down into his lungs, he was coughing as he filled the kettle. He felt much better.

His mate Brendan was picking him up in the van soon after seven for another fit-out job at Harefield. With any luck he should be back by the end of the afternoon. He might be in time to nip round to the shop and see if Sheena was back.

Gary knew he would be thinking about her all day. He did not like not knowing what was going on. While he was pouring tea he saw the business with Gravel and Old Peter as part of the same picture. The whole situation was unsettling. Now, Gravel had stopped calling on him. Another disappearance. Was there a pattern here? Were they connected? And Marnie? What was her part in it all?

He tried to fathom it out. Sheena … Gravel … Old Peter … Marnie. Four people who had become prominent in his life in the past few weeks. Now three of them had faded from the scene. Just like that.

He slurped hot tea and let his mind settle. Was it so strange? Marnie had worked on the boat and gone on a trip. No mystery, she had just decided to go off after collecting her supplies. No reason why she should not change her mind – she was a woman – and no reason why she should explain her plans to him.

What about Gravel? He came and went. That was what people like Gravel did. They turned up when you least expected them. Such men did not make appointments. But they did expect results. That was what worried Gary. He had nothing to show for his efforts. Excuses did not count. Sooner or later, Gravel would be back. It brought little comfort.

And Old Peter, what was he up to? Those conversations with Marnie … She came from nowhere, and suddenly they were big buddies. How could that be? She was a stranger, supposedly new to the waterways, but somehow managed to get in with a man who lived like a recluse and only knew about boats.

Now that he thought about it, Gary realised something had been bothering him for a while. That time in the tunnel. He thought he would give Marnie a scare, just for a laugh. Instead, she kept the boat straight on course until the last second when she flicked the tiller and bumped him. He was sure it was deliberate and thought, perhaps she fancied him. But could it have been a warning? *Don't mess with me!*

He poured a second cup. The tunnel incident still did not explain her connection with the old man. What if it was totally innocent? She had had a problem with the boat. He helped her. She went round to thank him. Easy. Then why were they still meeting?

They had nothing in common. He was a lonely old bloke who had lived all his life on the cut. She was up-market crumpet. No connection. On the other hand … What if she knew about … *something valuable?* How could she? That was what he had to find out. That was what Gravel wanted.

Gary's thoughts kept coming back to Sheena. Had she been hiding at the back of the shop the day before, or had she really phoned in sick? She had been fine when they had parted the previous day. This did not feel like the heave-ho. He could always tell when that was coming. It usually began with the same questions. Didn't he want a proper place to live? Was he content just to stay on a boat for the rest of his life? Didn't he want a proper job with a regular income?

Outside in the street a car horn sounded twice. Time to get going. Locking the boat, Gary looked at his watch and wondered what time the chemist's closed that evening.

———————

Marnie pulled over for breakfast, slipping in to moor, stern against stern, in a patch of sunshine behind a boat called *Foxcote*. She quickly turned off the engine. To celebrate the passage of the tunnel, she popped two rolls into the oven, put the kettle on and poured a glass of orange juice. She was setting up the folding table on the deck, when the stern door of the next boat opened and a bleary face looked out. A middle-aged woman stifled a yawn and smiled.

'You're up early.'

Marnie smiled back. 'I wanted a clear run at the tunnel.'

'Going far?'

'I was going to Llangollen, but now it's Oxford.'

'That's a lovely trip. Betty Atkins.'

'Marnie Walker. Can I offer you coffee?'

Betty looked over her shoulder. 'Why not? There's no sign of life in there.' Wrapping a dressing gown round herself, she stepped onto the towpath and went aboard *Sally Ann*.

They sat together in warm sunshine, chatting about places to visit. Betty spotted Marnie's sketch pad and camera on the lid of the gas-bottle container.

'Don't mind me asking, but are you an artist?'

'No. I just sketch as I go along.'

'May I?'

Marnie nodded. Betty picked up the pad and began browsing.

'Bridges and locks. My Ken would love these. Before he retired, he was a civil engineer with the county council.'

'Someone taking my name in vain?'

The voice came from behind them. A fleshy face was framed by the stern door on *Foxcote*. Introductions were made. Marnie offered breakfast and it was accepted.

Ken looked slowly through the sketchpad. 'Beautiful bridges … lovely shape.'

'You'd like the Llangollen canal.' Betty pronounced the name with some deliberation. 'The aqueducts are brilliant … Chirk and that other really big one.'

'Pontcysyllte?' said Marnie.

Ken smiled and shrugged. 'We never quite manage the pronunciation, but I admire the engineering.'

'Ah yes … Telford's masterpiece.' Marnie expected ready agreement, but Ken and Betty glanced at each other without a word. 'Er … have I got the wrong engineer?'

Betty leaned forward as if confiding a secret. 'It's a bit of a hobby horse of Ken's.'

'In what way?'

Ken made a dismissive gesture. 'Oh … I don't want to bore you.'

'No, really.' Marnie inclined her head towards the sketchpad. 'I'm interested in that kind of thing … structures … design.' The words brought an earlier conversation to mind.

Ken began hesitantly. 'Well … it's *said* to be Telford's … but he wasn't the *chief* engineer.'

Marnie delved into her memory. 'William Jessop?'

Ken's face lit up. 'Ah … you *do* know about these things.'

'I read about it somewhere … in a magazine, I think.'

Ken was away, explaining about the difference between being in charge of projects and doing the actual design work.

'… so it could be the chief's design or the senior engineer's … difficult to be sure. But sometimes, when I look at the details, I have doubts about whose it really was.'

'But all Jessop's papers have disappeared, haven't they?' Marnie was confused. 'I didn't think it was possible to check his designs.'

'Ah … that's the thing. His papers, plans, drawings … all vanished. And if you read Telford's journals, you could be forgiven for thinking Jessop hadn't even been there.'

Marnie wanted to point out that a lack of evidence was hardly strong enough to make out a case. She held back. 'But despite that, you have suspicions based on …'

There was no need to finish the question. She knew the answer before Ken provided it.

'Every designer has a personal style, points of detail that are there to see if you know where to look.'

'Of course.' Marnie agreed. 'Like a *signature*, written into their design.'

'Exactly! A *signature*.'

'And you see that in the aqueduct at Pontcysyllte, for example?'

Ken pulled a face. 'If I'm really honest …'

Marnie understood. 'Without the papers or some kind of evidence, it's hard to be sure.'

'That's right.'

'But you have your suspicions?'

'Like Betty says, it's become a kind of hobby horse … something I bore people with, given half a chance.'

'You certainly haven't bored me.' Marnie's quick reaction made Ken smile.

'I'm glad about that.'

'It was all a long time ago, anyway.' Betty's motherly tone of voice was intended to bring the discussion to a close.

'Eighteen hundred and five,' Ken confirmed.

'Wasn't that the same year they opened ...?' Marnie gestured with a thumb towards the tunnel.

'Exactly. Men of genius, they were.' Ken turned towards the portal. 'Genius and strong passions.'

—∽∾∽—

Gary was tired of hearing that woman's plummy voice.

The person you are phoning is not available. Please try again later.

He had rung Sheena's mobile at intervals during the day. After the third message he had wanted to lob his phone into the canal.

For once, the journey back into London had been less of a nightmare, and the van had crawled at a steady pace through the late afternoon traffic to deposit Gary by the bridge in Little Venice. Instead of taking the path to *Garrow*, he set off towards the parade of shops. He mooched in the newsagents for five minutes looking at magazines until, on the dot of five-thirty, he spotted activity across the road at the chemist's. Two people appeared in the doorway. It was the first time Gary had seen the pharmacist. The man exchanged a few words with his assistant and went back inside as she walked off down the street.

Gary caught up with the girl before she reached the corner. 'Hi. I was in the shop this morning.'

She barely glanced at him. 'I know. You're Sheena's boyfriend.'

'Is that what she says?'

'I've got eyes.'

'So ... where is she?'

'I told you, she phoned in sick.'

'I'm concerned about her ... can't get a reply from her phone. Do you know where she lives?'

Hesitation. 'Harrow.'

'Harrow? Whereabouts in Harrow?'

The girl shrugged. Gary persisted.

'Can you get her phone number for me?'

They reached the corner of the street. The girl stopped, turned to face Gary and gave him the eyebrow.

'Look, it's not what you're thinking. We haven't had a row or anything. I just really need to speak to her. It's important.'

'You know how it works. We girls stick together. If she wants to talk to you, she'll phone.'

The girl set off again at a quick pace. Gary accelerated to keep up with her.

'But I need to see her.'

'Try her mobile.'

'I've been ringing it all day ... no reply.'

The girl frowned. 'That can't be right. She's always on that mobile.'

'She is?'

'Yeah, always … usually just quick calls.'

'Not when she's at work.'

'Oh, yeah. She pretends she's going to the loo. One day I followed her out the back. She went into the yard. I thought she was going for a quick smoke. But she was on the phone.'

'Who to?'

'How should I know?'

'Couldn't you hear what she was saying?'

'I didn't listen. It was *private*. Anyway the door was shut. I couldn't hear properly. I saw her through the window.'

'How often does she do that?'

'A few times a day.'

This was disturbing. They had reached the tube station. The girl slowed slightly but did not stop.

'Gotta go.'

'Listen –'

'I can't tell you anything else.' She walked towards the steps. 'Keep your mobile on … she'll call you, I expect … when she's ready.'

Gary watched her go. Nothing seemed right. The girl reached the foot of the steps and turned the corner. She did not look back. Not bad legs, Gary thought.

———— ∾∾ ————

Marnie was more than glad to pull over that afternoon. It was a day for sun-block and wide-brimmed hat, with time to let her thoughts wander, thinking about Ken's *men of genius and strong passions*. It fascinated her to think that while Brindley's *navigators* were tunnelling through the hills around her, Jessop's and Telford's men were building a wonder of the world in north Wales.

At lunchtime she called in at the chandlery by Whilton Marina to buy bread. She emerged with a box containing a loaf, butter, eggs, cheese, milk, coffee, magazines, oil and wicks for the lamps, candles, matches, torch batteries, salt and various books, including two about the *Idle Women*.

Wanting somewhere peaceful for a picnic, she watched a Virgin express rocket along the West Coast main line beyond the marina, while lorries jockeyed for position on the motorway behind her. There was nothing for it but to head for the Buckby flight and tackle the climb into the Northamptonshire Uplands.

Two hours were to elapse before Marnie completed the ascent and reached Norton Junction. She pointed *Sally Ann* west under the bridge towards Braunston tunnel. In a lonely stretch, with fields spreading to the horizon, she brought the boat over to the bank and tied up. When she switched off the engine, she became aware of another rumbling. Time to eat.

Marnie dived below, stripped to her skin for a perfunctory wash and donned a bikini. She quickly made a sandwich of salmon and mayonnaise with diced green pepper to liven it up. Settled on the stern deck, she sipped designer water, hearing the faint susurration of the bubbles and the clink of ice cubes. The sun was shining; she had the whole country to herself; all was peace and light.

She did not notice that two pairs of eyes were observing her. A heron was mildly resenting the invasion of her territory by this interloper. Further along the bank a solitary angler had no such objection. It made his day.

As soon as he reached the boat, Gary put his mobile on charge and kept it switched on to receive calls. He took a shower, all the while thinking about Sheena, convinced she was not the kind of person to go into hiding. If she wanted to chuck him, she would just tell him. But what else could it be? Perhaps Sheena had just phoned in sick. Maybe she really was in bed feeling rotten with her mobile switched off.

He came out of the shower and checked the phone: no missed calls, no messages. He thought about the meals they had enjoyed together while he made supper: two fried eggs, four rashers of bacon, fried tomatoes. Over the dessert course – the *Evening Standard* and a cigarette, washed down with a mug of tea – he decided to make enquiries.

The early evening crowd was settled in at the bar when Gary pushed open the doors of the pub. His eyes strayed to one particular table in the far corner. It was unoccupied. He spotted a mate at the bar and walked over.

'Hi, Vince.'

'No.'

It was not the greeting he expected. 'No what? I haven't asked you anything.'

'No to any more jobs with the JCB, Gary. Don't even *think* of asking me.'

'What are you on about? I paid you all right, didn't I?'

'I got in deep schtuck over that.'

'How come?'

'You said it'd be a nice little job, no one'd know about it, I'd have the JCB back at work before anyone even noticed it had gone off site.'

'So?'

'So when we pulled that stiff …' He grimaced. '… *bits* of stiff … out of the pool, it got plastered all over the front page of the bleedin' *Evening Standard*, didn't it?'

'Ah …'

'Too right, Gary. It was on the front page of the *Mirror* and the *Globe*. I was everywhere in the *Sun* apart from page three. It even made the news on telly. My JCB had more viewers that night than *Eastenders*.'

'All right, all right … I wasn't going to ask you to do a job with your precious JCB. I was just going to ask if you'd seen my girlfriend.'

'Which one?'

'Sheena.'

'Is that the blonde bird with the legs up to her –'

'Yes.'

'It's the same answer, then. No.'

Gary looked around the saloon. He could see none of his other mates. The barman came over.

'What'll it be, Gary?'

'I don't suppose you've seen Sheena, my girlfriend?'

'Is that the blonde with the –'

'Yes, yes, the blonde …with the long hair.'

'Not recently, no.'

Vince nudged Gary's elbow. 'There was something else you wanted to ask me.'

'Was there?'

'Yeah … and the answer is, I'll have a pint.'

An hour and three pints later, Gary left the pub. It had not been a bad evening. He had picked up two offers of work, but his enquiries about Sheena had led nowhere. He pressed buttons on the mobile.

The person you are phoning is not –

He silently mouthed a succinct reply to the plummy woman as he cut her off.

30
Braunston tunnel

Marnie liked early starts, avoiding the holiday traffic on the canal. That Thursday morning, with an overcast sky and a heavy dew glinting in the grass, she tugged on a sweater, started the engine and cast off. It was six o'clock and she aimed to navigate the Braunston tunnel before the world was stirring. The plan almost worked.

Entering the tunnel she flicked on the headlamp, but already the dimness was playing tricks on her. She blinked, trying to clear the spots before her eyes. Behind, the tunnel entrance was slowly receding. Ahead, the spots remained. She was not alone. Another early riser was coming towards her. But something was wrong. There were two lights, which meant two boats, but both seemed to be of equal brightness.

Marnie shut down the engine to dead slow. As she straightened up, the blast of a horn came down the tunnel. She reached forward and pressed her own horn button to acknowledge, startled by the volume of noise it made in the confined space. She pushed the gear lever into reverse and pressed the accelerator to bring *Sally Ann* to a halt.

Marnie could now see clearly the shape of two boats ahead, breasted up, low in the water. She tugged the gear lever into neutral and waited, uncertain about what to do, faced with two working boats closing on her with a combined weight of maybe fifty tonnes.

By now they were only a short way ahead. She was about to hail them, when someone beat her to it.

'Back off!' A harsh voice of indeterminate gender.

'*Back off?*' Marnie repeated to herself.

The voice sounded again. 'Come on, back off!' It seemed to be a woman.

Marnie pushed the lever into reverse and pressed the accelerator to half speed. It took an age to reach the mouth of the tunnel. She focused all her attention on finding a space wide enough to move over and let the working boats pass. She glanced forward and was alarmed to see the bows of the two craft almost nosing against her own. A woman was crouching at the front of the butty and made a gesture of annoyance as if sweeping *Sally* aside.

'Over there!' the woman called out, pointing to a space between clumps of trees.

Marnie threw the tiller hard over. Nothing happened. She knew *Sally* could not respond in reverse. There was no way of manoeuvring. She could only drift and hope for the best.

The woman yelled again. 'Over *there!*'

Marnie had had enough. It was time to make a stand. She reached down and reduced speed to idle, then straightened up and raised a hand. If the pair of boats wanted to pass, they would just have to separate and go by in tandem.

Marnie prepared to bellow. She took a deep breath. 'You –'

It was all she uttered before *Sally Ann* ran aground under the trees.

The working pair squeezed round her and pushed past, the woman in the bows of the butty now peering ahead for new obstacles. Marnie felt she had been dismissed.

The long twin hulls slid by. The big diesel throbbed. At the tiller stood a young man, tanned and long-haired, in jeans and singlet. Drawing level, he turned his head to speak. Marnie waited indignantly for an explanation.

'*Idiot!* Don't you know you have to give way to working boats?'

Marnie's mouth dropped open. The pair passed by, buffeting her with a turbulent wake.

It took Marnie ten minutes of heaving and straining with the pole before *Sally Ann* was free.

——————

Gary was in the chemist's as soon as it opened on Thursday morning. He was hardly through the door when the sales assistant came out to serve him. She walked briskly through the shop, took a tube of toothpaste from the shelf and held it out towards him. She looked at it pointedly.

Gary took it from her. 'Is Sheena here?'

The girl sighed. 'She's on holiday.'

'No she isn't.'

'She *is*, I've just told you.'

'What are you talking about? Yesterday you said she was sick, now you tell me she's on holiday. What's going on?'

From the back of the shop a man's voice called out. 'Do you need any assistance, Diane?'

'No, it's all right, Mr Pillbrow.'

Gary clenched his teeth. 'Who's he?'

'Pharmacist … the manager …our boss. Look, are you buying this or what?'

Gary took some coins out of his pocket and put them in her hand. They walked along the aisle out of sight of the pharmacist.

Gary kept his voice low. 'She never said anything to me about a holiday.' Diane shrugged. 'When did she decide on this?'

'They phoned in last night when the manager was locking up.'

'*They?*'

'The boss thought it might've been her dad.'

Gary was bewildered. 'I don't get it.'

'She might've just felt like a break after not feeling well. She was having a holiday in a couple of weeks, anyway.'

'How long's she going to be away?'

'Two weeks.'

'*Two weeks!*'

'Shush … keep your voice down.'

'I don't believe it.'

'That's what the man – her dad supposedly – said.'

'*Jesus!* What the *bloody buggering hell's* going on?'

A cough from the pharmacy. Diane nodded at the toothpaste.

'Do you want some mouthwash with that, sir?'

———✠———

Marnie's second attempt at the tunnel brought no oncoming traffic. She had braced herself for confrontation, but the passage was without incident, apart from the occasional splash of water down from the air vents. A wiser and tougher person from her earlier confrontation, she emerged from the tunnel and rediscovered her pleasure in the morning.

There was ground mist in the fields and sunlight shining through foliage. She lifted her eyes as a flock of birds flew overhead. The sight of them brought a smile to her face. She looked ahead again and the smile faded.

For as far as she could see, fishing rods were stretched out across the canal. It was a competition, with anglers encamped on the towpath at twenty metre intervals. She had read somewhere she should drop to half speed and stay in mid-channel so as not to disturb the fish.

The passage through the barrier of rods was a war of nerves. At the last second each rose like a drawbridge for her to pass underneath. Not a flicker of recognition came from any of the men on the bank.

After an age, Marnie was relieved to see a lock up ahead. It was occupied, and she waited for the oncoming boat to come through, directly in front of the angler at the end of the line. She expected more bad feeling.

'Sorry about this,' she called over. 'I've got to wait for this boat.'

'No problem. I've got all morning.'

Surprised by the fisherman's amiable tone, Marnie made conversation.

'Not a very good spot here.'

'Luck of the draw, I'm afraid.'

'It must be frustrating for you, trying to fish with boats coming by all the time.'

'Tell me about it! Boaters aren't our favourite people this morning. As soon as we started, two big boats charged through the lot of us. They were so low in the water, even the fish must've held their breath. I expect you saw them. They must've gone past you.'

Marnie smiled ruefully. 'No ...*over* me.'

———✠———

At lunchtime Gary changed out of his overalls, left the boat he was servicing and headed for the pub. Benny faced him across the bar.

'What'll it be, Gary?'

'You seen that bloke lately?'

The barman scanned the saloon, his expression world-weary. 'Take your pick.'

'You know who I mean ... *Gravel.*'

'Who?'

'That's what I call him on account of his voice. Don't know his name. You know him … black leather jacket, shaved head, ear-ring –'

'D'you want a drink or what?'

Gary pointed at a pump. 'Pint o' lager. You don't understand. I'm following up something for him. I need to get in touch.'

Benny reached for a glass and turned the beer-tap. 'Ever heard of the telephone, Gary?'

'I don't have his number.'

'I bet he's got yours.'

'I've *got* to get in touch with him.'

'That's not how it works.'

'That's the story of my life. I can't contact anybody, but they'll talk to *me* when it suits *them*.'

'So? That's how it is. He'll talk to you when he's ready.'

'Then why isn't he? Why's he disappeared all of a sudden? Where's he gone?'

Benny finished pouring the beer, his expression puzzled. 'Doesn't your bird know?'

'My *bird*? What d'you mean? Why should she?'

'She was in here the other night.'

'You said you hadn't seen her recently.'

'Officially I've not seen anyone and I don't know anything. And I've certainly not told anyone anything.'

'But unofficially …?'

'She came in.'

'Who with?'

'By herself.'

'*By herself*? No bird like Sheena goes into a pub *by herself*.'

'Gary, I'm telling you she was alone when she came in.'

'What day was that?'

'Dunno … few days ago. We were busy.'

'What was she doing?'

Benny moved Gary to the end of the bar, opposite the table that Gravel used. As usual it was vacant, even though Gravel was absent, as if surrounded by its own private minefield.

'Why are you asking these questions, Gary?'

'Did she meet him?' Gary was hearing alarm bells.

'You didn't hear anything from me, Gary. Not a word.'

Gary's mind was racing. 'Why was Sheena seeing Gravel?'

'Gary, she's *your* girlfriend. Why don't you ask her yourself? I'm trying to run a pub here, believe it or not.'

'I can't ask her because I don't know where she is. She's fallen off the radar.'

Benny looked alarmed. 'Since when?'

'She phoned in sick for work. I haven't seen her for days.'

'What's this got to do with your mate – wotsisname – Gravel?'

'I've no idea. They've both disappeared.'

Benny tried to look cheerful. 'So maybe they've eloped together. Come on, Gary, it's just a coincidence.' He looked over his shoulder. 'Gotta go. I've got customers dying of thirst.'

Gary sipped his pint, deeply troubled. Why had Sheena met Gravel? She was asking questions. Big mistake.

———— ⚉ ————

Even after clearing the flight of six locks, the day was still young when Marnie reached Braunston. After weeks of measuring progress on mileposts giving the distance to that centre of the network, she had finally arrived. It was a busy place of moorings and workshops, boatyards and chandleries, comings and goings.

Dolly reminded her of the important matter of breakfast. To the accompaniment of purring emanating from the saloon and the singing of the kettle, Marnie showered and put on jeans and a T-shirt. Sitting out on deck in bright sunshine, she realised she was under no pressure to do anything but relax. It was the kind of pressure she could handle.

After eating, she dropped a load of washing in at the laundry room and found a phonebox. No messages on her answerphone, no reply from Jane, but Mrs Jolly answered at the third ring.

'Apologies in advance, Marnie. We may get interrupted. I'm waiting for *the man from the gas board* at any minute to service my boiler.'

'How are things then, Mrs Jolly, apart from the excitement of the gasman?'

'Well, there are still lots of police around, making their enquiries. Otherwise things are fairly quiet. What about you … are you having a –'

'Police? What enquiries? What's happened?'

'Oh, hadn't you heard? There's been quite a to-do. Apparently they found a – sorry, that's the doorbell. The gasman cometh!'

Marnie was left dangling. She reminded herself she was supposed to be away from it all. There was nothing for it but to get on with her jobs and put London out of her mind. Waiting for the washing machine to finish, she brought the boat up to the water point to empty the *Porta Potti* and fill *Sally Ann's* tank. Back on the mooring, she hung the washing on the whirligig and set off to explore downtown Braunston.

In the main street she noticed her reflection in a shop window and went looking for a hairdresser's. When she found a salon, its name brought a smile to her face: *The Cut*. Of course.

They offered her an immediate appointment for a shampoo and trim. Draping a towel round Marnie's shoulders, the hairdresser admired her tan and asked if she had been somewhere nice on holiday. Marnie's reply – *Rickmansworth, Leighton Buzzard, Stoke Bruerne, Blisworth* – brought a blank look.

'I thought maybe you'd been to Ibiza or the West Indies, somewhere exotic like that.'

'No, just the good old Grand Union Canal.'

The young woman settled Marnie back to the wash basin and ran the water, testing for the correct temperature with her fingers.

'Come to think of it ... wasn't there something about canals on the news this morning?'

'Oh? What was that?'

'Can't remember ... I think it was something unpleasant.'

Marnie relaxed and closed her eyes as the warm water flowed over her hair. *Something unpleasant* ... She hoped it was the sudden sinking with the loss of all hands of a pair of working boats south of the Braunston tunnel.

———※※———

Gary had a frustrating afternoon fitting a new gearbox on a boat down by Paddington Basin. It belonged to a middle-aged couple, the fulfilment of a lifelong dream. Instead of leaving him in peace to get on with the work, they hovered over him, bombarding him with questions, plying him with cups of tea. They assumed he shared their enthusiasm. It was hard work for Gary trying to pretend it was more than just another job. Shortly before five he was glad to pack up, pocket his cash for the day and go home.

On the way, he pressed a speed-dial button on his mobile.

The person you are phoning –

Shit! At this rate he would use up his entire month's allocation of calls listening to an answerphone. He was having a more steady relationship with the plummy woman than with his own girlfriend. He stuffed the mobile back into his pocket, turned the corner on to the bridge opposite the news-stand and stopped dead in his tracks.

He stared across the road at the billboard. His brain went numb. His heart stopped.

WOMAN'S BODY FOUND IN CANAL

Gary felt his stomach turn over. He looked round into the pool of Little Venice, as if expecting to see Sheena floating in the still water.

He told himself to calm down. There were eight million people in London, plus all the commuters and tourists. These were long odds. Of course it wasn't Sheena. Why should it be? She worked in a chemist's shop and was no trouble to anyone ... except him. But she did ask questions.

Gary checked his watch and turned back towards the pool. He ran under the bridge to the Little Venice management office. One of the secretaries was just leaving.

'Is Mike in?'

'No. He's gone off to a meeting. I'm the last one out. What's up?'

'I saw the headline ... this body in the canal ... wondered what it was about.'

'Ooh, I *know* ... *dreadful* business –'

Gary wanted to shake her. 'Not another death in Little Venice was it? I hadn't heard anything.'

'No, it's not round here. You weren't needed with the JCB this time, Gary.'

'What? Oh, yeah. No, I was just wondering what had happened. Do you know?'

'Not really. It was down the other end … somewhere like Mile End, I think.'

'Who was it?'

The secretary looked blank. 'How should I know?'

Gary went to the news-stand and bought the *Evening Standard*. There were few details. The woman was unidentified. She was in her twenties and had been found that morning between Mile End and Johnson's lock. The police were treating her death as suspicious.

If anyone had any information about a missing woman they should come forward.

Marnie checked her hair in a shop window and liked what she saw but was anxious to get back to a phonebox. This time there were two messages on the answerphone: Beth confirmed their return date in September; Steve was going to Crete on holiday and staying on for two extra weeks to start a joint project with its university. He added in an encouraging tone that he would be in touch. To Marnie it sounded like a threat.

She quickly made another call. Jane Rutherford answered, and Marnie explained about her change of plan.

'So, Jane, what excitement down in the Big Smoke?'

'You've heard about the body?'

'My god! In Little Venice?'

'No, Mile End.'

'Another gangster?'

'Who knows? It was a woman … not identified yet.'

'Could it have been an accident?'

'The police don't seem to think so.'

'Has anybody gone missing?'

'Funny you should say that. I bumped into Gary. He seems worried about his girlfriend.'

'You're *kidding*!'

'She's apparently gone away … an unexpected holiday … but Gary has doubts.'

'Has he been to the police about her?'

'*Gary*? The *police*? Now *you're* kidding.'

'Well, someone has to identify the body.'

'I think that may be what he's afraid of.'

On the way back to the boat Marnie re-ran the conversation in her mind. *Funny you should say that*, Jane had said. Thinking of the body lying on a slab somewhere, Marnie did not think *funny* was the word.

Someone must have loved her.

31
Braunston

Marnie liked the bustle of Braunston and decided to stay there a few days. Splicing new mooring ropes, laying in stores, touching up paintwork, she felt like a seasoned boatman.

Caring for *Sally Ann* had become the core of her daily routine, no longer a holiday interlude but a fixed part of her life. Tying a new pipe fender in place, she suddenly realised she would not be giving up the boat at the end of the trip.

What would Beth and Paul think? Marnie shrugged. Like Dolly, *Sally Ann* had adopted her. There was no going back.

On Friday Gary listened to every news bulletin, desperate to find out more about the woman in the canal. He learnt nothing new. He rang Sheena's mobile several times and gave up.

Returning from the pub that evening, he was sitting in the saloon on *Garrow*, smoking a last cigarette of the day with a whisky chaser, when he heard a knock on the side door. He froze. It had to be Gravel. A louder knock. Gravel must have followed him. He stubbed out the cigarette and went to the door. Surprise.

'Jesus, Benny! What are you doing here this time of night? I might've been in bed.'

'I just knocked off work. Anyway, I saw you ten minutes ago in the pub.'

'I thought you people stayed up till the early hours clearing up.'

'Yeah well ... the guv'nor said I could hop off for a change. Look, are we going to stand here talking about pub working hours or what?'

'You'd better come in.'

Gary put a glass on the table in front of Benny and reached for the whisky bottle. Benny shook his head. 'I never touch the stuff ... rots yer brains.'

'Why've you come? You got news of Sheena?' Gary was dreading the reply.

'You were asking about that bloke ... the one you call Gravel?'

'Yeah?'

'Someone else has been asking about him. Turns out his real name is Dave Naylor.'

'Dave Naylor? Who told you that?'

'We had two coppers in the pub tonight. They asked if we knew him or where they could find him.'

'Go on.'

'They said they'd interview all our customers if we couldn't tell them anything. On a Friday night, I ask you! We told them Gravel – Naylor – hadn't been in the pub for over a week.'

'Did they tell you what they were after?'

'Nah. They never do.'

'You didn't tell'em about me?'

'Gary ... what d'you take me for?'

'Sorry.'

'Mind you, with them asking around like that, it's only a matter of time before they find out you've been seen with him.'

'Thanks for the warning. I owe you.'

'No, you don't.' Benny looked around. 'This is cosy.'

'It's all right.'

'So ... any sign of your bird, then? What's her name?'

'Sheena. No. She's supposed to be on holiday.' Gary sounded doubtful.

'You don't really think she's gone off with this Dave Naylor, do you?'

'Not really.'

Benny noticed the papers on the table. The items about the dead woman were on top. Gary could almost hear his brain working.

'What is it, Benny?'

'Not sure. Everyone's asking questions these days: you ... your bird ... now the law. It makes you wonder what's going on.'

Good question, Gary thought.

———✺———

Saturday morning, the weekend, for Marnie a day like any other. There was increased activity in the marina and on the canal; pottering day for boat owners, changeover day for hire boats. Trying not to feel superior to the weekend fraternity, she set herself the task of attaching new fenders.

It was a busy day and a lazy day, plenty to do but without pressure of deadlines. There was time to nod at passing boat crews, time to sit out for a break with a mug of something hot or a glass of something cold.

The sun climbed to its highest point and Marnie, in broad-brimmed hat and anointed with sunblock, set off with camera and sketchpad to record the life of the waterway. It would extend that summer into the autumn and winter that followed when she eventually returned to the real world.

———✺———

On Saturday morning Gary patrolled the pavement by the tube station for almost half an hour, glad of the gentle exercise to clear his headache. After Benny had left the previous evening he had stayed up for an hour with the whisky bottle for company. He was no clearer in his mind about Sheena, but he had reached one conclusion: Diane knew more than she was saying.

When Diane appeared at the top of the steps and saw Gary she barely altered her stride.

He fell into step beside her. 'Will you come for a drink with me after work?'

'When?'

'Tonight.'

'It's Saturday, Gary.'

'I know that.'

'People make *plans* for Saturday nights. It's called a social life, remember?'
'So?'

She spelled it out for him. 'I have a boyfriend.'

'Ah ...'

'Also – in case you've forgotten – *you* have a girlfriend. Her name is Sheena.'

'It's Sheena I want to talk to you about. You know that.'

'I've told you all I can, everything I know.'

They reached a corner. Turning it, Diane increased her pace, leaving Gary trailing. He watched her draw away from him, saw the neat auburn hair, the shapely legs.

He called after her. 'The police are asking questions about the body of this woman they found in the canal.'

Diane stopped abruptly and turned. She looked shocked. 'You don't think ...?'

'How can I know what to think when nobody will give me a straight answer to any of my bleedin' questions?'

'But it's not possible –'

'How do you know what's possible? What aren't you telling me?'

Diane stared into the distance. Gary waited.

'I'll see you after work on Monday. You know we shut the shop at five-thirty?'

'I'll be outside.'

'No. I don't want anyone to see me meeting you.'

'Do you want to come to the boat?'

She pondered. 'I'll come to the pub ... the one over the bridge ... not your usual.'

She turned and quickly walked away, her brain in turmoil. She knew it was time she told Gary of her suspicions.

———※———

'What you drawing?'

The question took Marnie by surprise. So did the questioner. It was a quiet Sunday morning and she had heard no footfall on the towpath. She turned on her stool to find a small child staring at her.

She gave it a friendly smile and held up the sketchpad. The twin wrought-iron bridges at the junction of the Grand Union and Oxford canals. The infant gaped at the picture for several seconds and ran off.

Minutes later Marnie heard a babble of hushed voices behind her. A whole tribe of children of assorted shapes and sizes was standing at a respectful distance, watching every stroke of the pencil as the picture took shape.

———※———

Gary had a lie-in on Sunday morning, conscious of the cool empty space in the bed beside him. He thought of other Sunday mornings and turned his head to sniff Sheena's pillow.

Every trace of her scent had gone, as if she had never been there.

His eyes fell on the mobile phone on the cabin floor. Even as he switched it on he knew he was wasting his time. He did not even bother to curse when he noticed that he had forgotten to put it on charge.

— ∽∽∽ —

Marnie had never been so busy or so well organised. At least, that was how it seemed on Monday morning.

She returned from the local food shops, dropped her bags on the galley floor and headed off to the marina's laundry room. The washing that she had put in the machine on her way out had just finished its cycle. She loaded it into the basket and trudged it back to *Sally Ann*. While the kettle heated, she hung the clothes on the whirligig.

By the time she had stowed away her provisions, the water was ready for a pot of Earl Grey. Marnie spread maps and cruising guide out on the saloon table and began detailed planning. The silver highway was beckoning.

— ∽∽∽ —

Gary was already in the pub when Diane walked in on Monday evening and asked for a tomato juice. The place was busy with tourists and locals.

'Heard anything from Sheena?'

Diane shook her head. 'No.'

'So what can you tell me?'

She looked nervous. 'I'm not sure. It's very warm in here.'

'You haven't come to talk about the weather.'

'I've come because I'm concerned about Sheena.'

'We both are.'

'I know that. It's just …' Gary let her find the words. 'You unsettled me by talking about that … person they found in the canal.'

'So what have you got to tell me?'

Diane sipped her drink and frowned. 'They usually put a dash of Worcester sauce in these.'

'Diane …'

She sighed. 'There may have been something … I'm not certain … it's just a feeling I had. She was making these kind of secret calls … on her mobile?'

'I know that. You've already told me.'

'Well, there was another thing. Until now I didn't want to mention it …'

'There's another bloke.'

'How did you know?' Gary gave her the *I-wasn't-born-yesterday* look. 'Well, it might not have been like that. I dunno, but … I'm pretty sure, at least I think, something was going on.'

'Like what?'

'Sheena said something about seeing someone.'

'She was seeing someone else? I know it's logical, but I still find that hard to believe.

I mean, I think I'd know if she was. You can usually tell.'

'Not like that, I don't think. It was more like … she was going to see someone to have a word with them. You know what I mean?'

'Who?'

Diane shook her head.

Gary leaned forward, his voice low, urgent. 'Look, Diane, this is no time to be coy. I'm worried that Sheena may have been pulled out of the canal with her throat cut, and you're getting touchy in case she's been chatted up by some bloke. Tell me what you know.'

'She was going to see this person after work, or it may have been later on that evening.'

'What evening?'

'Not sure … just before she phoned in sick … the day before.'

'What did she say?'

'Well … I was coming out of the loo … I heard her say 'see you later'. She saw me and said she was going to see a friend.'

'You don't think it could've been me?'

'No. I'm sure it wasn't you. She seemed excited about it.'

'Thanks very much.'

'And she looked somehow … sheepish … in a way *nervous*.'

Gary lit a cigarette. 'Go on.'

'Just a feeling, really. It was like she had something on her mind for the rest of the day.'

'Something or someone?'

'I can't really explain. She kept finding jobs to do in the shop … keeping herself occupied. She was sort of … withdrawn … like she was thinking about something?'

'And you've no idea what it was?'

'I did wonder if it had something to do with some bloke she'd met, but … I think there was more to it than that. If that's what it was, she would've talked to me about it … girl talk, you know.'

'And she was going to see this person that evening.'

'Yes.' She sipped the tomato juice. 'Oh … and there was something odd she said. It was when I overheard her on the mobile. It sounded as if she called him …*old boy*.'

'What?'

'Yeah. I'm pretty sure I heard her say that. It struck me as really weird. I mean, nobody calls anybody that these days, do they? It's what old blokes with pipes and handle-bar moustaches used to call each other in black and white films.'

'Old boy?' Gary repeated.

'Yeah. I'm sure of it.' Diane lowered her eyes and stared at the tomato juice. 'It was the last time I ever saw her.'

———

Walking home from the pub after supper on Monday evening, Marnie noticed that *Sally Ann* looked better by moonlight. The shortcomings in the welding and the odd blemish in her paintwork were camouflaged by the shadows.

She had left a light burning on board to welcome her back and as she drew near to *Sally Ann* she stopped and took in the scene. The boat was no longer a collection of mysteries. The canal had stopped being a cause of anxiety. Now, it seemed like her natural element.

Looking down the long line of moored boats, some with lights, most in darkness, Braunston felt like a safe haven. *Sally Ann* looked peaceful, nestling at the bank, but her water tank was brimming, the fuel tank was replenished and a new gas bottle was stored in the locker. With each day that passed, Marnie sensed that both she and her boat were becoming restless.

———————

Gary went to take a cigarette from the packet and found it was empty. He read the government warning: Smoking can seriously damage your health. So can women, he thought.

Wanting to keep a clear head, he had barely touched a drop all evening. Earlier in the pub with Diane he had only drunk half a pint of lager. But back on *Garrow* he had smoked a whole pack of Marlboro that evening, and the boat was like a kipper factory.

He threw the empty packet along with the *Standard* into the waste bin. The paper only carried a brief piece about the body in the canal. The police were still asking for information about missing people. Was Sheena *missing*?

He was rationing his phonecalls to her mobile now: morning, noon and night. Once each. Time for the night call. He pressed the buttons and heard the answerphone voice, idly imagining her adding something to the message:

The person you are phoning is not available. Please try again later … old boy.

Diane must have misheard Sheena. Why would she call anybody 'old boy'? It was daft, she –

He stopped in mid-thought. *Wake up, Gary!* She wasn't saying 'old boy' to someone; she was talking about an 'old boy'.

And that could only mean one person.

———————

By Tuesday Marnie was beginning to feel like a local. The staff in the marina and boatyards recognised her and greeted her as she passed. In the shop she amazed herself, buying no fewer than seven waterways books and was delighted to see her library growing on the shelf in the boat.

She rang Jane and Mrs Jolly for a chat, but felt no need to phone Philip at the office, even to *touch base*. Her stylish London friends were mostly away on holiday in exotic locations, Antigua, the islands of the Aegean, Thailand, the Red Sea. Here she was, living on an old tub of a narrowboat, adopted by a black cat, temporarily staying in a village in Northamptonshire that no one outside the canal world had ever heard of.

Everything about her situation seemed right.

———————

Gary spent the whole of Tuesday driving a waterbus. Still no word from Sheena. But he had had plenty of time to think about what had been happening and he had got it all worked out. Nearly all.

This was how he saw it. Sheena had met Gravel and told him that Gary could not find out anything about Marnie or her connection with the *old boy*. Gravel had not taken offence – Gary could work out why not – and he had talked to her about Old Peter and his valuables. Gravel had thought Sheena stood a better chance of getting information out of him than Gary. That would explain the secret phone calls about the *old boy*. It would also explain Sheena's excitement. She had her eye on the chance to get a share of whatever might be going. *The pot of gold at the end of the rainbow.*

Gary had been looking out for Old Peter all day but had seen nothing of the old man or his boat. The words of a pop song came into his mind: *Everyone's gone to the moon.* It must be getting crowded up there, he thought.

After work Gary found a note tucked into *Garrow's* side door. Mike Brent wanted to see him at the BW office the next day. He hoped it meant more work. He also hoped it did not involve asking Vince for the use of his JCB.

32
Totteridge

Wednesday morning started cloudy and cool, though the forecast promised sunny periods.

With her usual mug of coffee steaming on the hatch, Marnie pressed the starter button. The engine turned over and stopped. She pressed it again with the same result. Mentally she ran through a checklist that she knew by heart.

She switched on the fuel pump and pressed the button, letting the engine turn over for several seconds on the starter motor. *Sally Ann* coughed smoke from her exhaust pipe and rattled into life. Marnie kept the engine running for five minutes and switched off. After five more minutes she went through the starting routine again. The engine fired first time.

We're both in need of exercise, Marnie thought as she cast off. They eased past moored boats towards the junction and followed the main line under the left-hand bridge. The North Oxford led away to the right.

The contrast with Braunston was immediate. Within minutes Marnie was heading south-west through a deserted landscape of rolling open country, with scarcely a house in sight. She stretched her limbs, feeling glad to be underway again. She took a deep breath and turned her eyes towards the hills on the horizon.

In little more than an hour they reached Napton Junction. With the sun breaking through the morning clouds behind her, Marnie steered *Sally Ann* into the South Oxford Canal.

Gary stepped out onto the towpath on Wednesday morning and turned his face up to the sun. He took a deep breath. This was a wonderful summer and no mistake. Too bad he was lacking a girlfriend to share it. Too bad his throat felt like sand paper.

As usual Mike Brent was the first one in the office. Instead of chatting in reception, Mike led him along to his room. This made Gary suspicious. The two of them were alone in the building and Mike had closed the door.

'Look, no pressure, Gary, no hassle, but … the police have been asking about you.'

'About *me*?'

'They want to see you.'

Gary was astonished. 'What for?'

Mike shrugged. 'It seems they were talking to some people in the pub. Someone mentioned you'd been asking around about a woman … who'd gone missing?'

'Missing? Well, not *exactly* …'

'What then?'

'I haven't seen her for a while, that's all.'

'So where is she?'

'Dunno.'

'I think that's what the police would call a missing person, Gary. It seems a fair description.'

'Why would they be interested in my girlfriend?'

'You know they're making enquiries about this woman they found in the canal.'

'Yeah?'

'Like I said, Gary, no hassle but … you didn't think it was worth contacting them about your *missing person?*'

Gary made a dismissive gesture. 'She's not a missing person. She's just … away on holiday.'

'Then why are you asking everyone if they know where she is?'

'Mike, who's side are you on?'

Mike raised his palms upwards. 'I'm just passing on the message. It might look odd if she's just gone on her holidays and you're asking if anyone knows what's become of her.'

Gary slumped into a chair. 'Yeah. I know. What do they want me to do?'

Mike picked up a business card from his desk. 'They said you should contact this officer. Tell her about your girlfriend.'

Gary read the card, Detective Constable Anita Griffiths, and tucked it into his back pocket. 'Did this detective tell you anything about the, er … person they found?'

Mike shook his head. 'I don't think that's how they work, Gary.'

Of course not, Gary thought. *Silly me.*

———

After Braunston, the Oxford Canal felt like a bywater, rural and timeless. Marnie had not seen another boat since her departure. Ahead the land was rising and soon she was skirting Napton Hill, topped by its windmill.

The Oxford was a narrow canal, which meant the locks were only wide enough for one boat at a time. Even so, Marnie found the gates and paddles no less stiff to operate as she began working her way up the flight to the summit.

Nine locks, two and a half hours later, sweaty but exhilarated, she stopped beyond the top lock and walked back onto the bridge to admire the countryside. A secluded land of undulating meadows and spinneys, it seemed unaltered since the 1780s when *navigators* had dug the canal through fields that even then had changed little since the Middle Ages.

After a flannel lick over her upper body, a blast of deodorant spray and a fresh T-shirt, Marnie ate cheese and tomatoes on deck, shaded from the noonday sun by the parasol in the peace and solitude of the pastoral landscape.

She was ready to face the afternoon, but the engine coughed twice before starting. Pushing off, she pulled the lever into forward gear and pressed down the accelerator. She had reached mid-channel when the engine cut out. She engaged neutral and pressed the starter button. To her relief it fired at once. To her dismay it stopped as soon as she put it into gear.

Another attempt with the starter; another failure. Marnie grabbed the pole from the roof and began punting *Sally Ann* to the bank. The boat swung, the nose veered round and stuck in the mud of the shallows. They were now aground at one end, completely blocking the channel. All Marnie's efforts with the pole came to nothing. However hard she pushed on either side, the boat only became more bogged down, the pole harder to pull out of the claggy bottom.

Marnie laid the pole on the roof. Gobs of mud stained the cream paintwork and rivulets of gunk oozed down the side. She lifted out the deck panels. For all its bulk, the engine looked a simple construction. Marnie slid out the dipstick, wiped it with a tissue and checked the oil was up to the mark. She dismantled the fuel filter and inspected the bowl. It seemed okay but she cleaned it nonetheless.

She tried the starter again. The engine turned and turned but failed to fire. It had to be a blockage in the fuel line. She was opening the tool box when she heard the familiar sound of lock paddles turning.

Marnie looked towards the lock, fifty yards away. The gate swung open and a boat emerged. Her heart sank. She wished *Sally Ann* could do the same. It was the unmistakeable shape of a working boat.

After her experience with the pair in Braunston tunnel, Marnie expected no mercy.

———✺———

Gary broke the habit of a lifetime. No pie and pint for lunch in the pub that day. He grabbed a sandwich and a Coke from the floating café. His prompt return to the waterbus surprised the other drivers.

'What's up, Gary? Not feeling well?'

He shook his head. 'Short of staff … thought I'd work through.'

The small queue of passengers began boarding his waterbus. In the five minutes before departure he ate the sandwich and gulped down the drink. From his back pocket he pulled out the business card. *WDC Anita Griffiths, Metropolitan Police*. He had never seen her, but he guessed she looked about twelve. Where had the old-style detectives gone? Where were the square-jawed six-footers with trilby hats, size eleven shoes and belted raincoats? No *proper* detective could be called *Anita*. It was a kid's name.

Then why was he putting off seeing her?

———✺———

The working boat glided slowly towards *Sally Ann* and stopped a few yards short. A man stood up in the bows and looked down at Marnie. Without a word he reached into the hold and produced a rope, coiling it in his hands for throwing.

'If you fasten that to the T-bracket I'll pull you off.'

Marnie heard the rhythmic pop-popping of an old-fashioned engine and felt the power as the rope tautened and dragged her clear. They tied up at the bank in line astern.

Marnie tried the engine again, desperate to get it running, desperate not to have an arrogant working boatman sneering at her inadequacies.

'Thanks for your help.' She tried not to sound grudging. 'That was good of you.'

The man nodded. 'That's all right.'

'I've got engine trouble.'

Marnie explained the symptoms and how she had tried to resolve the situation. He listened, head on one side. When she finished, she waited for him to tell her the problem was childsplay and put it right with a flick of the wrist.

'Mm … you seem to have done everything you should. D'you think maybe you've got a blockage?'

'I was going to check the fuel line from the filter to the inlet manifold.'

'Can I give you a hand?'

'Well I –'

'I'm not brilliant at engines, but it's got to be worth a try.'

They worked side by side. Marnie undid the clip holding the fuel pipe in place and disconnected it from the filter. The newcomer held a jam jar underneath to catch any escaping diesel. He was tall and rangy, in his twenties, in check shirt and jeans, with sandy hair. John Lennon glasses made him look scholarly.

Liquid squirted into the jar and the smell of diesel filled the air. The young man shook his head, reconnected the pipe and crouched over the engine, running a long finger under linkages, cables and joints.

'You said you'd cleaned out the filter?'

'Yes.'

'What colour was it?'

'Pink.'

'Red,' he muttered to himself.

'Well it looked pink to me.'

He grinned at her. 'It is … only officially it's called *red* diesel.'

'Oh, yes … I knew that.'

He stood up. 'I think there's only one thing for it. I'll tow you to the nearest boatyard.'

'How far is it?'

'Best part of ten miles, I think.'

'I couldn't possibly impose on you like that.'

He smiled. 'Do we have any choice?'

'I hate to be a burden.'

'That's all right. I've always wanted a butty.'

Marnie hesitated. 'Then … I present the butty, *Sally Ann* … and steerer, Marnie.'

'I'm Andrew.' A mock bow. 'Of the motor boat, *Totteridge*.'

They shook grimy, oil-stained hands.

It clouded over in the afternoon as the butty, *Sally Ann*, trailed the motor boat, *Totteridge*, at a distance of about five yards. It was peaceful travelling in tandem without the clatter of the Lister, and Marnie concentrated hard, determined not to run aground.

She worried that the engine problem might be serious. Perhaps Gary had been right about needing a complete overhaul. Perhaps that was why he had tried to contact her.

Marnie waited for a straight stretch of water and pulled the mobile from her pocket. Holding the tiller under one elbow, she tapped out Gary's number and raised the phone to her ear.

———❀———

Gary was running on auto-pilot as the waterbus cruised down towards Regent's Park from the Hampstead Road locks. He was trying, and failing, not to think about Sheena, the woman found in the canal and the business card from WDC Griffiths that was burning a hole in his back pocket. All his worries were centred on women. The ringing of his mobile surprised him as he was reducing speed for the approach to the turn at Cumberland Basin.

He yanked the phone from his pocket to check the tiny screen. Sheena? He tilted the phone to get a better view of the name. Marnie! He was shifting his grip to press the answer button when a loud noise – a warning blast on a horn – startled him. The waterbus was already poking through the bridge hole, but an oncoming boat was making the turn.

Gary whipped the control lever into reverse to halt the bus, dropping the mobile in his haste. In panic, many of the passengers looked back at Gary, alarm in their faces. The mobile fell through the air, bounced on Gary's boot and dropped over the side to vanish in the murky water.

The other driver waved Gary forward. As the boats passed, Gary made a show of giving maximum attention to the manoeuvre. He briefly glanced over to acknowledge the generosity of the other boatman, who nodded back and shook his head.

The passengers were calm again, but Gary felt jangled. He had made a fool of himself. Worst of all, he had lost his mobile. Now, even if Sheena tried to phone him, she would fail. He groaned. It felt like losing Sheena herself.

———❀———

Marnie let the mobile ring, without taking her eyes from the towrope and *Totteridge*. *Come on, Gary!* If only she could talk to him, perhaps he could diagnose the problem and tell her what to do. At a stroke she could stop being the helpless female.

The call was answered. 'Gary? It's Marnie –'

A woman's voice, calm, efficient.

The number you are calling is not available. Please try again later.

Marnie disconnected. They were approaching a bend. It was worth a try, she thought. No harm done.

———❀———

Another hour passed. Marnie tried Gary's number at intervals and gave up when they reached the boatyard. Andrew signalled Marnie to bring *Sally Ann* alongside. He took hold of the centre rope and made it fast, leaving the two boats breasted up close to the marina's entrance.

While Andrew went off to make enquiries, Marnie reflected that *Sally Ann's* experience as a butty had come to an end. When he returned some minutes later, his expression was troubled. There was no mechanic available. Andrew had another plan.

'Our best bet is the boatyard at Banbury. Trouble is … that's over ten miles away and

– more to the point – about thirteen locks.'

'Andrew, I couldn't possibly –'

'You already have. I phoned ahead from the office. They can look at the engine tomorrow, but want us to get closer to Banbury. They'll meet you near the first lock at Claydon in the morning.'

'That's brilliant. Er –'

'No problem, Marnie. Is my butty driver ready for another stint?'

'How far is it?'

'Hour or two.'

'Let's do it … but there's one condition.'

———

They moored that evening within sight of Claydon top lock. Dinner was a simple salad of chopped tomatoes, cucumber, peppers, spring onions, hard boiled eggs and tuna. The dressing included Marnie's best balsamic vinegar and olive oil, with mustard and a touch of honey. She was putting a part-baked baguette in the oven when Andrew came on board. He had changed into fresh clothes.

'Sorry to come empty-handed. I've got nothing to bring you. This was all unexpected. I didn't like to pick the wild flowers, and the wine cellar on *Totteridge* is empty at the moment.'

Marnie laughed. 'Luckily the cellar on *Sally Ann* is well stocked.' She produced three bottles of wine, each of a different colour. 'There. You even have a choice.'

'That shade of pink looks nice for a summer evening.'

'Rosé.'

'It looks pink to me.'

She grinned. 'It is … only officially, being wine, it's called *rosé*.'

'Oh, yes … I knew that.'

33
Parcel

When Marnie got up the next morning she had two surprises. She had scribbled a note inviting Andrew to come on *Sally Ann* for breakfast, but stepping outside to deliver it, she discovered that *Totteridge* had left. She found the first lock empty, the lower gate hanging half open. Further on, the next one was in a similar state. Andrew was long gone, making up for lost time.

Turning back, she caught sight of movement on the towpath, a man on a bicycle. Her second surprise of the day, and it had barely begun. Seeing her by the lock, he slowed to a halt.

'Marnie Walker, by any chance?'

'That's me.'

'Adrian Poulsby.' He offered a hand. 'From Banbury.'

'You're an early riser, Adrian.'

'I wanted your problem out of the way before the boatyard gets busy.'

'You've come from Banbury on your bike?'

Adrian shook his head. 'Left the Land Rover by the bridge. I keep the bike in the back for jobs like this.'

'Have you had breakfast?'

He grinned. 'I salivate for bacon sandwiches on occasions like this ... but don't worry. I never get them. It's just a dream.'

'Dreams can sometimes come true.'

———✠———

Thursday morning was one of those days when summer takes a break and cools off. It brought a hint of drizzle. It also brought Gary back to the tube station to wait for Diane. She gave him no more than a sideways glance as he fell into step beside her, but she was the first to speak.

'Don't you have a job to go to, Gary?'

'Yes. It just ... varies from day to day.' He did not like being put on the defensive, especially by a woman. 'I'm self-employed.'

'I haven't heard from Sheena.'

'Is that good or bad news?'

'If she's on holiday it's what you'd expect.'

'If she's on holiday, wouldn't she send you a postcard?'

'Not necessarily.'

'So you're not worried about not hearing from her?'

'Only when you keep going on about it, Gary.'

'The police have been asking about her. They want to see me.'

Diane stopped suddenly. 'The *police?*'

'They want me to contact this woman detective.' He produced her card in evidence.

Diane studied it. 'Metropolitan Police ... this makes it seem really kind of ... official. They're treating Sheena as a ... *missing person.*'

'No.' Gary tried to sound reassuring. 'All they –'

'When are you going to see them?'

'Er ... dunno. I'm busy today –'

'Gary! This is serious. You ought to go round there now ... right away.'

'It's just routine,' he protested. 'If it was really serious they'd ...'

Diane waited, staring at Gary. She supplied the ending. 'They'd come and arrest you?'

Gary shook his head. '*Course not!* Don't exaggerate.'

'I know. They just want you to help them with their enquiries, don't they, Gary?'

'Yeah. That's all it is.'

Diane nodded. 'And we all know what that means, don't we?'

———⟋⟍⟍———

Adrian was wiping his hands when Marnie came to check if he was ready for that bacon sandwich. He peeled off his overalls and went below.

Marnie offered him a seat. 'So, what's the verdict?'

'Good news or bad news first?' He took a bite and rolled his eyes in bliss.

'Just tell me straight.'

'Fuel injector nozzles ... blocked ... as I expected.'

'Repairable?'

'I've cleared them for now, but they'll need looking at. I'll run the engine after breakfast. This is brilliant, Marnie.'

'You're welcome. And the good news?'

'That was the good news.'

Marnie's jaw dropped. 'Oh ...'

He finished chewing. 'It's your wiring ... probably original ... vintage nineteen-seventies.'

'Could it be dangerous ... catch fire or anything?'

'You've got some dodgy bits. We need to have a proper look. No serious danger, though.'

'Oh well ... could be worse.'

'It is. We're chocablock at the boatyard ... our busiest time of the year.'

Adrian munched thoughtfully while Marnie imagined herself marooned outside Banbury for the rest of the summer.

———⟋⟍⟍———

No one in Little Venice remembered the van. It parked on the yellow line under the trees overlooking the pool. Nor did they have a clear recollection of the man in plain overalls who took out the parcel and carried it down the towpath towards *Garrow*. In the middle of the morning he was unlikely to find Gary on board. He left the box by the stern door.

Soon after the man had returned to his van and driven off, another figure appeared on the bank beside the boat and looked down at the box. It was a cube, each side measuring about one foot square. There was no address label, no postage stamps or stickers. On the top surface was printed, THIS WAY UP. On the side was an inscription in black felt-tip pen:

GARY
N/B GARROW
LITTLE VENICE

The parcel felt curiously heavy.

———— ∿ ————

The offices of Lyle and Broadbent, solicitors, were situated not far from the Edgware Road, which made it convenient for Roger Broadbent to nip along to his boat, *Rumpole*, whenever he needed to.

That Thursday morning, returning to the office from a meeting, he stopped the car on double yellow lines by the railings that separated the pavement from the towpath. He looked up and down the street to make sure there were no traffic wardens lurking, and took a case of wine from the boot.

After sliding the case into a locker, he turned on the fridge and put two bottles of Chablis inside. He was locking the boat's main doors, just as Jane Rutherford was passing.

'Not at work today, Roger?'

He tapped the side of his nose. 'Spot of essential maintenance … on my way to a meeting. You?'

'Pupil in ten minutes.'

'Jane, do you know someone called Marnie Walker?'

'Has Gary got you on the case now?'

'Gary? No. Er … someone mentioned her the other day. Apparently she's been away for a while.'

'Everyone seems to be wanting her right now.'

'Any idea why?'

'I can guess what Gary might have in mind. He *says* he's worried her engine might give trouble. Is your *someone* concerned about Marnie's engine?'

'Not as far as I know.'

'Well, I'm sure you can't discuss it, but whatever it is, you're going to have to join the queue.'

'Do you know how to get in touch with her?'

Jane hesitated. 'Yes. Do you need to?'

Roger shook his head. 'It'll keep.'

Driving back to the office, Roger could imagine why Gary might be interested in

Marnie. But Old Peter? What was all that about?

———

Adrian pocketed his mobile. 'Got a piece of paper, Marnie? I'm going to give you an address and phone number.'

Marnie produced the logbook. 'You can write it in here.'

He wrote carefully in capital letters on a fresh page. 'Your contact is Peter Truscott at this boatyard. He'll be expecting you.'

Marnie looked at what Adrian had written. 'Oxford Boaters?' She sounded doubtful.

'Peter runs the second-oldest boatyard in these parts.'

Marnie closed the book. She wondered if Peter would be wearing, a striped blazer, a cravat and a monocle.

'Great.'

———

Gary got back to his boat that evening after another day on the waterbuses. He had spent most of the time thinking over his problems, trying hard to convince himself that once Sheena returned from her holiday everything would be made clear.

He was taking the keyring from his pocket when a head popped out from the next boat.

'Got a parcel for you, Gary.'

'Who from?'

'Dunno. Came this morning. I saw it on your boat … thought I'd better take it in, in case it grew legs and walked before you got back.'

The neighbour laughed. Gary smiled to be sociable and examined the parcel for markings. There were no stamps and no postmark. He weighed it in his hands.

The neighbour studied Gary's face. 'Heavier than you'd expect, innit?'

'Depends what you were expecting.'

'True. It's odd, but I was thinking it's about the size and weight of a human head.'

Gary laughed at the joke. 'Yeah. Funny you should say that. It's just what I ordered.'

'Two heads are better than one, eh, Gary?'

Gary laughed again and went back to *Garrow*. He put the parcel on the table in the saloon and sat down. Staring at it, he lit a cigarette. Somehow the thought of it sprouting legs and walking about did not strike him as very funny. Nor did the comparison with a human head.

———

Marnie was bone-weary by the time she reached Aynho Wharf that evening, but it was a good feeling. After several hours travelling on one of the prettiest canals in the country, she had lost count of the number of locks she had worked. Too tired to prepare a meal, she showered and headed for the pub.

Scampi in a basket with a white wine spritzer completed a wonderful day. Back on *Sally Ann* Marnie undressed and slipped into a fresh white cotton nightdress. When she laid her head on the pillow she had barely time to sigh before falling asleep. She did not even notice when Dolly jumped up onto the foot of the bed, curled into a ball and began purring.

———∽∽∽———

Gary stayed in all evening. He tried to ignore the parcel on the galley workbench, but it taunted him, daring him to open it. At one point he had sniffed the box and almost convinced himself that an unsavoury odour was seeping out, but he had been smoking and the inside of *Garrow* was a complete fug.

A breeze was blowing down the cut, and he opened windows and doors to clear the atmosphere. In the darkness he sat in the cratch well, unmoved by the lights of Little Venice reflected in the water. Sheena would have scolded him for letting the boat reek like a smokehouse. Sheena. She was never out of his thoughts.

He closed his eyes and saw her face and, as he pictured her in his mind, her head transformed itself into the cardboard box waiting for him in the galley. He shuddered and reached for the business card in his back pocket. Diane had been right. He would go to the police tomorrow … unless something spurred him on that night.

Gary clenched his teeth, stood up and ducked into the saloon, determined not to put it off a minute longer. He opened a drawer, pulled out a kitchen knife and sliced through the brown tape that sealed the package. He prized open the lid and peered inside. When he saw what it contained he slumped into a chair and put his head in his hands.

34
Banbury

Sunlight was spilling in through chinks in the curtains. Marnie lay for a few minutes basking in the comfort of the bed, aware of a lump beside her feet. It moved when she turned onto her side to look at the clock. Six-twenty. Dolly walked up the bed and pushed a whiskery face towards her. Marnie reached out and stroked fur like thick-pile carpet.

She yawned. The day like the canal – and the cat – stretched out before her. If she kept going she could reach Oxford by nightfall. If she was going to find herself stranded somewhere for a while, Oxford was a good place to be.

With a final scratch behind Dolly's ears, Marnie rolled out of bed and tugged the curtains apart. It was a beautiful day.

———— ᴍ ————

Gary had a lighter than usual breakfast that Friday; he had smoked all his cigarettes the night before. Stirring his mug of tea, he looked across the saloon at the cardboard box on the galley workbench and grimaced.

He reached for the mobile he had bought to replace the lost one, checked a phone number on the wall calendar and pressed buttons.

'Oh, hi … it's me, Gary … about your engine.'

'Good news?'

Gary glanced sideways at the cardboard box on the workbench. 'Yeah. That fuel pump I ordered for you … it's arrived. I wondered when you'd like me to come and fit it.'

'That's wonderful. Er … do you work on Saturdays? We could go to the boat tomorrow morning if that suited you.'

'Sure. No worries. Say, ten o'clock?'

'We'll be there.'

'Oh and er …'

'Yes, Gary, that's fine. We'll bring cash, as usual.'

'Thanks. Saves on the paperwork, you know … helps me keep the costs down.'

They agreed a price for the job and disconnected. It was business as usual. Gary was halfway round the pool on his way to the waterbus station when he remembered WDC Griffiths. He had left her business card in the galley. It would keep, he told himself.

———— ᴍ ————

Marnie made good progress that morning. A band of moist air had gradually spread over the country and wrapped itself round the boat like a clammy hand. Marnie welcomed the respite from summer heat, but the damp misty weather heightened her sense of isolation. She felt the need of human contact.

Passing Cropredy, she switched on the mobile phone and rang Jane.

'Marnie! I was just thinking about you. How's the trip going? Where are you?'

'North of Banbury. A spot of engine trouble, but it's okay. Why were you thinking about me?'

'There's someone else taking an interest in your whereabouts.'

Marnie stiffened. 'Really?'

'Roger Broadbent.'

'*Who?*'

'You don't know Roger. He moors near you. *Rumpole?* He's a solicitor.'

'Why would he be interested in me? Has Gary been using my mooring for illicit activities?'

'He asked if I knew you and could get hold of you.'

'Did you tell him?'

'He didn't want me to.'

'He didn't say what he wanted?'

'Nope. Just said it wasn't urgent.'

First Gary, then the stranger on the towpath, now a solicitor. Marnie thought she had never been in such demand. But why? She could find no answer to that question.

———⟋⟍⟍⟋———

Gary was seeing a group of Japanese tourists onto the waterbus when Eddy Waterman, the supervisor, came by and whispered in his ear.

'What time is it, Gary?'

Gary checked his watch. 'Five to two.'

'I meant, what time's the funeral?'

'Eh?'

'I assume by the look on your face that that's where you're going.'

'I don't get it.'

'What's up, Gary? These days you're such a miserable sod. You're supposed to be making the customers feel welcome. These people have come thousands of miles to see the sights of London. A trip on a waterbus through Little Venice is one of the highlights of their visit. And you look as if you're about to ferry them over the Styx.'

'What sticks?'

'Forget it. Just try at least to look friendly … all right?'

'I am friendly.'

'Then try showing it.' Eddy beamed at Gary. 'Get it?'

'Right.'

'What is bothering you, Gary?'

'Nothing. Everything's fine. Wonderful.' Gary turned towards the passengers. 'Come along, please, ladies and gentlemen.' He turned on his broadest smile. 'Welcome aboard. Pass right down inside.'

One elderly Japanese couple bowed towards him.

Gary bowed back and smiled again. 'Sayonara,' he said confidently.

The couple hesitated momentarily, but followed the rest of the group down the steps into the boat. They were looking forward to their trip. It was a highlight of their holiday.

———✕✕✕———

At Banbury the undulating countryside of meadows and pockets of woodland gave way to industrial estates. Marnie chugged through and found a mooring in the town centre within sight of Adrian Poulsby's boatyard. It felt reassuring.

A market was in full swing, a place of bustle and activity against a backdrop of cranes and scaffolding. Noticeboards proclaimed the construction of a leisure centre and museum. Half an hour in the supermarket and a tour of the local stalls replenished *Sally Ann's* store cupboards.

Casting off, Marnie cruised slowly past the boatyard and spotted Adrian deep in discussion with a customer. In the dry-dock another man was squatting to inspect the rusted hull of an elderly working boat with peeling paintwork. Adrian glanced over, recognised Marnie and smiled. She waved back, pointed down at the engine compartment and gave a thumbs-up. Adrian looked thoughtful as he watched her pass.

Turning her attention to the next stage of the journey, Marnie estimated that if she made steady progress she could be in Oxford by Sunday evening. She headed out into open country.

———✕✕✕———

It was another Boys-Night-In for Gary. He was wondering what had happened to his life when a thump on the boat's side doors made him freeze. Quickly he cleared dishes from the table into the sink and opened one of the doors.

Two men stood on the towpath, shoulder to shoulder, tall, broad, unsmiling. They reached into their pockets and produced warrant cards. Gary glanced at the logo of the Metropolitan Police, pushed open the other door and stood back to let the men down the steps.

Gary remained standing. 'Look, I was going to come round in the morning. I've been at work all day ... it's a busy time ... tourists and that, and –'

'Come round?' The card had identified the speaker as a detective sergeant.

'Yeah. Only I didn't think it was urgent.'

'What was urgent?'

'Sheena ... that's my girlfriend. She's not really *missing*, well, not the way you mean by that –'

'Let's start again ... at the beginning. You are Mr ...?'

'Gary. Everyone just calls me Gary. That's how it is on the boats.'

'That isn't how it is to the police, Mr ...'

'Greener. Gary Greener ... of *Garrow*.'

'Of where?'

'That's the boat.'

'This is your normal residence?'

'Yeah.'

'Now tell us why you were going to call round about something that wasn't urgent.'

'It's about my girlfriend, Sheena. She's ... well, she's away at present.'

'This is the missing person who isn't missing?'

'That's right. Diane from the shop says she's just away on holiday.'

'We wouldn't normally class that as a *missing person* as such, Mr Greener.'

'No. That's why –'

'It isn't urgent.'

'You got it.'

'Then why were you going to come round?'

Gary frowned. This line of questioning was confusing him. No wonder people confessed to things. 'Anita Griffiths left me her card ... said she wanted me to call in.'

'WDC Anita Griffiths?'

'Yes. Didn't she send you?'

'Nobody sent me, Mr Greener. I'm conducting enquiries.'

'About Sheena?'

'I haven't come to chat about your girlfriend's holiday. I want to talk to you about another of your friends ... Dave Naylor.'

Gary was confused again. 'Who?'

'The man you've been meeting regularly in the pub over the past few weeks, Mr Greener.'

'Oh ... him.'

'I understand you haven't seen him for a while.'

'That's right.'

'When exactly did you last see him?'

'Not sure. A week or two back.'

'Do you know where he is?'

'No idea.'

'Do you know where he lives?'

'No.'

'How long have you known him?'

'Like you said, a few weeks.'

'And the nature of your acquaintance?'

'Business ... sort of ...'

'What sort of business would that be?'

Gary was feeling uncomfortable. 'Look, what is all this?'

'You tell me, Gary.'

'I met this bloke in the pub, right? He tells me he's interested in boats, right? Asks me about how much they cost to buy, how much to run ... stuff like that. A lot of people talk to me like that. Boats are what I do. It was just casual chat in the pub.'

'So he was interested in buying a boat and asked your advice?'

'Maybe.'

'Was he or wasn't he?'

'Hard to tell. Sometimes people just like to chat.'

'That's all it was?'

'Yeah.'

The detective smiled. 'Well, that wasn't so painful, was it?'

'No. Is that everything?'

'I think so.'

Gary moved towards the doors and unlatched the first one.

'Thank you for your assistance, Mr Greener. Nice boat.'

'Yeah.' Gary pushed one door open and unbolted the second.

The detective who until then had not spoken, turned as he walked over to the doors. 'So where's she on holiday, then? Somewhere nice?'

'Who, Sheena?'

'Who else?'

'Er … I'm not sure.'

'Not sure? Didn't she tell you where she was going? No postcard … *weather great, food great … wish you were here?*'

Gary hesitated. 'No.'

'It's not so strange, is it, Gary? Women are like that.'

'No, I suppose not. You're right. It's not that strange.'

'They can be unpredictable.'

'Yeah.'

'Even so, you miss her.'

'Yeah.'

'Nice, is she? Good looking?'

'Oh yeah.'

'Blonde … good figure … legs up to her armpits?'

Gary swallowed. 'Something like that.'

Suddenly the detective sergeant turned and faced Gary at close quarters. 'I'll tell you what is, strange, Gary. You tell us you don't know your friend, Dave Naylor, very well. Yet he meets you in the pub and buys you double whiskies. I think I'd remember a friend like that. We'll talk again soon.'

The two men left without another word. Gary sat down in the saloon and opened a packet of Marlboro. He was wondering how, if the detectives had come to see him about Gravel, they knew Sheena was blonde and had legs up to her armpits.

35
The Henrys

For Marnie it should have been an idyllic weekend's cruising. Once clear of Banbury she was back in rolling country, the Cherwell valley, dotted with copses and spinneys, pastureland and water meadows.

But she was troubled by a niggling anxiety. Each time the engine note varied, she worried it would cut out and leave her stranded in the middle of nowhere. She travelled from one charming area to another, past old canal buildings and cottages, through a variety of locks, most of which seemed deeper than those on the Grand Union, their depth exaggerated by their narrowness. The exception was Aynho Weir Lock, which was diamond-shaped and more spacious than the others.

Her target for Saturday evening was Aynho Wharf and a pub supper, but having made good time, and with plentiful supplies on board, she changed plans and continued on towards Somerton. Only one obstacle lay ahead on that stretch: Somerton Deep Lock.

Descending in the chamber, Marnie felt misgivings as the stone edges of the lockside receded inch by inch above her. Down and down she went between the slimy walls. She had been in deep locks before, but this was unlike any other. Scarcely wider than the boat, it felt to Marnie as if she was being lowered into her grave.

Gary had never felt so restless. In Little Venice on Saturday night all was peace and quiet. It was quiet too on *Garrow* but Gary was not at peace. He had worked all day finishing off jobs on the boat with the new fuel pump.

That evening alone on his boat; he had no desire to go to the pub, but stayed in with a couple of beers and whisky chasers, worrying all the while about Sheena.

A thought suddenly occurred to him: was he still expected to contact WDC Griffiths, or had he now been passed on to the other two detectives? Anita Griffiths wanted to talk to him about Sheena ... and the dead body pulled out of the canal in east London. The two men wanted to talk to him about Gravel ... Dave Naylor. Marvellous. Gary had never been so sought after. He poured himself another whisky and mulled over his predicament.

The police were pursuing him on all sides.

It was evening and the galley smelled of freshly-baked bread. Marnie had just taken a baguette out of the oven and set it aside to cool. She added French dressing to a green salad and chopped chives into omelette mixture, pausing to take a sip of spritzer as a knob of butter melted in the pan.

Over supper, her thoughts returned to Iris Winterburn. Afterwards she took the books about the *Idle Women* from the shelf and thumbed through them, hoping to find a mention of one called Iris. No luck.

She hoped the old lady had recovered completely from her injury. Something about Iris Winterburn told Marnie she was a survivor.

———〜∞〜———

When the mobile rang out just after ten, Gary almost fell off his chair.

'Hallo?'

'Gary, it's Eddy … Eddy Waterman.'

'What's up?' Gary could feel his stomach knotting.

'Sorry to phone so late … hope I'm not interrupting anything …'

'What is it, Eddy?'

'I'm a man short for tomorrow. Robbie's phoned in to say –'

'You want me to cover for him?'

'Could you?'

'Sure. Usual time?'

'That's brilliant.'

'Cash at the end of the day?'

'Well … I'm not sure, Gary … that might be difficult …' Gary remained silent. 'All right.'

'Great.'

'Thanks, Gary. I wish all my problems could be solved that easily.'

So do I, Gary thought as he disconnected.

———〜∞〜———

Marnie set off early on Sunday morning, determined to reach Oxford that evening. The engine fired first time, thumping steadily with faint puffs of light grey smoke.

The canal was lined by willows, and as *Sally Ann* chugged along, Marnie had the waterway to herself. The only reminder of the outside world was the glimpse of a train beyond the fields scurrying north. By the time most holiday boaters were blinking a first eye in their cabins, Marnie was well south of Lower Heyford. She had passed through woodland just as the sun began to burn off the cloud cover, and rays of bright light splayed across the water.

More tree-lined banks followed, with here a view of a packhorse bridge spanning the river, there an abandoned mill. Everywhere trees threw their shadows over fields and water as the sun climbed higher and the morning wore on. A mile or so after Northbrook Lock, *Sally Ann* entered what appeared to be a tunnel carved from a forest, and Marnie imagined herself in the Amazon.

She was making solid progress, the weather was wonderful, the engine firing evenly. Leaving the next lock, Marnie permitted herself the luxury of a full-body stretch, rising on tip-toe with both arms spread wide, breathing deeply. In command of the situation, competent and capable, she knew what it meant to feel on top of the world.

———〜∞〜———

Gary felt jaded when he reported for duty on the waterbuses after another restless night.

He had already set off along the towpath from *Garrow* when he remembered he had not shaved. When Gary arrived five minutes late for work, Eddy Waterman was not pleased.

'For gawdsake, Gary, at least try to look cheerful.'

'Right. I'll tape the corners of my mouth to make a permanent smile if you like.'

'Good idea. Tell you what, you can have a promotion. I'll make you my number one driver if ever we get asked to do a canal funeral like in the olden days.'

'What are you going on about, Eddy?'

'There used to be funerals on the canals, right?'

'Yeah. I been to one or two. Old boat people got taken to the cemetery on a boat for burying.'

'Yeah. If we ever get asked to do one, you'll be my first choice as driver. It'll save me money. I won't have to pay anyone as mourner to look sad on the boat. You can do the job.'

Gary's expression did not change. 'Ha … ha …' he intoned slowly.

'That's the spirit! Now get that tape fitted on your mouth and start boarding the passengers. It's going to be another *wonderful* day.'

Wonderful is not the word, Gary thought, but he turned on his smile. He made a big effort not to appear miserable as he worked the waterbus between Little Venice and Camden Lock. He attempted to set his worries aside: Gravel, the stiff in the crate, Sheena, Old Peter, the dead woman at Mile End, the police. At any other time this would be a bumper year, with steady work and cash in hand. He could at least try to look cheerful. And yet …

In the middle of the afternoon he had to wait to let a boat come through Maida Hill tunnel. He brought the waterbus over to the bank by *Sally Ann*'s vacant mooring and tried not to think about Marnie and all his other troubles.

The oncoming boat nosed out of the tunnel and turned off its headlamp. He saw the familiar grey-green boat emerging into daylight and knew that at the tiller he would see none other than Old Peter.

———— ⚶ ————

Marnie's heart skipped a beat; she thought she had heard the engine do the same. She peered over the stern at the exhaust pipe, her head cocked on one side. No. Both cylinders were running evenly with no trace of smoke. She told herself she was becoming paranoid or neurotic. What was the difference? She would look them up when – if – she eventually reached Oxford, capital of the English language.

The locks had become less deep on the approach to Oxford, so that progress was marginally quicker as she drew nearer to the city. Marnie was beginning to relax and grow more confident of reaching her destination.

They reached the last lock before Oxford Boaters, and Marnie was relieved to find the chamber full. She cruised up to the gates, pushed them open and slipped in. Only the rasping sound from a garden machine whining in the distance spoilt the evening air. She watched the boat descend to the lower level, wishing the noise would stop and bring peace to the scene. To her surprise and gratitude it did. All was calm. When the lock had emptied Marnie opened the lower gate, vaguely sensing that something was different. She climbed the ladder down onto the gunwale and realised that the garden machine was not the only engine to have stopped. *Sally Ann* was silent too.

After several attempts to fire the engine, the starter battery was weakening. Marnie turned the selector switch to use both batteries together to boost her efforts, but a long blast failed to produce results.

She grabbed the pole from the roof and pushed against the gates behind her. *Sally Ann* eased forward, her nose clearing the lower gateway. Marnie hopped along the gunwale, picked up the long rope attached to the bow ring and jumped ashore. She heaved on the rope and fourteen tonnes of boat slid slowly out from the chamber.

It was early Sunday evening. No point trying to contact Oxford Boaters; the yard would be closed. Marnie felt frustrated at failing when so close to her goal; the yard was barely half a mile away. Looking at the long mooring rope in her hands, a plan began to take shape.

The first hundred yards or so were not too bad. In the second hundred she could feel a groove in her shoulder. Bow-hauling was not destined to become a new hobby. As she reached the first bridge a cluster of people looked down at her. Raising her head, a bead of sweat dripped into one eye. Marnie backhanded it and saw four young men leaning over the parapet. Her stomach tightened. A flashback to the skinheads in the rain.

'W-why are you doing that?' A slurred voice.

'What's the game?' Another voice, equally imprecise.

Not a bunch of skinheads, Marnie thought. Hooray Henrys. But were they harmless? It could go either way, especially as they seemed the worse for drink. She ignored them and passed under the bridge, straining on the rope. They were watching for her on the other side.

'Is it a bet or a dare or something?' The first voice again.

She gave them her parting shot. 'I'm saving up for the horse.'

Hoots of laughter. To Marnie's relief their voices receded. She changed shoulders and tugged on the rope. She counted twenty paces before she had to stop for breath. Looking round she was dismayed to find *Sally Ann* nosing into the bank. There was more to this bow-hauling lark than she had imagined.

Wearily she pushed the bows away from the edge and waited until the boat had drifted out to mid-channel. Picking up the rope, Marnie took the strain and trudged on. Before she had reached the second bridge, she turned and saw the boat almost back beside the towpath. Worse, a man and woman were coming towards her arm in arm, quizzical expressions on their faces.

'Broken down?' said the man.

Marnie wanted to shout *sod off!* but had to draw breath to speak and thought better of it.

'No … Woodville College … experiment in surface tension … its effect on hull dynamics and steel structures at low speed.'

The couple looked at *Sally Ann* and nodded their understanding.

'Are you doing a doctorate?' the young woman asked.

Marnie drew another breath. 'No. My doctorate was on step-growth photopolymerisation ... rather elementary, of course. I wanted my post-doc research to be more challenging.'

The couple regarded Marnie in awe, sensing they had been in contact with a great mind.

Marnie pushed the boat away from the side. 'Well, must get on.'

Marnie vowed that the next person who asked what she was doing would get the short version of her reply. She was taking up the slack on the rope when she heard laughter again. Advancing on her from behind came the Hooray Henrys.

'Hey, what are you really up to?'

By now Marnie's patience had worn to the bone. Breathing heavily, she stared at them.

'What does it look like? I've got engine trouble, so unless one of you's a mechanical genius, I'm lumbered with hauling my boat to the nearest yard for repairs.'

'Why's the boat keep swinging in to the bank like that?'

It was a good question, even if slightly slurred. Marnie thought about it.

'I suppose it's because I've got the rope attached to the nose ring.' She pondered. 'Perhaps it'd work better if I shifted the rope further back along the handrail on the roof.'

'And had someone to steer to counterbalance the pulling,' one of the Henrys suggested

Oh no ... Marnie was not going to hand *Sally Ann* over to a bunch of tipsy revellers who would probably crash her into the next bridge.

'Thanks for the offer, but I ought to be on my way.'

The man stepped forward and took hold of the rope. Marnie felt the first stirrings of unease. Hooray Henrys perhaps, but they could cause trouble in a pack, and she could not stand up to them alone.

She began, 'Look, I think –'

'Why don't you get back on the boat ...' He squinted at the name on the bows. '... get back on good ole *Sally Ann*, move your rope thingy and we'll pull you along. The boatyard isn't far.'

Marnie was suspicious. 'How do you know it isn't far?'

'If it's Oxford Boaters, they're just opposite my digs.'

'But this is the long vacation. I thought the students weren't around.'

'Postgrads ... we press on to the end.'

Another added. 'Especially when we're a little behind in our work.'

It figured. 'Well I –'

The man took the rope from Marnie's hands. 'You get back on board ... we'll be the horse.'

Only half-reluctantly Marnie let them pull the boat back to the towpath. She tried the engine, but it coughed and wheezed and spluttered, so she altered the position of the rope and took the tiller.

'Push away!'

The four men laid hands on *Sally Ann* and heaved. When she reached mid-channel they began towing, marching in single file.

One of them piped up. 'I suppose this is what's meant by being roped in.'

The others laughed, and Marnie allowed herself a smile. She found that by steering against them she could keep more or less on a straight course and idly wondered how many men it took to equal one horsepower. Another bridge came into view, and Marnie could see people leaning against the parapet watching the strange convoy draw nearer.

She heard voices from the bridge and then a strange sound like the moaning of the wind. It rose in pitch and gathered strength, and Marnie realised she was listening to the song of the Volga boatmen.

'Yo heave-ho … yo heave-ho …'

The Henrys were chanting as they pulled, and any hope Marnie might have entertained of making an inconspicuous entry into the city of the dreaming spires was thrown overboard. Laughter broke out from the bridge followed by sudden movement. More young men clattered down onto the towpath and took up the task of hauling the boat on her way.

So it was that Marnie and *Sally Ann* completed their journey to the heart of Oxford amid hilarity and bonhomie, propelled by the most unlikely crew ever to handle a narrowboat on the waterways.

36
Oxford

'Mm … oh dear … oh dear …'

Marnie looked down in anguish at the back of the mechanic's head as he poked about in every corner of *Sally Ann's* engine compartment. She knew the *oh dears* would add up to an expensive total and that he would soon be doing the *good news – bad news* thing.

She had awoken that Monday morning moored a short step along the canal from Oxford Boaters, where the Hooray Henrys had brought her the previous evening.

After some minutes and several more *oh dears*, Peter Truscott extricated himself from the engine.

'Well, d'you want the –'

'Bad news first,' Marnie interjected.

'New fuel injector nozzles.'

'I suspected as much.'

'Also …'

'Is this the good news bit?'

'No. It's your electrics. One battery is probably on the way out and your wiring could do with improvement.'

'Meaning?'

'If it was my boat … I'd want it completely rewired.'

'How long would it –'

He was shaking his head. 'Not feasible. First, I haven't got the time … second … I haven't got the manpower … third … you wouldn't want to be stuck here waiting while I fitted the job into the schedule.'

'But I wouldn't want to be lurching from boatyard to boatyard all the way back to Little Venice, breaking down every five minutes.'

'No … and that's the good news.'

'I was beginning to wonder.'

'I can do the nozzles and sort out the batteries.' He looked back at the engine. 'Maybe …' Marnie waited in silence. 'I could tidy up the wiring … bring the isolator switch panel inside.'

They agreed on a modest programme that Peter could fit in over a couple of days. He went off to his office and returned with the battery charger and a hook-up to connect *Sally Ann* to mains power during her stay. He also brought a set of keys.

'We don't usually let people stay on their boats, but as you've got nowhere else to go …' Holding up the keys, he pointed towards the two large black-painted gates that gave access to the yard. 'This is for the Yale lock. The big one fits the deadlock. Make sure it's turned twice for security. You'll be okay here. You can come and go as you please, but at night there's no one else around on this side of the canal. You'll have the place to yourself.'

———〰———

Gary's mate, Brendan, was not best pleased. They were sitting in the van on double yellow lines opposite the entrance to the tube station, watching out for Sheena. The trouble was, they should have been battling through the Monday morning traffic on their way to a job. The owner had promised a bonus if the work could be completed before Wednesday and Brendan was counting the minutes.

Brendan suddenly pointed. 'Look, there she is.'

Gary was half out of his seat before he spotted the girl. 'Nah ... that's Diane, you plonker ... it's the girl she works with.'

They watched Diane walking briskly along the pavement.

Brendan checked his watch. 'Well what time does she usually get in to work?'

'About now.'

With Brendan so fidgety, Gary feared he would drive away at any second. He opened the van door.

'I'll go and wait by the exit so as not to waste time when she comes out.'

Brendan wound down the window. 'Just a quick hallo and fix a time to see her, right?'

'Sure.'

A few minutes went by before the next load of passengers came up the steps. No Sheena. When the last person rushed out, Brendan called across the pavement.

'Come on, Gary! We gotta go.'

'Just wait for the next train ... just one more. She's bound to be on that one. It'll only be a minute.'

It was almost three minutes. Brendan was drumming his fingers on the wheel when he spotted the traffic warden. 'Gary!' He yelled and pointed down the street. 'It's lovely Rita. We go ... now!'

———〰———

Marnie spent the day wandering round Oxford visiting bookshops, galleries and museums. She bought some postcards and went to a café to write them. It was in the café that something strange happened.

A waitress had come across to clear the table. As she bent down to gather up the crockery, she hesitated momentarily, her face close to Marnie's shoulder. It was odd, but Marnie had the distinct impression that the waitress had sniffed.

She ordered a cappuccino and a sandwich and went to the toilets. She checked herself in the mirror: hair was fine, a discreet touch of eyeliner, a light sheen of lipstick, nothing smudged, nothing smeared.

On leaving the café she posted her cards and went back to the boat. It hit her as soon as she pulled open the doors and stepped down inside: that smell. Marnie had become so accustomed to it, she was unaware it pervaded the atmosphere on *Sally Ann* and followed her in diluted form wherever she went. The waitress had been literally *sniffy* because of

Marnie's individual perfume – *eau de diesel*. Or should that be *odour diesel*?

Marnie could not wander round one of the most beautiful cities in the world smelling like an oily rag. She dragged her clothes from the locker and sorted everything into two piles on the bed. With a handful of coins, she headed for the laundry room, leaving her clothes revolving in soap suds, as she set off into town.

On her return she placed the bags from a small boutique in Little Clarendon Street in the cratch, the furthest point from the engine. Having piled all the washed clothes into the tumble drier, she made a pot of tea and took a mug out to Peter. He was working at the other end of the yard, kneeling in the stern of a short trailboat. It was sitting on its trailer on the slipway, and Peter was showering the air with sparks from a welding gun.

Back on board, Marnie tried on her new outfit. The trousers were pale blue loose-weave cotton, tied at the waist with a white cord. The top was in soft white cotton with a scoop neck and short sleeves, and it hung loosely just below the waist. It was the first time that summer that she had even been inside a clothes shop.

That evening she would eat out on deck to celebrate the new clothes.

———— ∞ ————

It had been a frustrating day, especially for Brendan, who was quietly seething as he drove back into London. Beside him in the van, Gary was able to look on the bright side. They may have been held up with their job because the spare parts they needed had not arrived, but at least he would now be back in time to see Sheena when she left work.

Just along the street from the chemist's was a café. Gary sat at a pavement table where he could keep the shop in view and settled down to wait for the quarter of an hour till closing time.

Promptly at five thirty-two, Diane came out alone and began her rapid walk to the tube. Gary leapt up and blocked her way.

She spoke without hesitation. 'Have you talked to her?'

'I haven't even seen her. She hasn't come out of the shop yet.'

Diane frowned. 'Not *Sheena* … Anita Griffiths … the *police*.'

'Griffiths can wait.'

'I'm not sure she can.'

'Look, Diane, I'm waiting to see my girlfriend – supposed girlfriend – right? I'm not here to talk about the police.'

'But you haven't talked to them, have you?'

'Not yet. I've been busy. Where's Sheena?'

'I haven't seen her.'

'What are you talking about?'

'She didn't show up for work today.'

'Why not?'

'Dunno.'

'Didn't you ask?'

'Course I asked. Mr Pillbrow just said she wouldn't be back for a while, if at all.'

'Why was that?'

'He didn't say.'

'What did he mean … *if at all?* Is that what he said?'

'Yes.'

'And?'

'Gary, Mr Pillbrow's the boss-man. I can't interrogate him. Now if you'll let me pass, I've got a train to catch.'

'What about Sheena?'

'Your guess is as good as mine.' She side-stepped him and walked off, turning back with a parting shot. 'You ought to contact the police, Gary.'

Her remark made people sitting at the café tables look up in surprise and curiosity. Gary bowed his head and walked away. He felt guilty, but he did not know why.

Marnie was humming to herself as she prepared supper, a feta salad. It had been a good day. The boat was aired. All her clothes were clean, dry and odourless, packed in black plastic bags in the cratch. Work was in hand to cure *Sally Ann's* engine problem. It was a fine evening. She was wearing her new things and looking forward to settling down with her notes to write up the logbook. What could be better?

Music played softly on the radio while she ate out on deck. Dolly made herself comfortable on the lid of the gas bottle container, folded her paws and closed her eyes, the perfect companion.

After the meal Marnie sat in the saloon with a glass of wine, while Dolly curled up on the opposite chair. A joss stick was burning, just like her student days, scenting the air with sandalwood. She read through the notes in the logbook and began writing up the latest instalments of the journey, becoming so absorbed that she was surprised to look up from her writing to discover that dusk had come down.

She lit the oil lamps and went out on deck to enjoy the quiet of the evening while the globes warmed, leaving the interior bathed in a dim half-light.

Marnie leaned over the tiller. On her side of the canal the boatyard was in darkness. Stars were beginning to appear between bands of cloud, and lights were coming on in the houses on the opposite bank. Somewhere close by she heard a faint splash. A fish had jumped, rippling the still surface of the water.

She stepped down from the boat, gazing across the canal, remembering that one of the Hooray Henrys had his lodgings over there. She did not notice the movement in the shadows.

What happened next lasted no more than a few minutes, but to Marnie it felt like an age. Turning back to the boat, she heard another splash close at hand, but this was no perch jumping. Something big had hit the water. She spun round and saw it at once. Already too far from the bank to be reached by hand, someone was in the canal, sinking in the murky water.

Marnie raced to *Sally Ann* and grabbed the boathook from the roof. She sprinted back and lunged at the body. The brass end with its point and hook came down hard on her target and she heard a groan as it struck. Praying that she had not harpooned the person she was trying to save, she twisted the handle of the pole in an effort to hook onto him before he could vanish below the surface. Kneeling on the ground she pulled hard on the shaft, tugging him towards her.

Every second felt like an hour until finally she had the man within reach. She seized his clothes, pulled him nearer and held his head clear of the water. All attempts to drag him out were futile. Although alive, he was unconscious, a dead weight. She bellowed for help as loudly as she could.

Panting from her exertions, she tried to think straight. She was squatting on the canal bank with an unconscious man in the water, possibly seriously hurt, certainly in need of urgent medical attention. There was no way she could get him onto the bank, no way she could leave him while she ran for her mobile.

Marnie stared at the face, its features indistinct in the gloom. 'Can you hear me?'

A groan. She leaned closer to speak into his ear. He smelled of mud, oil … and alcohol. 'Can you give me your arm?'

No reaction. Again she yelled across the canal, again the houses ignored her.

Marnie took a deep breath, gripped the man's clothing in clenched fists, summoned all her strength and strained every sinew. After an eternity of struggling, she slumped to her knees, gasping and exhausted.

Alone in the boatyard, marooned in darkness, she was close to weeping with frustration and anger. The words ran through her head … darkness … boatyard … Her breath quickened. It was a boatyard … with a slipway. *The slipway!*

Raising herself to a squatting position, she took hold of an arm and began duck-walking along the bank. Absurdly, it made her made her think of bow-hauling *Sally Ann*. Then suddenly she tripped over an unseen mooring ring and went sprawling forward, her chin hitting the dusty concrete. Still holding on, she brushed off the grit and picked herself up, feeling the way along the canalside.

She almost screamed with joy when her fingers found the edge of the slipway. The trailer was still in place, taking up most of the width, but there was room for her to steer the inert body round the corner and onto the slope. Now the man became heavier, but the shallow rise of the ground was in Marnie's favour and she heaved him half out of the water. After a pause, she tugged again with both arms and he was clear.

Marnie knelt on the bankside, elated at her achievement.

'Don't go away!' she gasped, too weary to laugh at her joke.

She stumbled back to *Sally Ann* and found the mobile in the galley. She hit three nines, asked for an ambulance and gave directions. She grabbed the boatyard keys from the hook and dashed out to tackle the gates. Diverting to check the man on the slipway, she regretted she had forgotten to take a torch. He was still lying in the shadows, but seemed to be moving his head.

'You'll be all right. Help's on its way.'

He groaned. Marnie sprinted to the gates and turned the key in the deadlock before twisting the Yale open. The ground bolt was long and stiff and she had to struggle before it yielded. By the time she had pushed both gates apart and fastened them in position, she could hear a siren in the distance, steadily growing louder.

She jogged the short distance to the end of the street and signalled to the ambulance when its flashing lights appeared round the corner. Speeding back down the cul-de-sac, she entered the yard just ahead of the vehicle. It stopped inside the gates. Two paramedics in dayglo jackets climbed out, a man and a woman.

Marnie was panting. 'He's over there by the water.'

The man screwed up his face. 'Whereabouts?'

Marnie pointed. 'By that trailer. He's on the ground in the slipway.'

The woman had a bag like a small suitcase and set off in the direction Marnie had indicated. The man took hold of Marnie's shoulder.

'What about you? Are you injured?'

'Me? No, I'm fine. It's *him*.'

'Your chin's bleeding.'

Marnie raised a hand to her face. It was sticky. 'Really, I'm all right. He's the one who needs your attention.'

The man looked over her shoulder. 'Perhaps not.'

Marnie turned. The other paramedic was standing by the trailer, shaking her head. Marnie's heart almost stopped beating. Three letters flashed in her mind: DOA – DEAD ON ARRIVAL. She swayed. The man caught hold of her.

'No,' she gasped. 'It's not possible. He was moving … groaning.'

Marnie broke loose from the paramedic and stumbled towards the trailer. Sliding to a halt, she realised there was no man lying on the slipway. Apart from the trailer, it was empty.

'He was there … I dragged him out.'

She squatted down to look under the trailer. Straightening up, she felt dizzy and put a hand to her head. The paramedics exchanged glances.

'Look, he must have rolled under the trailer … or something.'

The man took a torch from his belt and searched around them. 'Have you had a fight with your boyfriend?'

'*What?* Of *course* not. I've no idea who he was. I just heard a splash and –'

'How did you get that cut on your chin?'

'I tripped over a mooring ring while I was dragging him. We've got to find –'

'Can you describe this man?'

'No. It was dark. I couldn't –'

'You didn't recognise him.'

Marnie breathed out heavily, exasperated. 'I've told you, I couldn't see him properly. Look, why don't we search the yard? He was unconscious, he can't have got far. He's probably –'

'We'll do that. I'll look around. You go back to the ambulance with my colleague and get that chin cleaned up. You may need stitches.'

With that the man walked off while the woman led Marnie away. Before they reached the ambulance Marnie broke free and ran back to the canalside.

'He must be here! We should all be searching for him.'

'That's what we're trying to –'

'Look!' Marnie pointed.

She knelt down at the end of the slipway and stood up holding a shoe. It was dripping with mud and full of water. Marnie turned it over to empty it.

'He was here.'

37
Lombard

Marnie slept badly and woke with a headache. She got up, took two painkillers and slipped back under the duvet, hoping that Peter had no plans for drilling steel or operating a power saw. If he did either, her head would fall off.

After a while the tablets took effect. She got up again and splashed her face with cold water. The previous night after the ambulance had left, exhausted, grimy and dripping blood, she had stripped off and washed all over with a flannel before collapsing into bed.

The headache had been a bad start to the day, but it took a turn for the worse when Marnie saw her clothes lying on the floor, *brand new* clothes that she had worn for the first time for just a few hours.

The trousers were smeared with dirt, mud and oil, one leg torn at the knee. The top, previously white, was almost as dirty and stained with blood. Marnie padded along to the stern doors and tipped the ruined clothes out onto the deck. She checked her chin in the bathroom mirror. It was sore but clean and needed no stitching.

She pulled on shorts and a T-shirt and headed over to the showers. On the way back she met Peter crossing the yard.

'You had an accident? Your knee's bruised … and your elbow's grazed.'

'What hurt more was the damage to my new clothes.'

'Bad?'

'Ruined.'

'I'm really sorry, Marnie, if something here has –'

'No, no.'

'It's one of the reasons I don't normally let people stay on their boats –'

'It wasn't the yard … well, not directly. I wasn't going to mention it, but …'

She told him about the incident as they strolled towards *Sally Ann*.

'You saved his life, Marnie.'

'I'm not sure he wanted to be saved.'

'Whatever … you didn't find him.'

'No. He just vanished.'

Peter's eyes strayed to the water. 'You're sure he didn't …'

'No. We got torches and searched everywhere … including the canal.'

'Did you get a good look at him? Would you know him again?'

Marnie shook her head. 'No … and no … in that order.'

———✧———

That Tuesday Gary was presented with an ultimatum.

'If you want the work, we leave by seven. Your choice.'

There was no way he could persuade Brendan to wait outside the tube station. Driving out of London, Gary sat thinking about Sheena. He went over all his anxieties and confronted his fears. He was not just worried, he was mystified. There seemed to be a conspiracy surrounding her. Brendan broke the silence when they were stuck in a queue of traffic at a roundabout.

'What is it with you these days, Gary?'

'What d'you mean?'

'Well … you always used to be good company … told jokes … had a laugh … Now, you just sit there.'

'It's nothing.'

'Don't give me that. I'm not stupid … or blind. It's obviously to do with this girl. What is it … she pregnant or something?'

'Nothing like that.'

'What then?'

'She went on holiday and hasn't come back … no contact …not answering her mobile … not a postcard … not a word … nothing.'

'You mean all this is because some bird's given you the elbow?'

'Nah … there's more … it's just … I dunno …'

The traffic crept forward.

'What more? I don't get it, Gary. You're talking in riddles.'

'The police want to talk to me.'

Brendan froze. 'What about?' Gary said nothing. 'Sheena?'

'Yeah.'

'Why? I don't get it. You said she'd just gone on holiday. Why would the police want to talk about that?'

'I was asking about her … in the pub. Someone told the police.'

'Gary, the more you tell me, the less I understand. I've no idea what you're talking about.'

'You remember that woman at Mile End, the one they fished out of the canal?'

Brendan put the van in gear as the stream of traffic began to roll.

'Jesus!'

'Exactly. Look, Brendan, you asked me what's on my mind, now you know. It's private.'

Brendan had to concentrate on the road. It was a while before he could take up where he had left off.

'You've been worrying that the woman in the canal in Mile End was Sheena?'

Gary sighed and said nothing. Brendan persisted. 'Have I got it right?'

'Yes.' Gritted teeth.

'You needn't have worried.'

'Why not?'

'Remember Leroy Monroe?'

'Rings a bell.'

'It should do. He was the kit of parts you pulled out of the pool in Little Venice a few months back.'

Gary had a mental image of the dismembered body spilling out of the broken crate.

'What's that got to do with –'

'The word is … the Mile End woman … was his sister.'

'His *sister?*'

'Larissa. Seems she was more than a tad mixed up in her brother's activities.'

'Bloody hell!' Gary stared through the windscreen.

Brendan smiled. 'So … not Sheena.'

'No.'

Brendan chuckled. 'I bet you were pretty … *cut-up* about her.'

———∞———

Marnie needed to be out of the way while Peter worked on *Sally Ann*, but she lacked the energy to do the Oxford tourist thing. The sight of her new clothes lying in a filthy heap on deck gave her an incentive: retail therapy.

She retraced her steps to the boutique to buy trousers and top identical to the ruined ones. The owner of the shop recognised her and when Marnie explained what had happened, she offered a generous discount on the replacement items.

Marnie stopped off in a pub for a sandwich and got back to the boat as Peter was replacing the deck panels. He wiped his hands on a rag.

Marnie grinned at him. 'Don't give me the good-news-bad-news routine.'

'You're in a good mood.'

'Who wouldn't be? The owner of the boutique took pity on me and gave me a discount for the replacements.' Marnie nodded at the boat. 'So what is the news, good or bad?'

'Could be worse. We don't have to replace both batteries. I've got a new starter one on charge. I'll install it this afternoon.' Peter looked beyond Marnie towards the far end of the yard.

'And the wiring?'

'I'll check that later. First, I've got to sort out the little tiddler on the slipway.' Another glance over Marnie's shoulder.

She looked round. A man was walking across the yard towards the trailboat.

———∞———

At another boatyard, about forty-five miles south-east of Oxford, Gary was trying hard to concentrate on fitting a new rudder post. He switched off the welding torch and pushed up the visor of his face mask to inspect the joints. He was also trying hard to adjust to the new situation concerning Sheena.

The good news was, she had not been dragged from the canal at Mile End. The bad news was, he still had no idea what had become of her or why she had made no contact with him for the past weeks.

When Brendan had told him that the Mile End murder victim was probably Larissa Monroe, a feeling of relief had swept over him. It had been short-lived. Before they reached the marina he was already asking himself the obvious question.

If the Mile End victim wasn't Sheena, where the hell was she?

———✂———

Marnie left Peter to speak to his visitor. She took her bags inside and left them in the cratch, returning to deal with the ruined clothes that had been pushed to the rear of the deck. She was stuffing them into a bag to throw in the rubbish bin, when she spotted the shoe. It was caked in mud, inside and out. She knelt over the side to rinse it in the canal, holding it up by a lace to examine it as she pulled it out.

'Perhaps you should try using a different fly.'

Marnie's head snapped round.

'Sorry if I startled you.'

She had been unaware of anyone's approach. The man facing her was dressed in dark blue trousers and a pale yellow shirt. He was fortyish, tall and of slim build with dark hair, perhaps a little pale for the time of year. His voice was pleasant.

'I never had any better luck when I went fishing as a boy.'

Marnie smiled. 'Sorry, I was slow off the mark.'

The newcomer continued looking at the shoe. 'Is there some reason for washing that?'

Marnie had no real desire to explain, but felt drawn into conversation.

'Someone … fell in the canal last night and left this shoe behind.'

'And you rescued it. Do you know its owner?'

'No. It was dark. I didn't see him properly.' She turned it over. 'Interesting …'

The man moved forward for a closer look. 'In what way?'

'It's a good make … hand-made … repaired not long ago … and this lace looks new.'

A telephone bell began ringing loudly across the yard. Marnie saw Peter walking quickly to his office.

'Are you sure?'

'Yes. You can see it is … even with the mud.'

'You could be right.' The stranger looked at Marnie. 'Are you going to deduce all sorts of things about the owner?'

Marnie studied the shoe from all angles. 'Let's see … it's in a classic style, hand-made in Earls Barton by a top shoemaker. I'd say this man had good taste. Obviously he wasn't usually short of money.'

'*Usually?*' The man frowned. 'Why do you say he wasn't *usually* short of money?'

Marnie pointed at the sole. 'Look how it's been repaired.' The man came nearer. 'These shoes carry a lifetime guarantee. The makers will rebuild them as often as the owner wishes. It's not cheap, but you always get top quality work.'

'Go on.'

'Well, these aren't very old … perhaps a couple of years? You can tell by the marks on the leather.'

'Even though it's just been fished out of the canal?'

'I think so. Look here. These repairs were never done by the makers … more likely one of those kiosk places.'

'So what do you conclude?'

Marnie reflected. 'I think … the owner has a sense of style … he's had the means to indulge it, but now … he may be down on his luck. That might explain why he came to be floating in the canal last night.'

'This is very interesting.' The stranger sounded impressed.

Marnie could see Peter in his office, apparently immersed in conversation on the phone. She had things to do but couldn't abandon the newcomer on the canalside.

'It looks as if Peter isn't going to be finishing your boat for a while. Would you like a cup of coffee?'

A minute later the man was settled in a safari chair on deck, one leg crossed over the other. While Marnie was occupied in the galley, Dolly came out and sniffed at his foot, rubbing her head and flank against it. Marnie returned with a tray to find the cat sitting on the stranger's lap having her ears stroked.

'Put her down if she's a nuisance. I wouldn't want her spoiling your nice clothes.'

'She's no trouble. I'm fond of cats.' He took his coffee and poured in a measure of cream. Dolly caught a whiff of it and, ever hopeful, jumped down to investigate her bowl in the galley. The visitor took a sip. 'Is this your boat?'

'I'm looking after her for my sister.'

The man's eyes came to rest on the damaged clothes stuffed into the rubbish bag. Marnie felt compelled to offer an explanation. He let her reach the end of her story before speaking.

'Brand new and ruined? It was very selfless of you.'

'What else could I do? There was no time to change … he might've died.'

'Of course.'

'My only worry is what became of the man. I'd dearly like to know.'

The visitor drank from his cup. 'This is excellent coffee. Do you mind me asking what you do … I mean, apart from leading a nomadic life on the boat.'

Marnie explained in outline about her sabbatical while the man listened in silence. Then he said something that surprised her.

'I suppose you realise that sabbatical leave isn't about going away. It's about going back.'

Marnie hesitated. 'Yes. I know what you mean … and I'm sure I will go back to my company … when my journey's completed.'

'So … an interior designer … not a detective.'

Marnie laughed. 'Not a detective, no. I'm probably quite wrong about the drowning man. He was probably a drunken old tramp, who'd just been given those shoes from a charity shop.'

'Drunken?'

'Oh, yes. Didn't I say? I'm sure he'd been drinking. I could smell alcohol on his breath.'

The man drank again and looked at Marnie over the cup. 'Your reasoning is sound.'

'You think so?'

'The first part of your analysis seemed very fair. The drunken part … most perceptive.'

'I just smelled it on his breath.'

'Even so.'

Marnie smiled. 'I thought my deductions about the shoes were the best bit.'

He shook his head thoughtfully.

Marnie was surprised. 'You don't think so? I felt quite convinced about that.'

The man put down his cup. 'I think you overlooked another possibility … if you don't mind my saying so.'

'What was that?'

'The shoes … It needn't have been a question of money … of being *down on his luck*, as you put it.'

'How do you –'

'Did you not consider that the man might just have given up caring?'

'Then why bother having them repaired at all?'

'Could it just be that they were letting in water and had to be repaired?'

Marnie felt suddenly annoyed that her carefully thought-out theory was being rejected. She retorted mildly. 'I think that's cobblers.' A pause. 'Oh dear … I can't believe I said that.'

The man put down his cup, threw back his head and laughed. 'Wonderful!'

'And rude of me –'

'No, priceless and very apt.' He looked at his watch. 'Sorry. I have to go. May I offer you dinner this evening?'

'Oh … I don't think that's –'

He stood up. 'Are you leaving to continue on your journey?'

'Not today.'

'Then let me help make up for your spoiled clothes. I know a restaurant not far from here.'

'It's kind of you, but I … well, I should eat on the boat … I've got food on board that has to be used up.'

'I understand. Then I'll bring the wine. Shall we say eight o'clock?'

'But I don't even –'

The man reached out his hand. 'My name is Lombard. Ralph Lombard.'

———❦———

Marnie set off at a rapid pace armed with a list of things-to-do. She noticed Peter's legs protruding from the trailer of the small boat parked on the slipway.

'Peter, can I ask you something?'

A voice from under the hull. 'If you don't mind me not getting up.'

'The owner of this boat. How long have you known him?'

'Not long. But it's *her* not *him*. She's just bought it.'

Marnie was bewildered. 'It wasn't that man who came in the yard?'

'No. I'd not seen him before. He was interested in boats. I said he could look round. He didn't give you any trouble, did he?'

'No, not at all. I'm sure you're right, Peter … probably just … interested in boats.'

On the way into town Marnie had an idea. Her first stop was Blackwell's, the biggest bookshop in Oxford. She made her way through its labyrinths until she found the reference books section. The latest edition of *Who's Who* included an entry for *Lombard, Ralph Anthony MA, DPhil (Oxon), economist, Fellow of All Saints' College, Oxford.*

There was his life, summed up in one neat paragraph: born 1953 in London, PPE at Balliol College, MA 1974, DPhil 1979, married Laura Gregson 1980, widowed 1988, no children. There were his appointments from assistant lecturer to his present post as Reader, followed by a few lines of book titles. Marnie was surprised to discover one that she recognised: *We're Going Wrong.* She knew it was also the title of a famous song, but she had definitely heard of the book. When it came out in 1982 Lombard, still in his twenties, had been snapped up by the media, becoming famous, even notorious, for denouncing the government's economic policies. The pro-Thatcher press had pilloried him.

Lombard became an icon for the radical tendency. For a time his opinions were received like Holy Writ, his books best-sellers. He became the darling of the intelligentsia. Students wore T-shirts emblazoned with his name.

Who's Who listed a few more books, but nothing in the past few years. The entry gave his interests simply as 'thinking'. Marnie slotted the hefty volume back onto the shelf and walked through to the enquiries desk.

'Do you have *We're Going Wrong?*'

The young woman at the counter thought for a few seconds. 'The music department is next door.'

'Not the song … not *Cream*. It's a book on economics.'

'Who's the author?'

'R.A. Lombard.'

'Doesn't ring a bell.'

'What about *Public Need versus Corporate Greed*? Same author.'

'Lampard?'

'Lombard.'

'Just a moment, please.' She turned to a man who was checking a list of orders behind her and spoke quietly in his ear. He looked up at Marnie.

'Lombard?' he said. 'It's a while since we had those in stock. I think they're out of print. Are you with the Galbraith Colloquium?'

'The what? Er, no.' Marnie felt she had strayed into a parallel universe. 'I just wanted to read the books.'

'Try the second-hand section.'

Marnie gave up and went to the market. Buying vegetables in the everyday world seemed normal and reassuring. But as she picked her way among the stalls her thoughts kept returning to Lombard, his rise to fame and his apparent fall. Where had *he* gone wrong?

—✦—

'This is *very* good.' Lombard looked out of place on *Sally Ann*'s stern deck. In fawn slacks and cream silk shirt, with light tan slip-ons, his style was more suited to a cruise liner than a narrowboat moored in an urban yard. 'How do you make it?'

'Avocado … plus a few bits and pieces.'

'A secret handed down by generations of the Walker family?'

Marnie grinned. 'I think it comes from the Galilee. I doubt if many Walkers are living over there.'

'I'd really like the recipe, then, if you don't mind.'

'You take one ripe avocado and scoop out the flesh. That was one of the reasons for suggesting we eat here tonight – the *very* ripe avocado. Chop up two hard-boiled eggs and half an onion … add them to the avocado with a tablespoon of mayonnaise and seasoning. Mix it all together. Serve cold with a French stick and butter, accompanied by a very good claret brought by a guest.' She raised her glass.

'I could make that.'

'Shall I write it down for you?'

'Thanks. I'm always interested in new dishes. You see, I'm a widower. I live alone.'

'I know.' Marnie bit her tongue.

'You know?' He smiled. 'You've done your homework.'

'I hope you don't mind, Dr Lombard.'

'Ralph.'

'Ralph,' she repeated. She poured him some more claret. 'I must check the salmon.'

They ate the rest of the meal in the saloon, lit by candles and oil lamps, and Lombard asked Marnie about boating and canals. She found it easy to talk to him about feeling stale and needing a break from work. He was a good listener.

While Marnie stacked crockery, Lombard admired her small waterways library and picked up her sketchbook.

'This is an extraordinary experience … sitting here, enjoying a delicious meal … charming surroundings … excellent company. It's hard to imagine we're in what I used to think of as a *canal barge*.'

Marnie chuckled. '*Narrowboat*.'

'As I now know. I can't imagine all *narrowboats* are as stylish as yours.'

Marnie shrugged. 'Styles vary as much as people. You meet all sorts on the waterways.'

Lombard lowered his voice. 'Including the ones who end up drunk in the canal.'

'Accidents will happen.' She poured the remains of the red wine into Lombard's glass, aware that he was watching her.

'When did you work it out … that it was I who …?' His voice trailed away.

'When I found out that you had no business in the boatyard … other than coming to see me. I did wonder how you knew I was the one …' Marnie's turn to leave the sentence unfinished.

'It was easy.'

'So you weren't unconscious?'

'I must've been, at least part of the time. I vaguely remember thinking I was about to drown … I didn't care. Then something hit me very hard on the back of the head.'

Marnie grimaced. 'Oh god, yes … sorry about that. It was the boathook.'

'I was already pretty groggy from the brandy. I'd drunk as much as I could hold down – almost a whole bottle – and I was passing out fairly rapidly. Your boathook must've completed the process.'

'I had to pull you to the bank. I suspected I'd probably made things worse.'

'You certainly prevented me from being able to resist.'

'I thought I'd nearly finished you off.'

'I heard a voice coming from far away. I felt I was out of the water … I didn't know how. I tried to get back in the canal.' Ralph was almost whispering. 'Then the voice was there again. I squinted up and something came into focus above me. I saw this lovely face in the dim light, filled with concern, someone telling me I'd be all right. Suddenly – don't ask me why – I knew I *wanted* things to be all right.'

'But you disappeared before the paramedics could help you.'

'I had to, Marnie. I couldn't risk people finding out what I'd done. I couldn't pretend it was an accident, so I slipped away in the dark when the ambulance came.'

Marnie put cups and saucers on a tray. 'Coffee outside? It's such a mild evening.'

'Marnie, I wanted to explain –'

'Ralph, you don't owe me any explanation. Really not.' She took a carton of cream from the fridge. 'On the waterways you have the right to privacy.' She smiled. 'That's how it is here. We don't go in for *kiss and tell*.'

Ralph started to get up from his chair. 'Can I do something to help?'

'Just relax and be comfortable. There's no room for extra hands in this galley. I don't have any cognac to go with the coffee, I'm afraid.' Marnie regretted it as soon as she spoke.

'Don't worry. I had more than enough last night.'

'Sorry, Ralph. That was stupid and thoughtless of me.'

To Marnie's astonishment, Ralph laughed.

'You could say I had enough to last me a lifetime … almost literally.'

38
Fall from grace

Wednesday morning began dull and grey. Marnie skipped across the yard to the shower block amid sprinkles of rain. That day, Peter would replace the injector nozzles on the engine, and *Sally Ann* would be geared up for the next stage of the journey. Turning her lathered body under the hot spray, Marnie knew it would soon be time to move on and she was ready. She would certainly not forget Oxford in a hurry.

Working shampoo with both hands, her thoughts strayed to Ralph. He did not owe her an explanation, but she had anxieties about him nonetheless. Now she would never know the rest of his story. He had left not long after ten the previous evening with a polite handshake and a peck on the cheek.

Towelling herself dry, Marnie pondered the obvious question: would he make another attempt on his life? She heard his voice, barely more than a whisper.

... someone telling me I'd be all right. Suddenly – don't ask me why – I knew I wanted things to be all right ...

He had certainly seemed to be in a more positive frame of mind during their evening together. But would it last? She would probably never see him again to find out.

———〰———

Gary was at a loose end that Wednesday morning. They were held up by a lack of parts on the refit, and Brendan had gone to price another job. Gary was not needed on the waterbuses. This left him free to loiter by the tube station. He arrived early and kept out of sight so that when Diane arrived she did not see him. Pacing up and down the pavement between trains, he watched and waited. By nine-thirty he had had enough.

Outside the chemist's he peered in through the window. Only Diane was visible, stacking shelves. Grimly he told himself this was one day he would not be seeking an excuse to talk. And he would certainly not be speaking to her. He waited until Diane retreated to the back of the shop before he went in, strode direct to the prescriptions counter and came face to face with the pharmacist.

'Good morning. Can I help you?' The man in the white lab coat was holding out his hand to take the expected prescription.

Gary at once felt at a disadvantage, having to explain himself to someone in a kind of official uniform. He cleared his throat but kept his voice low as he heard another customer enter the shop. 'I want to speak to Sheena.'

'Sheena?'

'That's what I said.'

'Sheena isn't here.'

'Why not? Where is she?'

The pharmacist looked flustered. 'I'm afraid I … I can't tell you that.'

'What d'you mean? Look, she's a friend of mine, right? She's been away for longer than a normal holiday. No one knows where she is. I want you to tell me … now.'

'But it's company policy not to –'

'I don't care about policy.' Gary's voice was getting louder. 'I just want to know what's happened to Sheena and you're going to tell me.'

'We never reveal –'

'Don't give me that bullshit!' Gary was shouting. 'Just tell me where she is.'

'Please keep your voice down.' Mr Pillbrow was now very agitated and shooting nervous glances over Gary's shoulder. 'There are customers in the shop.'

'I don't care if a coach party's just arrived from Swindon. I want to know –'

'Here, just take it easy.' It was a woman's voice from behind him.

Gary was furious. Even the customers were ganging up on him now. He whirled round to face the woman and tell her to mind her own business. She was holding up her hand as if to defend herself. Then he noticed what she was holding.

On one side of the card was an emblem that looked vaguely familiar. On the other was a name and number, also familiar: WDC Anita Griffiths.

A light drizzle was falling when Marnie came out of the shower block, rolling her towel as she had done as a child at the swimming baths. When she looked up she saw a man ahead of her advancing slowly, stealthily, towards *Sally Ann*. With a start of surprise she recognised Ralph Lombard.

Her sandals were silent on the concrete as she fell into step not far behind him. What *was* he doing? He seemed to be carrying something, so that his posture was slightly stooped as he moved quietly closer to the boat. When he reached the stern, he glanced round to see if he was being observed. At that moment he came face to face with Marnie. They both jumped.

'Oh my god! … you startled me.' Ralph brought one hand up to his chest.

'What are you *doing*?' Marnie was incredulous. The situation was like a Whitehall farce and she had to struggle not to laugh.

Ralph looked discomfited. 'You took me by surprise.'

'Not for the first time.' She wished she hadn't said that.

Ralph held out his other hand. In it was a spray of tiny roses, white and pink and apricot. Attached to them was a gift tag with a message. It read simply,

Thank You.

Gary could hardly believe he actually had a woman detective sitting in the saloon on his boat. Anita Griffiths had accepted his offer as a chance to speak in private. He knew she wanted to check out his place and was annoyed that his failure to contact Griffiths put him on the back foot.

'Look ... er, I was going to come and see you.'

'Really?' She sounded unconvinced.

'Yeah. It's a busy time for me, the summer ... lots of work coming in. I can't afford to let it go.'

'You found time to go to the chemist's this morning.'

'I know. I had to find out about Sheena. I was going to come on to the station afterwards.' He knew it sounded like an afterthought.

'What about Sheena?'

'I just wanted to know when she was coming back from her holiday.'

'That's why you were shouting at her boss?'

'Yeah. He was being ... awkward about telling me.'

'Why?'

'I dunno. Ask him.'

'Were you asking for her address?'

'Er ... well, yeah ...'

'You'd expect an employer to give out private details of a female member of his staff to some man he didn't know?'

Gary raised his voice. 'She's my girlfriend, right?'

'Then why did you have to ask where she lived?'

Deflation. Gary had no answer.

'If she really was your girlfriend ...' Gary started to protest, but Griffiths raised a finger to silence him. '... I'd expect you to know where she lived. So let's try again. Why were you asking for her address?'

Gary murmured. 'She just sort of disappeared.'

'What do you mean?'

'Just that. One day she was here ... then she wasn't. It was *weird*. That was *weeks* ago.'

Griffiths pulled out her notebook and flicked over the pages. 'She phoned in to work saying she had a stomach upset. That was on the Wednesday. She was off sick for the rest of the week. Then she went on holiday –'

'She wasn't planning to go on holiday that weekend –'

'She had to bring her holiday forward because of the course.'

'*Course?*' Gary was puzzled. 'What course?'

'She was offered a place at the last minute on a company staff training course.'

'She never told me about any course.'

'A place came available ... someone dropped out. Sheena altered her holiday plans so as to take it up.'

Gary searched his memory. None of this rang true. Griffiths was studying him closely.

'What I want to know –'

'What *I* want know,' Griffiths interrupted, 'is what concerned you so much about

Sheena that you began making enquiries.'

'I just got worried about my girlfriend when she went away like that. That's not suspicious. It's natural.'

'Had you had a fight?'

'*No!*'

'Have you any idea why she didn't contact you to let you know what was happening?'

'No.' Less emphatic.

'She presumably had your mobile number?'

'Of course she ... Oh ...' Gary closed his eyes.

'Oh what?'

'My mobile ... *Bugger!* I'd forgotten.'

'Go on.'

'I lost it.'

'Really?' Griffiths sounded unconvinced again.

'No, honest. It fell in the canal when I was driving a waterbus. I had to get a new one. It came with a new number. No way Sheena could've known it.'

'When exactly did this loss take place?'

'Not long after she left.'

'So you have a new phone?'

Gary pulled it out of his pocket and passed it over. Griffiths inspected it. It bore the stains of oily finger marks.

'You realise we can check with the phone company when this mobile was sold?'

Gary stood up and rummaged in a drawer. He pulled out a slip of paper and passed it to Griffiths.

'Receipt.'

She looked amazed. 'You keep receipts?'

'They come in handy sometimes ... tax claims and that.'

Griffiths stood, handed the receipt back to Gary and made for the door.

'I may need to talk to you again. In the meantime it'd be a good idea if you kept away from the chemist's. And don't you decide to go on any sudden holidays without letting me know, right?'

'Sure. So ... what about Sheena? What happens now?'

Griffiths paused before mounting the steps. 'I'd have thought that was obvious.'

—— ⚏ ——

Ralph Lombard may some time have been a world class economist but Marnie concluded he would have made a useless commando. In the spotting drizzle she had invited him inside and grinned to herself while she prepared breakfast.

'You know it's been a long time since I had a guest for dinner who was still around at breakfast time. Sorry ... that makes me sound like a hussy.'

Lombard was laying the table in the saloon. 'A *hussy*?' He feigned shock. 'It's a pity I haven't come in my scarlet-lined cloak, and I don't have a moustache to twirl.'

Marnie turned slowly to face him, her expression sultry and smouldering. 'Would you like … cornflakes or Weetabix?'

'Just toast would be fine.'

Marnie completed the table and they settled down to breakfast. She gave a progress report on the repairs.

'So when will you be off on your travels again?'

'Probably tomorrow if *Sally Ann's* running okay.'

'That's a pity.'

Marnie shrugged. 'We're taking up space in the boatyard … mustn't outstay our welcome.'

'That would be impossible.'

'Even so …'

'And I'm only just getting to know you.'

Marnie looked serious. 'Whereas I know very little about you.'

'I thought you'd checked up on me … thought I had no secrets from you.'

'That was just a few lines in a book. And talking of books … I couldn't get hold of your famous ones. They said they were out of print.'

'That's me … out of print … out of fashion.'

'I don't understand. Ralph, I've no wish to meddle in your affairs, you know that, but seeing you again … I can't help feeling …'

'Curious?'

'*Concerned*. But I know some things can be too painful, and it's better to think of the future than dwell on the past.'

'I couldn't agree more.'

'Good.'

Lombard looked at his watch. 'I'm afraid I have to go … a meeting.'

Marnie stood up and held out a hand. 'Thanks for dropping in. Oh god … I mean –'

'It's okay, I know what you meant.' Lombard smiled tentatively. 'I was just wondering …'

'Yes?'

'Would you be free for dinner this evening?'

Gary locked up *Garrow* after Griffiths left and walked a short way along the towpath. He had a paint job to price and even though he could do it in his sleep, he found it hard to concentrate as he calculated quantities of paint and materials.

His head was filled with questions. How could he contact Sheena? Why had Diane not told him about the training course? Why had Sheena not told him? It felt like a conspiracy, though he had to admit it was largely his fault; he had forgotten about the lost mobile.

At one point he looked up from his measuring to see the grey-green boat passing by with Old Peter at the tiller in his Panama hat. More questions raced into his mind. Where was Gravel these days? If Gravel made one of his sudden appearances, Gary would have nothing to report. That would not be a good move. He would go and see the old man the next day.

How would he broach the subject of Old Peter's valuables? Gary would have to think of something.

———⟐———

Lombard met Marnie at the boatyard gates and they walked to a small Italian restaurant about ten minutes away. Having dinner together for the second time in two days seemed strange, but Marnie told herself she would probably never see Ralph again and they still had things to talk about.

The service was attentive but unobtrusive and they sat at a corner table where they could talk.

'You know, Marnie, I've been thinking about what you said. You mentioned my books, the famous ones – some would say *infamous* – that propelled me into the public arena.'

'I wanted to see why they made the headlines.'

'You have to remember we were in the middle of the Thatcher Revolution. Labour had collapsed into its own private ideological civil war. People were feeling uneasy about so much change. My books spelled out what was happening in straightforward language.'

'You became the opposition?'

'I provided an objective commentary on the new policies.'

'I vaguely remember a lot of fuss. I was at art school then. Your books were all the rage.'

'The media spotlight. I did the round of TV chat shows, got serialised in the Sunday papers, became a guru.'

'What went wrong?'

'The establishment struck back. I'd rocked too many boats, become too influential.'

'What happened exactly?'

'A chair came up at my old college, a professorship. I was tipped as the hot favourite. It was just after I'd coined the term, the *loadsamoney society*. Words were whispered in influential quarters … I became *persona non grata*. The chair went to a worthy but unexciting American as part of a much-heralded brain-gain.'

'So much for academic freedom.'

'A question of patronage, Marnie. Once the powers-that-be had damaged my reputation they could destroy me behind the scenes. No more chat shows, no more prime-time. My next book received brief reviews. I was out of step and became untouchable.'

'Must have been a nightmare.'

'The worst was yet to come.'

'Things could get worse than *that*?'

Lombard lowered his voice. 'My wife was diagnosed with an incurable illness and within six months …'

'Ralph, I'm so sorry …'

'Yes.'

A question was forming in Marnie's mind, but she could not think how to frame it without seeming heartless and insensitive. She could hardly say, *why did you wait so long before attempting to commit suicide?*

'Thanks for sharing all this with me, Ralph.'

'You had a right to at least some explanation. I didn't want you to think you'd just pulled some habitual drunk out of the canal.'

'I didn't think that.'

'Good. I expect you're wondering … why now? Why didn't I try to kill myself back then?'

Marnie said nothing.

'Hopelessness can take time to grow. The loss of someone you love is devastating but it can numb the spirit. It took time for me to realise that everything I'd based my life on was finished. Can you understand that, Marnie?'

'I think so.'

'You said you felt stale … that's why you decided to take a sabbatical when the offer of the boat came along.'

'Yes, but … actually there was more than that. My marriage broke up a few years ago. Not quite the same thing as your experience, Ralph.'

'Maybe not, but a tragedy nonetheless.'

'That's how it felt.'

'And you tackled it by …?'

'Throwing myself into my work.'

'And now your sabbatical with *Sally Ann*.'

'That's part of it too.'

Lombard laughed quietly. 'You threw yourself into your work. I threw myself into … Well, what you did seems more sensible than what I did.'

'A desperate measure.'

Lombard was serious again. 'Thanks for listening. I hope I haven't bored you.'

'Of course not. Tell me, though, what were you trying to escape from? Was it being passed over, professional isolation? Or was it that you had nothing more to say?'

'All but one of those.'

'Which one didn't apply?'

'I still have things to say.'

'Then why don't you just set yourself the task of saying them?'

'It might not be as simple as that.'

'Yes it is.' There was a hard edge to Marnie's voice. 'Just do it. It can be as simple as that.'

'Just do it,' Lombard repeated.

'Why not? If you have something to say, say it. It's got to be better than what you tried to do the other night.'

'I thought drowning would be simple and relatively painless.'

She grimaced. 'It's not a way I'd choose to go. Rats … do things in the water.'

Ralph laughed, a deep, spontaneous chuckle.

'Shall we have coffee on the boat, Ralph?'

'Why not? I want you to tell me more about boats. You've given me an idea.'

They walked back to the boatyard and sat out for the last time. On the stern deck Marnie lit two small candles. In the dusk the only other light came from the windows glowing in the houses opposite. The canal looked like smoked glass.

'So, Ralph, what's this idea you've had?'

'I'm due to have a sabbatical next year. The plan is to write a book. Ever heard of the scholar gypsy?'

Marnie delved into her memory. 'A poem I remember from school … Matthew Arnold?'

'Exactly.'

Marnie caught the implication. 'Are you serious?'

'Why not?'

'*You* … travelling around on a *canalboat*?'

'So? Whatever happened to *just do it*?'

'Wouldn't you need access to libraries?'

'Not all the time. There'd be plenty of room for books. I've got a lap-top. I can work anywhere. There must be a way of charging the batteries.'

'You'd need a generator.'

'There you are, then. Of course you may think that after what happened, I shouldn't be allowed anywhere near a canal ever again.'

'Nothing like that is going to happen ever again, is it, Ralph?'

'You sound pretty confident.'

'Absolutely.' Marnie laughed. 'The scholar *water* gypsy …'

'Is it so unrealistic? After all, it's what you're doing.'

Marnie leaned towards him. 'Promise me something. If you write that book … send me a copy?'

'You'll have to let me know how to get in touch with you.'

'I'll give you my business card.'

'So you don't discourage me?'

Marnie replied in a firm voice. 'Just do it.'

39
Postcard

Marnie had mixed feelings that Thursday morning. She went to see Peter in his office and paid him for the works. Back on *Sally Ann*, she checked the boat from bow ring to stern button.

Everything mechanical and electrical had been sorted out, at least enough to get her safely home. Diesel and water tanks were full. The empty gas bottle was replaced. All fluids were topped up. The stern gland was packed with grease and the rudder post oiled.

The store cupboards on *Sally Ann* were full, the cratch lockers packed with non-perishables as stand-bys for the next leg of the journey. Marnie could not imagine there would be supermarkets lining the lush banks of the Thames.

But for all this, Oxford felt like unfinished business. Marnie tried to imagine Ralph Lombard spending his sabbatical year on a boat. Would he *just do it?* Perhaps she might one day receive a book through the post sent by a secretary at the publisher's office, just another name on the author's list for a complimentary copy.

Peter came over to see her off and stood by as she pressed the starter. The engine fired without hesitation. They grinned as Peter pushed *Sally Ann* away from the bank.

'There you go, Marnie. All ready for a fresh start.'

The engine was beating steadily as they slipped through the water that early September morning and left the yard behind. It felt good to be getting underway again.

Gary was lurking on the street corner, one eye on the tube station exit a hundred yards away, the other watching out for Brendan's van along by the towpath.

Suddenly Diane appeared. Gary legged it along the pavement to meet her halfway. As usual she shot him a quick glance without breaking stride.

'Hi Diane.'

'Look, Gary, you're not –'

'I know, I know. But this isn't the shop. I just want you to give this to Sheena.'

'What is it?'. Diane eyed the slip of paper with suspicion.

'My new mobile number. That's all I'm asking, okay?'

Diane grabbed the note and accelerated as fast as her heels permitted. Gary eased off and watched her go. Definitely not bad legs, he thought. Turning, he raced across the road and headed back to the boat. No sign of Brendan.

He checked his mobile was switched on and climbed on board. A small scattering of mail littered the floor at the foot of the steps. Among the junk was a picture postcard showing a rocky coastline with a brilliant blue sea under a cloudless sky. The address read:

Sally Ann's Summer

Gary Greener,
Narrowboat Garrow,
Little Venice,
London,
England

The greetings came from Cyprus. The message was from Sheena.

Hiya,

Mobile doesn't work here for some reason, yours is switched off. Weather perfect – 38 degrees! Food good – wine better!! Going on a coach trip to the mountains. Wish you were here. Love, Sheena xx

Gary told himself he had never really doubted her and it was as much his fault as hers that they hadn't spoken. Now the new mobile would put that right.

It began ringing sooner than he had expected. Diane must have contacted Sheena as soon as she got to work. He pulled the mobile from his pocket.

'Hallo, darlin'. I knew you wouldn't let me down.'

A gruff voice. 'Let you down? It's bloody Parcel Force has let us both down. I'll murder the bastards. What's this *darlin'* business? You feeling all right, Gary?'

'Oh, Brendan … thought you were … what's with Parcel Force?'

'They promised the parts would be here this morning. They're not. Now they're telling me the parcel is *out for delivery*, whatever that means.'

'What does it mean?'

'It means we can't sit around all day waiting for them to turn up when it suits them. Sorry, Gary. I've got other work I can fit in, but it's a one-man job. I'll ring you.'

Gary was stymied as far as work was concerned. He had planned to bring paint back from Harefield in the van. Without transport he was stuck. Then it occurred to him. There was something he could do.

———— ⚒ ————

Marnie steered *Sally Ann* down the Sheepwash Channel and took the turn left towards Osney Lock. She looked back at Oxford and wondered if the roofscape included All Saints' College where Ralph lived and worked.

Progress through the city was slow, with boats moored everywhere. It was a good time to use the phone. She rang Jane Rutherford and left only a brief word on the answerphone to say she was in Oxford.

She had better luck with Mrs Jolly and gave edited highlights of the journey, omitting the drowning man episode. Mrs Jolly laughed at the Hooray Henrys.

'I don't suppose you've noticed Old Peter, have you? A sturdy man … grey-green boat … Panama hat?'

'Let me think … yes, he seems familiar, though I don't think I've seen him for a day or two. Is he a friend of yours?'

Marnie hesitated. 'Yes.'

———❦———

On the way round to the Paddington Arm, Gary moved quickly and decisively, confident that although he did not know exactly what question he was going to ask Old Peter, he would not be accepting *no* for an answer. If there were valuables hidden somewhere, he would find them.

The grey-green boat was at its mooring, as Gary had expected. He had *willed* it to be there. The door was unpadlocked; he banged on it with a firm hand. There was no reply. A glance through the window of the caravan revealed it was empty.

Gary banged again on the door of the boat. That noise would wake the dead, he thought. The idea made him feel suddenly uneasy. He pulled at the door and it swung towards him. Gary stuck his head in and called *hallo*. A second and a third call brought no response. Gary felt compelled to investigate. He had barely reached the bottom step when he saw the old man sprawled face down on the floor.

'Jesus!'

He knelt beside Old Peter, detected shallow breathing and reached for the mobile. At that moment, it began to ring in his pocket. Without hesitation he killed the incoming call and pressed three nines. A calm voice told him an ambulance would be on its way and he should wait by the boat. He made sure the old man's collar was loose and put a pillow under his head. All thoughts of hidden valuables vanished from Gary's mind. He was wondering how long the old guy had been lying there – he was fully clothed – when he heard the siren.

Gary waited on the towpath. The ambulance crew soon brought Old Peter out on a stretcher and loaded him into the ambulance. Watching them drive off, Gary remembered the mobile. A message in the window told him he had one missed call. He pressed the button. One word stared out at him from the screen: Sheena.

He activated call-back with a smile on his face and found himself listening to a voice he knew so well.

The person you are phoning is not available. Please try again later.

40
River boat

Gary checked the mobile, plugged into its charger, as soon as he got up. He could hardly wait to try Sheena's number again. Estimating that she would be up and about, he pressed the speed-dial button.

'Hallo?'

'Sheena, it's Gary. Please don't hang up.'

'I know who it is.'

'So, where are you?'

'What about the *nice-to-talk-to-you-did-you-have-a-good-holiday-thanks-for-the-card* bit?'

'Oh yeah … did you? I got your card. Thanks.'

'I tried phoning but –'

'My mobile – the old one – fell in the canal.'

'That explains it, then.'

'You went off so suddenly. I was worried.'

'Were you? That's nice.'

'Sheena, where are you now?'

'Liverpool.'

'*Liverpool?* Blimey! And, er … are you going to stay there?'

'No fear! They all talk funny up here. It's just for an induction course. I've got a chance to better myself.'

'So you are coming back to London?'

'At the weekend.'

'Going back to your shop?'

'Yes, temporarily. But you can't see me there. Diane says you had a row with Pillockbrow – sorry, I mean, Mr Pillbrow.'

'Then … where can I see you?'

'Up to you. What d'you have in mind?'

'Would you like to go out … for a meal or something?'

'That'd be great.'

Gary felt relief wash over him. They agreed to meet on Saturday evening and he would take her to the Café Laville in Little Venice for dinner. It would be like old times. A smile spread slowly across his face. The world was getting back to normal.

Then he remembered Old Peter in hospital. The smile vanished as Gary pressed buttons on the phone again.

———⚓———

Sally Ann had become a river boat. Marnie bought her visitors' licence in the keeper's office at the first lock and was now officially registered for the Thames.

The journey took on a different tempo. Marnie no longer had to work the locks by hand. Here, they were long and wide, operated electrically by lock-keepers in uniform who marshalled the traffic, took her rope and secured her to a bollard. Cruising the Thames valley was a leisure activity. Marnie felt more like a tourist than a traveller.

Sally Ann took her place among craft more varied than those she met on the canals. There was a preponderance of white cabin cruisers, including a few really smart Gin Palaces with smoked glass windows and twin 75hp diesels gleaming in polished engine rooms. The clanking of *Sally's* twin cylinders, beating out thirteen horsepower, was comfortingly reassuring now, but clanking nonetheless.

Marnie found the upper reaches of the Thames beautiful, with charming scenery, desirable residences and picturesque towns. They had a Sunday-best flavour. But as she travelled on, she found herself impatient to be back tugging at balance beams and heaving on the windlass. She was looking forward to taking *Sally Ann* home.

Gary checked that a visit was allowed and bought a bunch of grapes on the way to the hospital on Friday afternoon. He was concerned for Old Peter's health, but felt happier than he had been for weeks. There was plenty of cash in the box under his bed, and the keys to Old Peter's boat were hanging safely on a hook in the galley. The warm weather matched his mood.

More than anything, Sheena was back. He had phoned her again quickly after speaking to the hospital and told her about the old man.

Sheena had read his mind. 'So you've got the keys to his boat now.'

'Yeah.'

'And?'

'And what?'

'You know *and what*, Gary. You have to do the right thing.' Gary stayed silent. He did not want to blow it before he'd even had a chance to see Sheena again. 'You have to look after the boat and make sure no one gets on it and searches the place ... *no one at all.* That's right, isn't it, Gary?'

'Yeah.'

'Sorry, the line's not very good. I didn't quite catch what you said.'

'Yeah ... that's right.'

'Good. I knew you were a reliable sort of fella.'

'That's me, sunshine.'

41
Gold

Marnie knew it was Saturday without looking at the calendar by the increase in traffic on the river. The fine weather could not continue much longer, and the boating fraternity was out in force.

The day had begun strangely with an unexpected visitor at breakfast time. Marnie had been drinking orange juice in the saloon, reading the log when she heard the sound. Dolly heard it too and stopped eating from her bowl, pricking one ear and looking up. Something was on the roof of the boat.

The sun was breaking through low cloud cover and at the window Marnie saw a shadow extending across the path like a radio mast. The sunlight gained in strength, the shadow deepened and Marnie smiled. A heron was using Sally Ann as a perch. By the time she had swabbed its calling card from the roof, it was time to set off.

At the first lock Marnie was amazed at the number of boats queuing to go through. She was counting them when she became aware of a man in uniform waving and calling to her from the lockside. His words were indistinct, but his gesture was clear. He signalled Marnie to go forward.

Under the stares of the other boaters, she drove *Sally Ann* past the fleet of shining cruisers and took her place at the head of the lock. She had read about this in the cruising guide; steel boats were brought in first to avoid damage to GRPs. Marnie was in pole position as the lock-keeper looped her rope round a bollard and began bringing the other boats into the chamber. She felt as if she had strayed into a formal reception wearing an old pair of jeans.

———————

Gary had felt strange all day, like a teenager on a first date. When he met Sheena at the tube station he knew why. She assured him that after a week on the course the suntan was fading, but she looked stunning. Her hair seemed blonder, reaching down to shoulders that shone like gold.

In Little Venice's most stylish restaurant, Sheena told her story.

'I'm not sure where to begin really. Shall I tell you about my holiday?'

'You left so suddenly. One minute you were here, the next you'd gone. You didn't even tell me you were going.'

Sheena looked thoughtful. 'Yeah … it was all a bit … unexpected.'

'What was?'

'Promise you won't get angry or do anything silly.'

'I couldn't get angry with you, darlin'.'

'Not with me … with Mr Pillbrow.'

Gary looked blank. 'What's *he* got to do with it?'

'Everything, really.'

Gary glowered. 'Just say the word and I'll –'

'Gary! You promised. You keep calm or I go home ... now.'

'Calm's my middle name.'

'Good. So ... Mr Pillbrow ... though really it goes back before then.'

'Before when?'

'Remember you telling me about that bloke ... the one you called Gravel? Well, I thought you were pussyfooting around too much. He's only human. I thought you should just tell him straight.'

Gary looked alarmed. 'Tell him *what*?'

'Old Peter didn't have any *treasure* ... you didn't know where Marnie was.'

'I remember thinking it wouldn't be a good idea.'

'You were right.'

Gary frowned. 'Go on.'

'I ... I thought I'd try to explain to him.'

'You *what*?' Incredulous.

'Yeah. Anyway, he wasn't in the pub that night so I didn't tell you about it.'

'When was that?'

'When it all started. First I heard that Gravel – his real name's Dave Naylor, by the way –'

'I know. Keep your voice down.'

'Right. Anyway, he wanted to see me. Someone must've told him I was looking for him.'

Gary groaned. 'I don't believe this.'

'But you told me he wanted Marnie ...' She looked round the restaurant. '... *taken out*. Remember?'

Gary nodded. 'People like him think they can get away with murder.'

Sheena looked startled. 'Too right. Seeing him was a big mistake. I was really worried ... heard about this dead woman pulled out of the canal at Mile End. I phoned in sick, but I went in to see Mr Pillbrow after closing time. I told him I wanted a transfer. He asked if I was unhappy there. I said I really liked the job but needed a change. He said he could make things better for me with the company ... much better ... if I wanted ... if I had a manager's recommendation ... said I was a bright girl ... play my cards right and I could go far.'

'I know how far this is going.'

'That's right.' Sheena placed a hand on Gary's. 'This is where you remember your promise not to get angry or start shouting, right?'

'Er ... right.'

'Mr Pillbrow wanted to go far as well. We were alone together at the back in the pharmacy. I told him to keep his hands to himself ... I yelled at him ... gave him a real shock, said I'd tell the area manager if he ever tried anything on again.'

'The rotten little –'

Sheena raised a finger. Gary subsided.

'Then I asked what he meant by *making things better for me with the company* … how I could *go far*. He said there were training opportunities. They wanted people to train up as pharmacists. I could do part of the training … on the job.'

Gary spluttered. Sheena shook her head.

'No, Gary, not … Anyway, it was a new scheme. Mr Pillbrow said it was too short notice, but I could apply for next year. I told him I wanted to go *now*. End of. Long story short, he phoned up, got me a place for this week's course … agreed I could take my holiday a bit earlier than planned. Next day I got on to the travel agent and they said they could change my booking. It was like fate, Gary, a chance to better myself.'

Gary looked doubtful. 'You reckon?'

'I do. The firm will sponsor me to do the A levels and then college. And straightaway I've got a new job title: assistant pharmacist (trainee).' She shook her head in wonder. 'That's *trainee* in brackets.'

'But you never told me any of this … you just left.'

'I just had to get out. I'm not kidding, Gary, I was *really* worried. I did phone you when I got to Cyprus, but I couldn't get through.'

'Yeah. I was worried too … thought you might be …' He stopped. If he said he thought she might be the dead woman at Mile End, she'd be back in Liverpool before you could say *stiff*.

'Thought I might be what, Gary?' She looked serious.

'Going to give me the elbow.' He hoped he sounded convincing.

A golden smile. 'Oh Gary. As if I would …'

———※———

For Marnie and Dolly Saturday evening was Girls'-Night-In. Marnie sat in the saloon writing up the logbook, feeling pleasantly tired.

She had spent the day cleaning up the boat. The sight of the smart Thames cruisers had made her cast a more than usually critical eye over *Sally Ann*. She had found a quiet bank and given the bodywork a good wash. Then, armed with paint pots and brushes, she had worked her way steadily round the boat, touching in every scrape and scratch. By late afternoon she was satisfied that *Sally Ann* was as presentable as her venerable steelwork would allow.

They celebrated by splitting a tin of red salmon, though Dolly abstained from the mixed salad and chilled Orvieto.

———※———

For Gary, everything was wonderful again. He had made a special effort to tidy up *Garrow* and had kept the windows open for much of the day to clear away the odour of cigarette smoke. Now that Sheena was back he would be cutting down on smoking. It had occurred to him that Sheena could carry a Government Notice: Knowing this Woman could be

Good for your Health.

In the cabin he lay back with his head on the pillow, feeling languid and relaxed. A cigarette would have been just right, but he refrained for Sheena's sake. She lay beside him, her perfume making a welcome return. He wondered what she was thinking.

'It's nice, being on a boat, Gary.' Her voice was little more than a whisper.

'Yeah. I think so.'

'Sort of … romantic …'

'Yeah.'

'… special … different from real life.'

Gary knew what she meant. 'It certainly suits me.'

Sheena agreed. 'Yes. It's lovely … for the moment.'

42
September

In her days on the Thames, Marnie found it hard to believe she was cruising just a short commuter journey from the capital. It was idyllic, pastoral, rural, all those and more. There were parks, gardens and woodlands everywhere, a huge variety of boats, from steam pinnaces with broad funnels to slipper launches gleaming with acres of varnished teak. Could this really become that wide brown river flowing through London?

Summer seemed to get its second wind, and only the early mists hovering over the water and fields reminded Marnie that it was already September. Each day she expected the weather to turn, but each day it remained determinedly sunny. Though the days were warm, the nights were cool, and every morning the temperature was slow in rising. The angle of the sun, the condensation on *Sally Ann*'s steelwork, the earlier dusk, the later dawn, the tinge of colour in the foliage, all were foretastes of an autumn that seemed hesitant to arrive.

On waking, Marnie would wash quickly and stand out on deck in the semi-darkness while the kettle boiled. With the air cold round her ankles, she would watch the day coming to life, colour-washed in pale grey. Every evening she performed the same ritual while the light faded. She had never felt so in touch with the seasons.

———⬗———

Gary was the first to wake up in the sleeping cabin on *Garrow* on Sunday morning. He knew Sheena had said something significant the previous night, but could not remember what it was. She stirred beside him. All thoughts of what she might or might not have said disappeared. Her face was half concealed by hair; he brushed it aside with his fingertips. She murmured and breathed out slowly. He waited, knowing what would come next. Gradually a smile spread over her features.

'I know you're looking at me, Gary.' Her voice was husky and low.

'Why wouldn't I?'

Sheena yawned, a slim golden hand emerging from under the duvet to cover it. Pink varnish on tapered fingernails.

'Little Venice ...'

'Glad to be back?'

'Mm ... Funny place, though.'

'Funny?'

'Strange people.'

Gary had never thought of Little Venice as *funny* or its people as *strange*, at least no stranger than anywhere else.

Sheena spoke again, her eyes still closed. 'What is it about Little Venice, Gary?'

'How d'you mean?'

'Is it a Black Hole or what?'

'Black hole? I don't get it.'

'People seem to come and ... well, disappear.'

'Like you, you mean?'

Sheena opened her eyes wide. 'I hadn't thought of it like that. I was thinking more of ... you know ... Gravel ... Dave –'

'I know who you mean.'

'Do you know *what* I mean?'

'I think so. The point is ... it's better not to go round asking questions.'

'I suppose so. Talking of questions ... have you seen him lately?'

'No.'

'Do you know where he is?'

'No.'

'Is he likely to come back?'

'How should I know?'

'What will you tell him if he does?'

'Don't ask.'

That Sunday, *Sally Ann* was underway long before anyone else on the river. Marnie steered down the centre channel as the sky turned from pink to grey to blue and the other boaters were not yet up or even on the way to their moorings.

She wondered if the smart boaters regarded her on the old tub *Sally Ann* as a *Water Gypsy*, or even a *river rat*. There certainly seemed to be a different relationship between river and canal people. On the canals, passing crews exchanged a friendly word. On the Thames, boats went by without even a glance from the other steerer.

At first Marnie had wondered if the boaters in the white cruisers regarded a narrowboat as inferior. But gradually, she thought there might be a simpler reason; the river was much wider. Perhaps the natural British reserve was the default setting. Perhaps narrowboaters acknowledged each other simply because they passed in closer proximity.

Marnie tried an experiment. She began giving a cheery wave to oncoming boats, even the most opulent gin palaces. It worked. The steerers waved or nodded back. Then she noticed another difference. When she encountered a narrowboat, the greeting was almost a conspiratorial smile ... between water gypsies.

Gary walked Sheena to the tube. He was sorry she could not spend Sunday with him, but she owed her parents a visit and, she reminded Gary, she had work to prepare for her training course. He felt proud of her.

From the station Gary went to the pub. It was just on noon but already all the tables on the pavement were occupied with people out for a pre-lunch drink in the sunshine. In the saloon bar nearly every table was taken. Gravel's table remained unoccupied as usual.

Gary took a stool at the bar and ordered a pint and a pasty. While Benny poured the beer, Gary expected him to ask about Sheena but he said nothing.

'You all right then, Benny?'

'Not bad. Overworked, underpaid. Get you anything else?'

Gary passed him a tenner. 'Packet of Bensons.'

When Benny counted out the change, Gary inclined his head towards the empty table.

'Seen Gravel lately?'

'Who?'

'You know … Dave Naylor.'

Benny made a face and shook his head. 'Can't say I recall the name.'

Gary began forming a question, but thought better of it.

43
Henley

Marnie felt relaxed and liberated. She enjoyed those mild, calm end-of-season days and realised she had adapted to cruising the river, with less work than on the canals – being cosseted in the locks – and much to explore. Under no pressure to reach journey's end, she passed the time watching Victorian and Edwardian architecture glide by or wandering round the towns and villages along the banks.

She spent the evenings writing up the log or reading, with music playing softly in the background. At times, the only sound in the cabin was the bell on Dolly's collar, tinkling against the edge of her feeding bowl, Dolly the stowaway, first in a series of encounters at the very start of the journey. Flicking through the logbook, Marnie thought of the others: Anne (with an 'e'), Jack Hadley, Iris Winterburn, Attila, Andrew, the Henrys. Where were they now?

Then there was Ralph Lombard. Would he *just do it*? Would he spend his sabbatical year travelling on the waterways, become a *scholar water gypsy*? By a quirk of synchronicity, Classic fm was playing music from the movies, including the original soundtrack version of *As Time Goes By* from *Casablanca*, one of Marnie's all-time favourites. On that evening she had poured herself a brandy and could not help but remember Ralph's face.

Of all the canals in all the world, you have to fall into mine …

She shrugged. It was more than probable, she thought, that she would never see Ralph or any of them ever again.

———

In the days following Sheena's return, Gary wondered when Gravel would make a comeback but the prospect did not worry him. With Old Peter in hospital, he had a readymade excuse for not putting the screws on the old boy and he could point out that he had been on the spot when the heart attack had struck.

Most days Sheena rang, but not as often as before. The drawback with the new job was that she had to study in the evenings, and they could only see each other at weekends. She explained that, as *assistant pharmacist (trainee)*, her days were busier and she spent more time working alongside Mr Pillbrow. Yes, she assured Gary, the old lecher was keeping his hands to himself. The 'new responsibilities' meant that her calls had to be briefer now.

'Hi, Gary, it's me. Just time for a quickie.'

'I'll be right round darlin' …'

'Gary!'

———

After a few days' cruising, Marnie tied up at Henley and went in search of stores. In the town centre she spotted a phonebox. Her first call was to Beth. No reply; she left a message. The next was to Jane.

'Marnie! We thought you must have sunk.'

They exchanged news. Jane assured Marnie that Gary had not let her mooring to anyone else. The rumour in Little Venice was that Mrs Jolly had had radar installed. Gary had no way of penetrating her security.

After disconnecting, Marnie had two more numbers to ring. Both made her feel apprehensive, but for different reasons. She took a deep breath and dialled the first.

'Biology Department.'

'I'd like to speak to Dr Boyd, please.'

There was a click.

'Stephen Boyd.'

'Steve. It's Marnie. You left a message. Sorry to take so long replying. I've been travelling.'

'That's fine. Look, I'm just going into a meeting, but I would like to talk to you. Could I pop round this evening? Are you free?'

'I am free, but I'm in Henley.'

'Henley?'

'On the Thames.'

'Yes, I know where it is.'

'I expect to be back within a week.'

'Oh … this is rather awkward.'

'I don't want to make you late for your meeting.'

'No. It's just … well … I'm going off to a conference … tomorrow … to Padua … in Italy.'

'I know where it is. That's nice.'

'I'm er … not going alone.'

Marnie felt *hugely* relieved. Before she could frame a reply, Steve continued.

'I know this must come as a shock to you, Marnie –'

'I quite understand.'

'I'm really sorry to break it to you like this, but … with you being away all this time …'

'No, it's okay, really.'

'Thank you for taking it so well.'

God, you're a pompous prig, she thought. 'Not at all. Well, have a good trip and, er … enjoy your conference.'

With a burden lifted, she dialled her last number.

'I'd like to speak to Philip Everett, please. It's Marnie.' She waited for a few seconds to be connected.

'How's it going?' Philip sounded strained. 'Where are you?'

'In Henley-on-Thames. Everything's fine. You wanted to talk to me?'

'Yes. Er ... when d'you think we could meet?'

'That sounds a bit ominous.'

'It's just ... I can't discuss it at the moment.'

'Shall I call back or ... come to see you? I should be around next week.'

'Ring me when you get back. We'll put something in the diary.' He lowered his voice to a whisper. 'It's slightly embarrassing.'

—⚒—

Gary was towelling himself dry after a shower when his mobile started chirping in the saloon. He padded through the boat, hoping it was Sheena finishing work and suggesting they meet. As he grabbed the phone a smile was forming.

The call was a surprise. Old Peter was leaving hospital that morning. Still damp, he threw on some clothes, left the boat and took off at top speed.

—⚒—

Later that week Marnie moored just above Teddington Lock, opposite the film studios, and outlined her plans for the next leg of the journey to the lock-keeper. He agreed her calculations and advised her to phone ahead to Brentford to let the keeper know she would be coming through next morning.

With a little apprehension about going on to the tidal section, Marnie sat in the saloon on *Sally Ann* that evening, with the cruising guide on the table and Dolly in the opposite chair. A Brandenburg Concerto was playing on the tape machine, a joss stick scenting the air with snow jasmine.

According to the tide chart, they should go through Teddington Lock just before eight to catch high water. They would run against slow current for about an hour. Then the tide would turn as they were nearing Richmond and they should reach the entrance to the Grand Union at Brentford about half an hour later. It all seemed quite straightforward.

'Is anything straightforward where boats and water are concerned?' Marnie said out loud, closing the cruising guide.

Dolly only looked up briefly from washing her tail. She knew it was a rhetorical question.

44
Tide

The Teddington Lock gates opened to release *Sally Ann* at precisely eight o'clock that pale grey Friday morning. The boat was dripping with condensation, and Marnie could feel a late September chill in the breeze. With a final wave to the lock-keeper, she pulled up the collar of her jacket and turned to face the rising tide. At this stage in its cycle it was running against her at about one mile an hour and offered little resistance. They chugged steadily down to Richmond where elegant buildings rose from the banks in layers and Marnie noticed that the river had ceased to run. Slack water.

Sally Ann cruised on, the tide now slowly turning in her favour, past ranks of barges moored in the channel. Within less than half an hour Marnie saw the sign on her left marking the entrance to the canal at Brentford. She pushed the tiller hard over to bring the bows left and for a moment thought she would over-run, miss the turning and float on past. But *Sally* responded, aimed herself at the canal entrance and scampered round the tight bend under full throttle.

The first lock was operated for her by the keeper. He noted the name and ticked her off his list. They motored on between old factory buildings to the second lock. Marnie made ready to secure the boat when a man appeared up ahead and waved her forward.

As *Sally Ann* rose in the lock chamber, Marnie called over to the keeper.

'Any more manned locks on this stretch?'

He shook his head. 'From here on, you're on your own.'

———— ∿∿ ————

While the tea was brewing in the pot, Mrs Jolly walked through to her sitting room and moved the lace curtains apart with a finger. It had been part of her routine all summer, ever since that man with the cheeky face had let Marnie's space to another boat. *Sally Ann's* mooring was clear.

After breakfast Mrs Jolly promised herself a baking session. Marnie's homecoming should be marked with a proper celebration.

———— ∿∿ ————

The journey was not yet over. The pale sunshine may have belonged to the first days of Autumn, but it still had the strength to warm. Heading north away from the Thames, Marnie tugged off her jacket at the first lock. By the next, she was down to jeans and T-shirt. So far she had not encountered a single other craft travelling in either direction.

The landscape was partly industrial, partly suburban, with occasional views over parkland, the canal hemmed in by roads and railways, criss-crossed by bridges. The map showed eight more locks ahead, raising the canal nearly a hundred feet.

A piece of paper fell out of the guide and landed at her feet. She read the message:

BITCH
TIME YOU THOUGHT ABOUT IT
LET ME KNOW
G

The note made her smile, but also reminded her of the need to think about *Sally*'s hull. There was always some job waiting to be done. It did not occur to Marnie that it might not be her responsibility. Before one more day was out, her role as boat skipper would be over.

At the top of the Hanwell flight, Marnie was hot, weary and ready for food. She found a pub near the towpath, sat under a parasol in its garden and ordered pâté and toast with a glass of cider.

Waiting for lunch to arrive, she rang Mrs Jolly, who invited her for coffee on Sunday morning.

The afternoon was as hot as almost any that summer. Marnie changed into shorts and washed over the bodywork. In an hour *Sally Ann* was shining in the sunlight. Next, she tidied the interior. It still pleased her as it had at the start, but now it looked and felt like home. Marnie knew that she too had changed. She had become part of the boat as the boat had become part of her.

───·ᚱᚱ·───

The evening was warm enough to eat out on deck. Marnie sipped a spritzer while tossing the salad and chopping herbs into the omelette. Only the occasional jogger passed by as she sat out in the warm air, watching the sky turn to pale grey and pink as the sun went down. Music wafted out from the cabin. From her limited collection of tapes she had chosen Vaughan Williams' *Fantasia on a Theme by Thomas Tallis*.

Marnie waited until darkness had fallen before going inside. It was the last evening of *Sally Ann*'s summer.

45
Procession

Marnie woke at six-thirty on Saturday morning. The cabin felt chilly. She sat up in bed and parted the curtain. The world was grey. She yawned and wiped condensation from the window. Still grey.

Outside all was silent. The cold air smelt of damp earth, and from the stern deck she could see up to the bows but no further. The bushes on the other side of the canal floated in mist.

Ten minutes later, dressed for warmth, Marnie cast off and took the boat through the last two locks of her journey. Nosing out of the top lock she switched on the headlamp and running lights. The suburb of Norwood was invisible. Fog enclosed *Sally Ann* as she headed slowly north towards Bull's Bridge.

After half an hour, Marnie scanned the right-hand bank intently, looking for the white-painted outline of the bridge at the entrance to the Paddington Arm. In about four hours she would reach Little Venice.

All London seemed to be sleeping in the mist while *Sally Ann* groped her way along the canal. Marnie tried not to become mesmerised by the grey air and could only judge progress by noting the numbers on the bridges that she passed.

Hours dragged by. At one moment the sky brightened and for a few seconds Marnie glimpsed the sun. She estimated that this was the approach to Kensal Green and she strained to pick out the hulks of the gasholders that should be standing over to her right. Somewhere round the next bend she would see the supermarket opposite the old cemetery.

The sun strained through again, turning the mundane stretch of waterway into a painting by Turner. The extra light merged water, sky and the damp condensed air into one swirling vapour. Marnie stood transfixed, suspended in time and space. Looking up, she saw the sun piercing the clouds and its light blinded her.

She eased the tiller over to take the long bend and at once sensed movement ahead. Her eyes were trying to focus but could find nothing to hold in the dazzling opaque light. Marnie blinked furiously. There it was. A boat was turning across her path, the steerer intent on the manoeuvre, looking the other way.

Marnie swung the tiller. Passing round the stern, she quickly dropped the engine to idling and steered back to mid-channel, realising in that instant that another boat was ahead. Over went the tiller. Again *Sally* turned and headed for the bank, where a third craft was pulling in.

Marnie had no time to think, weaving her way through this armada. She sensed rather than saw other boats. The sun was still struggling through the mist. Reflections dazzled and confused her, like a conjuror's stage-set of smoke and mirrors. A shadow appeared ahead and she veered left. What was going on?

A shape loomed up on her left, a working boat, its tarpaulins fastened back, was passing through the water with hardly a ripple, at the edge of Marnie's field of vision, half hidden in the mist. She stared. On a platform in the middle of the boat, covered with a huge three-coloured cloth, lay a coffin. She had inadvertently blundered into a funeral procession. The coffin-boat glided past in silence.

More boats came by, the steerers concentrating on their passage through the fog. And then the cortege had passed. It had been the most bizarre incident of the summer. All Marnie's thoughts were on the strange procession, the ghost-fleet on its way to the cemetery, the simple dignity of the coffin-boat.

The sun only began clearing the mist on the final approach to Little Venice. Marnie switched off the headlamp. In her mind she saw again the outline of the coffin. Only then did she realise that its shroud had been a flag, the tri-colour of Ireland.

46
Homecoming

'Ah … the water gypsy returns!' Beaming, Mrs Jolly kissed Marnie on both cheeks. She took the flowers that Marnie had brought and led her through to the kitchen.

'It's nice to see you looking so well, my dear. I've made a few biscuits to welcome you home. How does it feel to be back?'

'It's lovely to see you again, but it feels odd in a way, being back … rather an anti-climax.'

Mrs Jolly put the flowers in a vase and stood back to admire them. 'It's not surprising, really, after all your travelling. And then there's what I call London Sunday Blues, how strangely quiet it can seem.'

Marnie agreed. 'It was the same yesterday, too. Little Venice seemed curiously *deserted*.'

Mrs Jolly ushered Marnie towards the sitting room. 'It was very misty for much of yesterday, of course. That always quietens things down.'

'I suppose so. But I – Oh …'

Marnie stopped in her tracks as the old lady opened the sitting room door. Table lamps were glowing and the fire was alight, reflecting off Mrs Jolly's best china. The low table had been laid with plates of biscuits of various shapes and sizes. The chintz covers on the furniture made Marnie want to flop down forever.

'This looks *wonderful*, Mrs Jolly … a *real* homecoming.'

'I'm so glad you like it, my dear. I hope you don't mind me saying this, but you seem a little sombre. Are you sorry you've finished your journey?'

Mrs Jolly reached for the coffee pot and offered Marnie an armchair.

'Actually, there's more to it than that, Mrs Jolly. I think the place was deserted yesterday because of the funeral.'

'Oh. I didn't see it.'

'It was at Kensal Green cemetery, a waterborne funeral. I ran into it – almost literally – on the canal in thick fog.'

'I didn't realise they had that kind of funeral.'

'They did yesterday.'

Mrs Jolly leaned forward to pour the coffee. Straightening up, she glanced towards the window.

'There's that man again, hanging around *Sally Ann*, the one who rented out your mooring space.'

They both went to the window.

'Actually, Marnie, I saw him there last night just before I went to bed. At first I thought it might be you, so I looked out.' She giggled. 'Do you think I'm becoming a curtain-twitcher?'

Gary turned and begin walking down the towpath. He had barely gone a few paces when he was joined by a woman.

'That's your friend, isn't it, my dear?'

Marnie nodded. 'Jane Rutherford.'

Gary and Jane spoke briefly together before Gary went on his way. Jane waited for several seconds then turned, let herself out of the towpath gate and crossed the road.

'I think she's coming here.' Mrs Jolly went to the door.

When the three of them were sitting comfortably, Jane asked about Marnie's journey, but it was obvious she had something on her mind.

'Is everything all right, Jane? We er … we saw you talking to Gary just then.'

Jane smiled. 'The radar.'

Mrs Jolly looked puzzled.

Marnie replied. 'Yes.'

'Gary wants to see you, or – more precisely – Roger Broadbent does.'

'Who's Roger Broadbent?'

'*Rumpole* … along the towpath from you.'

'Why does he want to see me?'

'He's a solicitor.'

'Oh?'

'I ought to start at the beginning.'

'Good idea. I only got back yesterday afternoon. I'm obviously out of touch.'

Jane frowned. 'Yesterday?'

'Yes, I came through the fog and –'

'So you saw the funeral?'

'I inadvertently drove through it.'

'So you've heard the news?'

Marnie looked blank. 'What news? I had to weave through the procession and by a miracle I didn't hit anything. I was going to call round to see Old Peter. I figured he'd know all about it.'

'Marnie … it was *his* funeral. We were there to bury Old Peter.'

Marnie felt a hollow sensation in her chest. She breathed in deeply. 'Oh …'

She stood up and moved towards the window. Looking out, she saw Old Peter passing on his grey-green boat, hat fixed firmly on his head, pipe clamped firmly in his mouth. She blinked several times and looked again. The canal was empty, with not a ripple on the water.

Mrs Jolly stood up and put an arm round Marnie's shoulders. 'That's very sad news. Are you all right, my dear?'

'Yes. It's just rather a shock. I had no idea he was …' Her voice petered out.

Jane spoke softly. 'He was a good age.'

Marnie and Mrs Jolly sat down. 'How did it happen?'

'A heart attack on his boat. Gary was passing by chance and found him.'

'So at least he died on the canal.'

'Not then, Marnie. They got him to hospital. After a few days he sent for Gary to take him back to his boat. He wouldn't stay in hospital, though he must have known he was dying. Gary told me Old Peter said, *I was born on a boat ... I'll die on a boat*. Gary was with him at the end.'

The doorbell made them jump. Mrs Jolly went out and returned, followed by Gary and another man. Gary spoke first.

'Marnie, hi. I've er, brought you a ... messenger ... from Old Peter. You know about ...?'

Marnie nodded and turned to the other man. 'Mr Broadbent?'

'You're well-informed, Mrs Walker. Call me Roger.'

'Marnie.'

They shook hands.

'I gather you've just returned from holiday.'

'Yesterday afternoon.'

'And you obviously know about Old Peter.'

'Jane's just told me. I don't quite see what –'

'Perhaps I could explain. Some weeks ago he came to see me. I'd never met him up to then, though I'd seen him passing, of course. He asked me to give you something when you returned.'

'Really?'

'An envelope.'

Marnie was bewildered. 'Why? What was in it?'

'He didn't say. All he said was to give it to you and you would know what to do with it. He thought you'd understand.'

'Understand what?'

'That is the question.'

'Do you have the envelope?'

'Not with me. I wasn't expecting to see you today. It's kept in the safe in my office.'

'Shall I come there on Monday?'

Roger hesitated. 'I know this will sound odd, but I'd prefer to give it to you here, in Little Venice. Somehow, it seems more fitting.'

47
Legacy

Marnie was not surprised to see Gary waiting beside *Rumpole* when she arrived at ten o'clock Monday morning. She knocked on the boat's side door. When Roger opened it and saw Gary, he raised an eyebrow.

'I've no objection to Gary being here,' Marnie said. 'After all, he was a friend of Old Peter … to the end.'

In the saloon Roger handed Marnie the envelope without explanation. Inside she found a single piece of lined writing paper, its message written in ballpoint, the handwriting clear and well-formed. Gary was practically stretching his neck to breaking point to try to see over her shoulder, and Marnie could sense that even Roger was consumed with curiosity.

'I could read it out loud, but I don't want to hold you up. Would you prefer me to take it away?'

Roger looked serious. 'Entirely your choice, Marnie, of course. It's a private matter between you and Old Peter.'

In the background Gary cleared his throat.

'Okay, I'll read it out. It starts without any greeting.'

My family has had some documents for a very long time. I don't know how long or how they came by them. I was once told by my grandfather that his grandfather had worked on the canals when he came to England from Ireland as a boy.

Marnie looked up. 'He was of Irish extraction?'

Gary nodded. 'Yeah. He told me he did have family over there.'

Marnie could hear Old Peter's voice: … *the three worst things ever invented for engines … dust … no maintenance … Irishmen.* Irony. She continued reading.

When I was a young man my father passed the documents to me before he died. He told me I had to take care of them and only give them to my own family to keep them safe. I have no family now. I want you to have them. They are yours now. They may be valuable. I don't know. You will find them on my boat. You will know what to do with them for the best. Thank you.

The letter was signed: *Peter William Gibson*

Gary broke the silence. 'That's not right.'

Marnie turned to face him. 'You don't think I should have them?'

'No. I mean, it's not right that the things are on his boat.'

Roger stared at Gary. 'You've searched the boat?'

Gary looked down at the letter. 'No … well, not exactly *searched* … but I know there's nothing on the boat … unless it's just a small envelope or something like that.'

Roger looked at Marnie who was rereading the letter. 'Is that everything, Marnie? No mention of where to find these *documents*?'

'Nothing.' She turned the paper over. 'Ah, wait a minute … there's something else. It's very faint … in pencil.' She lifted the paper up to the window where the light was brighter. 'Odd … it's just a series of letters.'

PSCXXI

Gary leaned forward. 'Weird.'

Roger read it from behind her. 'Perhaps it would become clear if we visited the boat. Do you have time, Marnie?'

———— ∾∾∾ ————

Gary had the keys to the grey-green boat, for *safe keeping*, he said. It looked as tidy as Marnie remembered it from her last visit. They began opening drawers, checking cupboards, under the bed, everywhere. Gary went out to inspect the caravan while Roger lifted up the mattress. Nothing.

Marnie sat down and scanned the cabin. 'It must be something obvious, otherwise he wouldn't expect us to find it, which would make the whole exercise rather pointless.'

Roger lowered the mattress and straightened the bedcover. 'I agree. He obviously took a lot of trouble to make sure whatever it is wouldn't be found by accident.'

'These … *documents* … didn't he say anything about them when he gave you the letter? What are we looking for, Roger?'

'Goodness knows. That mention of his grandfather … it's obviously an heirloom … deeds, perhaps. Maybe you'll find you own property in Ireland.'

'Why would he leave me anything like that? I hardly knew him.'

'Believe me, Marnie, it's not uncommon. An old man, no living family, meets an attractive young woman – I'm not implying anything, of course – and decides he'd like to make her a gift, make someone he likes happy to remember him.'

'But I don't deserve that.'

Roger grinned. 'That's not the usual reaction. It's usually: *how much is it worth?*'

'This isn't that kind of thing, Roger. I know it isn't. He's entrusting something to me to keep it safe … and it's here, staring us in the face, only we can't see it.'

'He never hinted at anything to you?'

'We hardly spoke. He told me about canals and engines and – wait a mo' … what kind of engine does this boat have?'

'Engine?'

'He once spoke to me about Lister engines. That might mean something.'

Roger walked through towards the stern. 'Gardner … vintage model … shining like new.'

'So not a Lister. Pity.'

Gary returned from the caravan. 'Bugger all over there – oops, sorry, not the kind of language Old Peter would've approved of.'

'One of nature's gentlemen,' Marnie observed.

'And religious,' Gary added.

'Religious?'

'Yeah ... RC. Used to go to Mass every week. I had to get a priest to come and give him ... what'ya call it.'

'The last rites?' Marie suggested.

'Yeah. Heard his confession.'

'You didn't happen to, er ... accidentally, of course?'

Gary shook his head. 'Priest asked me to leave ... heard it in private.'

Roger lifted the cutlery tray out of a drawer and looked in. 'Short of taking the boat to pieces I'm not sure what we can do here, Marnie.'

Marnie was working her way along a small row of books, mostly technical manuals plus the odd canal guide. Her finger stopped at an old bible. She pulled it out and flicked through the pages. It was well-thumbed. She tipped it up but nothing fell out. On the saloon table Old Peter's note lay face down. Staring up at her was the strange inscription.

Roger saw it and made the connection at the same time as Marnie. He looked at the Bible. 'A biblical reference?'

Marnie examined the writing closely. 'PS could stand for Psalm something, maybe?'

'Yes, CXXI ... one hundred ... twenty ... one.'

Marnie leafed through the pages. 'That's Old Testament, isn't it ... here we are ... Psalms. Ah ...'

'What is it Marnie?'

She looked up at Roger. 'It begins: *I will lift up mine eyes unto the hills* ... What hills?'

'*From whence cometh my help*,' Gary murmured quietly from behind them.

Marnie and Roger turned in surprise.

'Did it in RE at school.' He made a dismissive gesture.

Marnie altered her focus and lifted up her eyes. 'Is that a screw up there in the ceiling, Roger, above your head?'

'There's one here, too,' Gary added. He ran his finger along the tongue and groove lining. The dulled brass screw head was virtually invisible among the knots in the pine. 'And here's another one.'

Roger agreed. 'It looks as if this whole section is held in place by half a dozen screws.'

Marnie stood up for a better look. 'Could it just be the way the boat's constructed?'

'Is *Sally Ann* built like that, Marnie?'

'No idea. I've never thought to look.'

'That may be the point. You don't stand around on a boat examining the ceiling, even if it is just a few inches above your head.'

'Before we start dismantling the whole boat, I think we ought to check the rest of the ceilings.'

'Good idea, Gary.' Roger turned away. 'I'll inspect the galley. D'you want to try the engine room?'

Marnie stepped round the table. 'I'll look in the sleeping cabin.'

It took barely a minute to ascertain that only the ceiling in the saloon was held up by visible brass screws. Gary reappeared carrying Old Peter's toolbox. They moved the furniture aside and set about unscrewing the section above their heads and the three transverse battens that held the whole panel in place. Carefully they lowered that part of the ceiling to the floor.

Roger shook his head. 'It's just insulation. We seem to be back to square –'

'Hang on.' Marnie knelt down. 'This isn't padding. Look, it's folded over at the end.'

The ceiling panel had concealed a package roughly the size of a single mattress, about three inches thick. The covering was of strong brown paper, sewn all round except for one end. Marnie unfolded it, prised it apart and peered inside.

'It seems to be stuffed with paper. Roger, are there any scissors in that drawer? We're going to have to cut the thread to get a better look. It's all very tightly packed.'

Once the sewn end was cut, they pulled the package open. Marnie lifted the top sheet of paper.

'Old documents?' Roger asked.

'Well … they look like new … dozens of them … hundreds, maybe.' She slid out a drawing. 'This is superb draughtsmanship. Can you see a date anywhere?'

They pulled off the whole of the outer covering and inspected the contents of Old Peter's legacy. It contained batches of papers, many of them the size of architects' drawings. Some smaller items were tied in bundles with black ribbon, others in large envelopes. There were letters, accounts, bills, records, notes, quantities of plans and drawings.

The first surprise was their pristine condition. Initially Marnie thought they might be copies. But several of the working drawings bore finger-marks as if they had been handled during building works. Some had pencil notes in the margins. These were original documents, but whose?

The second surprise came when Roger noticed the box containing the details of the job, client, drawing and project number in a corner of one of the plans. Beside the title, *Engineer in charge*, he read just two initials: WJ. He stared at Marnie.

'What is it, Roger?'

'I wonder … Are there any letters in that pile next to you, Marnie?'

She passed him a bundle of papers. 'I hope these aren't in any sort of order.'

'I shouldn't worry about that. Everything here will have to be indexed and filed by an expert, probably an archivist … oh, I mean, if that's your wish, Marnie. They're your papers, after all.'

'I'm supposed to … *know what to do with them for the best*,' she reminded him. 'At the moment all I can think is that – Oh my *god* …'

It was the third surprise, and the biggest. With infinite care she eased a drawing out of its batch and sat staring at it.

Roger looked up from studying the letters. 'What have you … *good lord* …'

Gary, who had been untying ribbons, turned to see what had taken their attention so dramatically. '*Jesus Christ Almighty* … oh … sorry …'

They were staring at the drawing of an aqueduct, rising up on slim pillars from the floor of a valley to form graceful arches, the whole construction depicted in every detail, the ink as clear as on the day the aqueduct was built. For this drawing had been produced at that time by the man who had designed it.

In her head, Marnie heard a voice, an old voice, speaking slowly and precisely.

You like … structures?

'It can only be …' Roger shifted round for a better look. 'It has to be …'

Gary agreed. 'Yeah … the one with the funny name.'

'Pontcysyllte.' Marnie made a pretty good job of it.

'That's the one,' Roger said. 'But all these papers can't just relate to one aqueduct.'

'No. I think they relate to quite a few different projects. These seem to be a whole collection … my goodness … the papers of William Jessop …'

Roger corrected her. 'The *lost* papers of William Jessop, if I'm not mistaken … missing for almost two hundred years.'

'Must be worth a bob or two.' Gary looked up from reading one of the letters to find Marnie and Roger staring at him again. 'I only meant –'

'It's all right, Gary. We know what you meant.'

Roger got up from his knees and sat in a chair. 'I suppose the next thing is, you have to decide what to do with them, Marnie.'

Marnie frowned. 'But it isn't as easy as that. There are all sorts of questions to be answered. How did Old Peter come by them in the first place? Are they really his? What's best for them? How should they be treated? What's their value?' She glanced across at Gary. 'I mean, in historical terms.'

Roger steepled his fingers. 'Well, as a solicitor, I'd say it would be difficult for anyone else to prove title to them after all this time. As far as I know they've never been reported as stolen.'

Marnie got up. 'But equally, Old Peter's family surely can't prove ownership.'

'They might not have to. Of course, Jessop's descendants – if there are any – could contest that, but they'd have to produce a will that specifically mentions these papers. They relate to work Jessop carried out under contract to a company that no longer exists. We really need advice from an expert historian.'

'The devil's in the detail. Isn't that what you solicitors always say?'

'True, Marnie, but I think one thing is fairly clear. There's no evidence to suggest Old Peter's family misappropriated them. They haven't used them for gain. Quite the opposite. They've acted as their custodians, it appears, for generations. The country owes them a debt of gratitude.'

Marnie sat down, staring at the pile of documents at her feet. None of them spoke for some time. Eventually Marnie broke the silence.

'You're right, Roger. And I think I know exactly what to do with them.'

⎯⎯⎯∽∿∾⎯⎯⎯

Gary had to leave Marnie and Roger on Old Peter's boat to see a man about a job.

By twelve-thirty he was back in Little Venice meeting Sheena outside the chemist's for lunch. He was taken aback when she suggested the pub round the corner – Gravel's

Sally Ann's Summer

pub – but he let her have her way. Sheena was more definite about everything since her return from the course and her holiday. She knew what she wanted and expected to get it. Gary put it down to her new position of responsibility as *assistant pharmacist (trainee)*.

Approaching the bar, Gary glanced in the direction of Gravel's usual table, which was always vacant these days. He froze. On that day it was occupied. He saw the black leather jacket, the shaved head, the ear-ring. Three men were sitting there and, as he looked on, one of them rose from the table. Gary struggled to keep his expression neutral. At that moment, the shaved head turned and called out to the man heading for the bar.

'*Das Bier muß schön warm sein, Helmut. Nicht vergessen!*'

They all three laughed. It was not Gravel. Bikers. German, Gary thought.

Sheena had spotted an empty table in the corner. Gary left her reading a menu and went to order drinks.

'So where's our friend, then, Benny? Where's Gravel?' Benny looked up from pulling a pint. Before he could speak, Gary continued. 'And don't give me all that *I've-no-idea-who-you-mean* crap … Dave Naylor.'

Benny spoke quietly, watching the beer glass. 'Oh, I know who you mean, Gary.'

'Well, then?'

'He's done a Sheena.'

'He's what?'

'Gone on a mystery holiday.'

'What d'you mean?'

'I heard he'd gone off to the country where they take the siesta.'

'Benny, what are you talking about?'

Benny gave the final pull on the pump.

Sheena appeared at Gary's side. 'Ham baguette, no mustard.' She returned to their table.

More customers arrived, so Gary ordered the same and carried the drinks back, puzzling over why Benny was talking in riddles.

Sheena sipped her lime and lemonade. 'So what's on your mind, Gary … apart from the usual?'

'Nothing.'

'Don't give me that.' She smiled beguilingly.

'Well, there is something …'

'I can always tell.'

He looked over his shoulder and lowered his voice. 'Remember that business about the old boy and his, er … valuables?'

'Course I do.'

'This is all *very* secret, right?'

'Gary …' She sounded pained.

'Well, you know he died …'

'And?'

'It looks like we've found his stuff.'

'Go on.'

'He left this letter with a bloke who's got a boat here … solicitor. Like a will, almost. Anyway, he left his things … these *valuable* things … to Marnie.'

'Why am I not surprised?'

'I know what you mean, but she was surprised … *very*.'

'Really?' Sheena sounded unconvinced.

'Honest. She didn't see why she should have them.'

'Have *what* exactly, Gary?'

He leaned forward. 'Probably the lost papers of William Jessop. He was a canal engineer … two hundred years ago … very important.'

'How valuable is *very important*?'

Gary shrugged. 'Dunno. *Very* valuable to a museum, I suppose.'

'So all this fuss has been about a load of dusty old … *papers*?'

'Original plans and drawings of early canals … very good condition, from what I saw.'

'Amazing.' Sheena sounded underwhelmed. 'Oh well, it's a pity your mate Gravel isn't around, then.'

'Why?'

'He'd be pleased, wouldn't he?'

Gary stared into his beer. 'Ecstatic.'

———⚬⚬⚬———

Marnie immersed herself completely in sorting through the Jessop documents. She spent two hours spreading the papers out all over her flat, amazed at how much material there was.

Faced with the practical problem of what to do with the legacy, Roger had offered an immediate solution. *What are Volvo estates for?* He had fetched his car and they loaded the whole package into the cargo space, before travelling in convoy to Hampstead.

Alone in the flat with her legacy, Marnie laid out the plans and drawings in the living room, the notes and calculations in the guest-room, the correspondence in her bedroom and the bills and costings on the kitchen table. The apartment began to smell like a library. Dolly sniffed everything with suspicion. The next task was to stand several of the drawings around the walls, till the living room looked like a gallery.

Catching sight of the clock, she remembered she had to ring Philip to fix a meeting. The receptionist put her through, but a different voice answered.

'Marnie, it's Faye. Philip's at lunch.'

'Long lunch. It's nearly three.'

'That's how it is these days … long *working* lunches …'

'Is that good … lots of work coming in?'

Faye sounded surprisingly distant. 'Couldn't say.'

'I see … or perhaps I don't. Faye, is there a problem in the office?'

'Sort of.'

'But you can't talk about it on the phone in the office.'

'That's right. So, how are things with you, Marnie?'

'Actually, things are very interesting. I've just inherited – if that's the right word – a load of plans, drawings and papers from two hundred years ago, possibly the lost collection of one of the great canal engineers.'

'You're kidding!'

'They're spread out all over the flat. You wouldn't believe it.'

'How long have you had them?'

'Since this morning.'

'Let me guess. You've been so absorbed in them that you haven't eaten anything?'

'*Eaten?* Er ... well, yes, I suppose that's right, but –'

'Can I see this collection, Marnie?'

— ∾ —

Sheena insisted. Gary had to tell her all about Marnie's legacy. Between mouthfuls of baguette, he gave her the whole story, since Gravel first talked about it. He ended with the finding of the papers hidden on the boat that morning.

'So where are they now?' Sheena removed a tiny crumb from her lip with a perfectly painted fingernail.

'Marnie's flat. She's a dark horse, that one. I bet she knew all along the old boy had something valuable ...'

'Oh, I'm sure you're wrong about that, Gary.'

'Then why would he leave all those things to a woman he hardly knew?'

Sheena shrugged. 'No harm in it. She probably brought a little sparkle into his life.'

Gary grinned. 'You bring sparkle into *my* life, Sheena.'

'Yes, well, in Old Peter's case I don't suppose Marnie did it in quite the same way.'

Gary rested a hand on her knee under the table. She stood up, muttered 'Powder my nose', and walked off across the saloon. Several heads turned as she passed.

While she was away Gary wondered about Marnie. Had she known about the valuables? She was good-looking, all right, and could easily have charmed a lonely old man, but unlike many attractive women, she didn't flaunt herself. He was convinced that Marnie had not wheedled her way into Old Peter's affections with an ulterior motive.

Sheena emerged from the Ladies' room. Gary could sense radar antennae twitching. Every time he saw her, he could hardly believe his luck. Passing the bar, she stopped briefly as Benny spoke to her. She nodded and continued on her way. As she sat down, she crossed her legs. Gary tried and failed to avert his gaze.

'I've got a message for you, Gary ... from Benny.'

'A message?'

'I think it's about a car.'

'What car?'

'Something about ... a Siesta? Isn't that a type of Ford?'

Gary looked over to the bar; Benny was serving a customer. 'Are you sure that's what he said?'

'I think so. I don't normally run a messaging service, but I try to be accurate about things as a rule.'

'So what did he say about this … Siesta?'

'He said to mention that and then say one word: *cement*. Does that mean anything to you, Gary?'

Gary raised the glass to his lips. Riddles suddenly seemed to be the fashion in Little Venice. He puzzled over the strange message. *Siesta … cement …* Definitely a riddle … *cement … siesta …*

Sheena jumped in surprise as Gary choked on his beer.

Marnie greeted her visitor with a hug. Faye tottered, clutching a large box in one hand and a bottle in the other, trying not to trip over Dolly.

'Come in. Great to see you again. Hey, what's all this?'

'Not very original, Marnie, but I'm guessing you still haven't eaten so I've brought supper. King-size deep-pan pizza – Four Cheeses with extra Pepperoni – and a bottle of Chianti.'

Marnie grinned. 'Everett Parker Associates is running Meals on Wheels?'

'Not quite, but this could be useful practice. We may all soon be delivering pizzas full time.'

Marnie's smile faded. 'You kept a straight face when you said that.'

She took the pizza box and ushered her friend into the kitchen. Faye put the wine down beside a pile of Jessop's documents. Without touching them, she lowered her face and began reading. The item on top was a list of payments to workmen.

'So … the famous papers. I love the old-fashioned handwriting … it's a work of art.'

Marnie slid the pizza into the oven and beckoned to Faye who was stroking the cat.

'You've seen nothing yet. Come in here.'

'Okay, but first I've got a message from Philip. Could you meet him tomorrow at eleven.'

'That's fine. Will you be there?'

'No. I, er … I got the impression this was … just you, Marnie.'

'That sounds ominous.'

'I don't mean to speak out of turn. A lot of what I've heard is no more than gossip.'

Marnie led the way into the living room. 'Then we'll pay no attention to it. We'll just eat, drink and be merry, for tomorrow …'

'Don't say that, Marnie.' Faye walked into the living room. 'It can't be as bad as …' She came to a halt inside the doorway.

The room was filled with drawings, the like of which she had never seen before. She stood open-mouthed and uttered one long syllable.

'Wow!'

48
Designs

Marnie was surprised when Roger Broadbent phoned early on Tuesday morning and asked if he could call by before going into the office. When he arrived, his reaction to the picture gallery that had once been Marnie's living room matched Faye's.

'Wow!'

'That's the in-word at the moment, Roger.'

'Marnie, this is *extraordinary*. I've never seen anything like it.'

Marnie agreed. 'And to think Old Peter and his family kept them hidden all those years. Something's been bothering me. Why did they feel they had to protect the collection?'

'Good question, Marnie. I asked the curator of the National Canal Museum.'

'Did he have a good answer?'

'He said it was a mystery.'

'No wonder he's got to the top. Do you have any views, Roger?'

'Well actually, I do. It may be far-fetched, but I think there was a concerted attempt to suppress Jessop's role in favour of stressing the importance of someone else.'

Marnie had a flash of memory, a sunny morning near the Blisworth tunnel, a conversation over breakfast with Betty Atkins and her husband.

... It's a bit of a hobby horse of Ken's ...

'Thomas Telford,' she muttered.

'Exactly!'

'But why?'

Roger shrugged. 'Ego ... jealousy ... professional rivalry?'

'Is that what you came to tell me, Roger?'

'Not entirely. Partly, I was curious to see the collection. But there was something else ... two things, actually.'

'Oh?'

'When I spoke to the curator – Donald Stephens ... I know him slightly – I took the liberty of asking him how important these papers were ... and what he thought should be done with them.'

'What did he say?'

'He'd be very glad if you'd talk to him. Marnie, I hope you don't think I'm –'

'I'll phone him today.'

'Good. I think sooner rather than later, if you see what I mean.'

'Sure. I have a meeting this morning that's rather important and I've got some thinking to do, but –'

'Of course, Marnie. This is the return from your sabbatical, isn't it? You must have a lot on your mind.'

Marnie grinned. 'You know, I'm on such a high with all this …' She made a sweeping gesture around the room. '… I don't think *anything* could bother me at the moment.'

'I don't like to be a wet blanket, Marnie, but I think a single word might just do that. It's the other thing I wanted to mention to you.'

'Try me.'

'Insurance.'

———

Gary was up bright and early that Tuesday morning, another fine day in Little Venice. Everything was going right for him. True, Sheena had not stayed the night, but the previous evening she had proved she had lost none of her sparkle or inventiveness.

Sheena was now firmly back in his life, though she did seem to have a lot on her mind. Declining the invitation to stay, she had explained.

'It's called responsibility, Gary. In my new position …' She didn't have a job any more; she had a *position*. '… I've got more to think about, more to do, more to learn.'

That was something else he had noticed. She seemed to speak in threes these days. When he had pointed this out, she told him it had been part of her *presentation skills module*.

'You sell toothbrushes in packs of three?' She had rolled her eyes. He had persisted, with a twinkle in his eye. 'Talking of packs of three …'

'*Gary!*'

'What do you mean, then?'

With more rolling of the eyes, she had explained. 'It's management, Gary. On the course they taught us that you have to be multi-faceted, multi-skilled, multi … well all sorts of things, really.'

She used longer words a lot these days: objectives, brand recognition, positioning. She certainly knew a few things about positioning, he thought. He poured the breakfast tea and lit the breakfast cigarette. He had no problem with her new ideas, if it kept her happy.

After breakfast he had to call in at the BW office. Mike Brent, the manager, wanted to see him about a job. Setting off along the towpath, Gary's mind was filled with Sheena. He did not spare a glance at the pool. After the blip of her absence, the world was wonderful again.

Sheena was back, work was coming in, money was coming in. Three good things, he thought.

———

Marnie phoned the National Canal Museum at nine o'clock. Roger had alarmed her about what might happen to the Jessop papers if she was burgled or the roof fell in. Her home contents insurance policy would definitely not cover them.

'I'd like to speak to the curator, please.'

'Mr Stephens is in a meeting. Can anyone else help?'

'It's really the curator I need.'

'Could you give me an idea of the nature of your enquiry?'

Marnie took a deep breath. 'My name is Marnie Walker. I think I've just inherited the lost papers of William Jessop.'

In less than twenty seconds the curator was on the line. He arranged to come to London the following afternoon.

Now it all starts to happen, Marnie thought.

———※———

Gary was stunned. 'You want me to do *what?*'

'I know it's only about an hour's work,' Mike Brent said, 'but you'll get paid for half a day … usual rate.'

'Are you out of your tiny mind?'

'What's the problem, Gary? All I'm asking you to do is get a crane and lift that wooden crate out of the pool. You've done it before.'

'You are *definitely* joking. This is a wind-up, right?'

'No, Gary. It's a job. You're familiar with the term?'

'Yeah, and look what happened the last time I lifted a crate out of the pool.'

'Gary, that was a one-off. How many murders have we ever had in Little Venice? The place is as safe as houses.'

'You've got a short memory, Mike.'

'It's just a routine job.'

Gary shook his head. 'My mate won't bring his JCB this time, no chance.'

'This time, I can organise a salvage boat fitted with a crane. It's at St Pancras Basin, but you'd have to go and fetch it. I'm short of manpower, otherwise I wouldn't be asking.'

'I don't believe this.'

'Be reasonable, Gary. I don't want this crate bashing a hole in a tupperware and BW having to pay compensation.'

Gary turned towards the door. 'I can't do it. Out of the question.'

'That's your final word?'

'That's my final word.'

———※———

Marnie was in for a few surprises that morning. The first came when she looked in on her design group office before the meeting with Philip.

It was not the cards and flowers decorating her desk that made her stop in the doorway; it was the staring. All talking ceased as soon as she appeared. Fleetingly, she felt like a French aristo trundling through the streets of Paris in a tumbrel on her way to the guillotine.

Faye broke the silence. 'Welcome back, Marnie.'

She got up, crossed the room and gave Marnie a hug. The other members of the team quickly regained their composure and gathered round, everyone smiling, taking turns to kiss her on the cheeks. Once Marnie had torn herself away, Faye followed her out into the reception area.

'That was very odd, Faye.'

'I know. I should have foreseen that, but I didn't know how people would react.'

'To what?' Marnie could hear the blade of the guillotine falling. 'Do they know something I don't know?'

'No. It's just ... well, you have changed rather a lot.'

'In what way?'

'For a start, your tan wouldn't look out of place on the Riviera. Also ... don't mind me saying this, but ... you're slimmer than you were before you went off ... quite a bit slimmer.'

Marnie reflected. 'I suppose I have been getting a lot of exercise these past months.'

'More than that, Marnie. You've got a kind of ... *aura*.'

Marnie was incredulous. 'All I did was step into the office.'

Faye laughed. 'I know, but you somehow ... *exude* confidence. You look fit ... dynamic.'

Marnie saw Philip walking towards them. He looked worried.

'Let's hope it sees me through,' she murmured.

Gary lowered the crane head towards the water and stopped it a foot or so below the surface. Muttering to himself ... *I must be raving mad* ... he put the crane boat into gear. He had been muttering since he first collected the salvage boat, *Pigeon*, from St Pancras. The journey had given him time to prepare a plan. This time there would be no risk of smashing the crate.

Gary would nudge the crate towards Brendan, who was poised at the water's edge. Brendan would hold it against the side while Gary moored. Together they would manhandle it out of the water. At the first hint of anything unsavoury they would inform Mike Brent and he would have to sort it out.

A small crowd of onlookers was standing further along the bank. It was the start of the lunch period, and numbers grew as the word got round. A lugubrious curiosity was settling over Little Venice.

Gary swung the *Pigeon* round and approached the bank sideways on. Waiting for the boat to dock, he caught sight of a familiar shape. A blonde woman was walking slowly along the broad towpath. Sheena. Reaching the crowd, she spoke to a woman who pointed at Brendan, kneeling by the waterside. The onlookers were hushed, their excitement palpable even at that range.

Sheena took in the whole scene. When her gaze reached the salvage boat, Gary waved. For a few seconds Sheena stared. Then she turned and fled.

Philip looked dejected as he brought his presentation to a close. He sat back in the chair and checked his watch.

'That's more or less everything. I expect you've got some questions.'

Marnie had been taking notes. The other person in the conference room, Larry from the interior design group, sat stony-faced beside her.

Marnie looked up, breathing out audibly. 'I'm not sure what to say. That was very thorough. Have Willards actually withdrawn the contract?'

Philip shifted in his seat. 'Not exactly ... not yet.'

'But if I've understood correctly, they've rejected the interior design scheme for the pubs, so the other projects they've hinted at ...' Marnie looked at her notepad. '... new hotel, refurbishment of existing ones, extension of head office ... all of those could be lost.'

Philip looked pained. Marnie continued.

'All this just because they didn't like my scheme for the pubs?'

'Er ...' Larry's first contribution.

Marnie waited for more, but Philip replied.

'The scheme we eventually presented to them wasn't ... *entirely* yours, Marnie.'

'What d'you mean ... *not entirely?*'

'Er ...' Larry's second contribution.

Marnie turned to look at him. 'Speak to me, Larry.'

'Well ... this is really embarrassing. The thing is, Marnie, I didn't want to just take over your design. It didn't seem right.'

'But ... that's what we arranged. That's why I completed it before I went off.'

'I know, but somehow it felt like I was ... passing your work off as mine.'

'So what did you do?'

I er, ... modified it a bit.'

'Changed the colours?'

Larry nodded. 'I thought they could be a bit more ... definite.'

'You mean *darker*.' Marnie glanced at Philip. 'The whole point was to introduce a kind of *watercolour* feeling.'

Larry looked subdued. 'I know, but I thought it we could make it a little more ... bold ...'

Philip said quietly, 'We did think of reverting to your original lighter colours, Marnie.'

Marnie shook her head. 'It would look like tinkering. So what happens now?'

'Two Willards executives are coming in tomorrow for a discussion.'

'You think they'll wind up the contract?'

Philip nodded. 'This could go badly. It's not just this contract, but our whole reputation. There could be consequences ... for all of us.'

Gary tied up the *Pigeon* to a mooring ring and walked along to where Brendan was holding the crate against the bank. The crowd of onlookers had fallen silent.

'Can you smell anything ... in there?'

'Jesus, Gary. What kind of question is that?'

'Then let me put it another way, Bren. Does it seem to you that there might be a dismembered body rotting in that crate?'

'*God almighty!* I'd cross meself if I had a hand free.'

The box looked suspiciously like the other one. Gary shuddered. Was he about to come face to face – assuming there was a face – with Gravel? Was this another gangland murder victim?

'For *Chrissake*, Gary, have I got to kneel here all bloody day?'

Gary stepped forward, seized the crate and began to pull. Brendan added his considerable strength and gradually, tantalisingly slowly, the box rose from the water. On the lip of the bank, it teetered briefly as if about to topple back into the pool. Brendan gave it a mighty heave. The box slammed down onto the concrete and one edge came adrift. Water splashed out, spreading in a puddle around their feet. A gasp went up from the spectators.

Brendan grimaced. 'There's things rolling around in there.'

Before Gary could stop him, Brendan took hold of the loose cover and wrenched it apart. Several slimy objects rolled slowly from the crate. Every onlooker raised a hand to their mouth. Gary could hardly bring himself to look at what they had loosened. He noticed a word printed on the side of the box: Valencia.

'Spanish oranges,' he muttered.

Brendan looked at him. 'What?'

The cry of laughter that Gary let out echoed like the scream of a madman. It made the crowd step backwards and startled the pigeons in the trees. They fluttered from their branches and took off to fly in a great arc above the pool of Little Venice and away over the rooftops.

<hr>

After the meeting Marnie went home, hoping the plans and drawings would lift her spirits. They did, but only marginally. Lunch was a tomato and a yogurt, eaten while gazing out of the kitchen window. Only Dolly was getting proper meals these days.

She had brought the Willards folder from the office and set her design out on the drawing board in the guest-room. Compared with the hackneyed decor of some pubs, it looked fine. In contrast with Larry's modified scheme, hers would look like a pale imitation.

She was musing about possible newspaper headlines if she murdered Larry and left his body floating in the canal, when the phone rang. She braced herself for bad news, but it was a pleasant surprise: Anne (with an 'e').

'How are things, Marnie? Good to be back with your friends?'

'One or two problems. That's life. How about you?'

'School's fine. In fact my project about the canals … got top marks.'

Marnie wished she could say the same about hers. 'Brilliant!'

'Thanks … for all your encouragement. Things at home are much the same. Dad's got some temporary work … still trying to get a permanent job. So, what's your news?'

'I hardly know where to begin …'

Marnie told the story of the legacy.

'That's like … winning the lottery! What will you do with it all, Marnie?'

'Much as I'd love to keep them, they really belong to everyone. That's why the old man left them to me. He thought I'd know what to do with them for the best.'

'Absolutely. Everyone will want to see them. I hope I will, some time.'

'Of course you will.'

Anne became serious. 'Marnie, there's something I … I know it's a longshot but … do you think it might ever be possible for me to train as a designer and … work with you?'

'Ah …'

'I knew I shouldn't –'

'Anne, it's … the situation here is, to say the least, precarious. A big project has gone wrong while I was away.'

'At least no one can blame you, then.'

Unexpectedly, Marnie found herself letting it all out, the frustration, the sense of being let down, the feeling of betrayal … everything.

Anne sympathised. 'This person went behind your back while you were out of the way.'

'Yeah.'

Anne sounded thoughtful. 'It's a pity.'

'Understatement.'

'No, I mean … it's a pity you couldn't use the things you inherited … in your design.'

'How d'you mean? They're actual engineer's plans and drawings.'

'You know Paddington station, Marnie? They have huge murals where you come up from the tube – blow-ups of designs by Brunel – I photographed them for a project. They give the whole place a real 'wow' factor.'

'Wow?' That *in-word* again.

Anne continued. 'Yes, but I don't suppose your engineer worked on the canals round here, did he?'

Marnie's mind was racing. 'I think Jessop did the original survey for the Grand Junction Canal … I think I read that somewhere.'

'It was just an idea.'

'*Murals* … Anne, you're a genius! Gotta go. We'll talk again. Soon. That's a promise.'

49
Aura

Marnie swept into the office like a whirlwind, dropped her bag and a large portfolio on the desk and collared Faye Summers. It did not escape her notice that one seat was conspicuously vacant.

Faye blinked. 'Blimey, Marnie, you're chirpy for first thing on a Wednesday morning.'

'*First thing*? I've already had one meeting.'

Faye winced. 'What time did you get up?'

'About five-thirty.'

Faye wearily shook her head. 'Oh god, is this the shape of things to come from now on?' She lowered her voice. 'Or as long as we're still here ...'

Marnie was undeterred. 'Where's Larry?'

'Philip's idea ... gardening leave for a few days ...'

'Wise move. Come on!'

'Marnie, what was this *meeting* you've already had?'

'Photographic studio in Hampstead ... got some trannies processed. Are you coming or what?'

Faye trailed in Marnie's wake. She stopped by the coffee machine, guessing that Marnie had forgotten to have breakfast. By the time she entered the conference room, Marnie was loading slides into the projector and the table was covered with papers.

'Here ... breakfast ... coffee. ... two custard creams ... best I could do.'

Marnie, absentmindedly. 'Great ... now ... let's see if I've got these the right way up.'

She switched on the slide projector and focused the first image, a lock. The gates were old, water pouring though gaps, flowers and grasses growing on them. It had great charm.

'Pretty. You should drink your coffee, Marnie. The new machine isn't bad at cappuccino.'

Marnie persisted. 'It may look pretty, but you've got to see it as *engineering*. Look at this.'

The next slide was a plan of lock gates and mechanism, followed by a drawing of a complete lock.

'Is that ...?' Faye began.

'Yeah. The original design of that very lock ... 1793.'

'Beautiful!' Faye thrust a biscuit into her hand. 'Marnie, you should eat something.'

'And functional, Faye.'

Marnie began chewing. She pressed the projector switch and more images floated across the screen.

Faye watched and understood. 'This is the basis for a design.'

'Exactly. I've done one pub as a sample, with concept sketches for the others.'

'When did you do all this?'

'Last night ... and a bit this morning.'

'Did you get any sleep at all?'

'Concentrate, Faye. We haven't got much time before we meet the client.'

'You mean you're going to –'

'What's the alternative? We sit here and let them wind up the contract? Watch the slide show, look at my sketches and colour scheme and tell me honestly what you think.'

Twenty minutes later, Faye sat back. 'So you use mural panels with blow-ups of the designs and drawings –'

'Depending on the space available ... partial murals where it's limited ... tinted in appropriate colours.'

'Okay. And framed pictures for the walls ... documents ... sketches ... What about the old photographs of boats and stuff they already have?'

'Keep them ... reprint them if necessary ... maybe relocate for variety? We don't want the pubs to look like museums. What do you think?'

Faye scanned the papers. 'Stunning. I don't think anyone's ever done this before ... at least not in a pub.'

'It's a matter of scale ... proportion ... muted colours for a warm atmosphere. Let the strength of the images come through.'

'It's fabulous, Marnie. I love it. What now?'

'It'll be up to Willards. I've done all I can. Got any more of those biscuits?'

———✦———

Philip was surprised that the meeting went on so long. He had expected the Willards executives to ask for a renegotiation – essentially a winding up – of their contract. A prior meeting had prevented him from talking with Marnie. He was unprepared for what happened.

Marnie had immediately taken the initiative and launched into an outline of her approach to the design. The executives had not expected a presentation but were attracted by the slides and let Marnie take the floor. Philip thought the new-look, slimline Marnie, with her suntan and her ... *aura* ... also appealed to them.

When Marnie sat down and invited questions, the younger executive immediately spoke.

'We actually came here to talk about the other scheme.'

Marnie began. 'That was –'

'Sorry, can I just finish? What you've shown us was very impressive, but one thing bothers me. These documents ... they're all original eighteenth century material. Is that right?'

'Correct.'

'How can you be certain we'd get permission from the owners to use it? It could be expensive. You haven't presented us with any costings.'

'There's no difference to the agreed budget.'

'And the small matter of permission?'

'The owner is making everything available … free of charge.'

He paused. 'You've got that in writing?'

'You can have it in writing. The material is mine.'

The executives looked surprised. '*Yours?*'

'It was bequeathed to me and I'm arranging for it to go to a museum. But I'll make sure I keep the rights to use it in my work.'

The older man spoke for the first time. 'Very astute move.'

'It makes no difference to me financially. I just want to give the design a *wow* factor.'

The clients smiled. The younger man spoke again.

'I think we should take this idea back to the company.'

Philip leaned forward. 'With a recommendation to go ahead?'

'It's for the board to take the final decision, but …'

Philip smiled for the first time that day. 'Can I take that as a *yes?*'

The clients looked first at the scheme and then at Marnie.

'I think you can probably take it as a … *wow.*'

Gary was relieved that Sheena had agreed to meet him. When she had retreated from the canalside the previous day, he had wondered if she would ever come back. A message left on her mobile's voicemail – *the crate was full of oranges* – had done the trick, quickly followed up with an invitation – *pub lunch tomorrow?*

In the saloon bar, he glanced hurriedly towards Gravel's table. It was empty. Gary's heartbeat quickened as Sheena walked directly towards it. But why not? Perhaps he really could put his worries about Gravel behind him.

Life seemed good for the next three minutes, until Sheena delivered her double whammy. The first came while they were waiting for the food to arrive. Sheena sipped her mineral water and smiled at Gary.

'You know whose seat you're sitting in?'

Gary spoke in a hushed tone. 'Gravel's.'

'That's right. I met him here once. Gave me the creeps, he did.'

'You can say that again.' Gary took a mouthful of beer. 'Still, I don't suppose we'll see him round here any more … from what I've heard.'

'Who knows, Gary? I wouldn't be surprised if he was out there somewhere …'

Gary looked nervously towards the door.

The second whammy was even more scary than the first. Sheena smiled again.

'You know, I've been thinking.'

He knew it would be unwise to make a joke. 'Oh?'

'Yes … about your boat. It's nice, isn't it, having a boat … being on the water like that?'

'I like it.'

'That sense of freedom …'

He wondered where this was leading. 'That's how I feel about it.'

'Lovely ...' There was a dreamy look in her eyes. 'Like ... being on holiday.'

Was she going to suggest they take a holiday on the boat? 'Yeah ... it's ... great.'

'Still ...' She looked at him ... baby blue eyes ... long lashes ... golden complexion. She sighed. 'I suppose like all holidays ... like the one I had ... it comes to an end some time.'

Gary was struggling to interpret the signs. 'Does it?'

'Of course it does, Gary. You can't be on holiday all the time, can you?'

'I suppose not.' What was this all about?

'There comes a time when you have to think of something a bit more ... well, *permanent*.'

Gary's brows furrowed.

'Doesn't it, Gary?'

'Somewhere more permanent than a boat?'

'Exactly ... like a flat ... or a house ... and then ... a proper job.'

'Like you've got?'

'Yes, like I've got.'

Gary took another drink. The beer tasted flat. Sheena smiled cheerfully.

'So, a real place to live ... a regular income ... something more settled. Don't you think? ... Gary?'

———✑———

During the afternoon Marnie was at her desk working on the Willards programme when Beth rang.

'We're all ready to leave for the airport, so I can't stay long. Just wanted to say we'll be back in London late tonight your time. What's new?'

Marnie gave Beth a brief outline of the bequest.

'You mean, you've got the original lost drawings of this important guy ... what did you say his name was?'

'William Jessop.'

Beth considered the implications. 'Marnie, you're rich! You'll never have to work again.'

'Now hang on a minute. Don't go jumping –'

'Oh, no. Don't tell me ... You're about to come out with some goody-goody public-spirited gesture!'

'These aren't like a prize in a raffle, Beth. They're part of our history. No individual can own the national heritage.'

'Tell that to the Queen.'

'What I mean is, you can't try to make a profit out of a gift.'

'Tell that to British Gas shareholders!'

'Beth, I'm going to use the material in my work.'

'That's more like it. Any company would pay a premium to get hold of stuff like that.

No one could blame you for –'

'That isn't what I said.'

'I don't believe –' A voice in the background. Beth was distracted. 'Here's our taxi. Time to go. Marnie, don't do anything precipitate. Seeya!'

Marnie arrived back at the flat to find a man and a woman on the doorstep. The woman was about Marnie's age, petite, with auburn hair and a laptop bag slung over her shoulder. The man was tall, balding, fortyish, with square glasses. He introduced himself as Don Stephens.

'And you've brought a colleague from the museum?'

'Not actually.' The woman thrust a business card at Marnie. 'I'm Ginny Lang … *Guardian* features. I had a tip-off and er … Hope you don't mind.'

Marnie told her story and gave them the guided tour. The curator pored over the drawings, muttering to himself. The journalist typed notes on her laptop at high speed.

'What do you plan to do with the material now?' Her fingers were poised ready to pounce on the keyboard.

The curator looked up from the drawings. Marnie had a sudden fear he was about to announce that the documents were reproductions. He cleared his throat.

'These seem to be the original drawings and papers of William Jessop.'

Ginny Lang hit the keys. 'How important are they, in your opinion?'

Don Stephens paused before replying, aware that anything he said today could be in the newspapers tomorrow.

'I think – or rather I believe – we have reason to conclude that these drawings, subject to verification by other independent experts, could eventually prove to be the ones that have not been seen since the beginning of the last century. If that is the case, and of course it is yet to be established beyond reasonable doubt, but if it is, then these drawings add considerably to our knowledge of the work of Jessop. They could in turn lead to a reassessment of the relative importance of the man himself and some of his contemporaries. Major reputations could have to be re-evaluated in the light of this find.'

A snappy soundbite, Marnie thought. The journalist pecked rapidly at her keyboard.

50
Fame

Marnie jogged down to the kiosk to get the *Guardian* at six o'clock on Thursday morning. The story made the Home News section under the headline:

Lost Treasure of Forgotten Genius
Exclusive

The phone was ringing when she opened the front door. She wondered if the call was a hoax.

'Did you say the *Today* programme ... Radio Four?'

'That's right. We've read about the documents bequeathed to you and we'd like to do an interview ... this morning.'

'You want me to come to Broadcasting House?'

'We're sending a radio car to Little Venice to do a feature. Could you meet it there? We'll get a taxi to pick you up.'

Marnie declined the offer and drove to Little Venice. Pulling into a parking slot, she found she had no change for the meter. The BBC radio car was conspicuous with tall antennae on the roof and a young woman – who looked about fourteen – in black trouser suit and carrying a clipboard, lurking beside it. She met Marnie and opened the car door. Inside, the sound engineer gave her headphones and a microphone and checked levels.

'So, Marnie, have you done this kind of thing before?'

'No.'

'It's quite straightforward. Just speak normally without raising your voice, like on the phone. Keep your answers brief and to the point and avoid technical jargon.'

He went over the details of the story and spoke by phone to the producer. In the background the programme was playing quietly on the car radio. They waited for several minutes. At one point her mind went blank and she had no idea what she would say or even why she was there.

She became aware of a voice beside her.

'Marnie ... I said we're on after this next item. Three minutes to go. You're on peak time.'

Marnie's stomach turned over. 'Fine.' A lie.

'You're not nervous are you?'

'No.' Another lie.

She sat and waited during those long three minutes, aware only that a traffic warden was walking steadily along the line of parked cars. The sound engineer tapped her arm and raised a finger. She concentrated and listened to the anchorman loud and clear in her headphones.

And now, one of those rare stories that dreams are made of. An extraordinary find of priceless drawings has been made as the result of a bequest from an old eccentric who died last week, leaving his treasure to a friend. That friend is now in our radio car in Little Venice, at least I hope she is. Marnie Walker. Good morning.

The interviewer made it easy for her, like a friendly chat. He asked just the right questions to let Marnie tell her story. For her part, she kept to the essentials without embellishment, and the interview seemed to be over almost before it had started.

Thank you for being with us, Mrs Walker. And the result of that great act of generosity will be on view in a few months' time for all to see at the National Canal Museum. Now Sue ... is the weather going to be generous to us today?

And that was it. Marnie removed the headphones and rapidly climbed out. The traffic warden had reached her car and was just taking out his pen.

Marnie called out. 'It's okay, I'm just going.'

The warden looked at her and then at the radio car covered with BBC logos and the aerials on the roof.

'Sorry, love, I didn't know I was going to book a celebrity.'

'You're not.'

'You mean you aren't a celebrity?'

'I mean you're not going to book me.'

Twenty minutes later, as Marnie walked into the foyer at Everett, Parker Associates, the new receptionist jumped to her feet. 'Marnie! The TV news have been on the phone for you.' Her eyes were dancing with excitement as she thrust the message forward.

Marnie took it, thanked her and walked casually towards the office. She just reached the door when the receptionist called after her.

'Marnie, it's the *Telegraph*. Liza Crawford, features editor, on the phone. Shall I put her through to your desk?'

'Er, no. Take a message. I'll call back. I have to work out how to deal with this.'

Faye Summers caught up with Marnie, grinning.

'Hey, Marnie. Would you believe I've just heard the new girl on the switchboard telling a caller you were – and I quote – *in conference at this moment in time!*'

They winced in unison. 'I heard you on the car radio. I could hardly believe my ears.'

'Was it all right?'

'Yeah, great. When you're ready could we have a chat about the Willards project ... or even a *conference?*'

They both hooted and Marnie pushed open the door to the design group office. A cheer went up from the team. Laughter was heard in the building again. It felt like business was back to normal.

———⚓———

In the afternoon Marnie was working on the Willards designs when the phone rang.

'Sorry, Marnie, I know we're holding all calls, but there's a woman on the line who *says* she's your sister ... just flown in from Boston.'

Marnie agreed to take the call. 'Welcome home, Beth.'

'Thanks. It's great to be here … in your wonderful country. How come I got the third degree from the switchboard operator?'

'You did well to penetrate my security shield.'

'I told her I knew your agent.'

'She must've thought you were Spielberg.'

'What a surprise, Marnie. Paul opened the *Guardian* at the airport and there you were. We got home, turned on the radio and people were talking about you. I come back to find my kid sister's famous!'

'Yeah … for fifteen minutes, as Andy Warhol said.'

Beth became serious. 'So you're giving the drawings away?'

'I'm just lending them to the museum.'

'Marnie, they're going to create a new gallery for them. That sounds pretty permanent.'

'It's the right thing to do. Also it may have helped save my job.'

'That sounds like the right thing to do. And it's being named after the old guy?'

'Yep … the Peter William Gibson Collection. They were his drawings. Look, Beth, I'd better get on. We've got a lot on here.'

'I know, and Spielberg's probably hanging on for you.'

'Biting his fingernails, I expect. Come round tonight for supper.'

'Great. You can tell us about your trip on the boat, though I expect you've got it out of your system by now.'

In the background Marnie became aware of the faint chugging of a diesel engine reaching her through the open window. A thousand images flooded into her mind from her travels on *Sally Ann*. A boat cruised slowly past.

'Out of my system? I wouldn't put it quite like that …'

Epilogue

The cemetery seemed deserted when Marnie arrived in the late afternoon. A gravedigger directed her to the corner where Old Peter lay buried. She walked slowly past the rows of headstones, the last resting places of the famous and the obscure, the loved and the forgotten. When she found the grave, the sun was slanting from low in the sky, picking out the fading colours on the wreaths that covered it in profusion. Beyond the plot, Marnie could see the railings close to the place where she had first met Dolly.

She lay the wreath by the simple wooden cross at the head of the old man's grave. Bending forward, the breath caught in her throat and warm tears pricked her eyes. She looked over her shoulder to be sure she was alone.

'Hallo, Old Peter.' She had never called him by name before. 'Thank you for your letter and your bequest.' She swallowed. The rest of her words had to be unspoken. 'I've done the right thing. I know you'd be pleased ... you *are* pleased.' She took a deep breath, looked towards the railings and saw the water shining between the bushes on the bank.

'Thanks to you, the history books will have to be rewritten. Things will never be the same again.' She smiled. 'Thanks to you ... and *Sally Ann*, neither will I.'

For more information about other books by Leo McNeir,
see the author's website: **www.leomcneir.com**